The Sulphur Priest

ADRIAN BOAS

The Sulphur Priest

Published by Wheatmark®
2030 East Speedway Boulevard, Suite 106
Tucson, Arizona 85719 USA
www.wheatmark.com

ISBN: 978-1-62787-869-2 (paperback)
ISBN: 978-1-62787-870-8 (ebook)
LCCN: 202092602

Bulk ordering discounts are available through Wheatmark, Inc. For more information, email orders@wheatmark.com or call 1-888-934-0888.

rev202101

The wise man, his eyes are in his head; But the fool walks in darkness.

And I also perceived that one event happens to them all.

Then said I in my heart: 'As it happens to the fool, so too it will happen even to me; and why was I then more wise?'

Then I said in my heart, that this also is vanity.

For of the wise man, even as of the fool, there is no remembrance forever; seeing that in the days to come all will long ago have been forgotten.

And how must the wise man die even as the fool!

Ecclesiastes 2. 14–16

The title of this novel, *The Sulphur Priest*, is taken from the poem by Dylan Thomas "It is the sinner's dust-tongued bell", The Collected Poems of Dylan Thomas: The Centenary Edition, Weidenfeld & Nicolson, courtesy of the Dylan Thomas Trust.

To Yochi

CAST OF CHARACTERS

Acre and Montfort, 1271

- **Squire Hermann**, a young German squire at the Teutonic hospital in Acre
- **Albert of Ulm**, an elderly German knight in search of his son
- **Bernard of Ulm/Weissenau**, the son of Albert and prior of a Premonstratensian abbey, Weissenau in southern Germany
- **Commander Ulrich**, Commander of the Teutonic hospital in Acre
- **Grand Commander Eckhart**, grand commander at Montfort
- **Jordon of Hildesheim**, castellan at Montfort
- **Walther**, the guest master at Montfort
- **Matthew**, the cellarer at Montfort
- **Geoffrey**, the Hospitaller sacrist at Acre
- **Hubert**, custodian of relics at the Teutonic house in Acre

- **Gunther**, cook at Montfort
- **Johan**, a brother who shows Hermann around at Montfort
- **Matheus**, the Hospitaller preceptor's chief clerk at Acre
- **Thomas**, a novice aiding the guest master at Montfort
- **Michel**, prior of the Premonstratensian house in Acre

Montfort, 1926

- **Robert Palmer**, former member of the British gendarmerie in Palestine and assistant to John Riley
- **John Riley**, American director of excavations at Montfort
- **Lawrence (Larry) Walker**, assistant of John Riley at Montfort excavations
- **Bel (Isabel) Knowles**, half Indian daughter of a British diplomat and sweetheart of Robert
- **Mr. Knowles**, Bel's father
- **Jim Townsend**, representative of the Palestine Department of Antiquities in Haifa
- **Captain Peters**, police captain investigating Walker
- **Father Nicephor**, Greek Catholic priest at Malia
- **Ra'ed**, the foreman at Montfort excavations
- **Abdul**, the camp guard at Montfort excavations
- **Salah**, the camp boy at Montfort excavations
- **Professor Gilford**, director of the Palestine Department of Antiquities
- **Dr. Felix Riedl**, German theologian, scholar of Biblical and Church history living in Jerusalem

- **Dr. Gustav Neumann**, German theologian, orientalist and Aramaic scholar, friend of Riedl
- **Otis T. Merrill**, American consul in Jaffa

The curator had given me directions: a door behind the first row of display cases on the left wall as you enter the southern gallery, then a spiral staircase within the wall, exiting on a ledge high above the gallery, and at the end of the ledge, another door.

It sounded simple enough, but when I emerged from the staircase onto the ledge, I immediately had misgivings. To be honest I was horrified: the ledge was no wider than two feet, with no railing, and at least fifteen feet above the gallery floor, which, for someone like myself who suffers from a fear of heights, might as well have been fifty feet. I eased out and flattened myself against the wall. Perhaps if I took it slowly, and didn't look down…

I don't know how I got across. I opened the door and literally threw myself into a dark, musty room, not much more than a cupboard. I found a light switch, surprised that it actually worked, and looked around. There was no furniture of any kind. Against the walls were stacks of cardboard boxes; a number of them had collapsed and fallen apart, the papers spilling out onto the floor. The room had probably not been entered in decades. I blew dust off the labels and read the names marked in faded ink. Then I found what I was looking for: a box marked – Montfort Expedition – 1926. Excitedly I leafed through the papers in it. Halfway through, I found the field diary, a thick exercise book with a decaying cloth binding. Its grey front cover was printed *with the words - LYONS DIARY - 1926 - HALF A PAGE TO A DAY. Lyons & Co., Jaffa Street, Jerusalem. Telephone 1631.*

I had seen it once before, about twenty years earlier when I was a student. The archive of the British Mandate period was still located in a room off the library stacks on the ground floor of the Museum, under the reading room. Going down there for something else I had chanced upon the Montfort box. Curiosity had got the better of me and, for well over an hour, I had sat leafing through the yellowing papers. A fascinating story began to unfold before my eyes, and I forgot completely what I had come for. The librarian came looking for me and being a stickler for the rules, made me replace the papers and get on with whatever my legitimate task had been. Several months later when I was again at the library, I furtively sought out the box, but it was no longer there.

As a second-year archaeology student at the Hebrew University I had already come across an item related to Montfort. A friend visiting the office of the Palestine Exploration Fund in London had somewhat covertly obtained a copy of a short text, only about thirty printed pages, prepared in 1898 for the unpublished fourteenth volume of the Palestine Pilgrims' Text Society. This was the translation into English, from the Latin original, of an account by a brother of the Teutonic Order named Hermann, who had been at the German house in Acre in 1271, two decades before the fall of that city, and had witnessed the siege of Starkenberg Castle (the German name for Montfort) in that same year. This text was translated and partly edited by M.L. Shaw from a manuscript located in the Bibliothèque Nationale in Paris; this had been purchased by the library in 1836 from an anonymous private owner, and a colophon records that it was a copy made by a monk named Thietmar in 1356 in the scriptorium of Lorsch Abbey. Although not a long text, it is remarkably detailed, bringing the period alive so effectively that I felt as if I myself had been in the city and the castle. In the following pages I have simplified its language somewhat to make it more congenial to the modern reader, while remaining faithful to its contents.

In the years that followed other interests occupied me. Eventually I recalled the expedition papers and asked the archivist what had happened to them. She inquired on my behalf. It was thought that the box had been taken from the room when the heating system was replaced, but no one seemed to know where to. Almost a year went by, and I had all but forgotten the matter when one day I received a phone call from the archivist saying that she had traced my box. And now I was sitting on one of the sturdier cartons in the little room, my feet on the floor's thin layer of dust, the field diary open on my knees. Most of the entries were fairly mundane and laconic: "Weather fair. Work commenced at six o'clock. Clearing of the large vault below the hall. No exceptional finds…" or "Stormy weather all day. Workers sent home…" Some entries were more detailed, mainly describing the various finds and making a few personal references, nothing remarkable, but as I leafed towards the end I realised, to judge from the stubs of torn out pages, that almost half of the diary was missing. The final entry consisted of just three lines dated 12 April - "Returned to work in the afternoon with four of the men in the area west of the keep…" The rest of this page and all of the following pages had been ripped out. Only a single blank page remained before the end-cover.

The abrupt ending left me disappointed. I wondered if this was the same diary that I had seen on that first occasion: although many years had passed, I found it hard to believe that my fascination with the material could have been founded on this single, insipid, epigrammatic account. There must have been something more. So, what had been torn out and why? I did not recall having seen missing pages, but it was, after all, a long time since I had first seen the diary.

As I closed it, I noticed something else that I did not recall having seen before. On the back-cover board was an inscription written in black ink, in a different hand. It read: "continued in new field diary." I looked through the materials in the box but there was no other diary and no trace of the missing pages. Nor did a systematic search through

the other boxes—the small room filling with dust – yield any results.
The only other material from Montfort was a few pages of salary lists
stamped with the finger impressions of the workers from the village of
Malia.

With this unsatisfactory glimpse into the Montfort expedition my
interest might well have lapsed again. But in 1997 the third piece of
the puzzle came into my hands. Attending the international medieval
conference in Leeds, I met a young historian from London University
who, in a chance conversation, informed me that the grandfather of a
colleague of hers had played a role in the 1926 excavations at Mont-
fort. Returning to London I phoned the number she had given me, and
a few days later I met with Mr Peter Palmer at his flat just off Russell
Square. His grandfather, he told me, had been the assistant of John Ri-
ley, the head of the Montfort Expedition, and while I waited in the neat
sitting room of his flat, he went to look for material he had put aside
to show me, returning a few minutes later with a shoebox. In it were
a handful of photographs, mostly of a man in his late twenties, some
taken on the steps outside the British Museum where he stood dapper
in his town clothes beside an attractive young lady of slightly oriental
appearance. In others he appeared in uniform; several were taken at
Montfort, and in these he was in a semi-military outfit, but wearing a
trilby, and standing next to a tall, elegantly dressed and considerably
older man, whom I assumed was Riley. Below the photographs were
a few letters, some hand-written, others typed on yellowed tissue-thin
paper, and then two things that made me catch my breath: a faded,
typed carbon copy of a ten-page Palestine Police report dated 30 June,
1926 entitled "Captain Peters' Report on the Investigation into Activi-
ties and Death of Mr. Lawrence Walker at Qal'at al-Qurain", and with
it what I had hardly dared hope to find but recognised immediately; the
grey cover with the printed words – LYONS DIARY. It was the missing
second field diary. It continued, as my memory served me, from the last

entry in the first diary before the missing pages. The handwriting was that of Mr. Robert Palmer, the same as on the hand-written letters.

It was while I was attempting to find out more about Captain Peters that I came upon the final and in some ways most exciting piece of this puzzle. In the archives of the Mandate period Palestine Police Department in Oxford, I obtained with surprisingly little effort the original copy of this investigation report. Attached to it with a rusted paperclip were the missing torn-out pages of the first field diary, folded and somewhat crumpled but easily recognisable as having the same form as the printed dates in the diary pages, and I immediately recognised the handwriting of the first diary although here it was in pencil.

I now had, more-or-less, the complete story. I had uncovered two narratives; the first, a medieval account written by a squire of the Teutonic Order, and the second, a description contained in the now complete diaries, letters, and other documents relating to an early twentieth-century expedition to the very castle where events recorded in the medieval account had taken place. Each of these quite dissimilar stories might well be worthy of publication on its own, but it occurs to me that there is a compelling connection between them. I have taken two considerable liberties with this material. The first is to intertwine the narratives as alternate chapters in a single volume (if so inclined, the reader can ignore this imposed form and skip the pages of one account or the other). The second, and perhaps more extreme liberty is my decision to write these accounts in the form of a work of fiction. If the reader is so inclined, he or she can of course search out the original material in the archives.

A. B. Jerusalem, 2020

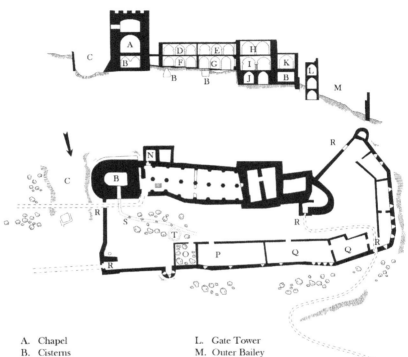

A. Chapel
B. Cisterns
C. Moat
D. Refectory & Dormitory
E. Knights' Chapel & Chapter House
F. Kitchen & Forge
G. Storage
H. Residence of the Master
I. Grand Hall
J. Vaults
K. Old Hall

L. Gate Tower
M. Outer Bailey
N. Latrines
O. Castellan's Garden
P. Guests'/Auxillary Workers' Quarters
   & Infirmary
Q. Stables
R. Gates
S. Secret Passage
T. Laboratory
U. Path to the Guesthouse/Mill

1 CASTLE HILL

He didn't know when exactly it was that he learnt how to slip from a mode of emotional involvement into one of impassive observation. It was an ability he had somehow picked up, and though it was far from perfected he was pleased to see how he was generally able to remain outside of the events that at an earlier time in his life would have entirely engulfed him. These past few weeks had been like reading a novel, which, to his great satisfaction, he found he could step out of almost whenever he wished.

The sun was high now, and the thick mist that had moved up the valley had already dissipated against the sides of the hill. The men had gone up an hour ago, and Robert had remained behind to finish his drawings. Now he could hear them clearly although they were some distance away at the far end of the castle. Every now and then came a shout or the heavy thump and roar as a load of rock and soil was tipped over the mountainside and clattered down the slope. He put his drawings into a file, lifted up the tent flap to put it on the foldaway desk, placing on it the heavy piece of carved marble that Riley had given him to use as a paperweight, and then stepped out again into the bright day. The camp-boy, Salah, was sitting on a crate by the edge of the camp. He waved to him, and the boy stood up.

"Should I make coffee?" he asked.

"No need. I'm off."

"No Coffee?"

"I'm going up."

"Yes sir."

Robert pushed his hat on. He could see Riley climbing up onto a wall at the very edge of the hill.

"I'll see you later."

The boy sat back down on the crate and pulled out of his pocket a tin box of cigarettes. Robert walked up the track from the encampment, skirting the outer enceinte of the castle almost hidden in the rampant spring growth of sage and small trees. On the side of the track, he saw a discarded whisky bottle. He shook his head as he climbed on up to the top of the track. When he reached the rickety ladder below the upper wall Walker popped his head over the edge above.

"There you are old boy. Thought you were taking the day off."

Robert clambered up the ladder taking Walker's outstretched hand as he reached the top and swung himself onto the smooth stone step that had once been the threshold of a gate into the central ward, but now gave onto mid-air. He could smell the whisky on Walker's breath.

"I've been working," he answered. "You might try it yourself sometime," but his voice was drowned under the crash of another pile of earth and rock tipped over the edge of the hill.

"Don't take offence."

"I never do," said Robert. "Where's Riley?"

"In the keep. Give him my best," said Walker with no attempt to hide his sarcasm. He moved his thin, lanky body aside as Robert passed and climbed the stairs. At the top he found Riley lying on a piece of canvass on the dusty floor of the keep, peering down through the opening of a cistern into the darkness.

"Anything to see?"

Riley raised his head and looked at him.

"I think I can see vault ribs."

"Really! Let's have a look."

He lay beside him and gazed down into the square opening and shaft that vanished below into a black void. It took nearly a minute before he could make anything out. At first the vague form of stones on a wall gradually emerged in the darkness, then the angle of a corner and another wall. And then he thought he could see a corbel and the stone rib springing from it, and it became clear and he could follow it up till where it was hidden behind the sharp rectangle of the opening shaft.

"I see it," he exclaimed. "What do you think? Rather unusual roofing for a cistern?"

"Yes." Riley pulled himself up on his knees and dusted himself off and Robert pushed up with his arms into a sitting position beside him. "Usually they're just barrel-vaulted."

A slight breeze ran over the floor shifting the thin film of dust that had settled there.

"What are you going to do about Walker?"

"I don't know."

"You'll have to deal with him sooner or later. You do realise that?"

"Yes, I know," Riley answered. He sounded exasperated.

The two men stood. Riley was so thin he looked as if he might blow off the side of the castle if the wind picked up. With the exception of his prominent nose, which had grown increasingly red in the sun, his complexion was notably pale. He was, as always, immaculately dressed - remarkable in this rough setting. Whereas Robert wore quasi-military dress, Riley was inevitably decked out in two of the three pieces of a fine, grey woollen suit and a thin grey tie, his only concessions to the field conditions being rather higher laced shoes than he wore at home, the pith helmet that he was

somewhat shyly proud of, a gesture he had made to the romantic
nature of his current employment and location, and of course the
fact that the third piece of his suit he had left hanging on a chair-
back beside his camp bed.

Riley picked up his cane, and they walked across the ruined
keep to the surviving inner face of its western wall. This fragment
of massive stonework indicated the monumental size of what had
once been the castle's stronghold. It rose to about twelve feet and
was formed of enormous buff-coloured ashlars that had turned
grey where they had been longest exposed. They were perfectly
tooled and joined and were stacked up like a giant's toy building
blocks. There was almost no mortar left between the stones, and
you could see right through the vertical spaces across the rest of
the castle and the green hills beyond where they rolled westward
towards the coast. To the left and right the steep valleys fell away,
and far below on the south-west in a clearing was the small camp of
four white canvas tents. To the north, at the foot of the valley was
the stream. Plane trees grew along its edges, taller than the other
trees and a paler shade of green; a touch of European forest in a
Mediterranean landscape. Further west the stream curved, vanished, re-emerged and ran through the valley to the sea. Riley sat
down, leaning his back against the cold stone and Robert sat beside him, took off his hat and ran his hands through his thick hair.

"He's been drinking again," he said.

"Yes. Well, there's not much I can do about it."

"You should warn him."

"I might ... I will if it gets any worse." They sat on for a few minutes in silence. Then Riley reached for his cane and pulled himself
up. "We'd better set a good example," he said, "I'm going to work
on the eastern vault again today. What are your plans?"

"I was thinking I would like to get that drawing of the hall
done, as you asked. I should start now before there is too much

light on the wall." He got up and walked to the staircase. A sparrowhawk was circling high above the keep. Robert descended into the central part of the castle. Walker was now directing a group of men who were attempting to lift a large stone onto a barrow. Robert walked past them to the far end, clambering up makeshift steps of wooden planking and passed through an opening in a massive wall that divided what had once been the domestic part of the castle from the western hall. He stepped out into a space like a stage hanging in the air, high against the jade backdrop of forest. An enormous stone column stood at the centre of a broad platform that had been part of the floor of the great ceremonial hall. It was formed of three monolithic, octagonal segments and rose to the springing level from where the vanished vaulting had once arched up, supported on broad ribs like a great fountain of stone. The only wall still standing was the twenty-foot-high mass of rubble and mortar with two large openings through one of which he had come. Nothing remained of the other walls to suggest what they had been like, but he imagined that they would have had large arched windows overlooking the sweep of hills that cascaded from high above on either side of the two converging valleys.

Against the column were a battered leather satchel and a board. He went over and picked them up. He found himself a position on the edge of the platform, took a sheet of paper from the satchel, taped it to the board and taking out a pencil began to sketch the scene.

The long morning passed with nothing of remark. After lunch he walked down into the valley to the ruined mill. At the bottom of the valley near the stream the path turned muddy and narrowed, almost vanished in a thick mass of blackberry canes. He walked in the shade of the plane trees along the edges of the stream and then into the cool shadow cast by the high façade of the mill. The building seemed almost intact although a large tree grew almost horizontally from high on the wall, its roots having bulged the stonework as they fingered their way within. On its trunk, a family of conies scrambled to safety in a gap in the wall, then reappeared, warily eyeing the intruder.

He peered inside the doorway. The mill had occupied the ground floor of the building. The walls were so thick that only a single thin shaft of light cut through the darkness from one of the windows. He took a few tentative steps. It was as cool as a cave. Perhaps it was his movements that caused minute fragments of lime mortar from between the stones in the vault above to drop into the thin shaft of light. He saw the particles fall silently, in their path a fine trail of dust that hovered for a few moments and settled. He heard the drone of unseen flies circling and, as his eyes grew accustomed, he could make out the form of the interior. The workings of the mill; the great wooden cogwheels and the millstones that had once turned in the flow of water from three chutes on the south wall; were long gone. There was nothing in the chamber but the soft dust covering the floor. A partition wall crossed about two thirds of the way down.

Stepping back out into the light he walked down the slope, crossed the stream at its shallowest, on flat stones that moved underfoot so that he almost lost his footing, and found himself a shaded position against the remains of the old dam wall where he sat to sketch the ruin. It was an ideal spot; the imposing façade of the mill, hall and tower against the wooded hill rising steeply behind, and the walls of the castle far above. As he worked, he listened to the soft rill of water in the stream as it came up against the stones of the ford.

He spent the early afternoon at his drawing, and then crossed back to the mill and took out a small hammer from his satchel and a short metal rod, which he hammered into the high ground at the eastern end of the wall. He slipped the ring of the tape-measure over the rod and wheeled out the thin white strip of numbered cloth tape, walking as far as the near side of the door, holding it high to adjust for the slope of the ground. He made some notes in a little book, then hammered in a new stake and continued the process along the front of the building. Without light there was no means of measuring the interior, and he determined to return with a lamp. He took up his satchel and drawing board and skirted the building on its eastern side, clambering up between the trees and fallen stones and entered the largely collapsed upper storey of the building. It was the first time he had seen these vaults. This level had once been a long gothic hall with four rib-vaulted bays ending in the west with a two-storey tower. Only a single bay of the hall was still standing, but it was overgrown and crumbling, with small trees and bushes growing out of the walls and roof. The other bays had long ago collapsed onto the floor. He estimated that he was about eight feet above the original floor level, and the collapsed debris rose nearly twice that height at the eastern and western extensions of the hall. The front and back walls, however, were standing to nearly their full original height. It occurred to him that this would make a very promising excavation, although it would be necessary to support the walls and the surviving bay. It was quite easy for him to reconstruct in his mind how the hall would have appeared when it was still intact. This was an exercise he liked to do. Huge stones that had fallen from the castle keep lay in the rubble, and he realised that this building must have collapsed when the Mamluks dismantled the castle on the hill high above it. He could imagine the thundering of these enormous stones rolling down the mountainside, shattering anything in their path and crashing onto the roof of the hall, so that the destruction of the castle above was echoed by destruction of this hall in the valley below.

As his thoughts were reflecting on these matters, he heard a rustling sound behind him and turning around saw Ra'ed the foreman, approaching.

"Ra'ed. Am I needed?"

"No, sir. Mr. Riley said I might check if you are in need of any help?"

"That was thoughtful of him, but I'm pretty much finished here."

"Have you walked along the valley Mr. Palmer?"

"No."

"Would you like to see the spring? It is very beautiful."

"Well, yes. I would."

The two men set off following the narrow path and made their way up-stream. The path ran close to the water, weaving in where it was deeper in the rock, out again where the valley broadened. Abandoned mills stood in ruin along the north bank, damp walls gradually sinking under fallen branches, moss and maidenhair. The woods were thick around the stream; tall oriental plane trees that reached up high, their pale foliage awakening fresh in the spring warmth. On the lower slopes above and all the way up, the walls of the valley were crowded with the smaller evergreens; bay, Syrian maple, Palestine oak, wild olives, and along the path were stands of yellow Spanish broom that honeyed the air. In the grass were purple and yellow vetchling and grey-leafed red cudweed with tight burgundy heads, and at the edges grew the tiny blue pimpernel. The path and all the ground on the slopes were covered with a constantly thickening layer of fallen leaves from the evergreens, and all the time scattered bursts of brown leaves rained down from the canopying trees together with dry, worm-like flower-heads that fell, and here and there caught at the end of hanging cobwebs, swaying then gently like tiny, silent wind chimes. The hills rose high, scarred with cave-ridden cliffs.

"That is Shqīf Abū-Shibān," said Ra'ed, pointing to a high forested peak to the right.

"What does the name mean?"

"Mountain of the Father of Shiba."

"Father of Shiba?"

"Shiba is that feathery grey plant. You see, on the slope?" he pointed to lower on the hillside which was bearded with Artemisia.

"Your English is very good, Ra'ed. Where did you pick it up?"

"My father was a soap merchant. He made a lot of money in trade with Egypt. The Egyptians favour the soap from Nablus, Haifa, and Jaffa because it contains no animal fats. When I was twelve, my father sent me to stay with his brother who ran the business in Egypt. I was there for two years and went to school at the English school in Cairo. That is where I learnt my English and a bit of French."

Further on they passed another hill that rose high against the blue. "That is Shqīf en-Nsūra, "Mountain of the Eagles." As if to prove the aptness of its name, two large birds were circling near the peak.

They walked on, bending under arched branches, manoeuvring rocks wrapped in thick, damp roots, the path sometimes breaking up and vanishing, Ra'ed leading, and Robert close behind. They continued talking as they walked:

"You must know this area well."

"I spent all my time here as a child. I know every tree, every stone. I think I could walk this blindfolded. I slipped on a rock once crossing the stream and came home limping and wounded. My uncle saw me coming into the village and asked me what had happened. I told him and he said someone must have put the rock there."

The path twisted back by the stream, and they saw the schools of tiger-patterned fish among the rocks jumping like salmon at a waterfall but without a salmon's talent to overcome the pull of the earth. In a wild rush the stream had slowly cut through platforms of rock forming deep crevasses and small pools, isolated after the winter rains, in which were fat black tadpoles and masses of mosquito larvae that looped their way to the surface to breathe and then darted back down to a murky refuge. Occasionally there was the squelchy croak of an unseen frog followed by a small splash as it plunged into a pool. Dragonflies, turquoise or blood red, with cellophane wings half-dipped in black, darted and hovered, levelling out to grasp the ends of reeds.

Riley was waiting when Robert and Ra'ed climbed back up. The sun had already dropped quite low in the west, and the men had packed their tools. Riley showed Robert a fine carved, stone boss that they had unearthed, a rosette formed of oak leaves that had somehow survived unscathed where it had fallen from one of the collapsed vaults of the upper storey. He showed him also a handful of bronze coins adhering to one another in a thick layer of green corrosion, their design still vaguely discernible. Walker was sitting on one side on a fallen ashlar, writing in the field diary. At five o'clock the workers lined up and, after pressing their finger onto an inkpad and then against their names on the payroll chart, they set out on their long walk uphill through the forest back to the village. The three men then headed down to the camp. Halfway down they could already smell the smoke of Abdul's fire and the meat he was preparing for their dinner. Salah was digging a drainage trench. The sun touched the crest of a hill to the west, and the castle began to take on a warm golden glow against the sky darkening behind them. Robert bent over at the edge of the path and picked up a tiny leaf-green creature, a chameleon. Its bright skin was formed of perfect minute scales like the careful artistry of an expert jeweller. It clung to his finger, rotated a conical eye in its hooded head, frowning with a grim, old man's mouth, its tail a tight wound spring.

2 STARKENBERG

We left the city by the Gate of Saint Anthony near the house of the Franciscans, Albert on the horse and I on foot. It was early morning and still cool and the good smell of the earth was in the air. Commander Ulrich had told me to take special care in looking after the old knight and had given me directions that I promised to follow to the word. The commander had grave doubts about the wisdom of such a difficult and dangerous journey for a man of his great age, but also, he instructed me regarding the route we were to take. We were to remain close to the escort as far as Coquetum where we would rest at the inn by the mill. From there we would follow a second escort to Castellum Regis. The last leg of our journey was a small matter; an hour's march down to the castle, for which we would employ a guide from the village of Terfile.

I walked close to Albert's horse as we crossed the moat together with the little group of travellers that comprised three mounted knights, some Provençal merchants on mules and a pair of monks who, to judge from their dress, were Carmelite brothers. There was little talk, mainly amongst the merchants, and we were distant enough behind them for this not to distract my thoughts. These were centred on the events of the past few weeks during which I had been assigned to take care of and aid the old knight.

Our little group took the road east, passing Mount Turon and walking across the plain for some hours. It was quite hot, and we rested for a short while under an ancient sycamore tree. One of the knights rode over to Albert and spoke briefly to him. After he had left, Albert turned to me.

"Did you follow that, Hermann?"

"No. I am not acquainted with the dialect."

"He told me that we must be careful not to fall back. It seems that there have recently been a number of raids by the Saracens in these parts, even down here in the plain."

This news reawakened my awareness of the dangers of the journey we were undertaking, dangers that I had put altogether out of mind. For the rest of the morning, we kept very close to the escort.

After some time had passed, we arrived at the Genoese manor at Coquetum. We stopped there to rest near the Genoese vaults where we had a frugal meal. The heat had grown, the road was dusty, and we were footsore and weary, wet with perspiration and glad of the rest. We remained in this place into the middle of the afternoon, then continued our journey into the foothills at Clie, walking as the day grew cooler towards nightfall. We walked for another three hours and the light was fast waning as we passed near our Order's castle of Judin. The road took us further east into the hills, and when the growing darkness became too great to see our way, we camped under a huge carob tree. By then we were extremely fatigued. We ate a small repast and drank some not very good wine.

I slept heavily that night and, other than some soreness in my feet, felt entirely recovered in the morning. Albert insisted that he was ready to continue, and we commenced our journey northwest, down valleys and into the mountains. After some time, we reached Castellum Regis, our old castle on a hilltop. We remained there that day and night. The following morning Albert was noticeably tired, and I persuaded him that we should remain at the castle for another day to enable him to rest and recover. We did so and set out the next morning, rather later than we had intended. The guide from Terfile accompanied us down through the forest until we were almost at our destination. The track we followed took us into an oak forest which was pleasant and cool, but being steep and rocky was difficult to walk. Albert began to complain of intense pains in his feet. Our guide suggested that we climb higher on the slope where there was a better path that had been made for the wagons carrying rock from the quarry at Terfile. We did this and found that this path was indeed a better one. We could not yet see the castle, but our guide informed us that we were very close and at this point, after giving instructions about how to proceed, he left us.

When we saw the castle for the first time my breath was taken away. To get a better view of it I tied the horse to a tree, left Albert for a moment in the shade and clambered up the steep side of the hill. The ground was very rough, formed of loose, rust-coloured rocks and covered with dry grass, thorns and stunted trees that clung to every pocket of soil. The ridge dropped steeply on two sides, and ahead it fell gently in the direction of the castle. I could only see the tower. Although it was still quite far off it appeared vast, and the buildings beyond it were entirely hidden. I had seen many great fortresses before, but none like this. The tower took up the entire width of the rock, rising against the sky in a solid curved wall constructed of enormous stones. Part way up on the wall was a row of arrow-slits, and high above I could see the guards moving between the merlons. As I stood, absorbed by the sight of this great tower, I heard a movement nearby, and from the corner of my eye saw the pale form of a serpent that slithered out between rock and dry grass on the edge of the scarp. A chill went through me, and I stepped quickly away, and then hurried back to where the old knight was waiting.

I untied the horse and we walked on along the path and then through the outer moat; a narrow chasm, half natural, half cut in the stone. As we skirted the hill below the keep, we could hear the sound of the men on the battlements above. We followed the path along the steep northern slope until we reached a gate where a guard stood aside for us to pass through. From here the path ascended to a large portal of the main building. The doors were wide open, and there was no guard here. An auburn-haired boy came over to us and took the horse, and we walked into a passage that led across the interior of the castle. We were immediately in the centre of a great deal of activity; a number of men were passing by, some going left, up a staircase into the great tower, others entering on the right into the basement of a large building that extended down to the west. Uncertain which way to turn, we followed the men who had entered the basement vaults. These were storage rooms. On one side men were carrying amphorae over to a large wine press, and the smell of fermenting wine was very potent. From the chamber to the south we could hear the roar of a fire and we felt the blast of hot air from within. The chamber was filled with enticing smells of cooking and, as we passed the door, I saw a man leaning over a grille, his face lit up by the fire, placing onto it large pieces of meat that sizzled and spat, and smoke rose up into a stone flue above. From further back we heard a loud repeated clanging, like the sounds of a forge. In an adjacent room came the sweet, almost overpowering smells from a large baking oven, and inside I saw two of the brothers working the dough and the baker at the door of an oven that glowed like an orange eye.

While we were standing there wondering where to go, a man

came over, looked at us inquisitively and introduced himself. He spoke in a very low voice as if he did not wish to add to the clamour all around us, and I had to strain my ears to hear his words.

"Welcome gentlemen. I am Walther. I am the guest master. I see you have just arrived. How can I assist you?"

Albert answered him:

"Good day, Brother Walther. My name is Albert. I am from Ulm. This is Squire Hermann from your house in Acre. He is helping an old man on an impossible quest.

Brother Walther looked at me then back at Albert.

"And what is that?"

"We are seeking my son. He came East about six years ago. Perhaps you have heard of him? His name is Bernard. He is the prior of the abbey of Weissenau.

"I know the abbey of Weissenau, but I am afraid that I have not heard of your son. I do not believe that he is here. I would certainly know if he was. I am sorry I cannot help you."

I could see the faint glimmer of hope fading from the old man's eyes.

"I did not come with the expectation that I would find him here, but in the hope that your grand commander might have some knowledge as to his whereabouts. Or perhaps that there may be someone else here who has some knowledge."

"You might speak with Brother Matthew, the cellarer, and certainly with the grand commander."

"That is indeed what I desire, Brother Walther."

"Then you will be staying?"

"Yes... that is, for as long as it takes to learn something, if indeed there is anything to learn."

"Very well. I will see to your needs while you are here. As you can see, there is much activity at present. In normal times the castle is as quiet as a convent... but these are not normal times. We have a great many new arrivals. The garrison has been increased by nearly forty knights and sergeants, and a large number of lay brothers and other labourers have arrived from Acre to work on our fortifications."

As he spoke, we stepped to one side of the passage to allow some men carrying timber to pass by.

"We are expecting more men this week," he said. "We have set up temporary quarters in the outer ward to house them. As you are staying, I will find you a place there."

I asked him how soon we could have an audience with the grand commander.

"That should not be a problem, although he is very busy at present, and it may take a few days. If you will come with me, we can find you a place to sleep."

We followed Brother Walther back through the outer door into a passage that ran parallel to the northern side of the building. The wall of this wing rose high above us, windowless at its base but with loopholes at regular intervals and large windows on the upper level. Below us the ground dropped steeply away, and a low wall below cut off the view of the lower part of the bailey and the outer fortifications. Along the sides of the path below the wall grew the same wild herbs that I had seen in the forest on the way: sage, rue, and others I did not know. I stooped to pick some leaves and crushed them in my fingers releasing their pungent smells. At the end of the path, we descended some steps and passed along the undercroft of what Brother Walther informed us was the Great Hall and above it, the grand master's apartments. We passed through a high gate-tower and down to some makeshift structures that, to judge from their appearance, had only recently been built against the outer wall. Along the edge of these apartments a path had been levelled, and Walther informed us that this was part of the ongoing expansions that included these low, roughly built structures that were intended to house the new arrivals. To one side, horses, mules, and camels had been herded into stables, and there was a livestock enclosure beyond from which emanated a variety of farmyard sounds and smells. The boy who had taken our horse reappeared, and Walther took him aside and spoke to him. As we waited, we had to move again to the edge of the path to make room for labourers directing ox-drawn carts loaded with building stone as they passed on their way towards the new fortification works that were being raised along the western slope of the hill. The path was covered with stone chips and fine white dust which covered everything; the walls, and the plants on either side; and rose in the air every time a cart passed by.

Eventually we were joined by Walther and the boy and were given a place in the dormitory. The beds were nothing but rows of sacks filled with straw and covered with rough woollen coverlets. They were placed quite close to one another on the dusty floor. Walther apologised for the conditions, which were due to the crowding:

"The foxes have holes and the birds of the air have nests; but the Son of Man has not where to lay his head."

"This is perfectly alright, Brother Walther," answered Albert. "I have only recently experienced much harsher conditions on the sea passage. Our ship was terribly crowded and filthy. I am rather tired now and, if you will forgive me, I think that I will lie down to rest for a while."

There was some time before Sext and the meal that followed, and the boy offered to show me around the castle. His name was Thomas and he appeared to be quite young, no more than fourteen perhaps. He was, however, an exceptionally good guide and well acquainted with the castle. We walked through the lower part of the main building, and at the far end he showed me the forge that he referred to as the great forge, for there was also a small forge in the lower ward. It was in a large timber lean-to and was abandoned now, but the smoke and smells and the warm orange glow of the fire in the coils were still there. Beyond was another chamber, partly constructed below ground level, and there were windows covered with iron grilles at the base of the wall, and from the darkness through these came voices and moaning sounds.

"What is this place, Thomas, and who are the people I hear."

"This should not concern you, brother," he answered, but my curiosity was roused, and I pressed the point.

"Since you enquire, Brother Hermann, I will tell you, but please do not mention that I have done so to Brother Walther. He would not approve."

"I will say nothing."

"This building houses a dungeon, and the people incarcerated in it are brothers who have broken the rule."

"Broken the rule? How so?"

"All I know is that there is a brother here who lost his sword and is in chains until such time as a tribunal will be held. And there is one brother who left the castle without having been granted permission and he will surely loose his habit. And there are two brothers..." and here he hesitated.

"Thomas. Be assured that I will tell no one what you have told me. It is merely my own curiosity."

"Well Brother Hermann, I shall only say that there are brothers here who are said to have conspired against the castellan."

"Against the castellan?"

"Yes. But I know not of what they conspired, and I really must say no more."

After this, as we passed through the various parts of the lower ward, he told me a number of things that I was unaware of, relating to the history of the castle. At the far end, beyond the stable and cat-

tle shed was a fruit and vegetable garden that had been levelled out
of the slope by the construction of retaining walls on two sides and
terraces in parallel rows, creating three stepped plots that extended
down to the outer fortification wall. He told me that the rich allu-
vial soil had been carried up from the valley. A drainage channel
had been excavated on its inner side to prevent winter flooding and
to carry off excess rainwater into a large cistern that served both
for the garden and for watering the animals in the neighbouring
stables. Larger plants had been placed against the fortification wall,
including small fruit trees and canes. The vegetables and herbs had
been arranged in neat beds around the walls, as in a cloister garden,
with a large stone basin at the centre of the broad central terrace. It
was well cared for and had a great deal of charm. Among the plants
there were beans, cabbages and onions and an abundance of herbs
including sage, rue and mint, and there were wild peony and pars-
ley and the fruit trees included pomegranates and oranges. There
were also some well-established rose bushes and the appearance of
this small orderly plot seemed quite out of place in the disarray and
chaos that surrounded it.

"This is an old garden," said Thomas. "It was made when
Grand Master von Salza was here. The forest is full of herbs but
Brother Georg, his very able herbalist, brought in new varieties
like the *Artemisia abrotanum* you see here," he pointed to a grey
feathery-leafed plant. It is of great use in the treating of intestinal
worms, which the hochmeister and many of the brothers suffer
from, and as a poultice for wounds. It is also said to counter sleeplessness, though I have had no luck with it in that regard."

"You are rather young to suffer from sleeplessness!" I remarked.

"Nevertheless, it is an ailment that I have had since I have been
here. Brother Simon the infirmarer gave me a draught made with

Artemisia and various other herbs, but it had no effect. In any case it is a useful herb, and here in the mountain it is used as a repellent of insects."

Just beyond the garden a second piece of land was planted with grape vines. The plot had not been levelled but sloped with the natural lay of the hill. I asked Thomas if these grapes were used to produce the wine that we had seen.

"They are for the table," he said. "The wine that you saw is from the grapes of the vineyards of Castellum Regis. We bring in better Cypriot wines from Acre. Excellent eating grapes are grown on land we purchased several years ago from Hugo Merlin and Guido de Renay just outside of the village. Unfortunately, we cannot harvest those grapes anymore."

"Why is that?"

"You must have seen when you came here. The countryside is abandoned. Some of our properties have been taken over by Saracen peasants and the threat of raids makes it too dangerous for us to work many of those that we still retain. We are bringing in almost all of our supplies from Acre."

"We saw the caravan on the Via de Tertille when we were on our way," I said.

I noticed then that a large area beside the herb garden had been walled off by a stone terrace above which was a thick wicker fence, doubled over so that it was impossible to see through it. The breeze from that direction carried an unpleasant smell and my curiosity was aroused. "What is behind there, Thomas?" I asked.

"That is the castellan's garden."

"The castellan has his own garden?"

"Yes. Brother Jordon has a great interest in herbs. He is a most remarkable man of many abilities. He is a great scholar with knowledge of botany as well as zoology and of the ancient arts and languages. He has himself written important treatises on these and many other subjects."

"Jordon? Jordon of Hildesheim?" I asked.

"You have heard of him?"

I had heard his name mentioned several times in the hospital in Acre, always, as I now recalled, with some reticence, and it seemed that he was regarded there with a mixture of reverence and fear.

"Yes," I said. "I have heard of him. What does he grow there?" I asked.

"I have no knowledge of that. Only the castellan himself goes there. But I know that there is a manure bed, you can smell it, and I have seen wagonloads of manure wheeled in, much more than could be needed for a garden, and charcoal and straw as well. I think it is for some experimental work the castellan is doing, but I have no idea what the nature of these experiments might be."

"Experimental work?"

"I only know what the grand commander has told us…" he added hesitantly, "that the castellan is doing important work for the benefit of the castle."

"With manure, straw and charcoal?"

"Perhaps. We do not question the grand commander… and, as I said, Brother Jordon is a remarkable man."

As we walked back towards the dormitory Thomas left me and Brother Walther came out, closing the door quietly behind him. He spoke to me about the old knight.

"He is sleeping now," he said. "He appears very frail. He must be very old. Are you sure it is a good thing for him to be making such a journey?"

"Not at all, Brother," I answered, "but he is determined. He has come all this way to seek his son and he will not rest until he has found him, I am only trying to be of service."

"Do not misunderstand me, Squire Hermann. I mean no criticism of you. It is just that, as you have perhaps heard, there is much talk of the Saracen successes in the north, and it is quite possible that they will turn to us next. Starkenberg is the last of the large castles near Acre."

"I know of the threat," I said, "but do you think that an attack is likely to occur soon? I thought we would have more time."

"I will be frank with you, Squire Hermann. All of the activity that you have witnessed is precisely because of these fears. At the last chapter, the grand commander spoke quite seriously of the possibility of an attack... perhaps in the very near future. I have followed the movements of the sultan, and my own feeling is that it may even come sooner than is generally thought. I am rather surprised that the commander at Acre permitted you and the old knight to come here. It would certainly have been safer to have remained in the city."

"We only plan to be here for a few days... until the grand commander can see us. Surely you don't think there will be an attack on the castle in the coming days?"

"Days? Perhaps not. But I would suggest to you that you return as soon as you can. Any place outside the walls of Acre or Tyre is unsafe. You are aware that the sultan is even now investing the great Hospitaller castle, Crac des Chevaliers. Even if he fails to take it, he will probably come south fairly soon and turn his attentions to us, and then perhaps it will be too great a risk to leave the castle."

"We will not stay any longer than it will take to ascertain whether Albert's son has been here and if there is anyone here who knows where he might now be."

"Then you must not delay in asking for an audience with the grand commander?"

"That is indeed our intention."

"I will see what I can do."

This discussion with Brother Walther distressed me greatly. It was not that I had not known of the movements and successes of the Saracens, but it had not occurred to me that the threat was so immediate. The old knight slept, and we did not disturb him. Walther took me up to the tower of the inner gate and through a vaulted passage and a small door below the Great Hall. There were a number of vaulted chambers here used as workshops for various crafts. In one of these I saw sacks of lime and iron bars, and there were massive beams of wood piled along the lateral walls. No trees in the forest could have supplied beams of this size and I wondered how they had been carried up here. From these chambers we descended the steps that led down as far as the new outworks where the wall was rising behind the wooden scaffolding. Worked stone had been brought from the quarry and stacked up here. There were stones prepared for arrow-slits, doorposts and other parts of the defences that were under construction, and there were masons here at work, their mallets and chisels laid out on the ground before them. I listened to the steady chinking of hammers on stone and admired the quality of the finished pieces, the tooling of which was fine and occasionally incised with tally marks: stars, arrows, and spirals. A roughly levelled path led down the slope, and most of the activity of the builders was at the far, lower end where the interior face of the wall was entirely encased in wooden scaffolding. This wall had already been raised to twice a man's height, and a large wooden treadwheel stood, idle now, against its inner face. While we were standing there and Walther was explaining the plans for these constructions, a bell rang out in the upper castle.

"We need to return. That is the bell for Sext."

We walked quickly up the path and through the gate tower,

then back down the north slope to the makeshift chapel where visiting brothers and guests were already gathering. Albert was not there, and I realised that he must still be sleeping. I decided not to disturb him.

He did not awaken that whole day. After chapel I went to see him and found him pale and cold, and breathing very irregularly. I called Walther. He sent a squire to find the infirmarer who came immediately and tried gently to waken Albert. After some time, he opened his eyes and answered our inquiries in a hoarse and very weak voice. He seemed more confused and concerned over our presence around him than ill, and almost immediately he fell back to sleep. The infirmarer did not seem greatly concerned.

"He is probably exhausted from the travel. You should let him sleep till morning and, if necessary, we will move him then to the infirmary."

"I will have Thomas keep an eye on him during the night and see how he sleeps," said Walther.

When I got back from morning mass the following day, I found Albert dressed and looking better, with more colour in his face. Walther came by and asked if we would like to come down the valley to see the guesthouse and the lake.

"Is it far," Albert asked.

"Not far, but a steep walk back up."

"Then perhaps I will decline. I will take a look around the castle myself if that is alright."

"Certainly. But let me get Thomas to show you around."

Walther took me down the path to the stream below the castle. On the near bank was the guesthouse. Walther told me that the mill occupied the ground floor. The stream in front of it was lined

with a thick growth of blackberry canes, and it was difficult to pass
through these and manoeuvre over the water-worn stones. It ran
from a sluice high on the stone weir that crossed the stream just beyond the mill. We came up to the mill where a number of labourers
were at work by the entrance unloading huge sacks of grain from
a cart, heaving them onto their shoulders and carrying them into
the building. The ground around the door was covered with a thin
coat of flour and scattered grain, which pigeons were making short
work of, strutting boldly between the labourers' feet. The upper
storey above the mill was the guesthouse which Walther explained
had been reserved for special guests but was not in use now because it was too far outside the walls to defend. The mill, however,
was indispensable and there was much activity going on. Walther
excused himself, saying that he would shortly join me and walked
over to speak to some men standing by the entrance. I crossed the
weir, along the top of which was a channel that carried water to
the mill. I walked down onto the opposite bank and crouched at
the edge of the stream. It flowed musically between the stones, like
knotted silver, deep and light, full of colour and shadows.

The narrow valley beyond the weir had been flooded to form
a small lake that spread over the width of the valley and extended back some distance along the old stream path. Although it was
mid-summer the water had risen nearly to the top of the weir and
gathered in one corner against it was a floating bank of duckweed.
When they built the dam, the brothers had introduced grey carp to
the lake, and some of these had grown to enormous size and moved
slowly through the water like sea monsters. Occasionally, when an
insect touched the water, with a surge of unexpected movement a
fish surfaced, kissing the skin of the water with fat white lips. Walther rejoined me, and we stood beside the weir. He told me that he
had been at the castle for nearly twenty years.

"When I came the castle was quite different from what you see now. The Great Hall had not yet been constructed and there were no outer fortifications at all."

"That would be at the time of Grand Master Günther."

"Yes, indeed. I see you have some knowledge of the history of Starkenberg."

"Some, yes. It was a quieter time then, no doubt."

"There were not so many people."

He was silent for a moment remembering.

"In places like this there is always a sense of being on the edge of the unknown. The real trouble began a decade ago; first with the invasion of the Tartars and then the Egyptians. We came under siege five years ago, and you can still see the damage that was done. But it has certainly never been quite as dangerous as it is at present. This is true throughout the land. You yourself must have experienced the sultan's attacks on Acre."

I admitted that I had been aware of them, but had not myself taken part in the fighting. He was silent for a moment, and then went on:

"Only a new army can save us, but there is too much division. I do not see any real hope. Since the death of the French king, much is discussed, but nothing is done. It was thought that the grand master would return. How are we to hold out on our own? It is beyond my humble mind to comprehend."

He sat then for a few moments gazing up at the castle on the hill above us, like a splendid ship riding the rock. I sensed the despair that Walther was expressing.

"We should perhaps be getting back," he said eventually. We climbed the path back and were up by the time the bell rang for Sext.

3 DISPUTE

Two weeks had passed since Riley, Robert and the camp-boy, Salah, had left Haifa. Departing early in the morning by car, they drove north, skirting the bay until the towers and green domes of Akko came into view, then continuing along the coast to ez-Zib and east as far the village of el-Bassa. They drove the car through olive groves into the village, along unpaved, rutted alleys between the flat-roofed stone houses, past mosques, and a small church. There were some new concrete houses built since the war, a few even with a second storey. In one of these lived the village sheikh. He greeted them and, as prearranged, they left the car there and mounted camels, the boy on a donkey, and continued on a winding track that led out of the village and into the foothills. The path followed one of the narrow valleys that rise gently to the east. Farmland along the valley was at a premium, and the dirt track was struggling for survival against the encroaching fields on either side. In places they had to ride over rows of tobacco plants or mount the banks in order to avoid approaching too closely to wooden beehives that had been set up directly on the path. In the fields were ancient olive trees, some entirely hollowed out by fire and worm, but surviving as broad rings of old and new growth, twisted, and writhing from roots to the masses of branches that spread above in a canopy of silver and green.

"This is something I never thought I'd do," Robert spoke, "riding a camel, I mean."

"It is strange," said Riley. "If my colleagues in New York could see me now! Imagine a photograph of me in the New York Times, on camelback in my three-piece suit… and the headline: "Fashion Reaches the Orient!""

Robert smiled at his boss's self–depreciating humour. Riley's almost dandyish care of his dress was amusing and his ability to laugh at himself was an attractive quality.

"You ride remarkably well," Riley said.

"You are doing quite well yourself."

"Do you think so? I feel as if I am just keeping my head above water. I was rather anxious about riding at all before I came out, so I took some lessons. Mind you, nothing prepared me for this. Riding a horse is far less daunting. This is steering a boat on choppy seas."

"Well. It seems the riding lessons paid off, anyway."

"I hope so. They were quite expensive. I had hardly ever ridden back home. When I was a boy my father once took me riding on a donkey, and I seem to remember that it did not go too well. When I was planning to come here, I went to a riding school on Long Island. The fellow who taught me was not the best of teachers. He was impatient and unsympathetic, although, no doubt I was a very trying student. The first time I mounted the horse I was mortified. I trotted around the yard, clinging to the poor animal's neck, terrified of falling off. I was afraid to move into the open space, but reluctant to ask the riding teacher to come to my aid because he acted towards me as if I was a useless child."

They rode on; passing a solitary hovel where a fawn-coloured dog tied to a stake bared its teeth at the camels as they passed. At noon they sat on a stone terrace and ate the sandwiches and fruit they had brought with them. A breeze ran through the grass at their feet, gently swaying the grass-heads and wildflowers, and the air was alive with sounds and the movement of insects. Salah gathered some brush and made a small fire, boiled a blackened and battered finjan and passed the two men tiny cups of sweet coffee. They drank and he refilled their cups. They took out their pipes and leaned back against a terrace wall in the shade of an almond tree. Robert was thinking that if this is the way things would be, he was going to enjoy this expedition. Riley opened an old leather wallet and pressed tobacco into his pipe bowl. As he passed the wallet to Robert, he noticed a cave in the rock outcrop opposite them. It stirred a recollection and he said:

"I haven't told you about my visit to the catacombs in Palermo, have I?"

"No. You have been to Sicily?"

"On the way here. The steamer docked at Palermo, and we were there for two days. There was a terrible storm, and I was glad we were on land, but for the first day I hardly stepped out of the hotel. Then this fellow traveller told me that he had organized a group for a short tour and asked if I cared to join them. I was enthusiastic, having nothing better to do, and in the early afternoon our small group was met at the door of the hotel by a monk from the nearby Capuchin abbey. The rain was coming down without a break, but he told us that where he was taking us would be quite dry. He was very mysterious about it. He refused to say what this place was, and if our travelling companion who had organized the tour had knowledge of it, he also refused to let on. Carrying umbrellas, we walked down a couple of narrow streets and found ourselves at the entrance to the monastery compound. I can't say that it was an especially encouraging sight; it was a pretty dismal group of buildings none of which appeared particularly old or of any architectural merit. However, we obediently followed our guide into the compound, and we entered a doorway and descended a staircase into semi-darkness. Once he had lit a number of lanterns and passed them around, we found ourselves in what I can only describe as the most bizarre and morbid, and at the same time the most fascinating place I have ever seen."

Perhaps for dramatic effect, Riley stopped for a moment to light his pipe, puffing the aromatic smoke out into the late morning air. Then he continued: "We were in a long corridor which occasionally broadened out to form narrow chambers. Some of the women in the group turned back at this point and we later heard at considerable length of their displeasure at the choice of venue for this excursion and at the fact that they had not been warned in advance. I suppose I can understand them. I was also quite disturbed by what we saw, but I am very glad that I did not miss seeing it."

Again, he stopped and puffed a few times on his pipe.

"Obviously you are enjoying dragging this out, John. What on earth was this place?"

"Have you ever seen pictures of the catacombs in Rome?"

"Yes, I think I have; all those human skulls lining the walls?"

"Yes. Well, it was a little like that, only I think even more macabre, though I have never visited the catacombs in Rome myself. These rooms and the passage we were in were … well … decorated, for want of a better word, with appalling human remains, hundreds of them. I think that what made them seem so awful was the manner in which they were displayed, dressed up as if for a pageant. There were monks in dark brown robes tied at the waist with rope, and they were perhaps not so remarkable though their faces gave me nightmares for some time. But it was the women dressed in once pretty frocks of silk and cotton, now stained and rotting and the children in particular, that sent shivers down my spine. Then we came upon what was the pride of the catacombs; the body of a two-year-old child, a girl named Rosalia Lombardo. Hers was the last body to be interred in these catacombs, just six years ago, in a tiny wooden casket. Our guide told us that her bereaved father had approached a local doctor named Alfredo Salafia as I recall, who was a noted embalmer, and he applied his knowledge with great effect. Doctor Salafia replaced the child's blood with a formula that he had developed himself. It was a secret, but the monk told us that it apparently contained formalin, alcohol, glycerine, salicylic acid and zinc; the combined effect being to dry and rigidify the body to just the right degree and kill any fungi that developed."

"How do you remember all that?" Robert interposed.

"I have a good memory for such things, and I put it all down in my diary. Anyway, at first observation it appeared to have worked exceedingly well. She looked as fresh and alive as if she had only just fallen asleep. Her pale hair was tied with a pink bow above closed eyes, a sweet little mouth and nose. She seemed not to belong here, surrounded by all of these ghouls. But I noticed that her entire body was covered with a dirty brown sheet tucked in under her chin and as I gazed at her I began to sense that this child's face was hiding something dreadful underneath. It was this contrast that I found so disconcerting; this beautiful child had become a lie, a fake, nothing but a mask covering the same decay that we had seen in the other terrible figures. I can tell you, it was a great relief when we left those dark chambers, though, as I say, I am not sorry that I had gone. But I was quite shaken for some time, most of all by that tiny child and her doll-like features."

Robert remained silent after Riley had finished his account and finally Riley spoke again.

"I'm sorry. I suppose that is rather a morbid tale. What about you, Robert? Have you travelled much?"

"Not really. Before the war I travelled a few times on the continent; you know, the usual school holiday stuff; bicycle trips in the south of France; that sort of thing."

"Actually, I don't know. Would you believe I had never been

out of the States before coming here? This has pretty much been the great adventure of my life. So, what sort of places did you visit on these bicycle trips?"

"Oh… castles and medieval villages mostly… some small towns to look at the churches."

After they had rested Salah kicked out the fire and they re-mounted and rode slowly out along the gently rising track. They still could not see the castle. The path continued in a steady mild ascent, the hills rising progressively steeper on either side. They had passed no one since they left el-Bassa, the only sign of life was an occasional pigeon in the air or black thrush thrashing about in the dry leaves under the trees. At one point they heard a strange call, and a flock of black goats came down onto the path before them, followed after a few minutes by a small boy with a stick. They waved at him, but he just stopped and stared as they rode past.

When they finally saw the castle, the suddenness of it, expect-ed, but no less startling for that, reminded Robert of the excite-ment he had felt as a child on the occasional visits to his grandpar-ents, when, coming down to the coast near St Ives, the thin strip of blue sea came into view between hills and trees, awakening the anticipation of adventures about to begin. Above the path was a stone wall, all but buried in the forest and higher up, a second, curved retaining wall and a tower, then more ruins beyond, rising steadily towards the highest part of the castle at the far end to the east. They stopped on their tracks and stood gazing at the majestic ruin on its hill.

The first days passed quickly, and the men settled into routine, organising the camp, making contact with workers from the vil-lages of Malia and Tarshiha, and when the equipment arrived, af-ter first clearing the ground inside the castle, excavations began in earnest. They soon were in a rhythm of work, and the pace rapidly picked up. They were up at the castle every day at daybreak, and as the weather was still not hot, they rarely came down before sunset. In the evenings they sat around a fire smoking and talking into the night.

There were more than forty years between Robert and Riley, but in the weeks that had passed since they first met, a strong bond and affection had grown between them, a type of relationship that easily overcomes quite different backgrounds. Sometimes they sat together with hardly a word passing between them, each one glad of the other's presence. Riley occasionally told Robert something about his work on Revolutionary War sites and Indian encampments. He worked for the New York Rapid Transport Company in the capacity of surveyor, a position that aided him in the discovery of many new antiquities. He had not been employed as an archaeologist; his training had been informal and there was little demand for that profession. However, over the years he had achieved considerable renown among the academic community through his discoveries. In recent years he had even been referred to in newspaper articles as the "old man of American archaeology", a title in which he secretly took much pride. He told Robert of the thrill of the first chance discovery he made when he was in his early twenties and first employed by the company. He had stumbled across a British camp site and collected a handful of brass buttons, belt plates and badges. He recalled how these modest finds had suddenly caught his imagination, opening in his mind an entirely different plane of existence, one that he had known of only from reading, but that now became more real through intimacy with these objects. He felt that a lifetime of work of this nature had now come to fulfilment in these entirely different surroundings.

Robert, for his part, had never before participated in an excavation, although in his schooldays he had visited many medieval castles in Britain and France. He told Riley of his three years in the gendarmerie, of the friendships he had made, of the difficult first year adjusting to life in the constabulary.

The third member of their party, Larry Walker, arrived at the camp on the second day, coming down on his own from Jerusalem. Walker was the son of an official in the colonial government, and it was through his father's connections that he had found temporary employment with the Department of Antiquities. Walker had been recommended to Riley when Riley was still in New York. The letter from the director of the Department of Antiquities, Professor Gilford, referred to him as a useful man, a good organiser who spoke some Arabic and Hebrew, and this was seen by Riley as a particular advantage, since he himself spoke neither language. Riley had met the tall red-haired boy in Haifa shortly after he arrived, and at their first meeting, as he later told Robert, it seemed the two would get along. However, although at the time Walker had behaved agreeably, something had bothered Riley right from the start—he could not quite put his finger on it—something about Walker's manner, things he half-said or did not say, and a certain self-assuredness that, as he got to know him, became overt, behaviour that seemed misplaced in someone so young and inexperienced. There was another thing that at the time Riley had dismissed; something about Walker's eyes. Soon, a previously unobserved brashness became evident, and by the time they had spent a week in close company, travelling by car to Jerusalem and later to Amman, it had become clear to Riley that Walker regarded him with contempt. He could not understand why. As far as he could tell he had not given him any reason for this; he had openly welcomed him in the post of assistant and in the weeks since they first met had treated him with courtesy and friendliness. Perhaps Walker disliked being placed in subordination to an American. Through derisive remarks and hints it became apparent that he regarded Americans as inherently inferior to the British. Perhaps, Riley thought, his behaviour stemmed from the fact that he, Riley, had no real training as an archaeologist or, for that matter, of any other kind. Desiring for him to feel more at ease, and being of an honest and open nature, Riley had early on made the mistake of acknowledging his informal background, information that Walker subsequently attempted to use to his own advantage. By the time Riley realised that he was going to be a problem, it was too late to do anything about it.

The doubts that had taken root in his mind very quickly proved to be soundly based. Walker's curt behaviour with the workers became increasingly aggressive, in speech and sometimes even accompanied by physical violence. From early on he attempted to undermine Riley's leadership. On one occasion, which Robert later heard about from Riley, he went so far as to take a group of workers, on his own initiative, to a part of the castle that Riley had decided not to excavate and set them to work there. When Riley went looking for him and the missing workers, he found them busy digging into the floor of a chamber near the western end of the castle.

"What the devil are you doing, Walker. I told you we were not going to excavate here." This was the first time Riley had raised his voice in front of the men. Walker reacted in a belligerent manner.

"Why not? This is a much more promising spot than where you're digging. Ask Ahmed here. The villagers believe that the gold was hidden in this part of the castle."

His attitude infuriated Riley who answered in a burst of anger. "I don't give a damn what anyone thinks about gold. This is not a treasure hunt. It's a scientific excavation." Riley's anger increased Walker's embarrassment, and he reacted with bold defiance and intentional familiarity, intended to antagonize Riley and lessen the blow to his own ego at being so curtly spoken to in front of the workers.

"Oh, come on John! You know as well as I do that's not the case. You simply think you'll find the goods in one place, and I think in another."

Riley was dumbfounded and all the resolve to retain his self-control was thrown aside. He grew red in the face.

"I'm not interested in what you think. I spoke to you about this. We have a plan. It is to systematically excavate this building. If we happen to discover objects of value, that will be a bonus. But it is not our aim. If I tell you to do something, I mean for you to do it!"

"For heaven's sake, old man … If that is what you want … no problem. No need to lose your temper." Walker stood with his hands in his pockets and a grin that was intended to feed Riley's anger.

"This is not about me losing my temper. This is about you carrying out my orders. If you are not willing to do so you're welcome to leave. But if you are going to stay, you will do as I say."

"Alright … alright. You're the boss," said Walker, winking at the workers as if to suggest that some alliance existed between him and them. But there was no alliance, and they observed this exchange with apathy, displaying neither support for him nor any particular interest in what had taken place.

"You will leave off this work now, and take these men back to where they were working before."

Riley's admonitions on this occasion had little effect on Walker, although for a while he was less openly hostile. He remained civil in his behaviour towards Robert, perhaps out of respect for Robert's former position in the gendarmerie. It was not very long, however, before matters deteriorated further. Walker had been drinking openly, and his outbursts with the workers were becoming noticeably problematic. A number of times he had been discovered by Robert in heated disagreement with the foreman, and on at least two occasions complaints had been made by the workers that he had been physically violent towards some of the younger men. Robert had tried to speak to him about this, but his reaction was like that of a stubborn child. He denied all accusations and placed the blame on the workers or on Riley's lack of leadership qualities that, he claimed, was undermining their authority.

A particularly worrying incident occurred one day during the lunch break when the three men were seated in the open space below the high wall of the ruined hall. Robert was in conversation with Riley, who had begun to tell him about a method he had devised for discovering Indian camp sites where there was nothing on the surface to indicate their existence. He told him that he had used a long, thin, iron rod which he pressed into the ground at intervals, feeling for irregularities and variances in the texture of the soil.

"It's largely a matter of experience, I suppose. I've been doing it since I was a boy."

Walker was sitting aside from the two men but within earshot.

"There's nothing remarkable in that," he interposed, "and it's really a bit ridiculous."

"What do you mean?" Riley turned to face him.

"A waste of time, I'd say. I mean … what do you find … a few broken arrowheads? There hardly seems to be any point in it."

"That just displays your ignorance, boy," said Riley. He was rapidly losing his patience in the face of Walker's constantly hostile attitude. "There is a great value in studying the past, even when the evidence for it is comparatively slim."

"I agree," Robert added.

"Well, if you like. But if you ask me, the sort of hobby you're describing hardly qualifies you to direct an excavation of this scale."

"Nobody did ask you," put in Robert.

"Keep your shirt on, old man!" Walker turned to Robert. "Can't a chap express his opinion?"

"Not if you don't have anything worth expressing."

"No, Robert," said Riley, trying to regain his composure. "Let him speak."

"I'm just saying I can't understand how they could let you be in charge of an excavation like this on that kind of experience."

"Well, if you put it like that ...", Riley attempted to remain calm and answered him with remarkable candour, "...you are quite right that I am not experienced in large-scale excavations, but I think that any man of intelligence and with a basic feeling for this type of work can pick it up, and I have to say, I have not at any time felt out of my depth."

"That's exactly where the problem lies," Walker responded. "You think you understand the work and you make all the wrong decisions and go bumbling your way, causing irreparable damage, and the sad thing is that you can't even see it."

"What damage?" In spite of his intentions Riley was flustered and deeply offended by Walker's remarks, in part because of a fear that perhaps there was a degree of truth in them. He was a man continually plagued by self-doubts; doubt about his abilities and about his qualifications. These doubts were rooted in his private life, and his lack of formal training had laid the foundations for them to rise in his professional life as well. Back home they were not such a problem; there were few professional archaeologists around, and he had largely overcome these feelings by building a reputation based on hard work, common sense, and good judgement; and no little good fortune as well. In this strange setting, far from his normal surroundings, his doubts would naturally have surfaced even without the taunting of his assistant. Before he could react to Walker's words Robert came to his defence:

"Walker. You are a fool. Mr. Riley is far more capable of doing this type of work than you or I are or ever will be."

Walker answered him as if Riley was not even present. "Oh really? Well, I disagree. Digging up stone tools on Indian camping grounds does not qualify a man for real archaeology. I at least have had some field experience. I worked at Gibeah in 1922. With all due respect, that was real archaeology… not arrow hunting on Long Island."

Riley stood up:

"I've had about enough of this, Mr. Walker. You had better watch what you say. You are looking to lose your job."

Walker realised that he had gone too far, and he answered in grudging conciliation. "Alright. I meant no offence." But he was obviously insincere, and it was clear he had achieved precisely the effect that he intended. Then, without another word he stood up and walked off.

Another incident occurred a few days later. Walker was in charge of work in two small chambers that had been identified by Riley as the kitchen area of the castle. He had been overseeing a group of workers who were carefully removing a layer of soil and fallen rubble. However, when the workers went on their morning break, Walker decided to speed up the operation by doing the digging himself. He took up a pick and swung it. When it came down it struck a hard object which he thought might be a stone, but when he looked, he saw it was a large sherd of pottery, part of an oversized storage jar. The blow had exposed additional pieces, and he bent down and pulled them free, placing them on the wall of the chamber and then began to hack away at the ground around the hole he had created, exposing, and knocking loose additional pieces. He made no attempt to work as he had been shown; to carefully expose as much of the vessel as possible without removing it in order to try to uncover it intact. Instead, he worked up a rhythm of labour, swinging the pick, bringing it down and lifting out the shattered fragments. It was of no interest to him that these were clearly largely complete vessels. He used all his strength hacking away, as if he intended to clear the ground, to leave no trace of the shattered vessels. He felt a sense of exhilaration in this act, like a child in a fit of destructiveness. When he was well into this, Ra'ed, the foreman, came by. He stood for a moment unobserved by the entrance to the chamber and then walked quickly away and spoke to Robert. Walker had not seen him. After a few minutes Robert came into the chamber.

"What the devil are you doing, Walker?" Startled, Walker swung around to face him.

"What? What do you mean?" he asked defensively.

"What are you doing?" Robert repeated.

"You can see what I'm doing. I'm digging." Robert walked up to him and grabbed the pick from his hand and pushing him aside stood looking over the ruin Walker had wrought. The floor of the chamber was covered with the fragments of a number of the large pithoi that he had managed to shatter down to their bases. He had piled the pieces of shattered pottery on the wall and there were enough there to show that several of these vessels must have been more-or-less complete before he had got at them.

"My god! Do you realise what you've done?"

"What do you mean? I've only been removing these pots."

"I can't believe you!" Robert shook his head. He was almost speechless at the scene of ruin. "How could you do this?"

Walker blustered:

"What are you making such a fuss for? I've been clearing the chamber. I did it on my own initiative … to save time. I'm nearly at the floor. You should be pleased. Riley will be."

"Are you a complete idiot, Walker? You have destroyed all of these vessels. Why?"

"What do you mean destroyed? They were already broken."

"Do you take me for a fool? You know this is not the way to uncover finds. You say you have had experience in archaeological excavations. Is this the method you learnt at Gibeah? You have single-handedly destroyed an important find."

It was only now that Walker seemed to become aware of the extent of damage he had caused. He spoke more quietly and apologetically:

"I was just trying to get things moving. I thought these would not be very important."

"Well, you were wrong."

"I can clean this up. We can put most of these pieces back together." He bent down and began to pick up some loose pieces still on the ground.

"Leave it!" Robert snapped. "Just clear out."

Walker dropped the sherd he was still holding and backed away. When he was at the doorway of the chamber, Robert noticed an odd and perturbing action by Walker. He quite suddenly stopped in his tracks, and Robert thought he was going to turn around and say something more. Instead, he looked up at the sky where in the far distance a sparrowhawk was circling slowly. He stood staring at it for a moment, then he turned back to look at Robert, and his mouth opened as if to say something, but no words came, and Robert saw in his eyes a terrible apprehension, as if that distant bird was somehow a threat.

4 ANTAGONISM

When they reached the camp, Riley entered into the cool darkness of the tent, leaned his cane against the fold-away desk, set down his notebooks and sat on the edge of his camp-bed. After some moments Robert pushed open the flap of the tent and stepped in.

"Take a look at these," he said, handing him the file with his drawings. Riley leafed through the drawings.

"These are very good."

"Yes… I have most of the measurements. I should be able to have a plan ready by the end of the week." Robert sat down on his cot. "Listen, John, I hate to bring this up again, but you are going to have to deal with Walker. When I was at the mill, I had a word with Ra'ed. He said that Walker has the workers up in arms. Apparently, he is demanding that they work on Sundays, and he threatened the lot of them with dismissal if they don't turn up."

"Oh, no! What is the fellow's problem?"

"Ra'ed said that Walker had warned them that if they don't come to work, he will bring new men in from Tarshiha. I'm telling you, John, if you don't deal with this, you're going to have a mutiny on your hands. Two or three of the workers have already left and are refusing to come back."

"Alright. I'll deal with it," said Riley. "He's gone too far this time."

Robert was about to mention the episode in the kitchen chamber that he had witnessed earlier, but before he had time to speak cries came from outside. The two men stepped out to find Walker almost on top of the camp-boy with his hand pulled back in a fist about to strike him. Salah, though a tall boy, was no match for Walker, and he had both his hands up to protect his face from the expected beating.

"Leave him alone, Walker." Robert pushed him off the boy.

Walker straightened up, brushing himself off with the flat of his hand as if he had been soiled. "Only way to deal with these people," he said indignantly. "I told him to have the place tidied up by the time we got back. Look at this… It's a pigsty. He should have had all these crates piled up and the finds from yesterday on the tables for sorting."

"That's no reason to strike the boy," said Robert.

"Let me deal with this, Robert," said Riley. "I want to have a private word with you, Walker."

Robert stood aside as Walker reluctantly followed Riley into the tent. Then he gave the boy a hand to get up.

"I'm sorry sir," Salah said, backing away.

"It's alright." The boy stood with his head down, as if he was ashamed of what had happened. "Are you alright?"

"Yes sir, Mr. Palmer. I am sorry sir."

"This is not your fault, Salah. Don't you let him worry you. Mr. Riley will deal with him."

Inside the tent a heated discussion was going on. With their voices raised Robert could not help overhearing the entire discussion. Riley sat down at his camp-desk and faced Walker who remained standing at the entrance, a look of insolent defiance on his face.

"Now listen to me," said Riley. "I've just about had it with you. Since we've been here you've been openly disrespectful to me…

which I can take, though I don't for the life of me know why…
but what I will not stand for is your behaviour towards the workers. You have managed to upset and offend them all. Some of the
men have walked off and are refusing to come back. You can't make
them work on Sundays. You have to treat with them with respect."

"You don't understand these people," said Walker. He fidgeted
with the flap of the tent as he spoke. "You don't know how to deal
with them. You have to keep them in line. They steal and they are
lazy. What do you think… they're going to church on Sundays?
Ha! That's nonsense. We can get Moslems from Tarshiha. They
work on Fridays with no complaints. You haven't lived here, Riley.
You don't know them like I do."

"I may not have been in this country as long as you" Riley re-
torted, "but I've been here long enough to know that half of the
problems here are caused by people with attitudes like yours. These
villagers are honest and hard working. I have had no problem with
them, and I won't have you stirring up trouble where there isn't
any."

"That's ridiculous. This isn't America. This is the Levant. You
have to be assertive if you want to get anything done. Otherwise,
they will take advantage of you. You'll be paying them and getting
nothing in return. I'm telling you; they are expert at avoiding work.
Anyway, you Americans are hardly the ones to give advice on how
to deal with natives."

"This has nothing to do with America. I am talking about be-
having decently to fellow human beings. You might do as you like
when you're elsewhere, but as long as you are here you will behave
with respect to me, to Mr. Palmer and to the workers. I'm telling
you this for the last time. I will not put up with any more insubordination from you. And another thing… I won't have you drinking
in the camp or at work."

"Drinking! What are you talking about?" Walker blustered.

His fist clenched around the piece of the tent flap he was holding. "I've hardly have had a drink since I've been here."

"I'm not an idiot, boy. There are empty bottles all over the place. I don't know where you are keeping the stuff, and I don't want to have to search your belongings."

"You wouldn't dare."

"I will if I think you are endangering the safety of the men."

"There's nothing wrong with a drink now and then. It's not as if I'm going around intoxicated. And don't tell me you don't touch the stuff."

"If you knew how to control yourself, I wouldn't have any objections." Riley picked up a pile of papers from the desk and waved them at Walker. "It's not only the drinking. How do you explain these?" He threw the papers onto the camp bed beside which Walker was standing.

"What are these?"

"Those are some of the bills from the purchases you ran up in Haifa before the dig."

"These are for equipment for the camp. Anyway, I don't owe you an explanation," Walker raised his voice.

"You most certainly do," Riley shouted back, dropping all efforts to retain his composure. "These are expenses charged to the expedition. There are a number of items here that I have never seen and, if I am not mistaken, some of these bills are for alcohol. I want a complete explanation of all of these expenses… and I want it today."

Walker stood for a moment with his mouth open as if he wanted to say something, and then turned to walk out of the tent. Riley spoke again: "I'm warning you, Mr. Walker. Either you change your ways or you're out of here."

Walker stopped and turned back to face Riley. "I don't have to account to you. My boss is in Jerusalem." He spoke now with increased malevolence and seemed to be throwing to the wind whatever caution he had previously exhibited. "I was given this position by the department. What did you think - they would let an amateur like you run this affair without anybody to keep an eye on you? If I let them know how you've been running this excavation you will be shut down before you can blink an eye."

"Why you insolent little..." Riley stood up glowering with anger and Walker stepped back against the side of the tent. He didn't wait for Riley's reply but turned his back and walked out and off to his own tent. Riley called out after him, "Walker, I'm not finished with you," but Walker ignored him, cursing under his breath as he pushed past Robert. Riley came out of the tent and Robert looked inquiringly at him.

"Damn him", said Riley. "The fellow has some nerve."

"Don't let him get to you."

"Did you hear? He threatened me! I should give him notice now."

"Leave it John. Deal with it when you calm down." Riley sat down on a crate, breathing deeply, his complexion slowly returning to normal.

"Yes... you're right. It's just... he's so infuriating. He is doing his best to undermine my authority."

"Wait till the morning. If there's any trouble tomorrow, give him notice then."

"I don't know... I'm half-minded to throw him out now."

"If you like I can speak to him."

"No... no Robert. I have to deal with this. As you say, I'll wait till tomorrow. But I swear, if he so much as raises his voice or repeats any of his impertinences, he is out of here."

The following morning Walker did not join them for breakfast. They were sitting outside when he suddenly emerged from his tent and without exchanging a word with them walked off up the hill towards the castle. The men watched him walk away. Salah heated a pan over the fire till it sizzled, broke in two eggs and then two more and when they were ready placed the eggs on enamel plates for the two men and poured for them hot coffee in two enamel mugs.

When they climbed the path up to the castle, they heard a faint squawking, and looking up they saw masses of migrating storks circling out in the blue void in an open spiral, like whipped up papers in a slow-moving twister.

Walker was already at work. Riley decided to wait and see how he would behave. He was sullen, hardly spoke to anyone during the day and was clearly sulking. Riley asked Robert to keep an eye on him to make sure he didn't take out his anger on the workers, and Robert spent the morning making drawings in the chamber where Walker and his team were at work. His presence there had the effect of restraining Walker from openly aggressive behaviour, but he made his feelings clear through curt speech and sour facial expressions.

Before lunch Robert went to look for Riley and found him in the castle's kitchen bent over an area of freshly exposed ground. He was examining the grey soil, and Robert came closer and gazed over his shoulder. He saw what Riley was looking at; a shallow bowl the size of a soup bowl. It was intact, although the dark line of a crack ran through its centre and fingered out across the surface in three directions. The rim of the bowl was impressed like the crust of a pie, and the interior was covered with a white glaze stained with dark green and ochre runs. Riley pushed the dry soil off the surface with his thumb exposing a lively pattern; an attractive childlike rendering of a knight standing between two upright palm branches. The knight was dressed in chainmail, wore a conical helmet and held a sword and a triangular shield.

Robert watched Riley as he worked. He dug a shallow area around the bowl and cleaned his way up to its edges, careful not to advance too quickly so as not to loosen the separate pieces. He wanted to observe the bowl in its context as he worked it free. When it was entirely exposed and the interior had been cleared of the adhering soil he stopped, put aside the small trowel, brushed the interior very lightly with a straw brush and took up his camera to photograph the bowl *in situ*. He wrote something in a small ledger in his very fine, neat cursive. Then he cleared under the bowl and with great care, using both hands, lifted it easily away from the soil. Freed, the pieces of the bowl came apart in his hands and Robert bent over and slipped his hand in to prevent the pieces from falling. The two men laid them in the cardboard box Riley had prepared. Riley took up his cane and rose, stretching to ease the stiff muscles in his neck.

Robert and Riley were not surprised when Walker did not join them at lunch but walked off and sat on his own. His anger was like a tiny flame that had kept its strength in the embers throughout the afternoon until, almost without warning, it flared up. A minor disagreement between Walker and one of the workers served as a pretext for him to raise his voice and threaten to throw the man out. Robert immediately intervened.

"Walker. Leave him alone."

"You stay out of this."

"There is no need to make threats."

"I'll do as I see fit. I'm in charge of these men."

"You won't be for long if you continue like this." The villagers had stopped their work and were watching the two.

"Don't try to undermine my authority," Walker snarled and then turned on the workers. "Get back to work."

"Walker. Listen to me…" Robert tried to calm him, but Walker turned on him and let loose all his spleen.

"You are no better than he is," he said. "I would have expected that someone who has had dealings with these people would understand."

"You're an ass, Walker." Robert looked across at the workers, wondering if they were following Walker's raving. If so, they could only find it offensive. "I don't care what you think regarding me or what your ideas are on discipline. But I can tell you this. You nearly got yourself fired yesterday, and if you don't change your ways, you are very shortly going to find yourself out of a job. And if that happens, you should expect that Mr. Riley will report your behaviour to Professor Gilford, which might make it very hard for you to get any employment in the future. I suggest that you take heed of my words."

"You take heed of mine," Walker shouted back at him. "Damn you and damn him! If I am fired, I won't be the only one out of a job."

"What do you mean?"

"I will destroy this dig and that American fool will be on the next boat home!"

"You think so, do you Mr. Walker?" It was Riley speaking now. Having heard the shouting, he had come in and had observed this latest outburst. He spoke very quietly and this time with complete self-control. "I want you to pack your things and leave."

"You can't make me go."

"Oh, but I can. You are a troublemaker, and I have put up with your insolence for long enough. You will leave in the morning."

"You are a fool, Riley. I'm glad to be out of here." He stormed off, stopping for a moment by the wall of the hall to have a last say: "I promise you… you will regret this. You have no idea who you're dealing with." He kicked a stone flying and pushed past Robert.

*By force I drive the weeping clouds, by force I whip the seas/
Send gnarled oaks crashing, pack the drifts of snow and hurl/
Great hailstones down upon the lands.*

Ovid, Metamorphosis 6.680-83 trans. Melville

The weather was changing. That night a storm gathered at sea, sweeping from the south into the north of the Sinai Peninsula and up the coast as far as Tripoli. The wind blew over the grey water, whipping up white crests and spray, lifting the mist in a boiling mass that rolled over the shore and inland, low across the plain to the north of the Carmel and in towards the hills where it billowed up, then fell heavily back to earth. Rain fell on the low scrub and rock along the spur on which the castle stood. It fell on the rocky crags and cliffs across the valley to the north. It fell on the oaks and the twisted red arms of the arbutus trees and continued throughout the night and into the morning. Water ran down the castle walls in rivulets. It ran down the hillsides carrying the soil that the workers had thrown. It ran into the cisterns, into the newly excavated trenches. The men in their flimsy tents slept through the storm, even through the flashes that momentarily lit up the dark valley, and the echoing rumble of thunder. In the morning they awoke to find themselves in a sea of mud. Abdul and Salah were already up, hoeing a trench to drain away the pool of muddy water that had formed around the tents. The rain was still coming heavily down, steadily drumming on the crates and on the trestle tables that stood along the edge of the small encampment and on the canvas of the four tents. Walker was nowhere to be seen.

Riley called over the noise of the rain: "Robert. Have you seen my cane? I can't find the damned thing."

"No. It's not in the tent?"

"I know it was here. Abdul... where is Mr. Walker?"

"I don't know, sir."

"Salah. Have you seen him?"

"No sir."

He turned to Robert. "He didn't say anything to you?"

"I only just woke up."

"Mr. Riley"

"What is it, Salah?"

"One of the camels is missing."

"What! It must be that fool. I don't believe it! Where could he have gone in this weather?"

"Here's your cane, John. I'm afraid it's broken," said Robert, bending to pick up the two snapped pieces.

"Are you going to manage without it?"

Riley shook his head I disbelief. "I don't really need it," he answered. "He wouldn't have gone up to the castle. I can't see how he could have got as far as Malia or el-Bassa in this rain. He must be mad to have left here in the dark."

But there was no sign of him, and it was apparent that he had indeed left in the night.

5 MISSION

The grand commander and his subordinates were busy directing work on the new fortifications, and Albert was promised an interview within the next few days. Meanwhile we had made ourselves comfortable in the makeshift dormitory in the outer ward. Brother Walther apologised for not being able to accommodate us in the more comfortable guesthouse in the valley. The dormitory was very crowded, and our pallets were up against one wall at the far end.

When I returned from the chapel after Sext, I found that the old knight was asleep again. His hair was very white, and his skin was pale, almost transparent. He suddenly seemed much older than he had. A number of times in the days that I had accompanied him, doubts arose in me as to the wisdom of his making such a great physical effort. But I knew that he would not give up and that to do so would probably be a greater danger to his wellbeing than the strains of travel and the risks of disappointment. In spite of his years something of the younger man could still be seen in his face as he slept, as indeed when awake, in his gestures and the occasional sparkle in his pale blue eyes. Watching him I thought about time and how things had changed for me over the past few years, how my childhood had fallen so quickly behind. How quickly, I wondered, had old age come upon him, and how quickly would it come upon me? He moved in his sleep, and I covered him gently with a blanket. I wished that I had someone to care for me as deeply as this old man cared for his son.

I had been two years at the German hospital in Acre when Albert arrived. I recall how I was seated in solitary contemplation in the cool dark chapel one morning after mass, when a brother brought an elderly white-haired knight over and introduced him to me as Albert of Ulm. I immediately observed a great gentleness about him, in both appearance and manner. Not wanting to disturb the other worshipers we went to the back of the nave and out through a door in the side aisle into the bright morning. We walked over to the shade of a small orange tree that grew at the centre of the cloister. This cloister, carefully tended by the brothers, was a most beautiful garden, one of the finest in the city. The orange tree was immaculately pruned. It had fruit but these were still green. A stone bench ringed the tree and around it a circular path from which four other paths ran diagonally out to the angles formed by the surrounding buildings. To the west a high ivy-covered wall sealed off the one side of the cloister that was not built onto. This wall extended beyond the buildings on either side to enclose the entire compound of the convent, including the hospital. Only the famous Turris Almani was outside of the wall. It rose mightily against the sky and was the tallest building in the eastern part of the city. It had been built as an unusual and remarkable act of bravado by one of the earlier commanders of our house in Acre, in blatant defiance against the masters of the Hospital and the Temple and perhaps even against the advice of the hochmeister, Gerhart von Malberg, who had urged caution in all our dealings with the greater military orders. The commander who built it had subsequently been replaced in his position, and some saw that as a rebuke for his audacity in this matter. But I had heard others claim that some financial irregularities lay behind his removal. Nonetheless, the tower remained and had become the pride of our Order. It could be seen even by ships navigating along the western shore and was one of the prominent buildings observed when one approached Acre from the east.

We sat down and, in a soft voice that was indicative of his age and gentle nature, the old man told me about himself. His conversation confirmed my impression of him as a man of most disarming integrity and courteousness. He said that as a youth he had served in the Emperor Otto's army in the disastrous battle against the French king in 1214. I realised then how extremely old must be. I asked him how long he had been in the East, and he said that his ship had arrived a few days earlier. The voyage had been very hard on him, and he had only just risen from his bed. He told me after a short hesitation that he had come East to look for his son. I asked if his son was in Acre, and he said that he did not know. He was not even certain that he was still in the Holy Land.

"How then will you find him?" I asked, and he opened his hands in a gesture expressing his lack of an answer. He told me that his son had been master of the novices at the Premonstratensian abbey of Weissenau in Upper Swabia and later became prior. About five years ago he had left the abbey to go on pilgrimage to the Holy Land. At that time there were almost no holy places still in Christian hands; Jerusalem and Bethlehem had fallen to the Saracens decades earlier; Nazareth had recently been taken, and it was in the year that he arrived that Caesarea had fallen, so that even the chapel and tomb of the Centurion Cornelius could no longer be seen. But Albert told me that he had later learnt from the abbot of Weissenau that his son Bernard's principal aspiration in coming over the sea, the true reason in fact behind his pilgrimage, was his desire to obtain for his abbey a most important relic, the arm of

Saint John the Baptist, which at that time was located in the German hospital in Acre. How it had come to be there Bernard had not
known, for it had formerly been in the cathedral church of Saint
John at Sebastia. Perhaps it had been removed from Sebastia at the
time that city fell to the Saracens. In any case it had somehow been
placed in the charge of the German custodian of relics in Acre. It
was indeed a most remarkable relic. It was said to be still covered
with skin and flesh which, though burnt, still gave forth blood. It
was wrapped in a cloth of purple silk and was contained in a gilded
silver receptacle, itself in the form of an arm and decorated with
precious stones. Bernard had told the abbot of Weissenau that it
had come to his notice that the Hospitallers also desired the arm
for their church, but he believed that he could obtain it first. Such
an illustrious relic would have greatly boosted the flow of contri-
butions to the monastery, and if he did succeed, the abbot had
intended to build a new church to house it. For this the duke of
Swabia himself, Conradin, who was titular king of Jerusalem, Sicily, and Germany, had promised to donate the costs of the church.
But nothing has been heard of Bernard since he left the abbey.

"I fear greatly for him," Albert said. He paused for a few minutes, then continued: "I had hoped that someone here might have
heard of my son, perhaps might know what has become of him, but
the commander told me that they had no knowledge of his whereabouts."

I asked Albert if he had spoken to the Premonstratensians who
are our neighbours in Acre.

"I have," he said. "It was the first thing I did. Their abbot told me
that he himself had only recently arrived in Acre, but he said that
he would raise the matter in chapter. But he found out nothing. He
suggested that I come to your house which had in any case been
my intention. I did so and, as I said, I spoke to the commander.
He made inquiries and sent me to speak with the custodian of the

relics who told me that no one had made an offer for the purchase of the relic except for the sacrist of the Hospital of Saint John, and it was now located in the Church of Saint John. It appears that no one in the German house has heard of my son."

Albert told me that he had decided to go to all the convents and hospitals and cemeteries in the city.

"Have you come alone," I asked.

"I have … against my wife's pleading. She said that I am too old, and she was right, but I will not go to my grave without knowing what has become of my son." There was a noticeable apprehension in his eyes when he said these words.

"You must love your son greatly," I said.

"Bernard is my only son and dearer to me than anything on this earth."

"How can I help you?" I asked.

"I hardly dare ask. I wish to trouble no one. I have come this far on my own."

"Do you wish that I go with you through the town? I have no office at present. I am sure the commander will permit it."

"I would be most grateful to you if you could, Squire Hermann," he said. "I hardly know my way in the city. I think that the brothers of the hospital of Saint John, perhaps the sacrist, might know something."

Over the following days we traversed much of the city. Albert said that he preferred to begin by visiting the cemeteries. He said that he would rather face the possibility of his son's death first. We began by exploring outside the city walls. On the first day we walked through the old quarter of Saint Thomas, which, since the English brothers had moved to the new city, had deteriorated into a pitiable warren of decaying hovels where some of the poorest residents now resided. We then continued through the gardens of Saint Romanus, an open area that occupied the north-eastern corner of the old city. As we passed near the old wall, we heard a commotion and saw that there were wrestling bouts going on between burgesses and servants. It was a colourful scene. They had hung banners in the surrounding trees, and a great crowd had gathered. From their costumes and the banners, it appeared that some of these men were from the Pisan Curia, and their opponents were servants from the Hospital. Nearby in an open place, a long trestle table had been set up covered with bright cloths, with benches beside it on which a host of guests were seated, and a sky-blue tent from which food was being carried to the table. There was much laughter and shouting, and this was clearly a celebration of a wedding, for on one side near the centre of the table sat a radiant youthful couple in lavish dress, and much attention was being paid to them by the surrounding celebrants.

It was a pleasant day, less hot and humid than most days over the past few weeks, and I greatly enjoyed the break from monastic routine. As we walked down the unpaved road in the direction of the city wall, we saw a flock of crows in the long grass under the trees stabbing the ground for worms. I recall this because I had not observed them until we were nearly upon them and, as we approached they flew up almost into us, and their loud caws were quite unexpected and frightening.

We passed the customs house and walked out of Saint Nicholas Gate onto the broad wooden bridge that crossed the eastern moat. Below, within the moat were makeshift hovels, even more miserable than those we had seen in the old English quarter. In the few years that I had been in Acre and on the few occasions that I was permitted to wander through the city I had seen a fair amount of change, mainly deterioration as the city became more and more crowded, taking in refugees from the towns and villages that had fallen to the Saracens. These hovels were an example of the lamentable overcrowding and the shortage of housing that had resulted throughout the city.

On the far side of the bridge, we passed through a portal in the outer wall. Just beyond lay the cemetery of Saint Nicholas. It was bordered by a low stone wall, and we entered through an arched gate, avoiding a wretched group of lepers who occupied the ground along the wall and who gave no warning of their presence, neither by rattle, nor cry as was required, but quite openly accosted us for alms. The cemetery was vast. It stretched most of the way along the eastern city wall and almost up to Mount Turon. In the north it approached the walls of the new city and extended south as far as the mouth of the Belus River. We walked between rows of tombstones all the way to the mills on the river where we saw the ruins of a small church. Seeing us, a priest who was seated on one of the tombs us stood up quickly. He was perhaps embarrassed at being found in this irreverent attitude, and he answered our greeting in a rather gruff manner. He spoke in a southern Italian dialect that I could not follow, though I have a rudimentary knowledge of vulgare Latinum. But Albert understood and later told me that when he had asked if the priest knew whether a Bernard of Ulm or of Weissenau was buried here the man had rudely answered:

"How could I possibly know? There are so many tombs. You should look for yourselves."

Ignoring his rudeness, Albert asked him if he knew what had happened to the little church, which had been thoroughly razed and was now nothing but a pile of stone and mortar. Only a large broken stone cross revealed its identity. The priest answered that it had been demolished together with the cloister during a recent Saracen attack. Nothing more could be learnt from him, and we began on our own to examine the tombs around the ruined chapel. They were positioned in irregular rows, and in some places, you could walk quite comfortably beside or around them, but in others they were so close together that it was necessary to squeeze past or even climb over them. Most of the tombstones were not of great age and could be easily read, although some were of a friable stone and had weathered badly and many that had their epigraphs painted rather than incised had faded so that little could be made out except for the remnants of painted crosses. I walked one way, reading just the first lines which usually contained the names of the dead: HIC IA-CET… in Latin "Here lies…" or ICI GIST in French and then the deceased's name; for example, †ICI GIST FRERE RICHARD QUI TRESPASSA EN L'AN DE L'INCARNACION NOSTRE SEIGNOR IHESU CRIST: MCCLX – Here lies Brother Richard who died in the year of the incarnation of our Lord Jesus Christ 1260. Other inscriptions were less formal, and some included in their epitaphs short verses referring to the decease's bones, the decay of his bodily form and the wandering of his soul at God's will and ended with a request that the visitor pray that it might pass safely to glory.

Albert followed slowly. He was finding it difficult to get between the tombs. This search seemed futile, there were so many tombs, and so many were unidentifiable that I quickly despaired. Nonetheless, we did this for well over an hour. Then I returned to Albert, who was exhausted from the effort and had taken a seat on a large stone in the ruins of the chapel.

"You have found nothing?" he asked, though it was perhaps not so much a question as a statement.

"I found no stone with his name. But there are so many."

He sighed, then sat in silence, but his lips were moving and seemed to be muttering to himself. Perhaps he was praying. I sat down beside him on the stone. Finally, he spoke:

"I don't know what we should do," he said. "We could search here for days."

"But, if, may the Lord forbid, your son is dead and is buried here, it would be under a fairly new stone, and I have examined most of those."

"Then I can still be hopeful," he said, though he sounded doubtful.

We sat there for a while, and perhaps it was in order to avoid dwelling on the dismal thoughts in both our minds that we spoke of various things, and somehow, we got onto the subject of his travels. Albert told me how his ship had almost run ashore in a violent storm somewhere between Tartus and Arachus. As if that was not enough, he said, they were assailed by a sea swine which he described as a horrid creature which is known when hungry to attack small ships and even tear them apart. He had not himself seen it, but he said that the sailors had told him of its presence and that it could only be fended off by being fed with bread or by their making angry and threatening faces at it. He did not know which method they had employed but the danger had somehow passed.

He told me other no less remarkable stories and after a while, when I could see that he had rested, I suggested that we head back. This time we walked across the open space approaching the city wall and then turned north along the moat, passing a small marble-faced building over the Spring of Saint William and, further on a sugar refinery where piles of red cane were stacked at the entrance. I was curious and looking inside I saw the glow of the furnaces. The air was sweet with the smell of boiling molasses. We turned west after passing the refinery and re-entered the city through the Gate of Saint Anthony.

We had now entered the new city, Montmusard as it is called. The road we were on passed by the Church of Saint Anthony near the house of the Franciscan friars and continued north past Saint Bartholomew and into the new quarter of the English, where their church dedicated to the martyr Saint Thomas was under construction. The streets here were broad and cleaner than in the old city, and the smell of sewage was notably absent. In the older part of the city, it was so perceptible that when one was there for a while it seemed to take on an almost physical presence.

Albert spoke to the English brothers but learnt nothing from them. Then we cut back across the neighbourhoods to the south, passing the Templar stables and the Hospitallers' auberge and crossing again into the old city. The moat between the new and old city was as broad as that on the east, but as it had long ago lost its defensive function and was now well within the city it had, over the years, filled with garden plots and squalid hovels and huts. From the bridge we could see these ugly, makeshift structures, built from any material available. Some extended from the old wall and reached out over the moat like the outstretched arms of a beggar, supported on beams of wood that were stuck into the wall or reaching up from below. The worst of them looked as if they would collapse in the slightest breeze.

Albert had grown tired, and the day had become increasingly hot. Anticipation, disappointment, and the physical effort had taken their toll, and I persuaded him to return to the hospice to rest. However, after Sext and the midday meal he felt sufficiently revived and insisted that we continue our search. I wondered where he found the strength. I was myself still tired from the morning. We left the compound again, this time walking directly into the heart of the city. Keeping to a slow pace we made our way west along an unpaved road in the open ground below the citadel and its three great towers. The warm afternoon air weighed with the fragrance of fig trees that grew in the shadow of the perimeter wall. These trees were full of fat ripening fruit, some already purple and split in the sun to expose their seedy pink flesh, an attraction to hundreds of small chattering birds.

At the end of the road, we turned onto a narrow alley with stalls here and there in porticoes and under the houses. After pass-

ing through an almost dark and empty vault we found ourselves
entering a broader street. Then we came upon a bazaar; tables
and benches piled with goods. Crates, barrels, and baskets were
stacked along the walls on the spaces between the doors of houses. We saw every colour and smelled every possible smell, and our
ears filled with the musical clamour of vendors selling their goods.
First, we passed through the butchers' market. I saw camel heads
hanging from hooks; necks of thick, pink muscle, roughly hacked
through, eyes wide open, jaws hung sideways displaying enormous yellow teeth. There was an inescapable rank odour. Whole
pigs lay on tables along with body parts of goats and sheep and
jars of sheep eyes and brains. There were hanging skinned animals,
some of which I could not even recognize; just masses of purple
flesh over which stretched torn transparent skins of pink-white
fat and tendons. Below the hanging carcasses lay bloody hides,
hair, wool, and various innards discharging thick, putrid, congeal-
ing ooze on the filthy stone steps. Wooden cages of pigeons and
small hens were stacked against the walls, one above the other in
rickety towers. Further on we passed a stall displaying cheeses.
There were wine stalls and others with fresh green and black olives displayed in straw baskets and open sacks of dried herbs, nuts,
beans and carobs, short-cut lengths of sugarcane and strings of gar-
lic-heads. There were stands piled with vegetables and fruits from
the gardens outside the city; among them bunches of yellow, cres-
cent-shaped fruits that I had not seen before. Further along I saw
a glass vendor selling all shapes of bottles and beakers, and inside
an adjacent shop was the furnace and the glassmaker at his work.
On the shelves and tables were his finer pieces; beakers decorated
with enamel that had come back from the painters' workshop and
were placed here together with their individual leather containers.
Some of these were painted with figures, heraldry and Arabic and

Latin inscriptions. I stopped to read some of the latter: "Master Roger made me" or "Don't break it!" In other shops there were vessels from the local potteries; cooking pots, storage jars, bowls; and there were imported table vessels, dipped, splashed, and mottled with yellow and green glaze and incised designs. The shopkeeper boasted that these were shipped from Syria, Egypt, Cyprus, Sicily, and even Spain. Then was an apothecary with trestle tables covered with spices and medicines, bunches of fresh and dry herbs, cones of white crystalline sugar wrapped in cloth, strange minerals, powders, and crystals; yellow and black, dull, and glossy. On one bench there was a large glass basin half-filled with water containing hundreds of sleek black leaches.

The street widened out and met a second market street, and here was an open area occupied by a seller of fine decorative stones, slabs of red and white marble, granite and porphyry stacked in piles and leaning against the side walls. Some were carved and engraved with intricate decorations, acanthus leaves, pinecones, and various animals. These were intended for buildings, and some had clearly come from dismantled structures. There was a timber yard and, alongside it were manufacturers of furniture, and the smell of freshly sawn wood pervaded. There was a forge where the smiths were manufacturing horseshoes, farm tools, weapons, chains, iron cooking-pots, sweet-sounding copper and brass bells that were to be attached to horses, and there were locksmiths who made their locks from iron and others who made them of wood. There were makers of spoons and ladles, knives, razors, hooks, and needles. We saw two men seated at a table; a smithy preparing fine iron wire, pulling, and cutting it, and a second man hammering the tiny pieces to construct chainmail for hauberks. There were stalls selling leather goods; parchment, ox-hides, buckskins, leather bags and bottles, saddles, shoes, and shields. There were stalls of brocades in various colours, violet, gazelle blood, indigo blue. I saw stacks of patterned silks of varying qualities, some of the utmost beauty, dyed in crimson, saffron, and vermilion.

The street narrowed again, and it was hardly wide enough for two people to pass between the crates, barrels and tables. Between our feet dogs and children were playing. And behind all the pleasant and surprising smells was the ever-pervading rank smell of the sewage.

We passed into a quieter residential street and quite suddenly found ourselves on the south side of the cathedral. Along its wall, in the recesses between the buttresses, alms-seekers sat in their sour rags, their filthy faces, brown and wrinkled like rotting windfalls in an orchard. You could see the lice moving in their hair. A retarded child among them was dressed in an adult's clothing. He opened a toothless grin as we approached, drooling, and flailing with his arms, his hands lost in the depths of his sleeves. The corner of the street opened onto the parvis before the cathedral. We stopped for a few moments to gaze up at the façade; the towering double belfries and pointed tracery windows soaring into the sky above the central door, sweeping arches, friezes, capitals, and abaci; leafed and crocketed, inhabited with carved animals, saints, demons, obscene creatures, and teems of resting pigeons. There were twelve almost life-sized saints around the hood arch of the main portal. We stepped into its cool shadow and through the doors into the dark interior where a murmur of prayer hung like a warm mist over dark figures crouched in the pews. Candlelight flickered in the side-chapels. I gazed up at the sweeping vaults, but Albert was already moving back to the door, and I followed him out again into the brilliant glare of the street.

This was the heart of the city. The houses were tall and pressed up one against the other with no end of annexes extending out and occupying part of the street. Every space was made use, of and walking became a hazard, not only because of the pressing of the crowds but because of the filth running in an open drain down the middle of the street. We went along more passages and past open doorways through which we could see into courtyards. We saw stables with horses, mules and camels, and smelt the sweet manure and freshly cut straw. Eventually we arrived at the portal of the hospital, a large, though unimposing building, outside of but belonging to the Hospitallers' compound. Between the two rose the great edifice of the church of Saint John the Baptist, almost as tall and no less splendid than the cathedral.

We entered into the semi-dark vestibule of the hospital and spoke to a physician there who took us up to the first floor to meet the hospitaller in his small office. Albert spoke to him, but it seemed that here too there was nothing for us. He knew of no Bernard of Ulm or of Weissenau among the patients, nor, after turning the pages of his books, could he find the name among his records.

As we were leaving Albert told me that the hospitaller had suggested we should ask in the hospice, where there might be more detailed records of guests and indeed of anyone who passed through the Hospital gates. He had suggested that we speak to the Preceptor's chief clerk, a brother named Matheus who was to be found in the Palacium, and he had directed Albert to turn right after the gate in order to reach the palace. The hospitaller had said it would be best if we asked the guard at the palace how to find the clerk. When Albert had asked him about the hospitaller sacrist who had purchased the relic, he repeated that we should ask that also of Brother Matheus.

Before we left, I looked through the doorway into the hall of the hospital itself. Rows of cots lined the walls and ran the length of the hall between the massive piers that supported the vaulting. There must have been hundreds of them. The hall was fairly dark and a closed, musty smell emanated from the doorway. I could

hear the heavy rhythmic breathing of the sleeping inmates and the
quiet moaning of some who were in pain. I hurried after Albert
who had begun to descend the stairs and followed him out into the
street. I could see the obvious disappointment on his face.

"Do not despair," I said.

"I have only begun my search, but I fear that my wife was right."

"There are many more places to look."

"I know, Hermann. I am disappointed, but do not think that I
have given up."

We walked back past the Hospitallers' church and skirted the
high walls and alleys around the compound of the knights then
entered at the main gate. After stating our business to the guard,
we were allowed to pass through the guardhouse into a dark passage and out onto a paved road leading through the compound
between tall buildings on either side. The guard had given us directions, which was just as well for the Hospitallers' quarter was a
collection of tightly placed buildings and narrow passages and was
crowded with people rushing about in all directions; knights and
pilgrims, labourers and churchmen, so crowded indeed that by
contrast, what we had witnessed in the town seemed almost tran-
quil. We made our way along a narrow passageway, then entered
through another gate into a broader street, on either side of which
were high-arched doorways. On one side these opened onto a series of gloomy, vaulted storerooms and on the other were stables.
We then came upon a broad paved courtyard to the left of which a
grand staircase rose to the first-floor entrance to the palace. We ascended and entered into another guard room, beyond which was a
large vestibule that opened onto various chambers. These were the
offices of the chief officials of the Order, and we were not surprised
to find ourselves subjected to intense questioning by the guard regarding the purpose of our visit. Once this was explained he handed us over to a young knight who led us through the preceptor's

offices and from there to one of the side rooms where we were told to wait. We could see here into the office of the preceptor's chief clerk, a large, spacious, and well-illuminated room with high windows facing the courtyard. There were a number of scribes seated at tables working on documents, a small, grey-haired man was passing between them taking up manuscripts or leaning over to see how the work was progressing. After we had been standing in the doorway for some minutes, he noticed us and walked over.

"Gentlemen. Are you waiting for me?"

"I think so," said Albert. "Are You the chief clerk of the preceptor?"

"Yes. I am"

Albert introduced us to him and explained why we had come. The chief clerk answered in remarkably good German.

"One moment. I will see what I can find out for you. How long ago did you say, he came East?"

"Six years. But I have no knowledge of where he went. He may never have set foot here?" Albert was preparing himself for the expected disappointment.

"We shall see," he said. "I have the records of everyone who has taken advantage of the services of the hospital and of our guesthouse. But it will take some time. Perhaps you will be seated here while I go to check the lists."

We sat on a hard, wooden bench near the door, and he went out through a small side door and was gone for some time. We sat in silence. Albert seemed deep in thought, and I was reluctant to disturb him. I looked up at the walls of this chamber. Even this vestibule and office was elaborately decorated with beautifully carvings and wall- paintings and sweeping rib-vaulting, and I reflected on the power and confidence of this great Order which so boldly displayed its wealth. The chief clerk was away for at least half an hour. When at last he returned, he had some news:

"I have perhaps found something. There were two Bernards of Ulm here in our guesthouse. One arrived in the autumn of the year 1262. He remained for only a few days. The other was here six winters ago. They may be two different guests or one and the same. Either one of them may perhaps be your son."

"No... no. Only the latter could be him."

"Well then, that answers it. But he is not here now, and I have no way of knowing what became of him after he left the hospice. If he is indeed your son, then it is quite possible that he made contact with other people in the city. Most pilgrims and travellers make use of the exchange adjacent to the Court of the Chain near the port. I know that they keep some kind of records... though I can't say how detailed they are. It might be worth your while to try there."

In spite of this meagre information, Albert's hopes were raised again, and there was a noticeable change in his bearing as we stood up to leave. He thanked the chief clerk and asked him if he would show us the way to the sacristy.

"Why do you wish to go there?" he asked somewhat cautiously.

"I would like to speak to the sacrist. He may have some additional information."

"I doubt if he can help you any more than I," said the chief clerk. I noticed how his manner had subtly changed and that his tone had become notably guarded.

"Nevertheless, I should like to speak to him.

"If you wish to do so you will find him in the sacristy below the church. Do you know the way?"

"To the church? Yes."

"Well then... if you enter the main door and turn to the right there is a small staircase adjacent to the south wall which leads down to the crypt. The sacristy is located there. But I think you will find that he will be of no help."

"I wish to speak to him all the same," repeated Albert.

We thanked the chief clerk and walked out of the office in the direction of the church. As we walked, I asked Albert:

"Why did you not mention the matter of the relic - not to the hospitaller and not to the chief clerk?"

"I have a strange feeling, my dear Hermann, that something is wrong. I can't tell you why or what it is that I feel because I do not really know myself... but until we are better informed, I think we should not say too much."

We returned in the direction of the church, but by a different road, and soon we found ourselves at the western portal through which we entered and stood for a moment in the great nave between the two arcades of piers. Above rose fabulous painted rib-vaulting, fanning out in gold, red and blue from painted capitals. A shower of refracted light filtered from windows high on the side walls onto the dark wooden pews and the smooth-worn slabs of the floor. The air was drugged with candle smoke and incense. In each bay a candelabrum stood, as high as a tall man. These were formed of twisted spirals of iron rising on tripod stands and branching out with finials in the form of pomegranates and flowers spiked with large candles. We saw a priest carrying lamps near one of the side chapels, and Albert stopped him and asked where the sacrist could be found. He did not answer but pointed to the small staircase half-hidden in the shadow of the aisle to our right. We descended the stairs and entered a series of gloomy windowless chambers that were divided with massive piers and faintly illuminated by hanging glass lamps. The priest had silently followed us down, and he gestured again towards one of the rooms. We stood hesitant in the doorway. We could see the sacrist at the far end of the room leaning over an altar. After a few minutes he straightened and turned, and we saw a tall man of considerable bulk, dressed in a black tunic. He was entirely bald with a broad face and a massive heavy jaw. His brows were dark and thick, and his eyes were like black caves beneath them. Becoming aware of our presence he walked towards us, in his hand a beautiful, gilded silver beaker.

"May I help you?" He spoke in a deep, cold voice that carried a vague undertone of annoyance. In spite of the presence of Albert, the sacrist addressed his question to me, and I found his countenance so alarming that I stuttered something in my very poor French and was glad that Albert immediately stepped in and answered him. As he later explained to me, for I had become so flustered that I hardly listened to or understood what followed, Albert told the sacrist who we were and why we had come, but almost before the words were out of his mouth the sacrist answered the still unasked question, denying ever having seen or heard of Bernard.

"Your son was never here," he said. "I know nothing of him."

When recounting this Albert said that he had thought it very strange that the sacrist had answered so unfalteringly, as if he had been expecting us and had no need to think the matter over. Albert spoke to him again.

"Are you quite sure of that? My son was certainly here."

"What makes you think so?" the sacrist asked abruptly.

"I know it for certain. He had come to here try to obtain the relic of the arm of Saint John for his abbey, the abbey of Weissenau. The relic was held by the German Hospital, and he had come to negotiate with them for its purchase."

"You are misinformed. The relic of Saint John was never negotiated for, except by me. It was I who contacted the German custodian of relics when he received it, and the matter was settled then, as was only to be expected. No one has a more rightful claim to the relic than the Church of Saint John. It is the logical place for it to be held. I'm sure you do not dispute this?"

His manner was aggressive, but Albert seemed unshaken.

"I dispute nothing, Brother Sacrist," he answered. "I merely seek my son's whereabouts."

"As I have said … I cannot help you."

"And you insist that you have heard nothing of him?"

"I have already said so. Do you doubt my honesty?" He almost spat the words out. "Now, if you will forgive me gentlemen. I have much work," and without further ado he turned and walked away from us.

Even without following most of this conversation I was shocked by the offensiveness of his manner. Albert turned back to the staircase. I could see the combined disappointment and doubt in his face. I hurried after him and spoke into his ear:

"That must have been upsetting. He was so discourteous."

"I believe he is hiding something," he answered as we ascended the staircase.

In spite of this disappointment and the unpleasant behaviour of the sacrist, Albert did not give up hope. Indeed, he almost seemed to be encouraged. When we were out in the open again, and after he had related to me the details of his conversation with the sacrist, he told me that he wanted to go off immediately to the exchange. He was sure that the sacrist was wrong or was hiding something. I, on the other hand, was very despondent. It seemed to me that the sacrist's words had extinguished any hope of a positive outcome for our quest.

"If he had seen your son, why should he deny it?

"I do not know." He stood a moment on the side of the street outside the church and seemed to be pondering the matter. "We must go to the exchange," he repeated.

"Perhaps we should rest first."

"I have rested quite enough in the office, Hermann. In spite of the words of the sacrist I am almost certain that he was here. I believe he met with the sacrist. One way or another I must find out. Perhaps he is still in the city."

"I do not wish to put a damper on your hopes, but it is possible that your son has not visited the exchange," I said. "If he has been in the East for several years, he would likely have exchanged his money long ago, or somewhere else."

"Perhaps… yes, you are probably right. I may be setting myself up for an additional disappointment, but I cannot help feeling that the answer lies here, in Acre. In any case, it is better that I know the truth, whatever it might be."

We walked back into the market street and passed through an open hall full of crates and barrels. It took us some time to find our way. We headed south through the heart of the city in the direction of the harbour. The poverty of the neighbourhoods we passed through was pitiful. The streets were narrow and poorly unpaved. Here, too, there were open sewage ditches and piles of stinking refuse outside the entrances to the houses. The air became increasingly foul as we passed a stone wall behind which was the piggery, and we could hear their noisy grunting and shuffling about in the muck. Entering the Vicus San Marco which skirted the Venetian quarter there were many signs of the recent conflict between the merchant communes that had been sparked by claims over the ownership of a Greek convent called Saint Sabas. I had heard a great deal about this conflict that a decade and a half ago had turned Acre into a battleground. The convent was located in the Genoese quarter, but it had been claimed by the Venetians. This dispute served as a pretext for venting the long-simmering hatred between the Italian factions and evolved into a decade-long conflict between virtually all inhabitants in the city, culminating in the sinking of the Genoese fleet and the expulsion of their community to Tyre. During the conflict, the quarters had been fortified with thick stone walls and gates.

Albert and I followed a small alley running east from the Hospitallers' quarter and turned down a second street that ran close to the shore. At the fishmongers' market there were numerous cats loitering about, hoping for offal, more than I have ever seen in one place. We walked through towards the Cathena. The walls of the city stretched into the sea like a mother's arms embracing the ships. Such a multitude of pilgrim ships was crowded there that the water could scarcely be seen between them. Thick white foam broke on the stones of the breakwater and the water in the harbour was black and filthy with floating refuse including rotting fruit, driftwood, dead fish, even the occasional corpse of a dog. It seemed as if all the sewage of the city ran into the harbour. The breeze coming off the water was fouler even than the air by the piggery. The port was nonetheless a remarkable sight. When I had first seen it, and every time since, it had captivated me. At that time, not only the harbour was crowded with vessels, but many more stood waiting their turn in the bay beyond the harbour towers where the great chain was hoisted up in the evenings. It was at this time that the English prince had arrived with his flotilla, and countless ships stood beyond the harbour walls. There were so many indeed that it seemed the entire bay between Acre and the southern shore below Mount Carmel, where the small town of Caifas could just be seen, had become a solid mass. Gulls careened in over the ships' masts, making high-pitched keee-oh calls, swooping low and landing on the rocks. All the merchants in the city were gathered here: Italians, Catalonians, Muslims and Egyptian Jews, and there were pilgrims of every nation.

The Cathena was a prominent structure rising over a tiny inner basin that was packed with smaller ships. Up against it were warehouses and market buildings, though none as high as the Cathena itself or as splendidly decked out in flags and banners. The ships that had docked in this basin were in the process of being unloaded of the merchandise they had brought from across the sea, and some were already being reloaded with local goods ready for the next sailing. Through the huge doorway of the Cathena we could see into a large hall in which clerks from the communes and representatives of the Court of the Chain were employed. I think that just about every language of the world could be heard. Labourers were carrying goods from the ships to loaded wagons that had been pushed into the Great Hall, where they were to be examined and recorded before being released. We passed a guard at the Pisan Tower and entered the Pisan quarter, walking along a narrow alley, as dark as if it was subterranean, between towers and tall houses. Then we came out again into view of the outer harbour. We reached the Cambium and entered. I had visited the exchange once before and was once again fascinated by the scene. Tables covered with piles of coins: copper obols, silver bullion from Chartres, local and Saracen silver coins and even some coins of gold; bowl-shaped gold numisma from Byzantium, dinars from Egypt, the gold bezants that are minted here in Acre. On the tables were scales and piles of documents. Albert questioned the chief clerk about the possibility of his son having been there. The chief clerk, who spoke some German, looked in his ledgers and after a considerable time he broke into a broad smile.

"He was here," he said. "You see." He showed us the name Bernard of Ulm, prior of the abbey of Weissenau, written in neat Latin script on one of the pages with a record of the transaction. "He was here about six years ago." Albert gazed some time at the inscription, pensively biting his lower lip. Here at last was concrete evidence of his son. But he seemed more agitated by the fact than relieved. Finally, he asked:

"He has not been back since?"

The clerk leafed through the heavy vellum pages but found no further reference to the prior.

"It must have been shortly after he arrived…" and turning to me Albert commented: "Just as you said, Hermann. I am afraid it will not help us now. But at least, I now know that he arrived safely here in Acre."

We left the exchange and headed back through the town by a different route. Albert appeared to be set on the idea that Bernard was still somewhere in the city and that if we walked through the streets around the town for long enough, we might simply run into him. We turned west, then north through a now-abandoned guard-house of the old Genoese quarter. Many of the houses here still showed in their broken walls and caved-in vaults, evidence of the conflict that had raged between the Genoese and the Venetians, although most of them appeared occupied. When we approached the northern end of the quarter where it bordered on the Hospi-tal, we could hear from somewhere nearby the rhythmic beat of a drum, which became progressively louder as we exited the gate of the quarter. The drumroll was joined by occasional trumpeting, and quite suddenly from one of the narrow streets a rowdy group of young knights appeared, five or six abreast and more behind, in a lively phalanx, laughing and shouting, taking up the entire width of the road and forcing anyone in their path to move to the sides of the street, into the shops and even the gutter. We hastily stepped into the entrance of the small shop of a wine merchant and wait-ed for them to pass. The interior was dark, and the heady sulphur smell emanating from the wooden barrels made my head spin. The shop owner who saw us enter realised that we had not done so by choice and ignored our presence.

"Who are they?" Albert asked me.

"I think that they are Hospitaller brothers, perhaps on their way to the bathhouse."

"And they are permitted to behave in such a manner?" He was clearly shocked.

"No… indeed, such conduct is explicitly forbidden in their rule. But, you know, rules are not always obeyed, especially by the young."

"You speak," he laughed, "as if you are not yourself young, Hermann. Surely you are no older than they are. Perhaps our German Order is more careful in guiding its young brothers."

As we walked out of the shop after they had passed, Albert spoke again. "I am grateful to you, Hermann, for your kindness in agreeing to accompany me."

"Not at all."

This must seem futile to you, and I must seem a foolish old man."

"No… no. I quite understand your intentions and honour you for them. I hope that I would be as faithful as you are to your son. I am very happy to help you, and if the commander will permit it, I will gladly continue to do so."

Albert paused for a minute:

"There is one thing," he said. "I hesitate to ask as you have been so kind…"

"Please. What is it?"

"When I spoke to Commander Ulrich, he told me that his predecessor is now grand commander of a castle called Starkenberg. This grand commander was here in Acre, at the hospital, at the time my son came East. It is possible that he might know something. It is perhaps too much to ask, but if Commander Ulrich will permit it, would you consider accompanying me to the castle? It would take just a few days."

"If the commander will give his consent."

Albert perhaps thought that I was reluctant. He stopped walk-

ing and turned to face me. "No. I have asked too much," he said.
"Forgive me. These are dangerous times."

"I do not fear the journey. It will be an honour for me to accompany you and a pleasure to see the countryside. I have hardly
been outside of the city since I arrived in the East."

Albert was noticeably pleased with my reply:

"We would have to wait until an escort leaves, but I understand that these go out at least once a week. As you have agreed,
I will speak to Commander Ulrich and ask his consent for you to
accompany me. I am certain he will allow it. He has been most
forthcoming so far." He was silent for a minute then spoke again.
"If you are quite sure."

"I am," I answered without hesitation.

"I am an old man, Hermann, nearing death," he said. "My
search can be no longer than the number of my days. Helping me
is a great kindness."

I had not been to Starkenberg Castle though I had heard much
about it from brothers who had been there, and in truth I had long
wished to see it, although of late this desire had been tempered
by the growing number of reports of attacks by the Saracens on
travellers in outlying regions and an increasing number of injured
travellers arriving at the hospital.

6 BEL

The disappearance of Walker proved to be even more disconcerting when they found that he had apparently taken with him their only rifle, as well as part of the field diary and the best saddle. The camp guard, Abdul, had heard nothing. He claimed to have been awake all night, and the heavy rain might explain his not having heard any movement or seen Walker leave. The following day passed without any resolution as to what had happened. The rain continued steadily, and no work could be done. The workers remained away, only Ra'ed arriving early in the morning on a donkey, soaking wet and leading the missing camel, which he had found wandering along the stream near the ruined mill. It seemed likely that Walker had ridden it in the storm as far as the mill and spent the night there. The men remained at the camp, sorting and writing up the finds. Robert worked on inking his plans and tried his hand at photographing the objects with Riley's camera. After breakfast they sat in the tent and discussed the situation.

"I never expected him to react like this," said Robert.

"He was pretty upset, and I told him outright that I wanted him to leave, but I can't believe that he would go off like that, in the middle of the night ... and in the storm. The fellow is definitely unstable."

"He may be in trouble."

"Yes. Well, he has brought it upon himself. We have to report this to the authorities in Haifa. And we will need to obtain another rifle. In any case, we need more supplies, and most of the workers will be away for Easter. I suggest that we take a few days' break. We should go up to Jerusalem together. But I want to stay here today, just in case Walker does come back. If the weather clears tomorrow, take one of the camels down to el-Bassa. Take the motorcar from there, where we left it by Sheikh Sayyed's house, and drive to Haifa. I will meet you there on Friday, and we can drive up to Jerusalem together. I need to speak to the professor, and I have to send a letter to New York. I'll leave Ra'ed here while we're gone, to watch over things."

By the following day, the storm had passed, and fine spring weather had returned. Robert rode to el-Bassa on one of the camels. The track was still muddy, and the camel lost its footing several times; more than once he was almost sent flying but managed to hold on and regain his balance. In spite of these near mishaps, he enjoyed the ride; the rolling motion of the camel, the pleasantly warm sun and being completely alone in the wild, beautiful country. The car was where they had parked it, under a large mulberry tree in front of the sheikh's house. Riley had left it there because it was the closest that they could get to the castle, and Sheikh Sayyed had promised that no one would touch it. Without that promise it would, in all likelihood, not have remained intact. However, everything seemed to be in order. He left the camel with the sheikh, cranked the engine into life and drove it onto the unpaved road, avoiding as best he could the numerous water-filled potholes. He headed to the Kabri road and then south towards Akko, passing low hills, isolated ruins, vegetable plots and the bustans of olive, fig and pomegranate trees that were half hidden behind stone walls. He saw stretches of untamed countryside, wondering at how such an old land could still have its wild places. Passing the green domes

and towers of Akko, he drove down the sickle-shaped bay towards
Mount Carmel. He saw the occasional Arab peasant on a donkey
and small children walking along the edges of the wet road. He saw
a mounted Jewish guard carrying a rifle and wearing large mous-
taches and a high, cossack-like fur hat. There was an endless caravan
of slow-moving camels carrying bricks and heading south under
the palms against the background of the sandy beach. Arab women
passed, carrying enormous piles of brushwood or earthenware jars
balanced on their heads. A falah was working in the field, guiding
an old stick-plough dragged by a reluctant mule, and in the meagre
furrow he had scraped a sleek white egret examined the upturned
soil. The land beyond swept away towards the mountain that had
taken on a purple hue in the morning light. Further on he passed a
small mound, the remnant of an ancient city. It rose abruptly from
the plain, its shape indicating a forgotten human intrusion in the
landscape. It was almost bare of vegetation, only a thin pelt of grass
gave it an animal-like appearance, like a large crouching rat. Along
its base were masses of grey thistles, remains of the dead season,
and below them the new green of one just born. Above, a hawk,
a fixture in this landscape, was circling slowly on a warm current.
Far above that, a single ethereal cloud moved on its lonely passage
across the otherwise flawless blue.

There were almost no motorcars along the way. On the Carmel the town had spread and scattered up the slopes, filing up the
open spaces. It was nearly three weeks since he had left Haifa. He
took the road up the mountain to Hadar HaCarmel. After passing through older suburbs, he turned into a street with five small
gable-roofed houses set well apart and parked the car under a tall
umbrella pine in front of the last house. There was no garden to
speak of, just a plot with a little grass within a wire fence, where a
few cypresses and oleanders clustered. He walked down the gravel
path, knocked on the front door and waited. There was no answer,

and he fumbled in his pocket, pulled out a key, unlocked the door and let himself in. The house was dark, silent, and stuffy. It showed signs of having been unoccupied for a long time; a thin coat of dust on the coffee table, long-dead flowers in a vase, a single fine cobweb hanging from the ceiling. He opened the windows and pushed open the heavy iron shutters, letting the morning light enter and fill the rooms. He threw out the flowers but did not bother to remove the dust from the table. He picked up a cushion and slapped it against an armchair, then sat down on it and closed his eyes.

After about an hour he got up, went to the door and out, drove into town and walked into the post office to check his mail. He picked up a letter from an old friend in England and a postcard from his aunt. There were some letters and telegrams for Riley and a large package from New York that he knew would contain copies of papers on the Middle Ages and medieval castles, which a colleague had sent, and which Riley had been expecting since before the excavation began. He lifted the stack of correspondence from the counter, but as he left the whole pile slipped from his hands and scattered across the floor.

"Blast!" he exclaimed. As he attempted to retrieve his post a young woman bent down beside him.

"Let me give you a hand," she said.

"Thank you," he answered with some embarrassment as he saw her lovely eyes. "It's alright. There's no need." He picked up the letters and the package, but almost immediately they slipped from his hands again. This time the young woman bent and picked up the letters before he could protest. As they gathered the papers together she introduced herself. Her name, she told him, was Isabel. She had also come to pick up her mail. She had dark hair; a mass of curls touched with auburn when they caught the light that streamed through the high windows into the post office hall. She had just the vaguest trace of the Orient in her eyes and in the graceful way she moved. He took the letters from her and thanked her a second time. Then, to his immense mortification the whole lot slipped from his hands a third time. Robert went red in the face and stood there not quite certain what to do.

"I don't believe this!" he said shaking his head. The young woman laughed and in spite of himself he laughed too, and they both bent down and picked up the letters again. He looked into her face. She had almond-shaped dark brown eyes.

"Thank you, Isabel," he said. "I hope I can hold on to them now."

"Call me Bel. It's my Indian name. My mother is Indian."

"Bell. That's a lovely name. What does it mean? Is it the same as in English?

"Just one "l". It means Jasmine flower. You haven't told me what your name is?"

"I'm sorry... Robert. Robert Palmer."

"Well, Robert Palmer. Which way are you going?"

"I live up in the hill, not very far. I have a motorcar."

"Then perhaps you can drop me off."

"Yes, of course! Where do you need to be?"

She gave him her address and they walked out of the post office. On the way she told him a little about herself. She was the only daughter of a British diplomat and his Indian-born wife. She wore a dark green silk kerchief bound around her rebellious hair that framed an exquisitely beautiful face. She was as tall as Robert and wore a cotton dress with a colourful floral pattern. As they drove along Herzl Street, he spoke to her. Not only had Robert regained his composure, but he also surprised himself with the ease he felt, and the feeling that he could speak forthrightly with Bel, as if he had known her for some time.

"You are very beautiful," he said.

She smiled at him, and her smile had a sweetness that increased his confidence, and he felt warmth overflow him as he had never before experienced.

"Are you always so outspoken with strangers?" she laughed.

"No… not at all. Quite the opposite, in fact. There must be some special connection between us." Again, he was surprised at his words, but he felt relaxed and unembarrassed.

After he dropped her off at her house, he drove down to the port to pick up Riley near the train station as they had prearranged.

"These are for you." He handed Riley the mail. He did not speak of his encounter with Bel, although it was very prominently on his mind. "I'm afraid my place is rather a mess. It looks like that woman I paid to come by hasn't been in since I left!"

"Don't worry. It will do for tonight."

They didn't leave for Jerusalem till the following morning. First, they drove to the police station to report the disappearance of Walker, not only because of the property he had taken but because Riley was quite worried about what might have happened to him. They purchased some supplies and obtained a new rifle to replace the one that had been taken.

The drive to Jerusalem was a long one. They took to the road early in the morning and drove south. For several miles the road followed the beach before moving back on the plain between the sea and the inland mountains. A low sandstone ridge ran parallel to the shore. Behind it the ruins of the north tower of the Templar fortress at 'Atlit rose dramatically, like a great stone shield on its peninsula. The road clung close to the ridge, and just before they passed the castle it entered through a narrow breach cut through the stone. They could then see the entire castle. In the shadow of the gaunt mass of masonry, scattered among the ruins, were stone houses and makeshift huts. This had been another of the great Crusader fortresses, the stronghold of Château Pèlerin, Pilgrims' Castle. Robert had passed here many times, but with his experience at Montfort his curiosity was now aroused, and he saw the ruins in a new light.

"Do you suppose…"

"…that we take a short look around?" Riley completed his request. "Yes. I don't see why not."

"How did you know that was what I was going to ask?"

"Because I was about to suggest it myself," Riley laughed. "It's pretty amazing, isn't it? I think we have time."

They drove onto a narrow turn-off that crossed railway tracks and led across a stretch of sand and past an ancient cemetery behind a low stone wall. Riley parked the car against the wall, and they walked through the graveyard towards a pebbly beach and the northern side of the peninsula where the castle's ruins rose abrupt and erratic, like a jaw of rotten teeth. A few surviving sandstone tomb-markers and hundreds of crumbling piles of rubble and mortar designated the graves of long-dead Templars. Windblown sand had piled up against the tombs along with scattered bits of salt-whitened driftwood, sea-worn shells, and fragments of glazed pottery. Beach wildflowers formed little patches of yellow, pink, and white. They came upon the remains of a fortification wall and shallow moat. These had once defended the small settlement that had grown in the shadow of the castle. Avoiding the pungent, rancid body of a decaying sea turtle, they followed the top of a half-buried wall that ran ahead, ending in a partly buried, high-arched gate. Beyond it was a second sand-filled moat. The water to the north was shallow with reefs and fallen masonry. They made their way along the outer fortification wall where it extended into the breaking waves and climbed a steep slope through a gap in the walls into the heart of the castle. The air was sharp and fresh with a pervading saltiness.

They now came up against the inner side of the great north tower. High on the surviving wall were three sandstone corbels that had once supported the rib-vaulting of an upper chamber in the tower. One of these was a carved head with curled hair. A second corbel was composed of three small heads with high crockets like peaked crowns and the third one displayed a bearded head. The features of all three of them had weathered into a blurred obscureness by seven centuries of wind and rain. The two men walked across the high part of the ruins, on a narrow path. This area, once an inner courtyard of the castle, was now occupied by shanty houses and small bustans. A few women were busy about their household chores and paid them no attention. Three small boys ran after them, laughing, and Riley gave them some coins. They walked down the slope on the west and into the ruins of an enormous broad hall. Centuries of stone robbing and erosion had taken a heavy toll and most of the hall had vanished, but the side walls were still standing and the great distance between them indicated its once vast dimensions.

When they were back in the car and on their way south the two men hardly spoke. They were well past 'Atlit before Riley broke the silence:

"You are unusually quiet, Robert."

"Am I?"

"Yes. Are you thinking about the castle? It is quite remarkable, isn't it?"

"Yes."

Riley noted his untypically terse answers.

"Is that really what you are thinking about?"

Robert hesitated for a moment:

"Actually no."

"I didn't think so. What is it? Walker?"

"No… hardly!" He hesitated for a moment, then spoke again. "Since you ask, I was thinking about someone I met yesterday."

Riley was interested. "A young lady?"

"Well… yes." Robert felt his cheeks flush, yet he sensed that he could speak of this with his friend.

"She must be very special to keep you this quiet."

"Are you hinting that I usually talk too much?" Robert laughed.

"No, no my friend. But I have a feeling this was not just a minor encounter?"

"I suppose I can tell you. You won't laugh at me?"

"I'll try not to." Riley promised.

"You know I went to the post office before I picked you up?"

"Yes."

"Well… there was a girl there. Her name is Bel." He hesitated for a moment. "John. If I'm being so open with you, can I ask you a personal question?"

"I suppose so."

"You told me you're not married but… have you ever met someone who completely bowled you over?"

Riley laughed and then caught himself. "I'm not laughing at you… just at your question. I'm a lone dog, Robert. But even I have been, as you say, bowled over."

"I didn't mean…"

"Robert. Don't be so serious! Anyway, it didn't come to anything. But yes… I have been there."

"It's just that… I mean, I've only just met her, and I can't think of anything else."

"Yes, my boy. That is how it works." Riley reflected for a moment. "I was extremely shy as a youth. Whenever I met a young lady I was certain to trip over or spill something, or just to turn red in the face. However, there was this one girl I met, her name was

Rose, and when I made an ass of myself with her it didn't seem to matter at all. I was in love."

Riley stopped speaking and looked ahead at the road. After a few minutes Robert broke the silence:

"What happened?"

"I don't really know. She liked me, but I guess she didn't feel as strongly as I did. It was all a bit embarrassing, and I suppose, I never had the courage again after that."

"I'm sorry."

"Don't be. It's all so long ago. I have had close friendships since then, but marriage was, I guess, just not on the cards for me."

They fell silent again. Robert wanted to say something but didn't quite know what. They drove on south, past the abandoned town of Caesarea where Bosnian refugees had settled among the ruins. They passed the Jewish settlement at Hadera, and the road curved away from the coast, through scattered fields and stretches of uncultivated land. As they continued south there were mild changes in the landscape; the soil turned a sandy red and there were more small villages. By noon they were passing rows of orange trees, occasional date palms and cypresses that rose against the clear blue sky like black flames, shading the sandy paths between the groves. They had reached the outskirts of the Jewish settlement of Tel Aviv, neatly laid out in the sands north of Jaffa. In the distance to the south, they could see the white walls and red-tiled gables of the ancient city, its minarets and bell towers rising on a low hill above the harbour. Passing through the new but already burgeoning town they drove by the train station and into the main square of Jaffa, under Sultan Abd al-Hamid's clock tower and stopped at the residence of the American consul, a Mr. Otis T. Merrill.

Riley had very briefly met the consul in Jerusalem shortly after he first arrived. Merrill had purported to take an interest in the expedition. His house was on a small street overlooking the port; a comfortable large-roomed residence with high ceilings and an eclectic mixture of European and Oriental furnishings. Upstairs was a reception room with three tall, pointed-arch glass doors opening onto a spacious balcony overlooking the port. They sat outside and a diminutive Arab woman served them tea and sweet cakes. The little harbour was crowded with fishing boats, and beyond the breakwater and the Rock of Andromeda a number of larger vessels were anchored, sailing ships and one huge steamship. Much further out at sea was another steamer on its way south to Alexandria. The Mediterranean spread back to the horizon where the blue took on a greater intensity towards its abrupt encounter with the paler blue of the sky. The three men sat around a table under a bright red and white striped canvas awning that flapped loudly in the breeze. Riley told Merrill about their experiences, skipping over the business of Walker. Robert noticed that although the consul asked an occasional question, he seemed hardly to be listening, and after a while Riley became aware of this too. The consul's occasional comments and interruptions made it obvious that he had no real interest in the expedition; his questions were stupid, and he turned out to be a bit of a bore. Riley was telling him about digging in the vault below the castle's hall:

"It is a large vault," he said, "about a third of it filled with rubble—collapsed debris from the hall above."

"Rubble? Yes…," said Merrill. "The cellar here was filled with rubble before I moved in… rocks and dust. You wouldn't believe it. It took days to get the place cleared, though it was well worth the effort and expense. It gave me a whole large room, part of which I use for storage. Would you like to see it?"

"Well… yes. Maybe later on," said Riley, who was taken aback by the consul's remark.

"But you were saying?" said Merrill, and Riley thought that perhaps the consul's interruption was a one-time slip.

"Well..." Riley returned to what his theme: "We began working in this vault because we had noticed some rather fine fallen stones in the rubble. Then..."

"Oh... and I must show you my wine cellar as well," said the consul.

Riley looked over at Robert. He was flabbergasted and Robert was trying to hide his amusement. Merrill, however, showed no sign of noticing and was apparently quite unaware that his behaviour might be considered offensive or indeed farcical. Paying no attention to the fact that Riley had stopped speaking he asked:

"What exactly do you expect to find on this expedition anyway?"

"Well... we would like to learn something about the type of armour that was used."

"But you can find plenty of armour in museums. Why should this be special?"

"Well, you can't always be certain of the authenticity of what you find in collections, and..." he added, "this is only one aspect of what we are trying to do. Obviously, we want to get a better idea of the nature of the castle itself... its history, how it functioned."

The consul turned to Robert, assuming a rather fatuous look of astonishment:

"I can understand wanting to excavate an ancient mound," he said, "There is so much there... so many layers of the distant past, of earlier civilizations."

"There is a great deal to be learnt from the more recent past as well," said Robert.

"Perhaps. But if you want to dig in the Holy Land, wouldn't you be better off working on something that you don't have in other places?" Before they could react to this he continued: "I mean...

what is the point in studying a ruined castle here when you have so many finer examples of castles, intact castle in Germany or France, or in the British Isles? And look… I'm saying this from personal knowledge." He was now sounding very much, the bore. "As you can imagine, as a diplomat I have travelled quite a lot. These bits and pieces of castles you find in the Holy Land are really pretty sad by comparison."

"I don't agree at all." Robert interjected. Have you been to Montfort?"

"Montfort?" he shook his head. "No."

"Have you seen the castle at 'Atlit?" Riley asked.

"Oh… I've passed it by on occasion."

"But you haven't been into the castle?

"No. But what does it matter? One doesn't need to go into every single castle. They're all pretty much alike. Anyway… I didn't mean to upset you, Mr. Riley. I'm sure you're doing a fine job."

Riley was quite glad to end this exasperating discussion, and the time had come for them to resume their drive. After thanking the consul for lunch, the men returned to the car. There, Robert could no longer hold in his laughter, and Riley was forced to join him.

"The man is an ass," he said as they drove off to a filling station near the railway. Refilling the tank, they headed inland. After some time, they arrived at the town of Ramlah, passing the desolate Moslem cemetery with its stone pile tombs and the tall square minaret of the White Mosque rising strikingly over the small houses. They continued along a thin strip of coarsely paved road through the sandy landscape. A large flock of starlings flew off a field, hundreds of birds in perfect synchronisation, rising and dropping across the contour of the land, the whole mass of individual birds in unison like a single creature, dividing, pulling ahead, dipping, breaking up and re-uniting, and finally vanishing over a rise. There were a few villages and the recently ploughed fields surrounding them were already covered with a fresh green that had come up after the recent rains. The road reached the edge of the Valley of Ayalon and serpentined down, then cut straight across and approached the foothills. It deteriorated in places where there were more ruts and potholes than road, and it required careful manoeuvring on Riley's part to avoid their finding themselves in the hedges of prickly pear that grew along its sides. At the far end of the valley in the Trappist monastery, among the cypress trees and vineyards, a new building was under construction, and behind on the hilltop a small village crouched in the ruins of another Templar castle: Le Toron des Chevaliers - Tower of the Knights.

From here they drove through the foothills and into the mountains, passing an inn at Bab al-Wad where the road entered a deep gorge. The hills rose ever more steeply from here on as the road ascended eastward towards Jerusalem. They were rocky, with little soil and hardly any substantial vegetation, but gently rounded like giant waves in a rolling sea of stone. Ahead, on the side of the road, they saw a boy riding a sorry-looking donkey and leading a second one by a short length of rope. Both animals were badly underfed, their ribs and backbones prominent under the grey scarred hides. Flies were swarming around their eyes, and they half-heartedly shook their heads and twitched their flanks. The second donkey was cruelly hobbled, tethered with wire wrapped tightly above its hoofs. The wire had become embedded in the flesh and the poor animal's failed attempts to keep up were rewarded with a lashing from a short thick stick against its side. Riley pulled the car up and got out. He walked in front of the leading donkey and shouted at the boy.

"Look at what you're doing to the poor creature!"

The boy looked at him doubtfully, clearly not understanding a word he said. Robert spoke from the window of the car.

"John. He can't understand you."

"Look!" Riley shouted again, pointing at the animal's bloody hoofs. Oblivious to his efforts for their wellbeing, the donkeys continued in their futile attempts at flicking away the flies with their ears and tails. The boy seemed equally oblivious, but turned his head and looked down, though he did not appear to see anything amiss.

"For goodness sake!" Riley was becoming highly agitated. "The poor animal! Look what you're doing to it." The boy just shook his head and made an expression that appeared to express the opinion that Riley had been out in the sun too long. Then he struck the beast he was seated on, and it let out a low bray and set off again at a slow trot. Riley was taken aback. He shouted out after the boy: "Stop! I'm speaking to you," but this had absolutely no effect. Robert tried to calm him.

"John … you are not going to change the Levant."

"We can't just ignore cruelty like that. You saw how he was beating the animal. Did you see its feet?"

"Yes, of course I saw. It's horrible. But you are not going to get anywhere by shouting at him. Unfortunately, this type of treatment is typical here. He doesn't see that anything is wrong with it, and shouting at him won't change that."

Riley reluctantly returned to the car, and they drove past the boy.

"I don't understand it," said Riley as they passed him by. "It is simple, wanton cruelty."

"You're lucky you are only here for a short time, John. You would have to grow a thick skin if you were to remain any longer. This is a brutal country, and unfortunately cruelty is not limited to the treatment of animals."

The road took them up through the weathered hills with their scattered scrub and occasional stunted trees. They drove through the small Christian village of Abu Ghosh and down to the spring of Belus and the medieval church, where a French speaking Benedictine monk led them into the dark interior, cool and heavy with the scent of incense. The monk showed them the medieval frescoes, and then they sat in the mottled shade of an ancient mulberry tree drinking sweet tea.

It was late afternoon before they reached the Holy City. They drove through the Jewish neighbourhoods and entered the Jaffa Gate. Riley pointed out an open niche just inside the gate, where beneath a twisted fig tree, two turbaned tombstones, according to popular lore, marked the burial place of the two unfortunate architects who had built the city walls in the sixteenth century by order of Sultan Suleiman, and who according to the legend were beheaded by the sultan for not having included the Mount of Zion within the new defences. They passed the high-walled citadel, parked the car near its gate and walked through narrow streets, now crowded for the festive season. Riley led the way through a confusion of stepped lanes until they arrived at the museum and offices of the Department of Antiquities, where a young man showed them into the director's office.

Professor Gilford was sitting in a small, book-lined office with deep arched windows, oriental rugs on the floor and large pottery jars placed strategically around the room for decoration. Although the day was not hot, a ceiling fan was slowly turning, and shutters cut off much of the light from the windows. The room smelt pleasantly of pipe tobacco.

"Do sit down gentlemen," said the professor.

The two men sat in chairs opposite a large oak desk. Professor Gilford was a small man, immaculately dressed in a dark suit and wore a small bowtie. He was balding and sported a carefully trimmed beard. Among the usual office paraphernalia on his desk were neat piles of official letters, a number of open volumes of an archaeological nature and scattered pieces of pottery. He fiddled with his pipe as he spoke with them, knocking shreds of blackened tobacco into an ashtray, refilling it and, with the aid of a bronze striker lighter, puffing it into aromatic life.

"Can I offer you something, gentlemen?"

"Nothing for me, professor" answered Riley.

"No thank you," added Robert.

"I don't think you two have met," Riley said introducing Robert. "This is Mr. Robert Palmer, our surveyor."

"Pleased to meet you, Mr. Palmer." The professor half rose and leaned forward to shake hands. "I have heard about you. You were with the Palestinian gendarmerie if I'm not mistaken."

"Yes," said Robert. "When they were disbanded, I decided to try something else for a while."

"And how do you find working on an excavation?"

"I quite enjoy it."

"Not too dull?"

"Dull? No. Not at all. Quite the opposite."

The professor then turned to Riley:

"I'm glad to see, John, that you have not allowed the Levant to lower your standards. In general, I find that chaps coming from cooler climates let themselves go to seed. You look as dapper as ever."

"Well, thank you Professor."

Listening to this brief exchange Robert thought to himself that this was if anything, an understatement. Riley was always carefully turned out, whether at a meeting or on the road, and most remarkably, in the field where, even on the warmer days he was never without suit and tie.

"So, tell me, how is the excavation progressing?"

"Well," said Riley, "the dig itself is moving along as planned. We have had no remarkable finds yet, other than some very fine architectural pieces, but I have a good feeling, and we are still well above the floor levels."

"I am sorry that I have not yet had time to visit the castle. I will see if I can do so while you're there. But I did manage to take a look at Kitchener's plan of Montfort before you came." He pulled the folded plan off the top of a stack of papers and opened it out on the desk, turning it around so that it was the right way up for his visitors. "Show me please where you are excavating."

Riley pointed to the area at the western end of the castle.

"We have been working in the easternmost of the two basement vaults below the hall. But now we are working in the keep, all the way over here." He pointed to the other end of the building represented on the plan. "There is something a bit odd about this plan," he commented. "It will be interesting to see how it compares to ours."

"How is that coming along?"

"Robert... You'd best answer that."

"I have the eastern end of the castle drawn and am about halfway across the middle section. I will certainly have it completed before we are through."

"And finds, John? You say nothing remarkable. You haven't found the armour you were hoping for?"

"Only fragments so far, I'm afraid. But we have found some other items of interest. We uncovered some very nice corbels and bosses from the vaulting and a rather fine carved head of a knight."

"Good... good." Professor Gilford puffed thoughtfully on his pipe, his eyes still on the plan laid out before them.

"And the labourers? How has that worked out?"

"The workers are fine. We have had no problems with them at all."

"And yet," he looked up into Riley's eyes. "I sense there is something bothering you. Am I right?"

"I'm afraid you are. It's that man, Walker. He has turned out to be a real liability. He's been drinking and insubordinate. I have had problems with him from the word go regarding purchases and excessive drinking. And he has been abusive with the men. Now he's disappeared altogether. He just left in the middle of the night. What's more, he took one of the camels, which fortunately we recovered, but also a rifle and some of our equipment."

The professor pushed his chair back during Riley's short speech, shook his head and sighed. His hands came together, touching at the tips of his fingers which seemed to signify an increased interest in what Riley was saying.

"He took a rifle!" he repeated. "I'm really sorry to hear this. I thought things would work out this time."

"This time?" repeated Riley questioningly.

"Well… Yes. I have to be honest with you. We have had trouble with Walker before. But I thought he had settled down."

"What sort of trouble?" asked Robert.

"Nothing very serious. He's never stolen anything until now. Let's just say, he has had trouble getting along with people. I had a long talk with him before I sent him out to you, and he assured me that things would be different this time."

"I wish you had told me," said Riley.

"Yes, I should have."

"And the drinking?" asked Robert. "Has that been part of the problem?"

"Well… yes. I really am sorry gentlemen. If I had had any idea this would happen again, I would never have sent him to you. His father is a good friend, and I understood from him that the boy had matured. I can see now that this is not the case."

"The question is, what do we do now?"

"Well, I can get you another man. It will take me a few days to organize but it shouldn't be a problem."

"No, no… That's not what I meant," said Riley. "There's really no need. We can manage fine as far as that is concerned. I meant… what do we do about Walker?"

"I assume that you have notified the police in Haifa?"

"Yes. We told them of his disappearance, and of course I reported the theft. But it is not only that. In spite of the trouble that he's caused, I'm worried about him. He went off in the dark, possibly drunk, and during a storm. He might have come to some mischief."

"Yes… I see." Professor Gilford sat silent for a minute and then spoke again. "But you know… there really isn't much we can do. I'm sure he's alright. He might come to his senses and return, although I doubt it. If he does, I suggest you discretely inform Jim Townsend in our office in Haifa. He should be back from London in a day or two. I will speak to him myself. Leave him to deal with it. Perhaps he can minimise the damage. Hopefully, the young man hasn't got himself hurt, and perhaps he will return the stolen items."

"You don't expect us to take him back?" asked Robert.

"No, of course not. But to avoid his causing more trouble if he does come back, let him think so… until Townsend arrives. He'll know best how to deal with this business."

"I don't know," said Robert. "I'm not sure you are aware of how much trouble he has become, with the workers in particular."

"Yes, Mr. Palmer… Robert. I think I know exactly how much trouble he has become. But it's best to deal with it this way, believe me. I will speak to the boy's father as well." He turned to Riley. "Are you sure you don't want me to get you a replacement?"

"Yes. We can manage quite well."

"Alright. Get in touch with Townsend. He will update me, and we'll deal with this matter. The three stood up and shook hands. "Once again, gentlemen… I am most sorry about this."

Outside, as they walked down the narrow street leading back in the direction of the city gate, Robert expressed his doubts.

"You know, if he does come back, we can't simply act as if nothing has happened, even if it's only until this Townsend fellow arrives. We are going to have to confront him on the theft, if nothing else."

"I wouldn't worry too much about it, Robert. I don't believe he will come back."

They spent the night at the new American School on Saladin Street. In the evening they sat for dinner at a long table in the courtyard garden under lemon trees and jasmine vines. Paraffin lamps shed suffused light over the courtyard and at the perimeter, pine trees and cypresses were beautifully silhouetted against the deep blue of the night sky. Among the guests that shared their table were three elderly sisters, each well over eighty, tiny mice-like women but lively and of adventurous spirits and not at all old except in years. There were also two young students of archaeology studying at the American school. One of them was a very pale, thin boy, painfully shy, with straight, straw-coloured hair and a weak attempt at a moustache, who hardly opened his mouth except to eat, and even very sparingly for that. The other was quite the opposite; stocky, dark-haired, one of those overly confident types who knew everything and made certain that this fact was generally realised by overtaking every conversation at the table. Another dinner guest was a rather morose-looking Anglican priest and there was a formidable spinster named Mrs Mooney, who gazed disapprovingly at everyone except, for some reason, Robert, next to whom she had placed herself and whom she informed in a sharp and generally audible whisper, that she was quite certain the elderly ladies were all senile, that the thin boy named Peter was suffering from a life-threatening disease and that his overbearing friend was there, not for the archaeology, but because his family in Baltimore had paid a great deal of money to make certain he remained in the East.

After dinner, Riley, who was tired from the drive, went to bed. Robert, however, was hoping to get another glimpse of the old city. He had only been in Jerusalem a handful of times and was always allured by its beauty and oriental strangeness that sometimes extended almost to grotesqueness. He walked out of the school and down the road that approached the Damascus Gate. The full moon rose above the city that spread out behind its walls like a stage set for a drama about to commence. Saladin Street was not very crowded despite the holiday season. At the gate he turned left into the street in what was formerly the moat that ran adjacent to the city wall. He walked past where the wall rose high on a rock escarpment, past Herod's Gate as far as the northeast corner of the city. From the corner tower the land fell steeply down into the dark valley in the east. He was deep in thought, ruminating over the discussion they had had with Professor Gilford and thinking about Walker and what might have happened to him. A strange, low moaning came from beyond the wall as the mu'ezzin on the Temple Mount began to call the faithful to the Eshaa, the evening prayer. It was soon echoed from another minaret, then another until the wailing call rose all over the city. Robert became aware that the street was not entirely empty. Some youths were sitting in the dark below the wall across the road. They watched him as he passed by, and he felt uneasy and decided to turn back.

The following day was Holy Saturday. Neither Robert nor Riley was a regular churchgoer, but Riley was eager to see the Orthodox celebration of the Holy Fire at the Church of the Holy Sepulchre and Robert was quite willing to accompany him, for no other reason than curiosity. They walked down the stepped market streets through the Muslim Quarter. Here the commercial activity was not affected at all by the Christian festival. Stalls in the bazaar were piled with goods for sale, and men and women rushed about carrying baskets of produce. One man held a tray full of sweet cakes, another carried cups of Turkish coffee on a tin platter and distributed them to the shopkeepers exchanging a short conversation with each. They followed a group of boys carrying chickens upside-down, three or four in each hand. The birds' legs had been tied with rope and their half-hearted protestations drew no sympathy whatsoever.

"It's as bad as those poor donkeys we saw in the mountains," said Riley. It seems no one here has the slightest regard for the suffering of poor creatures."

"The children are not much better off," added Robert as they passed some small urchins begging at the side of the road. They entered the Christian Quarter and approached the church. The narrow streets were filling with pilgrims. They had not anticipated the crowds, nor the pushing and shouting, which intensified as they entered the lanes leading onto the square outside of the church. Here they saw a growing throng that struggled to approach the single unsealed door. They had arrived early, well before Mass was to begin, but they soon found themselves being very roughly pushed about and pressed up against a wall and having to hold their arms up so as not to be crushed by the masses of pilgrims that surged and flowed into the narrow confines of the square. At first a line of stolid British policemen attempted to preserve some semblance of order in the square, but very soon they became irrelevant as the numbers of participants swelled and filled not only the church and the square, but all of the surrounding streets and alleys. Robert began to wonder if their curiosity had not incurred too great a cost. An elderly man with a vastly expansive stomach approached them. He was dressed in a dirty black suit and a battered hat out of which protruded a mass of grey hair. But he had a jolly face with rosy cheeks, a small fat nose, bright blue eyes behind wire-rimmed spectacles, small ears, and a bushy beard. Overhearing Riley speaking in English, he began to converse with them without any introduction.

"Gentlemen. Good day. You are pilgrims, yes?" He spoke excellent English, albeit with Germanic pronunciation. This, in contrast with his shabby appearance, suggested that he was an educated man, one who had apparently fallen on hard times.

"You might say that," said Riley.

"And you, I see, are an American. A fine country... America. I have never been there, but I have read much about it. You are just arrived in the Holy Land?"

Robert tried, in the crowded space, to avoid being pressed up against the man's large belly.

"Actually, we are archaeologists," Riley answered.

"Is that so? How interesting. Where are you working, if I may inquire?"

"We are excavating a Crusader castle in the Galilee."

"A Crusader castle! How extraordinary," said the fellow. "Well. This might interest you," and he produced from his pocket a small object and held it out for them to observe. Riley took it from him. It was a small lead flask, less than three inches in height and almost flat, with a broad neck, a wide opening at the top and small ring-shaped handle close to the base of the neck on each side. Its flat surfaces were decorated with a moulded design in low relief, rather like the pattern of a pinecone, and in the centre of one side was a circle containing a fleur-de-lis while on the other was a simple rendition of the Holy Sepulchre. "Do you know, perhaps, what this is?"

"Some sort of flask," said Riley, "for holy water?"

"Yes, yes indeed! You have hit it, my friend. This is a medieval ampulla, used, as you say, to hold holy water or oil. And it is, believe it or not, of Crusader date!" Robert passed it to Riley who took the small object and held it in the palm of his hand, then turned it over to observe the design of the fleur-de-lis.

"I have just purchased it from a dealer of antiquities. It is, he assures me, twelfth century, and it was made here and sold to pilgrims at the Holy Sepulchre." Robert handed the flask back, and the man went on speaking:

"You have come to see the Holy Fire? Perhaps then you are acquainted with the very interesting account of this event from the time of the Crusades by Fulk of Chartres, the chaplain of King Baldwin. No? Well, I will tell it to you then. Fulk attended the ceremony in the early years of the Crusader kingdom, I believe it was, shortly after the First Crusade. He described a sort of mixed service, Latin and Greek; mind you, not as mixed an affair as you will see today." He gestured to the multitude of varied humanity around them, and there were indeed devotees of several different sects present, varied in their features, the colour of their skin and their dress. "Apparently," he went on, "on that occasion the Holy Fire did not appear when it was expected in the ninth hour, as it had every Holy Saturday in the past, and indeed, ever since. There was, according to Fulk, a great consternation among the clergy." He gestured with his hands when he said this to emphasise the emotions that this must have aroused. "The patriarch called out 'Kyrie Eleison' three times but to no avail. He entered the tomb and prostrated himself, and then he came out in tears. Do you understand, my dears? In tears! This had never happened before." He gestured yet again to emphasise the point. "Fulk tells us that he himself went up to Calvary to see if the fire had somehow been waylaid there... but no. Evening came, and the entire night passed. There was overwhelming despair in the city. Nor had it appeared by the morning. The Latin clergy and the king with

his court followed by the townspeople, went in a barefooted procession through the streets to the Templum Domini, as the Dome
of the Rock was then called. Imagine the distress and emotion!
The Greeks and the other Eastern communities remained in the
church praying and in tears, tearing their hair in anguish. No one
could understand why this had happened, and at this of all times.
The city had only just been redeemed and at such cost. Surely the
sacrifice of all those knights who had fallen in order to recover the
Sepulchre from the Infidel... surely that would have pleased the
Lord? Finally, when all had despaired, as the patriarch was making
his way back to the church the light at last appeared in one of the
lamps above the tomb."

At this point the fellow abruptly stopped speaking and leaned
back against the wall of the building behind him. He did not continue.

"That's a fascinating story," said Riley eventually, but if you
have been so enlightening on this history, please tell us... what was
the reason for the delay?"

"Nobody knows. And it has never occurred since. The fire is
always there at the appropriate time."

"And you really believe in it?" asked Robert. "You do not think
it is a hoax?"

Seeing the man's reaction, he immediately regretted the question.

"A hoax?" the fellow repeated, opening his eyes widely with
incredulity. "No... no."

"I'm sorry. I mean... do you really believe that it's a miracle?"

"I understand what you meant." He seemed alarmed rather
than angered. "But you must know that the fire comes from heaven. How could it be otherwise?"

"I hope I haven't offended you," said Robert.

"No. Not at all. I am not offended, my dear."

"It was just that, as you described it, I thought you sounded sceptical."

"Sceptical of the Holy Fire? No. I have seen it for myself. When I first came to Jerusalem, I saw how the flame appeared at the oculus of the Rotunda and descend slowly onto the roof of the aedicule."

As he spoke these words a second man approached and uninvited, drew up close next to Riley and began to listen intently to their conversation. He was taller than the narrator, but similarly dressed. He had a harried look on his thin face. He reeked of whisky and his jacket gave off a combined smell of mould, perspiration, and camphor. Noticing him, the first man frowned, but continued speaking:

"Admittedly, there is a claim by the Moslems that it is a trick of the priests. They believe that someone is located on the top of the dome and that at the appropriate time he ignites an oiled filament that runs down to the opening on the top of the tomb. But this is nonsense." He dismissed the idea with a wave of his hand. "It is a true miracle, and in any case, this claim would not explain the fact that the fire usually appears in the Sepulchre itself. Only on occasion is it seen to descend from the roof of the Rotunda. And the patriarchs would not lie. They would certainly not play a trick!"

"No, no, of course not," said Robert, still regretting having expressed his scepticism. "And, as you say, you have seen it yourself."

"Yes, I have."

The second man now entered the conversation. Similar to the first fellow, he too spoke clearly and in a manner that stood in stark opposition to his ragged appearance.

"Ha, Felix, you old fool! You believe the lies of the clergy?"

The first man turned on him:

"They are not lies. It is true. I have witnessed it, I tell you."

"Well, you may think so, but this so-called miracle is nothing but fakery!"

"Then what are you doing here, Gustav?"

"Mere curiosity. I want to see how far the Church succeeds in fooling its followers. I, too, have read not a little on this ceremony. If I'm not mistaken, in the thirteenth century Pope Gregory IX denounced it as a deceit, and even more recently it was referred to as a "pious fraud" by the English historian Edward Gibbon in the concluding volume of his *History of the Decline and Fall of the Roman Empire.*"

"It is no fraud." The first man grew flustered. "Pay no attention to him gentlemen." You. You don't know what you are talking about." He had become almost apoplectic. But the other ignored him. Robert noticed that their little group had become the centre of attention. People around them turned to look, though most of them, he thought, would probably not have any idea what was being said.

"And the Greek scholar and humanist, Adamantios Korais," went on the newcomer, "referred to the ceremony as 'machinations of fraudulent priests.' He called it the 'unholy light of Jerusalem.'"

Robert and Riley listened to this heated conversation, fascinated but somewhat embarrassed. They were surprised by the apparent erudition of these shabby-looking characters. Meanwhile the crowd had begun to move, not actually to any place, but like liquid in a bowl, swaying and circling within the square. The man whose name they knew was Felix, in a physical act that was intended as a rebuttal of the second fellow's charges of fraud, turned away from him, sweeping his large stomach around towards Riley who pressed back against the wall behind him. He spoke now as if the other fellow had not been there.

"There has always been much rivalry over this ceremony, but it is the Orthodox Church that has had the upper hand. In 1099, after they took Jerusalem, the Crusaders replaced the Greek clergy and there were riots in the city until the king reinstituted the ceremony. In 1579, the Armenian patriarch, Hovhannes I of Constantinople, tried to usurp the position of the Greek patriarch by praying day and night in the hope that he himself might obtain the Holy Fire. However, the fire did not come until, of a sudden, lightning miraculously struck a column at the entrance to the church. The Orthodox patriarch, Sophronius IV was standing there and the candle he was holding was thus ignited. You can still see the crack in the column caused by the lightning. Do you see it?" He pointed to one of the columns on the left side of the western door of the church.

"Not really," said Robert. "There are too many people. How on earth do you remember all these details?"

Before he could answer the procession began. The Greek patriarch and his clergy came in the lead, the crowd moving aside to let them pass. They were dressed in their sacerdotal robes, singing hymns. They were followed by the Armenian patriarch and then came the Coptic bishop. The men joined in the movement and, despite the huge crowd, managed to enter through the open door of the church into the south transept where they could see the clergy as they walked three times around the Edicule, after which the Greek patriarch removed his vestments and entered the tomb. The Armenian and Coptic prelates remained in the antechamber. The 'Kyrie Eleison' was repeated and after some time the Patriarch emerged holding a cluster of burning candles. A roar went up in the crowd and the fire was distributed, passing from candle to candle. The worshipers held the candles aloft, and very quickly the entire square was filled with rapturous men and women and the lights of a thousand candles. In the flowing of this mass of humanity the fat man and his thin colleague quite unmiraculously disappeared.

On the following afternoon Robert wanted to take some photographs of the tombs in the Valley of Jehoshaphat. As it was the
Orthodox Easter Sunday he decided to avoid the crowds within the
city and to walk around the walls. He asked Riley if he would come
along, but Riley was feeling poorly, and he ended up going on his
own. He borrowed the camera, left the school, and walked down
Saladin Street. Against his intentions, curiosity led him to re-enter
the Old City through the Damascus Gate. He walked down the
Street of the Valley and past the first stations of the Via Doloro-
sa, but the crowds soon made him regret having gone against his
original plans. He turned and exited the city through Saint Steven's
Gate and took a dirt path running between the scattered tombs of
a Muslim cemetery below the city wall. The Valley of Jehoshaphat
fell away to the south. He took his time, stopping to examine the
great edifice of the blocked Gate of Mercy and the larger tombs
below it until, realising that it was growing late and that the light
would soon begin to fall off, he quickened his pace. He hoped to
photograph the ancient tombs and be on his way back before it
became dark; already the shadow was spreading out from the city
wall as the sun began its slow descent. Where the cemetery ended
the path turned sharply left, and ran as a thin pale line of dust between the tombs and thorns. It passed over the edge of the hill and
dropped with the hill as it fell steeply away. His pace unavoidably
quickened, and he broke into a full run. The camera was heavy and
swung as he ran. At the bottom of the hill, he managed to slow
down. He turned right and continued walking along the valley
where it passed between the city wall and the foot of the Mount of
Olives. The monumental rock-cut tombs stood splendidly above.
In the golden light of the late afternoon sun, they looked imposing. From close up they were even more remarkable than he had
expected, a strange and striking blending of classical and Eastern
architecture. He came closer, looking for the best position to take

a photograph of the Pillar of Absalom, the most exceptional of the monuments. It was cut of solid rock into a rectangular space in the cliff, behind which the buff hill rose, scattered with tombstone slabs and dusty rows of lugubrious cypresses. As he came close a boy emerged from behind the monument, followed shortly by a number of slit-eyed goats. Robert nodded and greeted him, but the boy only stared back. Then two more boys, youths really, came out from the shadow along the side of the tomb. One of them spoke to him in Arabic. He gestured by shaking his head and said that he did not understand. The other youth then spoke in broken English.

"Give me camera," he said.

"I can't give it to you, but I'll show it to you if you like," he answered. The youth repeated his request and Robert began to comprehend that he might be in trouble. "Shall I take a photograph of you?" he said, holding up the camera to his eye in a manner of explanation.

"Yes… photograph," answered the first boy.

Robert aimed the camera at the smaller of the boys and the other two came and stood beside him. He took a photograph and then turned the camera and directed it at the tomb. One of the boys came up beside him.

"Give me camera," he repeated.

"I can't give it to you. It's not mine." The boy put his hand on the camera and tried to take it. Robert pulled away. He grew annoyed and more worried as the second youth approached, and it became apparent that they intended to take the camera from him.

"What do you think you're doing," he said.

They were in the shadow of the valley and well below the city wall, and there was nobody to come to his aid. He drew back and the two youths came after him, the small boy watching from the side. One of them came up against him and snatched at the camera. He pulled it away, but the other youth took hold of his arms.

Then the first boy kicked out swiftly at his feet, unbalancing and knocking him down into the dust. One of them tried to pull the camera free while the other pressed Robert's arms against his chest to prevent him from fighting back. The boy holding him down was quite strong, and he could not free himself, and the leather strap of the camera, which was over his shoulder, pulled hard, burning the side of his neck. The youth pulled it down till the buckle broke, cutting his skin and the strap came away releasing the camera into the thief's hands. He got off Robert then, the second youth still holding him down, leaning hard over him. Now Robert fought back, swinging a fist in the direction of the one who still held him. The other was already fleeing with the camera. His fist struck the boy on the side of his face, and he let Robert loose, shouted something, and ran after his friend up to a cluster of stone houses on the upper slopes of the valley. Robert pulled himself up and began to run after them, but they had already distanced themselves, and after a while he stopped, breathless. It was hopeless. He bent over with his hands on his knees to recover, then straightened up, rubbing the wounded skin on his neck. The youths were gone, and he turned back. He saw the small boy with the goats fleeing over the other side of the valley, the goats straggling some distance behind. He cursed in frustration.

An hour later he walked back into the school and climbed the stairs up to his room. In the morning he came down and sat next to Riley at breakfast.

"How was your little adventure yesterday?" he asked, and then realized that something was wrong.

"Much more than I had bargained for, I'm afraid." Riley saw the red welt on Robert's neck, where the camera belt had been torn from him.

"What on earth happened to you?"

"I was attacked by a couple of boys. They got the better of me.

Worse than that... they took your camera. I'm so sorry, John. I shouldn't have borrowed it. I'll pay for its replacement, of course."

"No. Don't worry about the camera. But are you alright? I shouldn't have let you go alone."

"I'm alright. I am now. Just a bit shaken, and very annoyed, at myself as much as at them. I should have been able to stop them. They were only boys."

"We should report this to the police."

"It won't do any good."

"You never know. They might know the thieves. In any case, don't worry about the camera."

"We need a camera. I should pay for it."

"We have a few funds for losses and damage. I will see about replacing it. Perhaps the professor has one at his disposal."

7 CHAPTER

We were taken to a makeshift refectory set up in one of the chambers of the outer ward near our dormitory. After a rather fine meal, a brother named Martin who, like Brother Walther had been given the task of taking care of guests, took us to see another chapel on the first floor of the great tower, not a large room but one of considerable beauty with finely carved decorations and painted walls. At the altar he showed us a small, gilded chest in the form of a gabled building, studded with precious stones. "This contains our holy relics," he said.

"What relics are they?" I asked, my interest in relics had awakened since hearing about the quest of Albert's son.

"Well, for example, the hairs that the Pharisee Nicodemus tore from his head as he mourned over our Lord and aided Joseph of Arimathea in preparing for the burial." Then he opened the lid of the reliquary and showed us a tiny rock-crystal vial which he said held twelve tears shed by twelve widows who witnessed the agonies of the Lord as he passed by them on the streets of Jerusalem on his way to Calvary. "And here is the finger of Saint Thomas that touched the wound of our Lord on Mount Zion, and in this vial"—a beautiful cylindrical vessel of engraved silver—"are contained the peals of the bells of Jerusalem that rang out to announce the birth of our Lord in Bethlehem."

"These are indeed remarkable, Brother," said Albert, and though, having since then seen and heard many things, I might to-day question their authenticity, I must concede that at the time I too marvelled at the preservation of these wonderful objects.

After Compline we went to the dormitory, but the air was very still, and it was too hot to sleep. I lay for a long time on the cot listening to the rhythmic breathing of the brothers around me. Albert breathed heavily and occasionally spoke in his sleep. I wondered if he was dreaming about his son. In the dark I could just make out the thick timber beams of the ceiling above, and every so often I could hear footsteps as the guards moved across the flat roof onto the adjoining wall-walk along the battlements. An oil lamp sputtered on a ledge in the wall next to my cot, and moths and other small, winged creatures flickered in its frail yellow light.

I must have eventually drifted into sleep, for in the depth of the night I awoke, the jackals having entered my dreams. I heard them crying from the dark hills behind the castle. Lying on my cot I listened to a single high-pitched wail suddenly joined by a sequence of progressively higher, quavering howls that filled the night, then died away, and the quiet returned.

When the bell rang for Matins, a brother came into the dormitory with a lantern and shook awake those of us who were asleep. Although I had slept little I did not feel at all tired. I walked outside. The night was a vast cathedral, cool silence, the dark blue vault of the sky above. In the chapel many of the brothers were struggling to shake off their slumber, rubbing their eyes on the back of their hands and stifling yawns. Between readings I looked around at this mixed gathering. Like myself, all were of the Order, and all were visitors.

In the following days I had many opportunities to make myself acquainted with the castle. On one occasion I revisited the ground floor chambers that we had passed through on the first day. There

I met Brother Gunther who was in charge of the kitchens. He was basting a roast of pork on the grid, and other brothers worked at a large table, cleaning fowls and cutting vegetables. Gunther was enormous; indeed, his girth and stubby arms made it somewhat difficult for him to work at the oven, but he nevertheless managed remarkably well. He was not entirely clean; his tunic was spattered with spots of blood and grease - an understandable hazard of his profession; and he had a very red complexion, perhaps too a hazard of his profession, but he was of a decidedly jolly disposition, laughing frequently at almost any remark made to him in conversation. I later heard Matthew, the cellarer, praise him as a cook unequalled in the East, who constantly and good-humouredly complained of the shortage of supplies, but performed wonders with his cooking, which I can now vouch for as being decidedly better than any I had previously experienced, or have experienced since. However, for some of the brothers, his cheerful outlook and exuberance made him the object of censure. I heard Matthew remark:

"It is not surprising that there are those among the more righteous or perhaps self-righteous brothers who, while not hesitating to raise a well-spiced piece of roast meat to their mouths, will later condemn these repasts as inappropriate in the house of a Religious Order. They do so," he said, "secure in the knowledge that Brother Gunther will long continue to practise his art, and that they will have ample opportunity to partake of it."

One day, when we had been about a week at Starkenberg, Brother Martin took me to attend a special chapter that was to be held in the chapterhouse on the upper floor of the castle. Before we entered, I told him I was curious to see the other chapel, the one used by the knights. He pointed the way and I walked along the narrow passage to a splendid, framed portal, finely carved and brightly painted in black, red, and gold. Three slender columns on each side of the doors supported capitals with cloverleaf and lily designs inhabited by stunted, bearded angels, roughly carved and rather grotesque in appearance, but small in size so that they did not in any way detract from the otherwise charming decoration, but rather added to it an element of singularity.

While it was quite small, the knights' chapel was certainly one of the finest rooms I have ever seen. It was far more beautiful than the chapel in the tower and a world apart from the small and plain one for the guests and lay workers where earlier I had attended services. It was faultless in its proportions and in the striking but not excessively opulent decoration. The carvings and furnishings were simple and harmonious. The form of the lily was repeated in variations in most of the carved decorations in the chapel as well as on the painted ceiling and on the glass decoration of the windows on the southern wall. In a corner near the door was a large and wondrously carved stone basin of great antiquity that had originally served as a fountain and had a number of spouts on its sides, extending as carved figures of ancient mythology. It was supported on legs in the form of leopards, and Walther later informed me that it had been obtained at considerable cost from a merchant in Caesarea where it had been unearthed during construction of the fortification works, but the reason for placing it in the knights' chapel was unknown to him. Above the altar was a carved and painted wooden crucifix of Iberian style, which was quite old but in good repair. I gazed for some time at this heartrending work. It reminded me somewhat of a crucifix in my hometown of Freiburg. Everything about it was of grief, and this was expressed in a heaviness; in the bending of Christ's head, the drooping eyes, the slumping frail body with its pronounced ribs; so expressively carrying all of the weight of the Lord's impossible burden.

I must have been lost in contemplation of it for some time. The chapel floor was touched by the afternoon light coming through the windows high on the south wall. These had simple tracery and amber-coloured glass that at this hour flooded the chapel with gold. On the altar was a gilded altar cross decorated with a medallion at its axis containing a beautifully rendered figure of the Lord, and on the lower arm the Virgin; there were saints in medallions at the end of each arm, and when I walked over and examined it more closely I saw that there were more saints in low relief on the back of the arms. It must have been of great value. The altar itself was of a beautiful white marble, bled with green veins. It was partly covered with a fine piece of brocade decorated with rows of gold lilies.

After a while I recalled that I had come to attend chapter and I left the chapel and walked quickly along a passageway to the chapterhouse. Out of curiosity, as I passed by, I looked into the knight's dormitory. There were only a few men, knights, and squires, still in the chamber, as most had already left to the chapterhouse. It appeared that about thirty brother knights occupied this dormitory, and at the far end there was a separate chamber that I assumed was designated for their squires. Each knight had his personal equipment placed near his bed: his sword in its scabbard, battle-axe or glevîn, shield, hooded halsberc hanging in its wire bag, padded undergarment, and simple iron helm or topfhelme. On some of the latter were forged-on bariere and others had a painted wood and leather crest. All of these items far outshone my own humble equipment. The various tabards, banners, and shields with their painted emblems, although less colourful than others that I have seen, made a fine display hanging around the walls of the chamber.

A small room between the chapel and the chapterhouse held, as I later learned, the archives of the Order. It was sealed with a heavy wooden door on massive iron hinges, bolted with a beam and secured by a large iron lock.

I entered the chapterhouse, removed my cowl, and crossed myself, and was then directed to take a seat on one of the wooden benches that were reserved for guest brothers. The garrison knights occupied wooden stalls around three walls. There must have been at least fifty men in the room, guests included. The little commotion that there had been as I entered and took my seat soon died down and stopped completely when the grand commander and the chaplain entered and took their places at a table at the head of the room. I looked across at the grand commander who sat with his head bowed, the chaplain standing bent over him and whispering in his ear.

As we waited, I examined the chapterhouse, which was, in many ways, no less remarkable than the knights' chapel. I was astonished by the brilliant colours of the designs painted on the plastered ceiling. These were mainly in red and black and were very powerful images that spread over the vaulting: the great eagle of the Order, its spread wings, arched beak and cruel eyes, and the highly stylized lily. Around these designs the stone ribs swept up to large boss stones carved as oak-leaf wreaths. Through the dull glass of the windows, I could see the tops of the tree-covered hills to the south.

I had been so involved in the surroundings that I was almost startled when, breaking the complete silence in the hall, the chaplain clapped his hands.

"Good Brothers, stand up and pray to our Lord."

The *Veni Creator Spiritus* was chanted, after which the chaplain read the Gospel and gave a brief sermon, followed by reading of a section of the Rule. The grand commander then called for our attention, which was hardly necessary as we had been waiting for this, and when he spoke, all present listened intently to his deep, resonant but strangely emotionless voice.

"Dixit deus ad Noe: Finis universae carnis venit coram me: repleta est terra iniquitate a facie eorum, et ego disperdam eos cum terra." He paused for a moment for effect and then continued; "Make an ark of gopherwood; seven rooms you shall make in the ark, and you shall pitch it within and without with pitch. And this is the fashion which you shall make it of: The length of the ark shall be three hundred cubits, the breadth of it fifty cubits, and the height of it thirty cubits."

The grand commander now paused once again. Following his sonorous voice that had filled the chamber, the silence was powerful. Then he resumed: "Brothers. We have been building our ark now for over four decades. With the new outworks it is indeed three hundred cubits in length, its breadth is fifty cubits, and its height is thirty cubits. We are almost ready to withstand the floodwaters. But, Brothers, I fear they are already upon us … much sooner than I had anticipated. The Saracen army has had great success in the north. This is a time of trial, and we must prove our worthiness through our faith. Our salvation and that of all true believers, is firstly in prayer and devotion to the Lord. The sainted Augustine said: 'Prayer is the protection of holy souls, a consolation for the guardian angel, an insupportable torment to the devil.'" He paused yet again to let this sink in, then continued: "But along with building our ark, we have been taking other practical steps to defend ourselves against the pagan army. I have hinted to you in the past that our castellan, Brother Jordon, is wise in both ecclesiastical and secular matters. He has knowledge that may deliver us from our enemy. We cannot yet divulge the nature of this knowledge, or the form it will take, but I ask all of you to have faith in our efforts to protect you and to defend the holy soil. Now brothers … do any of you wish to speak?"

There was silence again but then, quite unexpectedly, Matthew the cellarer stood up.

"Forgive my audacity, Grand Commander, but if I may say so, I think that I have a greater knowledge of the strength and abilities of the Saracen army and of the Sultan than most others here and …"

The grand commander interposed:

"We are all acquainted, Brother Cellarer, with your fortunate escape from Arsur."

"I fear, Grand Commander, that your analogy of our fortress with the ark is only too apt. The flood waters are indeed all around us. But our ship has far too many holes in it to withstand the battering we are about to endure."

"Do you have a proposal to make, Brother Matthew?"

"I only wish I did, Grand Commander. Forgive me if I speak boldly, perhaps you will think impertinently, but I believe we should be allowed to hear what the castellan proposes to do to hold back the Saracen army. Has he found a way of completing the fortifications overnight?" There was a stifled snickering among the brothers and a loud hush from the dour chaplain. "I have heard," he went on, "that the Saracen army in Syria is composed of thirty thousand horsemen. How can our defences hold up against a force of that size? Even the great Hospitaller fortress of Crac is unlikely to hold out. And what are we by comparison? A flea on a dog's back! How can our poor walls hold out against their ballistae? Can we hide the sun with two fingers? Why should we not see and judge for ourselves the efforts being made to save us?"

Again, a hushed murmuring filled the chamber.

"Brothers… brothers. We walk by faith, not by sight," answered the grand commander. At this point the castellan suddenly rose and spoke angrily. His words cleared away any vestiges of indifference among those few brothers who had not been absorbed by the preceding discussion:

"Permit me to answer the cellarer," he said without actually looking at the grand commander, and he turned towards Brother Matthew. His face was almost purple, and a thick vein stood out on the side of his forehead. "What do you propose, Brother Cellarer? Would you suggest that we abandon the castle and return to Acre? Perhaps you have had enough of defending the Holy Land?"

Chapter 125

"No!" the cellarer protested. "I speak not out of fear, but out of concern that we are standing idly by while the enemy grows in strength. Why will you not share with us the measures you are taking?"

"Your words are evidence of a lack of faith, not only in me but in the grand commander who has entrusted me with this matter. I think, Brother Cellarer, that you speak only for yourself." He gazed around the room glaring into each and every face with ill-concealed anger, clearly challenging anyone to join this treasonous opposition. When no one spoke, he turned again on the cellarer. "Your words, are the words of a coward!"

The cellarer rose again from his seat:

"I am no coward. But I am not blind."

"Are you suggesting that I am blind, Brother Matthew?" the castellan spat out these words. "Again, I say to you that you are displaying a lack of faith in the grand commander. Your behaviour is outrageous."

"I have nothing but love and respect for the grand commander. But, Brother Jordon, if you have found the means of saving us, why do you refuse to share the knowledge with us? All of our lives are in danger here. Perhaps your methods will fail. Should we not hear of them first and have the opportunity to raise suggestions and to support or oppose them?"

The whole of the chapter was stunned by this dialogue and by the audacity of the cellarer and, though no one dared speak out, there were probably many who were of the same mind. The grand commander rose again:

"Please, please, brothers. Let us not lose our tempers. Brother Matthew… I have faith in the castellan, and if you love me then you too will have faith, unquestioning faith, in his efforts on our behalf. Perhaps…" he turned to Jordon, "you might wish to say something to ease the minds of the brothers in this matter."

Jordon opened his eyes wide and glared at the grand commander, then looked across at Brother Matthew. Then he rose again.

"I am surprised, Grand Commander..." he said, still facing Matthew, "that you put up with this insubordination. However, I will say this, and this alone. Most of you know that I have great knowledge of incendiary weapons and it is this knowledge that I am employing to save us. I have obtained, by means that you could not even imagine, a secret Syrian formula for an incendiary material that will make the *ignis Græcus* seem like water by comparison." He paused for a moment, then continued. "That is all I have to say about what I am doing. I am very near to completing this work and if I am not disturbed in it..." he emphasized the word "disturbed" and then paused again, looking around the chamber to make it clear that he regarded this chapter meeting as a disturbance, "I can assure all of you that when the Saracens arrive, they will find Starkenberg a hard nut to crack." With this he sat down and folded his arms across his chest in a gesture that made it clear that, as far as he was concerned, the matter was closed to further discussion.

As Brother Matthew now remained seated and no one else rose in his place, it was apparent that this was indeed an end to the debate. After a few moments of silence, the priest began again a quiet recitation. The knights sat bowed and reticent.

After chapter, Brother Walther came up to me accompanied by Albert and informed me that the grand commander was ready now to see us. As we walked in the direction of the Great Hall, I turned to him, but before I had opened my mouth he spoke:

"Squire Hermann. I must warn you that if you wish to discuss the matters raised in chapter, I cannot oblige you."

Chapter 127

"No, Brother Walther," I answered. "I wanted to ask you about the lily."

"Lily?"

"Yes. I noticed the very beautiful renditions of the lily in the chapel and the chapterhouse, and I recall seeing it in the chapel of our house at Acre. I was wondering if there is some special significance to it. I thought perhaps you might know."

"Well, yes I do," he answered. "The lily is a symbol of purity, and represents the brevity of life; *breve lilium*, Horace calls it. The three petals represent faith, wisdom and chivalry. But it may be that it was chosen by the Order not only for what it symbolizes, but also because it grows here in the very hills around this castle."

The audience with the grand commander took place in an anteroom of the grand master's apartments above the Great Hall. In the absence of the grand master, they were used by Grand Commander Eckhart. The anteroom was almost bare of furnishings. The most prominent object in it was a large oak chest placed against one wall and decorated with black, spiral-patterned ironwork. Above it hung a painted panel on which were two figures: one was a Teutonic knight in full armour standing beside a horse, the other was a young man in priestly dress. The only other objects in the room were a large throne-like chair finely carved with figures and beasts and scrolls of leaves and vines, and some simple benches opposite it. We sat on the benches after the grand commander had himself taken his seat. Seeing him from close at hand I was somewhat taken aback by his appearance. He was a small man of heavy build, but with a certain softness about the face that might have given a vague impression of weakness were it not for his startlingly blue eyes that introduced to his features a certain element of firmness. The other remarkable thing about his appearance was a repetition of the blue of his eyes in a magnificent ring that he wore on the second to last finger of his left hand. It was gilded and enamelled, with a black lily charge, a work of *opus Lemovicense*, the lily, that ever-repeated emblem, finely rendered on the brilliant azure field.

The grand commander nodded, and Albert spoke:

"It is most kind of you, Grand Commander Eckhart, to find the time to see me."

"Not at all. I understand that you were sent by Commander Ulrich?" I was impressed once again by the grand commander's deep and resonant voice.

"Yes. I am searching for my son, Bernard, Bernard of Ulm or possibly known as prior of Weissenau. He came over the sea six years ago. I have heard nothing from him since and have had no word of his whereabouts. Commander Ulrich was kind enough to permit Squire Hermann to accompany me." The grand commander nodded to me, and I bowed my head, "But so far we have found no trace of him. I am hoping that perhaps you, or someone else here at Starkenberg, may have knowledge of him."

"Bernard, you say?" The grand commander sat in silent thought for a few moments, looking down into the folds of the robe in his lap. Finally, he spoke. "I do remember a guest of that name at Acre, an interesting fellow… yes. A tall young man…" I looked across at Albert. "But no, I don't think this man was old enough to have been a prior. Of where, did you say?"

"Weissenau."

"I don't know… It might have been him. I recall that this man was involved in some transaction with the Venetians and there was some sort of dispute over a piece of land, I think. Could that be him?" Before waiting for an answer, he said: "Wait a moment. I will call the castellan. He was with me at Acre, and unlike me, he has a remarkable memory."

Chapter 129

The grand commander nodded to a brother who was standing by the door. The brother walked over to him, and Grand Commander Eckhart whispered some words into his ear. The brother walked out, and the men sat in silence for a moment. Then Eckhart spoke again.

"Our castellan, Brother Jordon, has been with me since I came to the East. He served me in Cilicia and in the hospital at Acre and we have been together at Starkenberg now for three years. He will certainly remember your son if he visited our house in Acre."

"I fear the Bernard you refer to could not be my son. He was not a young man at the time he came here. He came on some other business, and I don't think he would have had anything to do with purchasing land from the Venetians."

"In that case he is certainly not the man I was speaking of. Tell me, what is the reason for your taking such a dangerous and arduous journey? These are perilous times, and you are, forgive me, not a young man."

"That is precisely the reason why I have come. I am old and I am aware that my days are coming to an end. I wish to see my son and to hold him in my arms one more time before I give up this life."

"He has not written to you, nor sent word?"

"Not in several years. He visited me and his mother at Ulm before he left for the East, and he promised to correspond. But we have heard nothing. For some time, we lived in fear that some terrible fate had befallen him. Finally, after a year had passed, I went to his monastery and was told that they had no knowledge of what had become of him. Indeed, they had sent for word from their house in Acre and hearing nothing, presumed him dead. They had already elected a new prior in his place."

"Surely you knew of the dangers when he went East?"

"Yes, of course. And I thought that I could live with this knowledge. But I cannot, not without knowing what has befallen him. If he is dead, then I wish to be able to visit his burial place."

At that moment, the brother returned and walked over to the grand commander, speaking a few words to him, and after a few more minutes the castellan entered the chamber and Albert and I rose. This was the first time I had seen him up close. He was an extremely good-looking man of, I would estimate, about forty years, with fine features but a hard, almost cruel expression.

"Please be seated, gentlemen," he said. Then without a word to the grand commander, as if he was not even there, the castellan turned and spoke directly to Albert. "It is most unfortunate that you have come here now. You were ill-advised to do so. I'm afraid you will now not be able to leave. The risk is too great."

Albert was quite taken aback by this, as indeed was I. He half rose from his seat as he spoke:

"I have come regarding my son. Grand Commander Eckhart says that you may know something of his whereabouts. I am…"

"I know who you are. And indeed, I met your son in the hospital at Acre several years ago."

Albert's mouth fell open.

"You did?" said the grand commander, surprised. "Are you sure? Was it not perhaps that young knight who that came to us about his dealings with the Venetians?"

"No," he brushed aside the grand commander's remarks. "Your son was seeking to obtain a relic, the arm of Saint John the Baptist."

"That's right… yes indeed!" Albert sat bolt upright his eyes wide open.

"But I cannot help you."

"This man has come a long way, Brother Castellan," the grand commander spoke again. "Have you no information at all for him?" I was surprised by the deferential tone that the grand commander used when speaking to the castellan. It was almost as if their roles were reversed, but Brother Jordon continued to ignore the grand commander's presence and to speak directly to Albert.

"It was not a wise thing for you or your young companion to come to Starkenberg. I am surprised and sorry that you were not better advised by Commander Ulrich. You will certainly not find your son here and I can give you no information of his whereabouts. I'm sorry, but he may well be dead."

I saw Albert's countenance drop.

"But you have seen him … When? Where?"

"I met him briefly when he first came out. I knew of his intentions and of the opposition to his quest."

"Opposition! What opposition?"

The castellan ignored the question.

"But then he disappeared, and I have not seen nor heard of him since, and as I say, he may no longer be alive. You must remain here until you can be taken back to Acre. And then I think you would do best to return home." It was as if he was dismissing us. Turning to Grand Commander Eckhart he said in a very curt manner: "I must return now to my work. Please do not allow me to be disturbed again," and before the grand commander could answer he walked out of the chamber.

Grand Commander Eckhart turned back to Albert who sat stunned in his bench.

"I am sorry if he seemed rather unsympathetic. The castellan has much on his mind right now… as you certainly know, Squire Hermann. You attended the chapter, I think." Then, apparently observing and misinterpreting the astonishment still on our faces, he added. "It might seem strange to you that I treat him with such deference. You must understand… Castellan Jordon is a very learned man, a genius in fact."

"It is not that, Grand Commander," said Albert. "But he has

seen my son. And he speaks of opposition to his quest! I must know more."

"I am sorry. I will try to find out, but I can promise nothing."

Albert was much shaken by this conversation and returned to the dormitory to rest. After Sext I went to call him, but he was tired and did not wish to accompany me to the refectory. I washed at the small piscena below the stairs and waited outside the refectory with other visitors to the castle until it was our turn to enter. Then we were seated below a great window at a table especially assigned for guests. The food was carried in by serving brothers and placed before us – fowl and pork served with cabbage, onions, purslane, and beans. Wine was brought in in yellow and green Cypriot jugs. I sat in the silent room, buried in my thoughts. The chaplain read softly from the Holy Scripture, almost in a mumble that could not be properly heard, much less followed. I saw the grand commander enter and sit at his table. Brother Jordon was not present.

8 RETURN

At first it seemed that they had seen the last of Walker. When the men got back to camp, they were greeted by Abdul who informed them that he had not returned. However, word was going around among the villagers that he was still in the neighbourhood, and some of them expressed the fear that he intended to sabotage the dig. Riley dismissed this, but Robert was less certain that there might not be something in it. Walker's last words to Riley had threatened as much.

As they were not too tired from their drive, and the weather was fine, Riley and Robert, in the company of Abdul, walked up-hill to the south, and he showed them a particularly beautiful spot; an ancient olive grove where the trees were extremely old. Some of the villagers, he informed them, believed they had been there since the time of Saladin. The trunks were twisted and hollow and formed a myriad of writhing shapes. They were so old and gnarled that the silver green canopy above was a revelation. The grove was quite large, and the more distant trees seemed an almost ethereal shimmer, almost spectral in the sun. Riley was sorry he did not have his camera to take some photographs. The day had grown warmer, and the three men sat in the shade smoking, Riley and Robert with their pipes, and Abdul with a rather potent cigarette.

Once they had completed the little rituals so well known to pipe smokers, Robert started a conversation:

"I was wondering how you find the Levant, John, since, as you say, it's your first time outside of America?"

"Interesting might be as good a word as any... and somewhat disturbing at times. Why do you ask?"

"Oh... I don't know. I was just wondering whether you find that the people are very different?"

"Well, yes and no. To be honest, I sometimes find the people at home pretty strange."

"What do you mean?"

"Riley knocked his pipe on a rock and refilled it. "I suppose I mean that I'm quite often disappointed with folk."

"Really!"

"Present company excluded, of course." He was thoughtful for a moment. "I don't know... I imagine some people find me a bit disappointing too, a bit of an eccentric perhaps. I've always been a loner. That's why I like my job. It allows me to be on my own most of the time. I have to admit, however, that I have enjoyed working with you. This business with Walker has upset me, but, you know, it is perhaps not all that remarkable. There are a lot of disturbed people about."

"Disturbed?"

"Myself included," he laughed.

"I hardly think you are in any way like Walker."

"I certainly hope not. No. I guess I mean that I am aware that some people must think me a pretty strange bird. Perhaps not disturbed. More like... distressed. Ha... Well, that's an exaggeration too. But look... I live on my own; I have no family and no desire for one. I'm a self-sufficient type. I probably would have made a good monk, come to think of it."

The men sat conversing for some time when suddenly a shot

rang out from across the valley and echoed back between the low hills. Abdul stood up, without saying anything, walked across to the border of the grove and climbed onto a low terrace wall on the very edge, where the land dropped to the south.

"Someone hunting, no doubt," said Riley, lifting himself up with difficulty and missing his cane. Abdul said nothing but stood silently, and his intensity worried them.

"Do you see anything? Robert walked over."

"No. Mr. Palmer."

"A villager hunting, do you think?"

"I don't think so."

"Come make us coffee," said Riley, and Abdul walked back to where they had been sitting and began to pick up fallen branches and twigs. He made a small fire and, filling the finjan with water from a canteen, he placed it on the fire.

"Surely the villagers around here do a bit of hunting," said Robert.

"Yes... but not with pistols."

"That was a pistol shot?" asked Riley.

"Yes."

"We'll. I'll take your word for it. I have little knowledge of guns... But I wouldn't worry."

They did worry, nonetheless, all three of them. Each in his mind thought of Walker although no one mentioned him.

Later Abdul took them up to Malia. It was Robert's first visit there and they walked up the hill past the newer houses to the older part of the village on the hill where the small castle stood. This was Castellum Regis - the King's Castle. It was quite a simple structure, very different from Montfort, rather brutal and intimidating, but with none of the drama of Montfort's setting. It rose on a small hill, a crude rectangular mass dominating the village houses that had attached themselves to it like parasites, borrowing its stones, leaning on its walls, invading all the way into its heart. It had no complexity of form, consisting simply of four plain outer walls and three of the original four slightly projecting, corner towers. As they walked around the exterior they were followed by a group of small children and a dog that had seemed to emerge out of nowhere. On the top of the hill there was an open square and a small church. As they approached, they were greeted by the Greek Catholic priest, Father Nicephor, a young man in his mid-twenties. He wore a black wide-sleeved cassock and a chimney-pot hat, and had a short, untrimmed black beard. He took them inside the church that was modern and not particularly remarkable, and after they had taken a look around and expressed a polite curiosity about the age of the building, he sat with them in the shade of a trellised grapevine, just coming into flower on its ancient leafy branches. A boy served them tea and small, overly sweet, sticky cakes. Father Nicephor showed an honest interest in the progress of the dig, quite the reverse of that shown by the American consul in Jaffa.

"I've been meaning to get down to see you," he said. "How is the work progressing?"

"Very nicely on the whole," answered Riley. "We are working in the central part of the castle. You should indeed come and visit us."

"Have you found the chapel? I should be interested in seeing that."

"Not yet," said Riley, "but I think we will find it, or at least evidence of where it was. We are now digging in what must have been the service rooms below the knights' dormitory and refectory. I would imagine once we get down to floor levels everything will become much clearer."

"Do let me know when you find it," he said. "I have been busy with the festivities, but I will try to come down soon in any case. Have you taken photographs of the finds? I should like to see them."

"We have taken some, but we have run into a problem in that regard. Our camera was stolen when we were in Jerusalem."

"Stolen? But that is terrible.! Father Nicephor looked quite shocked. He thought for a moment. "My friends," he said, "I think that I can help you. I have a camera, a rather good Graflex which you may borrow."

"Could we, really?"

"Yes, indeed. Wait, I'll get it for you," and he went into his apartments, coming out after a few minutes with a large leather case and handed the camera to Riley. "Please gentlemen... use this. There is all you need in the case with the camera."

"But this is most kind of you," said Riley.

"I am glad to help. This way I feel as if I have a small role in your work. But there are two conditions attached... firstly that you are very careful with it. I use this camera on my pilgrimages, and it is a valuable possession. I will show you perhaps my photograph collection." He turned and spoke in Arabic to a small boy standing nearby and the boy ran off into the house. "The second condition is that you take a great many photographs and show them to me when you have the time."

"This is wonderful," Riley said taking the case and opening it. Inside was the camera with all the plates and film and other paraphernalia.

"This is a better model than the one we had," said Robert. "Thank you so much, Father. I have been most upset by the loss of the camera, especially as it was from me that it was taken."

"This will enable us to continue our photographic record," said Riley. "Of course, we accept both of your conditions."

"Have you reported the theft to the police?"

"It seems that there is not really much point in involving the police," said Riley.

"This sort of thing happens all the time," Robert added. "The police are far too involved in security matters to deal with petty thefts, even when they are accompanied by assault."

"Assault? The thieves attacked you?"

"Yes. But unless the injuries incurred are serious the police will not deal with it. I know this from my own time in the gendarmerie. Anyway, the injuries were to my pride more than anything else. I was as much upset by my inability to react effectively as by the theft."

Just then the little boy emerged from the house carrying in his arms three enormous photograph albums.

A week went by without anything particularly eventful occurring. The villagers uncovered some interesting finds, and it seemed as if the work was settling into a good routine. The weekend came around and Robert and Riley drove back to Haifa. Robert was excited at the prospect of seeing Bel again. He dropped Riley off at his hotel.

"I'll pick you up early Monday morning... about five."

"I hope you'll be up to it," Riley laughed, slapping his back in a friendly gesture. "Go on... and have a good time. I'll see you then."

Before he drove up the hill Robert stopped at Bel's house. She answered the door and smiled. Seeing her again, with the anticipation that had been steadily growing, he was overwhelmed with emotion. It amazed him that in so short a time he could become so impassioned by someone, to the extent that all the other things in his life, great and small, dissipated the moment he was in her presence. He asked her if he might take her for a drive and it was arranged for him to come by on Sunday morning.

Robert found Saturday a burden. He regretted not having made arrangements to see Bel then as well, but he was reluctant to appear overly eager and fought off his desire to change their plans. He found the day endlessly long and dreary. He tried to occupy himself with a book and took a long walk in the afternoon, but it seemed a waste to be on his own a whole day, and he wished that he had the boldness to ignore formalities and drive right over to see her.

On Sunday morning he picked her up and they drove to Stella Maris. They took the road up along the ridge of Mount Carmel. There was a place here that Robert knew, a field of wild grass that stretched along the side of the road overlooking the blue expanse of the Mediterranean. He parked the car; Bel took out the sandwiches and they sat on a blanket beneath some tall pine trees.

"Tell me about yourself," she said. "I still know so little about you."

"There's not all that much to tell really," he said. "I grew up in England. My parents are both dead. My father was an officer during the Great War. He served under General Horne. He was killed at Arras in the Second Battle of the Somme. My mother was always frail. She fell ill immediately after receiving the news and died within a year. I have one sister. She is married and lives in South Africa, and I have an aunt in London. That's about all my family."

"When did you come out here?"

"Just over three years ago."

"What made you come?"

"So many questions!" he laughed. "I don't know... for some reason I can hardly understand myself. I suppose it was chiefly to get away from things. I was bored with my life and didn't know what to do. I didn't have a profession and it seemed like an adventure. I volunteered to serve in the gendarmerie. But then I found that it was not quite what I had expected. Many of the fellows were former Black and Tans. Have you heard of them?"

"No."

"Auxiliary police who had served in Ireland during the Rebellion of 1919. They were a rough lot, and I saw a lot of things I didn't like. A few months ago, the gendarmerie was disbanded. Rather than go back or do what most the other chaps did and be reemployed in the Palestine Police Force or enlist in the Trans-Jordanian Police, I decided to leave the service and find something else to do here for a while until I was ready to go back." He ran his hands through his straight, black hair. "I suppose I was putting off making a decision about my future and by chance I ran into John Riley and ended up joining his expedition. I'm glad I did."

"Yes. It must be quite an experience. I'd love to visit."

"Well, you should."

"What is your boss like?"

"I hardly think of him as a boss. He's more like a friend. He's a really decent chap. I'll see if I can arrange for you to come out if you'd like."

"Yes, please do. I'd love to see the castle. Tell me a bit about the dig. It must be terribly exciting."

Robert stretched and lay back on the grass, gazing up into the trees and the expanse of blue sky. "Well, it is sometimes. But there is a lot of time when it's just work. I am doing the surveying. I've done a bit of survey work in England, and I suppose I'm good with the pen. On the whole, the experience is quite different from what I had imagined," he said.

"What do you mean?"

"Well… the dig itself is pretty much as I expected it would be.

The castle is amazing and John, as I said, is a fine fellow. But the other chap, a fellow named Walker, has turned out to be a complete disaster."

"In what way?"

"Well, you see… he was supposed to be an assistant to John and to act as a sort of liaison between him and the locals. John doesn't speak any Arabic."

"Oh, I see."

"Professor Gilford, he's the head of the Department of Antiquities, he recommended Walker. I guess he didn't really know the fellow. It is now apparent that he was a very poor choice for the job. Completely unreliable. Not only is he useless with the workers; he's a bit of a thief as well. Last week he had a huge fight with John and then he left in the middle of the night, taken some of our equipment, including a rifle."

"He walked off? Just like that? What was the reason?"

"He'd been stirring up trouble with the workers and drinking too much. John was reluctant to deal with him at first. He warned him a number of times. Then things came to a head. John questioned him about some business over unexplained expenses billed by Walker to the expedition, personal expenses apparently, probably alcohol. The chap went completely overboard. Anyway, then we caught him attacking the camp-boy, for absolutely no reason. The poor boy didn't know what was happening. He even thought himself to blame. That was the last straw. John had it out with him and then he just went off in the middle of the night in that huge thunderstorm."

"Perhaps he's just gone to cool off a bit. Don't you think he might come back?"

"Well… quite frankly, I think it would be better if he didn't. Anyway, as it stands it looks as if the man's not just a petty thief. He could even be dangerous."

They were silent for a moment. Then Robert sat up and looked into her eyes.

"Now," he said, "I have been monopolising the conversation. What about you? Tell me about yourself… your family."

She told him that her father traded in teas and spices. His work was centred in Bombay, but he had recently moved to Palestine in the hope of opening an office there. Her mother was of Indian origin. She was a beautiful but sickly woman. Bel showed him a small photograph of her in a silver locket she wore on a fine silver necklace. He examined the image of the attractive woman, not unlike her daughter in appearance but of a paler complexion and with darker hair. She was sitting by a lead-framed window, dressed in a white lace blouse and with a thick fur wrap over her lap. Holding the locket in his hand brought him close to Bel's face and he gazed at her as she spoke. Bel had grown up in India, then in England and recently had come with her parents to Palestine. Her mother, because of her poor health, was often back in England and she lived mostly alone with her father.

"Are you close?" he asked.

"I love him. But he is not an easy man. And he's extremely busy. I am really closer to my mother."

"That must be hard on you."

"I have some friends here, but I am rather lonely at times. Sometimes. I wish…" she hesitated.

"What? What do you wish?"

"It's nothing. I shouldn't complain." She hesitated again for a minute and then said: "I sometimes wish I had had a more stable childhood. I have no siblings and we moved so often."

He looked at her face and its flawlessness, the perfect eyes, slightly oriental, the shapely lips. Suddenly he said: "Do you have any idea how beautiful you are?"

Bel half-smiled and did not answer. He took her hand in his

and they sat in silence together, he, looking at her, and she, looking down in her lap.

"I think I am falling in love with you," he said eventually. She looked up into his eyes. They were silent now. There was no need for words. He held her warm body in his arms and their lips joined.

As the morning wore on, whatever inhibitions there had been between them, dissolved. The sun filtered through the mass of pine needles above. They talked, laughed and were silent for long stretches. Robert lay back and looked at her sitting beside him hugging her knees, gazing off towards the bay. The sun picked out the fine down on her upper lip and highlighted her hair like flame. He watched her breathing, her breasts rising and falling. He sat up and kissed her again and she responded, opening her mouth to his. A quiet drone came from above as a small white airplane passed slowly across the bay, moving parallel with the coast, then inland, over the mountain and back out to sea.

Early on Monday morning Robert picked up Riley and they drove off in the half-light. The sea was dark, and the hills rose in misty grey.

"So, my friend," Riley spoke after a while. "How was your weekend?"

"It was wonderful, John. We drove up to Stella Maris. I thought Bel might be reluctant to go. I was a little worried, I suppose, that perhaps I was moving too fast, but it was wonderful. She is wonderful!"

"So it would seem. Do you think you will be able to get your mind back to work?"

"Of course I will. How was your weekend?"

"Not quite as good as yours, I imagine. Mr. Townsend invited me to attend an outdoor banquet held in a field at the foot of

Mount Carmel just below the Bahai gardens. It was a colourful event; Egyptian servants dressed in white galabias with red sashes and wearing red tarbushes, and pipes played by a band of Seaforth Highlanders. The food wasn't too bad either."

The following morning started on a worrisome note when Abdul reported to Riley that some more equipment seemed to be missing, mainly hoes and one of the barrows. Riley spoke to Ra'ed who promised to speak to the workers. Ra'ed was insistent that none of them would have taken the equipment. Later on, Salah came and told Riley that he had found the missing tools dumped in a pile just below the perimeter of the camp. No one seemed to know who had placed them there. Robert temporarily took over some of the tasks that Walker had previously handled including the morning roster, and he watched over a team working in one of the two large barrel vaults beneath the ruins of the hall. This new responsibility meant that he had little time for his drawing, but he did not really mind the change and enjoyed the closer contact with the villagers. He experienced a continually growing level of excitement as earth was uncovered and they excavated closer to the floor levels. This was the first time he had participated in the actual excavation work, and he found that he was tremendously intrigued in all aspects of it. Rather than stand on one side to oversee the workers as he had imagined he would do, he hovered over them, peering over their bent shoulders as they hoed and trowelled the soil. He delighted in the smell of the freshly exposed earth and looked on with fascination at every little object that was revealed in the grey soil: green-glazed ceramic sherds, a lump of corroded copper coins, bent iron nails, arrowheads, the bones of a tiny animal. There were as many women as men on the team, and Robert was impressed by their physical abilities that almost equalled those of the men and occasionally surpassed them. Six of the workers were involved in the actual digging, first with picks, then hoeing the loosened soil into straw baskets. The debris that had fallen from the upper storeys when they collapsed had formed a steep slope from the inner side of the vault. The men piled the larger stones on one side and then the baskets of soil were heaved by a team of men and women up the slope to where the last man in the human chain swung a basket onto his shoulder and carried it to the edge of the slope. A path of wooden planks had been laid to prevent slipping, and from here emanated the crash of rock and soil that intermittently smothered the quiet chatter of the workers. Every so often one of the diggers would slow his pace, sensing he was coming upon something. Almost instinctively Robert became aware of the change and would come closer and watch as some object was slowly exposed. Quite often these discoveries proved to be nothing more than an interestingly shaped rock, a quantity of broken pottery sherds or a piece of badly rusted iron. But sometimes a finely carved stone was uncovered or a small object of interest such as a piece of worked bone, and one time, a handful of silver coins packed with soil in the fragments of a broken flask.

When the workers took their break and Robert had little to do, he found himself daydreaming about the castle and the knights who had once occupied it. He wondered what life would have been like in such a community of warriors, cut off from the world and enduring the strict regimen of monastic routine. He thought about the siege. In his mind he could hear the shouting of the attackers and the noise of the battle, and he tried to imagine the smell of the smoke, the fear that must have engulfed defenders.

In the early afternoon, the workers resumed their labour, and at one point he was called to another part of the castle to witness the excitement of discovery when a huge cross-shaped stone was cleared and with the use of a pulley, hoisted out of a cistern and onto the ground. It was in beautiful condition, a superbly carved bossed keystone that had fallen from one of the vaulted bays. It was decorated with a rosette, still intact despite it having fallen from the upper storey through the basement and into the cistern, a drop of about 60 feet. The design on the boss was a wreath of oak leaves that were so carefully and confidently rendered in the hard buff limestone that they almost seemed to be moving in the slight breeze. Robert imagined how splendid, with decoration like this, these halls must have once appeared.

Shortly after this find, the workers uncovered a second very different but no less thought-provoking object. It was a fine necklace formed of amber beads. It was found next to a stone staircase on the western side of the domestic ward, lying on a fallen ashlar, neatly spiralled in a double loop as if it had only just been put down. Without being asked, the worker who had uncovered the object handed Robert a brush and moved aside to allow him to take over. With immense care Robert cleaned the individual beads, using the edge of the brush and with great concentration so as not to move the pieces as they emerged from the dust. The copper or bronze chain that had held the beads had turned into a green powder, but some links were still intact, and the amber stones were all in the exact position they had been when it was first placed here. There were two gilt lion-head clasps, and a number of gold beads at intervals between the amber that appeared as unblemished and bright as if they had only now been fashioned by the jeweller. As he was progressing Riley joined him and watched the younger man tentatively brush the fine dust away.

"You work like a professional, Robert," he said. "You seem to have a natural talent."

It took a good half hour to uncover the entire necklace and remove all the tiny adherences of dust and soil. Riley then called for one of the men to bring the new camera and carefully took a photograph of the object *in situ.*

"Well… What do you think?" Robert asked.

"It's very fine… but I must say, its presence here raises some questions."

"Why is that?"

For one thing, what is a piece of jewellery doing here? Remember this is the castle of a Military Order. That means that it was occupied by men living a quasi-monastic life under monastic rule… and, only men. There should not have been women present here. Jewellery would seem to be out of place, except maybe rings and pendant crosses and the like!"

"I see what you mean. So… how do we explain it? Were the brothers wearing jewellery, or were women perhaps spirited into the castle perhaps, contrary to the regulations?"

"I very much doubt the former." Riley smiled at the thought. As to illicit women… I don't know. That might have been managed in Acre, or in lesser castles, but could they have been brought in here without being observed. This was the most important castle of the Order. The German leaders, even the grand master, resided here at times.

"Perhaps they were openly here, for some legitimate menial tasks… laundry or cooking?"

"Possibly, though those were usually labours carried out by the brothers themselves."

"Couldn't the jewellery have been kept here for its value, part of a treasury perhaps, or for trading?"

"That is certainly a possibility. But, if that was the case, why is this necklace here on its own? If we had found a trove of jewellery, I would agree that it might have been kept for its worth rather than for being worn… but a single piece? I don't know. And another thing is mysterious here. This stone on which it is placed is not in its original location. You can see that it has fallen, yet the necklace had been carefully placed on it. That must mean that it was placed here during or after the destruction of the castle. Perhaps it did not belong to inhabitants of the castle at all."

"But then... to whom? The Muslim soldiers? That would make no more sense than if it belonged to the Germans."

"Possibly, Riley wondered aloud, "someone left it here after the castle was destroyed?"

"Do you think so?" asked Robert.

"Not really. Think about what we have removed from above it."

"About two feet of rubble."

"Precisely! It was found within the debris of the collapsed vaulting, which we assume fell here during the destruction of the castle. That means that it could not be later than that destruction, which, as we know, took place almost immediately after the siege."

"Yes. I see."

"Another thing...," said Riley. "You note that these beads are amber."

"Yes?"

"Well. Where does most amber come from?"

"I've no idea."

"Mostly from the shores of the Baltic Sea. And do you know who ruled in much of that region in the thirteenth century?"

"No."

"The same people... the German knights! From what I have read, they had established a Teutonic state in Prussia at the same time that they were active here in the Levant. Of course, that doesn't necessarily prove anything, but it might suggest that you are right about it being kept for its worth, part of a treasury, and perhaps our knights were involved in some sort of trading activities?"

In the early afternoon, a group of children came down from the village and joined the workers—small, dark-haired, thin-legged boys dressed in baggy trousers, white shirts, and vests. One boy had brought with him a yellow puppy, an excited little creature that ran about under their feet, darting and yapping at anything that moved, generating an occasional angry warning that neither child nor dog took any notice of. In the following days, this puppy became a constant presence at the dig, appearing without the boys when the workers arrived in the morning and always about, often underfoot, filling the air with its noise but never exciting more than an occasional curse, and even doing its bit, digging away with enthusiasm when the mood struck it. If it got out of hand, they would tie it with a piece of rope to a post and it would yap away for a while, whine a bit and eventually settle down and lie in the dust and watch the work. It had no name and was simply referred to by all as the kalb.

The following day Townsend arrived on horseback, riding down from Malia. He was not alone, and when he came up to the castle, they saw from a distance that his companions were another man in uniform and a young woman who, Robert was delighted to discover, was Bel. The uniformed man was a quiet-spoken po-liceman whom Townsend introduced as Captain Peters. Robert greeted Bel warmly and held her horse while she dismounted. He introduced her to Riley and then he took her aside.

"Well. This is a surprise!"

"I told you I wanted to come," she said, "and it appears that we have mutual acquaintances. Jim Townsend is an old family friend. He told me he was coming out and I asked if I could join him. I hope you don't mind?"

"No, of course not. I'm surprised. I had planned to bring you out myself."

"Well then, I've saved you the bother. I was worried about you. So… you are glad to see me?"

"Yes, of course I am. I didn't know you could ride!"

"There's a lot you don't know about me, Robert."

"Won't your father be worried?"

"Perhaps" she answered with a slight smile. They sat down on some large stones in the shade of one of the walls and Bel listened as the men talked over the matter of Walker.

"You say that he went off without letting you know?" asked the officer.

"Yes," said Riley. "…during the night, apparently. As I told you, I had some harsh words with him the evening before. I told him he was to leave in the morning."

"You fired him?"

"Yes. But the fellow walked off in the middle of the night, and during a violent storm. It was absurd."

"And you are quite certain he took the rifle."

"Yes, of course… as well as a camel and some other things."

"Well. Thank you, Mr. Riley. I should like to have a talk with some of the workers now."

"Certainly. I'll call the foreman."

Robert took Bel up to the excavations and Townsend and Peters spent most of the morning interviewing the workers. When they got back Townsend spoke once again with the two men.

"Are you aware that some of the villagers claim to have seen Walker, or at least someone who might have been Walker, wandering about the hills near the village."

"Yes. We have heard about that, but it was only from a distance," said Riley.

"And several of them say that they have heard shooting at night. Have either of you heard any shooting?"

"Well, we did hear a shot fired the other day… you remember Robert? Abdul said it was a pistol shot."

"Did Walker possess a pistol?"

"Not that I know of."

"Is it not possible that he had one that you didn't know about?"

"I suppose it is."

"And you haven't seen anything yourselves?"

"We would certainly have mentioned it if we had."

At noon, Townsend, Bel and Captain Peters rode back and the two men went up to the castle.

"Well Robert, now I see why you are walking around in a daze," Riley teased him. "Your girl is certainly a beauty!"

"She is, isn't she?"

They got back to the camp well before dark. Robert had come down first, and as Riley had suggested that this was a good opportunity to sort through the finds they had so far recovered he took several of the cardboard boxes that were stacked about and emptied them out on a table and then began to divide them into categories; ceramics, objects of metal, bone, wood and glass. At first, he did this without much thought, simply moving each type of material into a separate pile on the sorting-table. Then he moved between them, dividing the finds into still smaller piles so that, for example, among metal finds there was a small pile of arrowheads, a handful of coins, a number of bronze buckles, a large pile of heavily corroded iron nails and, on its own, a perfect, small, bronze archer's thimble. There were also two large and complete, though badly corroded claw-head hammers. In a similar fashion he divided the ceramics into glazed and unglazed pieces and into those he could identify as cooking pots, bowls, and storage jars. As he worked, he began to take interest in certain items and to hold them up in the light and occasionally he noted down items on a sheet of lined paper, carefully taking measurements and noting these down as well. He paid particular interest to the wood finds. The burning of the castle had produced a thick layer of lime from the burnt limestone, and this had turned to slake in the winter rains and acted as a preservative, enabling wooden objects within it to remain in almost perfect condition. Most of these pieces had come from one of the two chambers under the hall where the fire appears to have been particularly intense. He took up an object whittled out of pale wood, about 20 inches in length and slightly bent. On the upper part were a notch and a simple, carved heraldic emblem. Alongside this he placed a number of thin pieces of painted lengths of wood, round in section. These were arrow shafts. They were painted in red, white, and blue and some had designs like eyes painted on them, perhaps for ownership identification or to make them conspicuous in dry grass and branches, and thus recoverable after a battle. There were three wooden spoons, one of them almost complete. They had long, slightly curved rat-tail handles and oval bowls.

While Robert was so occupied, Salah had roasted two chickens over the fire. The pleasant smell filled the air and whetted his appetite. Salah had placed on the table a variety of vegetables and spreads and some pita bread that he had brought from the village. Riley at last came down and joined them. They had a jug of ice-cold water that one of the workers had carried from the spring further up the valley to the east. Later they placed a lamp on the table and sat around reading and smoking, but after a while this became quite difficult as a multitude of winged creatures were attracted to the lamplight and spiralled around it, a living mass of tiny flies and moths, gnats with their dangle of legs, and a single large rhinoceros beetle, shiny black as a new car. They put out the lamp and sat with their pipes long into the night.

Robert met Bel again the following weekend. The morning was pleasantly warm. He picked her up and they drove along the coast, parked the car, and walked to the edge of the beach. A boy and a dog ran across the sand before them. They found a place to sit and sat there for some time looking out over the water and talking about themselves.

"You do realise," Bel said, "we could never do this back in England."

"Do what?"

"Meet un-chaperoned, of course."

"Thank heavens we're not in England!"

Bel wore a pale blue dress and had her hair tied up. He could smell the scent of her cologne on the sharp sea air, and he stole glances at her when, in the intensity of the conversation she gazed across the blue expanse. When she caught him at it, she laughed and tossed her head, and he felt a little embarrassed and a great deal in love. He took hold of her hand, and she rested her head on his shoulder.

9   TROUBLE

Another weekend came around. Robert drove over to see Bel. Her father opened the door. Bel was dressing, he said, and he showed Robert in. The two men sat down in the sitting room and a rather formal conversation developed:

"So, you are the young man. Robert, is it?"

"Yes sir. I'm glad for the opportunity to meet you and your wife."

"Bel's mother isn't here," he answered. "She is back in England. I understand that you were in the gendarmerie?"

"Yes, sir."

"And you are an archaeologist?"

"No. Not really. Well, not a qualified one anyway. I'm working as assistant to an archaeologist, but I have had no training myself, although I am beginning to think now about the possibility of studying to become one."

"Really?" Something about the way he said this made Robert think that Bel's father doubted him. There was a vague hostility in his voice that had caught Robert off guard.

"It's just a thought," he said.

"You're considering staying out here?"

"Certainly, for the moment, yes."

Robert fidgeted with his tie. He had begun to feel a bit uncomfortable under the intense scrutiny of Bel's father.

"That is your choice. But I should think that there are better studying opportunities in England… that is, if you are serious about studying to be an archaeologist."

"Well, as I say, it's only a thought. Anyway, there are the British and American Schools in Jerusalem, and this country is certainly the place for field experience."

"Yes… I don't have any particular interest in archaeology. Do you think you can earn a living from it?"

"I don't know. I haven't really thought it through." Bel's father asked nothing more and appeared to show no further interest in Robert, even to the point of picking up a newspaper, which seemed to Robert to indicate more than just a lack of interest in him or in his prospects. An embarrassing silence ensued and continued until Bel walked into the room and joined them. Robert was greatly relieved by her arrival. He rose as she entered and then sat back down. Her father nodded to her and shortly afterwards put down his paper, stood up and left the room. After he had left, Robert took Bel's hand and spoke:

"I'm afraid I didn't make a very good impression on your father."

"Don't be silly. He's like that with everyone. I'm sure he liked you."

"I don't think he does. In fact, I think he has a fairly poor opinion of me… though I'm not quite certain why."

"You're mistaken. How could he help liking you?"

"Well, not everyone does. But it is nice of you to say so."

"What did he say to you?"

"Nothing very much. He just asked me about my plans."

"Then you're imagining it. I'll speak to him."

"No, no, please don't. Maybe you're right. Anyway, it doesn't matter."

"Yes, it does. I want him to like you."

"You can't make someone like someone just because you do."

10 ASSAULT

The following Sunday Riley went to Haifa to deal with some financial matters and pick up his post from New York. Robert decided to do a bit of hiking on his own. He took with him a small pack with some fruit and biscuits and a canteen of water. He had no particular direction in mind but liked the idea of exploring on his own. He left the camp, heading east through the valley south of the castle. The rough track had once been broader, cleared by the villages as a path for pack animals coming up from the coast, but the lower part had been little used, and the forest had regained its hold. He climbed up through the trees and cut across the ridge behind the castle, heading north and intentionally keeping off the track because the sun had grown quite warm. As a result, he had to pass through dense scrub, and the going was increasingly rough and sometimes almost impenetrable. The trees were oaks and bays, and wiry vines hung from the branches. The undergrowth was mainly of aromatic herbs: sage, rue and artemisia, and in the damper places among the rocks various types of ferns and moss. The slope became steeper, and he found it necessary to grasp hold of branches for support. Crossing the shoulder of the mountain where the ground dropped away, he was glad to be alone and felt the sort of exhilaration in the freedom he had not experienced since childhood. Eventually the ground levelled off and began to rise again, and after a while he came up onto the edge of a limestone formation at the highest point over the northern valley, where the land began again a gentle decline towards the cliffs above the stream. The limestone exposure was worn and shattered with endless fissures, many of them several yards deep and wide enough for a man to fall into. In the ages since this feature had formed, the rock had weathered enough to enable trees to take root in rust-coloured pockets of soil. When, in the early mornings the clouds rising from the Mediterranean rolled inland they drenched these fissures, and the vegetation here grew particularly luxuriant. There were not only oak and bay trees, but carobs and pistachios. And there were some striking arbutuses with their rust-red branches twisted as if by the wind that ran through them, the bark cracking and peeling into scrolls that exposed the green fresh growth beneath. Their leafy branches, recently terminating in masses of tiny ivory campanulate flowers, had now developed the strawberry-like fruits that the forest birds so favoured. It being the end of spring, the flowering plants—cyclamens, wild hyacinths, and perennial orchids—had passed their season, but the air was still full of the hum and buzz of insect life.

He descended in the direction of the cliff. The sun shone down, pleasantly warm. He reached the very edge of the cliff and made his way around an outcrop onto a narrow ledge, then sat down on a flat shelf of rock, his feet over the edge of the abyss, a vast emptiness dropping out below him. Between where he sat and the distant cliffs on the other side of the valley a sparrowhawk sailed, riding the warm air on broad wings. He could touch it in his mind, sense how it felt, the warm air holding it up, the breeze fingering the soft feathers on its breast and under its wings and tail. He imagined how its yellow eyes penetrated the distant grass and stone below, observing the tiniest movement.

Three uneventful days went by. On the fourth, a series of oc-
currences took place that shook the whole community; the workers and the expedition team. As they walked up from the camp at
daybreak, Riley and Robert heard from a distance a considerable
commotion. Reaching the castle, they found the men gathered in
the central part where work had concentrated over the past few
days. The men were standing around a deep trench excavated in
what had formerly been the castle's kitchen. At the bottom of the
trench was a small red and yellow object that Robert thought at
first to be a piece of clothing, but as he came close, he saw to his
horror that it was the battered body of the puppy. One of the men,
using a hoe, lifted the small bloody pup, took it over to the edge of
the castle and flung it far into the thick bushes on the slope. Nobody knew what had happened. It was seemingly a small matter,
but it upset the men and cast a cloud over the morning.

The second event occurred at about midday, shortly before
the workers were to take their lunch break. At the time, Robert
was standing on the platform of the hall overseeing a group of men
piling heavy mangonel balls in a stack against the wall. Six of these
huge stone missiles had been found in the rubble on the floor of
the hall. Robert was wondering where they had been hurled from.
The nearest position was the slope of the hill to the south, and as
he walked over to the edge of the platform and glanced down the
valley something caught his attention. Concentrating his gaze, he
realised that down to the west a small plume of white smoke was
rising, hardly noticeable. It was coming from their camp. His first
thought was that it was the campfire, but then he noticed a touch
of brilliant orange, and he could clearly see that one of the tents
was on fire. The flame rose on the side of the white canvass, and
the faint swirl of smoke rose above it. He could see a figure, apparently Salah, and at this distance his rapid movements appeared like
a dance.

Robert told the workers to take a break. He hurried through the opening in the wall into the central part of the castle, calling to Riley as he ran.

"What's the matter?" Riley asked as he came up to him.

"Quick! There's a fire in the camp."

Riley ordered one of the men to take over, and Robert rushed down the hill to the camp, Riley following more carefully in his wake. By the time they reached the camp they found the equipment tent was fully ablaze. Salah, however, was nowhere to be seen, and there appeared to be nobody about. They shouted his name. Robert ran to the water tank at the far end of the camp, but found that it had been sabotaged, the tap had been left fully open, and a silver ribbon of water was running out down the slope. He turned off the tap and went to look for a bucket. He found one and filled it with water, but by the time he returned he found Riley gazing almost bemusedly at the remains of the tent, now completely burnt away exposing a pile of smouldering objects within. Robert threw the water on the already dying fire.

"Help me get more water."

"There's not much point now," said Riley. "The tent has gone, and so has most of the equipment."

"This was no accident! The water tap was left open, and I can't find Salah? I saw him from the castle. He was here when it was burning. Where has he gone?"

A worried look returned to Riley's face. "Are you sure it was him? It might have been Walker?"

"Walker? You think he did this?"

"Well … what do you think?"

"I don't know. I suppose so. We had better put this out and see if we can find out what has happened to Salah."

"Where are the buckets?"

"I found only one. There were a couple of new ones in the tent!"

Riley pushed aside a piece of smouldering canvas and found the new buckets. They had been tied together, but were now pulled apart and had been punctured, apparently by a pick. There was no doubt that the fire had been intentional, and they both now presumed that it had been Walker who set it. They managed to put out the remains of the fire, and after looking through the other tents, which appeared to have been untouched, they sat down on a couple of crates. It was then that they heard shooting, a whole volley of pistol shots from across the valley to the north.

"Come on," said Robert. "It's from over there."

"Wait," said Riley.

He went into one of the tents and came out holding something wrapped in a piece of cloth. He walked over to Robert and unwrapped a Smith and Wesson revolver.

"Where did you get that?"

"Townsend handed it to me the other day just as he was leaving. He said it might be better if one of us has an extra gun. Robert. You must be better at this than me. Would you take it?"

"Yes. Of course," said Robert. Riley handed him the gun. "Listen. Perhaps you should stay here."

"I don't know. You can't go on your own. Walker is armed and dangerous – if it is him."

"Do you have any doubts that it's Walker?"

"No, not really." They were standing at the edge of the camp, and they saw Abdul and some of the other men coming down the hill towards them.

"I should hurry. He might have taken the boy."

The other men joined them, Abdul carrying a rifle.

"Good," said Robert, seeing the rifle. "Abdul. You come with me. You other men, stay here with Mr Riley until we get back. Does anyone else have a weapon?"

One of the men produced from under his jacket a short, curved dagger.

"That won't be much use. But I doubt if he will come back here. Come on Abdul. Let's go."

"Be careful," Riley shouted after them as the two went off. They headed down a narrow track, cut across the field through the low scrub in the direction from which the shots had come. After a short distance they reached a broader path that curved around the western side of the castle hill and joined another path along the southern bank of the stream. As they came down the hill, they could see a fair way along the path and down to the stream where a thicket of blackberry canes almost smothered the path below the plane trees that followed the stream. Where the path levelled out, they came through into the open again. Robert signalled to Abdul to stop.

"We have to be careful," he said in a hushed tone. "We are completely exposed here." They continued cautiously along the path approaching the mill and climbed up through the collapsed western side below the remains of a guard-tower. They trod carefully between the fallen stones and brush, trying to make as little noise as possible. Riley signalled again to Abdul to wait while he climbed the ancient stone staircase in the wall that had once given access to the collapsed upper level of the tower. No one was there. They descended to the path and approached the main door of the mill. Both, at once noticed fresh marks in the soil around the doorway. It was obvious that something or someone had been dragged here. Cautiously they entered the doorway. Standing on one side of the entrance Robert called into the dark.

"Walker. We know you're in there. You might as well come on out." There was no answer. As his eyes adjusted to the dark, Robert could see more marks on the floor. These were undoubtedly made by a man having been dragged through the entrance and across the chamber. Robert called again into the dark:

"Come on, Walker. There is no point to this. Come out and we can talk this through." Still there was no answer, nor any sound to suggest that he might indeed be there. Robert called again:

"Listen, Walker. We are armed. You will make this much easier on yourself if you come out now." No sound came from within. "Alright. We're coming in."

Followed closely by Abdul, Robert moved through the doorway and peered around the edge of the wall into both sides of the dark vault. Then, taking a chance he stepped directly into the chamber, exposing himself entirely to Walker, if he was there. Abdul was behind him. They could hardly see in the gloom, only the vague curve of the vault rising above. However, their eyes quickly grew accustomed to the darkness, and they began to make out, faintly at first and then more clearly, how the chamber extended some yards to the left of the doorway and considerably further to the right. There appeared to be no one here, but some way to the right there was a broken partition wall that partly obscured the far end of the vault. As this emerged in their vision Robert thought he could hear a sound coming from behind it. He called again into the dark "Walker, come on, for heaven's sake. We can work this out." They could both now hear a low muffled moaning sound rather like a whimpering coming from behind the wall. "Alright. We are coming in." There was a muffled moan now.

"Salah! Is that you?" and in answer the moaning became even more distinct. Dropping all caution, the two men moved towards the partition wall, their guns raised. Behind it they found Salah lying on the dirt floor. His hands were bound with rope and a gag had been tied tightly over his mouth. Robert removed the gag and Abdul untied his hands. "Are you alright?"

"Yes, sir. My head hurts," he said, raising his hands up to the back of his head, and then looking at them. Even in the dark he could make out the matted hair and blood.

"He has hurt you!"

"He hit me hard with the rifle, Mr. Palmer."

"Damn the fool!"

"It was Mr. Walker, sir."

"Yes, we know, Salah." They helped him to his feet. As he stood up, he rubbed his wrists and raised his arm again, rubbing the side of his head.

"I don't understand. Why did he hit me?"

"You're not to blame, Salah. It's nothing you did. Mr. Walker is a sick man. Here. Let's get you out into the light and take a look at that wound,"

Salah leaned on the two men, and they stumbled with him, out of the dark vault into the sunlight. They could see that he had a nasty gash above the hairline and a swelling on the back of his head. His hair was damp with blood, and he also had a bruised area above his right eye. He raised his shirt and they saw another large bruise over his right shoulder blade. Robert took out a handkerchief and tenderly pressed it to the wound on Salah's head.

"I think the bleeding has stopped," he said. "Tell us exactly what happened, Salah."

"He came up behind me. I did not see him come. He hit me before I could say anything. I asked him to stop but he cursed me, Mr. Palmer. What did I do? He made me go with him with his gun. He fired in the air. I was scared and he dragged me here. Then he left... just a few minutes ago. Please, Mr. Palmer... was it my fault? I did not mean to make him angry."

"It's not your fault Salah. Mr. Walker's behaviour has nothing to do with anything you might have done."

Salah sat down.

"You say he just left?"

"Not very long ago, Mr. Palmer. About five minutes."

"Can you walk?"

"I think so."

"Alright. Listen. You go back to the camp with Abdul." He turned to face Abdul. "Have him bandaged and take him back to Malia on one of the camels. Is there a doctor in the village?"

"Yes, Mr. Palmer."

"Good. Get him to the doctor. I will take a look around to see if I can find any signs of Walker. Tell the men to go home for the day."

"Mr. Palmer. You shouldn't go after him on your own," said Abdul. "He is dangerous."

"Don't worry. I'm only going to take a look around. We will get the police in."

Robert was uncertain which way to look. He was aware of the possibility that Walker might be hidden somewhere in the thick forest above the mill, but he may have headed off along the stream to the east, or west towards the coast. He would likely not have gone north as the hill rose very steeply and the path up to the flat area high above was almost treeless and exposed. If he attempted to escape in that direction, they would certainly have seen him. He looked around the mill building and the lower part of the hill, but he could discern no signs that might show which way Walker had taken. For no particular reason he took the path along the stream to the east. He held the gun ready, walking along the edge of the stream, his eyes sweeping the trees on either side. If Walker was watching from among the trees, he thought, he probably had decided against a confrontation. Robert walked for several miles upstream. The path was a pretty one, the stream flowing rapidly at places where it narrowed through exposed rock, more leisurely where it broadened out. When he reached the spring several miles upstream, he decided that it was pointless to continue. He turned back, retracing the path to the mill, and then skirting the castle hill back to the camp.

When he walked into the camp, Riley and three of the workers were sitting on crates around the remaining tents. Riley got up as he approached.

"Any sign of him?"

"No. I went all the way upstream but didn't see a thing. He must have headed in the direction of the coast. But we did find Salah."

"Yes. I saw. Abdul brought him here and they have just now left for Malia. It's a good thing you didn't run into Walker. He's dangerous. I've been worried the whole time that it might come to a shoot-out. The police need to deal with this."

"Yes, of course, you are right. He has to be apprehended. The fellow is clearly unstable. I don't think he will stop at this."

"There's no point going on with work until this is sorted out. Listen Robert. Can you take over here?"

"Of course."

"It will be best. I'll go back to el-Bassa and drive to Akko. If I leave now, I should be able to see Townsend today. I will be back by midday tomorrow."

"If you're going to el-Bassa you'll need to be on the lookout. Walker might have taken that path. You shouldn't go alone."

"I'll take one of the men with me."

"I could go with you. Or I could go to Akko instead of you."

"No. It's better this way. I need you here. Anyway, I'm not much use with a gun if he does come back."

"Yes, but if you should run into him …"

"I'll take Ra'ed with me. He can take Abdul's rifle."

After Riley and Ra'ed had left, Robert set about getting the camp back into shape. He and the men who remained took down what was left of the burnt tent, placing the still usable equipment on one side, and whatever was burnt beyond use, which was most of it, on another, together with the remnants of the tent. It took them the better part of an hour. There was neither sign nor sound of Walker, but they remained constantly alert to make certain they were not taken by surprise. When things were more-or-less in order Robert sent the men home, leaving only two of them to serve as guards until Abdul's return. He then went over the boxes of finds to make certain nothing was missing or damaged, although he did not expect that Walker would have had the time or the inclination to take anything.

Thinking about Walker's motivation for this strange and violent behaviour, he could only conclude that it was the outcome of some sickness of the mind. Walker must have been offended by Riley's criticism and aspersions that he had mismanaged the expedition's funds, but his actions were entirely out of proportion. And what would happen now, he wondered? They would have to hunt him down. Otherwise, the continuation of the expedition would be in jeopardy. The villagers would be up in arms over what had happened to Salah. Things could so easily get out of hand. He knew how in Palestine the most insignificant events could serve as pretexts for outbreaks of violence. The past few years had been relatively quiet ones in the relations between the Arabs and the British authorities. It would be disastrous if this expedition should provide the catalyst for a renewed outbreak of violence. If Riley could not assert his authority, some of the younger men might want to take things into their own hands.

There were, however, no more disruptions during the day or the night that followed. Nonetheless, Robert slept uneasily. He awoke in the middle of the night and lay in his camp bed thinking about the events of the last few days. Perhaps Walker would realise he had gone too far. He surely knew that the police must now be called in. Hopefully, he would leave the area altogether and they would hear no more of him.

The following morning the sun rose high over the castle, filling the valley with light until every tree and plant stood out in its particular form. The long grass above the stream path hung down like loose hair. Sunlight broke in shafts through the thick canopy of the forest. North, along the stream bed, Judas trees painted a path of pink.

The workers arrived on time. There was a great deal of talk about the abduction of Salah, which was seen as an attack on the community as a whole. Abdul told Robert that after much discussion they had agreed to return to work after Abdul had informed them that Riley would engage the help of the police and that Walker would certainly be arrested. Robert assured him that Riley had indeed gone to Akko. It appeared that Abdul's intervention had stemmed the dissension and that work could carry on as long as there were no subsequent attacks by Walker. In order to make certain that this was the case, Robert had two of the men, one of whom was armed, remain in the camp, and had Abdul take a revolver and locate himself on the keep, which was the best position to overlook the castle and the surrounding slopes. If Walker did try to approach again, there was a good chance that he would be seen in advance.

The morning passed uneventfully. It was a pleasant early summer day. A mild breeze played in the trees along the sides of the castle. The anxiety that Robert had felt in the morning dissipated as the day wore on. He even opened a new area of excavation, putting some men to work in the cistern beneath the keep. Riley had suggested this earlier, and indeed the cistern seemed to be Riley's chief interest since the beginning of work at the castle. There was something remarkable about it. The vaulting seen through the narrow opening shaft seemed unusual for a cistern, a structure that was not intended to be entered. Several days earlier they had cleared the shaft of fallen rocks, but for a variety of reasons Riley had put off work in it. Before he left for Akko, he suggested that if there were no further trouble, Robert should begin clearing it. Cisterns and sewers, Riley had pointed out, were often of particular interest in an excavation because of the tendency people had to unintentionally drop things into them; complete ceramic vessels were often recovered and, on occasion—when, for example, a building was abandoned during a siege—objects of value were often hidden in cisterns in the hope that the opportunity would arise for recovering them.

At first the work was fairly simple. Two men were employed within the cistern working with spades, scooping the soil into wicker baskets. By mid-morning, a fairly broad space below the shaft and the upper vaulting had been cleared. There was still only enough room for the two men working crouched within, as the cleared area gradually expanded to the sides. It was hard toil, and the cistern was soon filled with dust. By midday they had removed several feet of earth and rubble below the opening. So far nothing of importance had been found—a few bits of broken pottery, but little else.

Riley and Ra'ed returned in the early afternoon. Together with them on horseback were Peters and another officer. Riley told Robert that some troops had been sent directly on to Malia and after interviewing Salah would begin a systematic search of the area.

"Their presence should make a difference," he said. "Even if they don't find him, they're bound to scare him off. How is Salah?"

"Abdul says he's a bit shaken, but he suffered no serious injuries."

"I feel bad for the boy. I might go up and see him myself."

"I'll go with you."

"You're not too tired?"

"No. Not at all."

"Fine. In that case we should head up pretty soon so that we can be back before it gets dark."

It was decided, and after Riley had bathed, he joined Robert on the steep walk up to Malia. After passing below the castle the track entered the cool, shaded forest. Halfway up they had to pass the carcass of an enormous black boar lying across the middle of the path. The nauseous, sweet smell of death and decomposition was robust, although the beast appeared only very recently dead. They held their breath as they skirted it.

"I wonder what killed it," said Robert once they had got past and could breathe freely again.

After fifteen minutes they came out of the forest and the countryside opened up, still rising steeply to the east, with small fields of wild grass and olive groves bordered by wire fencing. To the north the hills rose as a barrier, beyond which was the Lebanon. They continued to climb the track, which was partly a former stream bed, became very rough here with the rocks that had washed down the slope with the recent winter torrents, but slowly it levelled off.

At the top of the rise, they took a few minutes to rest, sitting on a rock outcrop below a carob tree. Then they continued along the path, crossing a dry wadi bed and more olive groves before they finally arrived at the village. Climbing the road toward the village castle, they then turned off down a narrow alley and arrived at Salah's house. It was a stone building with a variety of wooden annexes, surrounded by a vegetable garden with several fruit trees and an ancient grape vine that trailed on its thick stem up onto a trellis on the roof, the twisted branches just coming into fruit. Under the vine on the flagstone-paved courtyard was an assortment of well-stuffed chairs and wooden benches and a dilapidated couch on which they found

Salah seated beside an old and wizened man. Salah rose when he saw the two men approach.

"Don't get up," said Riley.

"This is my father," Salah introduced them to the wizened old man who held out his hand.

"Salaam Aleikum," he said, half rising from his seat and smiling broadly. They shook hands and Riley turned to Salah:

"How are you feeling?"

"I am alright," he said. "I am sorry I did not come in to work today."

"We didn't expect you to come, Salah. You need to rest."

"I wanted to go… but my mother… she said no," and as he said this his mother, a diminutive, dark-haired woman, came out of the house and walked over, greeting them as she came. She signalled for them to sit, and they sat on chairs facing Salah.

"She does not speak English," said Salah.

"Tell you parents that we are sorry about what happened." The boy said some words. His father nodded his head, but his mother broke out in a long, high-pitched monologue in Arabic. When she finally finished, he answered her and then turned to Riley:

"My mother says something bad will happen again. She does not want me to go back. I said to her not to worry and the police have come."

"Yes. Have they spoken with you?"

"Captain Peters came this morning. I told him what happened, and he wrote it down. He said they will arrest Mr. Walker."

Salah's mother spoke again and went inside coming out shortly after with a tray on which were glasses of cool water, and sweet cakes.

"The water comes from the spring," said Salah. "It is very good," as indeed it was.

The walk back down to the camp was easier. They arrived just as the sun was setting. Abdul, who had remained with another armed man in the camp, greeted them and it was with a sense of relief that they heard of the quiet afternoon that had passed in the camp. Even with the anticipated arrival of the police troops, the possibility of Walker's return remained in their minds.

Next morning Riley, who was overseeing the men working in the keep, came looking for Robert. He found him drawing in one of the western chambers. Riley looked worried.

"Robert. You had better take the camel and ride up to Malia. Captain Peters was here just now. He's waiting for you at the church."

"Why? What's happened?"

"Your young lady has been there."

"Bel?" A cold fear ran through him. "Where? Why was she there? Has anything happened to her?"

"Don't worry. She is unharmed."

"Unharmed? By what?" he asked with increasing apprehension. "What has happened?"

"It seems she came up to see you this morning. Some friends had arranged to drop her off at Malia. They knew people in the village, and she planned to get one of the villagers to bring her down by donkey or camel to the castle. Apparently, she had the whole thing worked out. Of course, she had no idea what had happened here. She had hoped to surprise you. However, the villager who was to accompany her had asked her to wait on the road as he had to change the mule he had brought, that proved to be lame. While she was waiting, she ran into Walker."

"Walker! Did he hurt her?"

"Not physically. But he gave her a good scare."

"Oh, no!"

"She said that they got to talking, and at first he seemed quite friendly and she did not notice anything strange, but once she mentioned you, he began to behave strangely, and she became suspicious and realized that it must be Walker. I understand you had told her about him. Anyway, he made some derisive remarks about me and began to curse, and she took fright and tried to get away. She began to run along the road back to Malia and he started after her but just then the fellow with the mule returned."

"And she's not harmed?"

"No, no. Only frightened."

"Oh, God! I don't believe it. It is my fault. I must see her."

Accompanied by Ra'ed, Robert headed up the path to Malia. When he reached the church, Robert found Peters waiting with Father Nicephor.

"Hello captain. Where is Bel?" he asked.

"I sent Miss Knowles back to Haifa with my sergeant."

Later that day Robert arrived in Haifa together with Captain Peters. He entered the police station and Bel was there, seated beside her father who stood over her protectively. When he saw her father's face it became clear to Robert that her father regarded him as to blame for what had happened. Bel, however, seemed quite calm. She rose from her seat as soon as she saw him. Robert came over to her and took her tenderly by the shoulders.

"Bel. I'm so sorry about this. I never imagined that he would hurt you."

"I know." She held onto his arms. "I'm alright. Really." But her father intervened.

"Isabel. Sit down and wait here. I wish to speak to this gentleman in private." He took Robert out into the vestibule and began immediately to berate him:

"I want you to know that I hold you responsible for what has happened. You had no right to involve her in this business."

"But sir. I never…" Robert attempted to protest.

"Don't interrupt me, young man. You knew about this Walker fellow. The officer has told me he has already attacked another person, yet you allowed my daughter to come out there on her own. Anything could have happened to her. This is inexcusable."

Robert tried again to speak:

"I had no idea she was coming. I would never have had her come out."

"That is a lie! I know from her that you suggested she come."

"Sir. That was before this trouble. And I meant to escort her myself."

"So, are you saying that it was all her idea? Why," he spat out the words, you are not even a gentleman!"

Robert was affronted. "Please. That is not fair! I did not want her to put herself at risk. But Bel is not a child. You can hardly expect me to make decisions for her."

"What I expect is that you will keep away from her." Bel's father grew increasingly angry as he spoke. He had raised his voice and his words could be heard throughout the station and certainly by his daughter in the next room. "If you were still in the gendarmerie, I would inform your superiors. I don't want to see you around my daughter again. Do you understand?"

Robert was mortified, but held his ground. "With all respect, sir, I think that is for her to decide."

"I have no interest in what you think. I am warning you. Break off your relationship with my daughter now. Otherwise, there will be consequences, and I promise you, you will regret it if you defy me." Without waiting for an answer, he stormed out of the room.

Robert was at a loss. But he had no intention of leaving without speaking to Bel. Shaking with emotion after the clash with her father, he went back into the office, but Bel was already leaving with her father.

"Bel."

She turned, and but her father was almost forcefully leading her out of the door. "Robert. I'm sorry," and she gestured with her hands to express that there was nothing to do. "I can't speak now."

"Please… Bel…" he called after her, but she turned away and followed her father out of the station.

Townsend watched them depart, then turned to Robert. "I'm sorry about that, Mr. Palmer. It seems Mr. Knowles is a very protective father. I think you should let things cool off a bit."

"Cool off a bit? He blames me! It is not fair."

"Give him time. I'm sure the young lady does not hold you responsible for what happened."

"What exactly did happen? I've only heard what Captain Peters told me. Walker attacked her?"

"I'll tell you what she told me," he said, and more-or-less repeated what Robert had already been heard from Captain Peters.

Robert spent that night in Haifa. The following day he went to Bel's house. Bel opened the door. She appeared very pale. She smiled, but immediately the smile faded as if it was a sort of spontaneous gesture without any meaning. She fidgeted with her skirt.

"Bel. Are you alright?" he asked. She didn't answer but looked down at the folds of her skirt.

"What is wrong?"

"Nothing. I'm sorry. There's nothing wrong. But you shouldn't have come."

"Please Bel… what has happened? Are you angry with me?"

"No, no… of course not…" she hesitated. "It doesn't matter," but she knew from his eyes that she could not leave him without an answer. "It's me," she broke into tears. "I was so stupid. I should never have come out. I thought it would be amusing. It was so foolish."

"It doesn't matter. As long as you are not hurt." He put his arm around her, but she gently though firmly pushed it away.

"I can't Robert. I'm sorry. My father… I'm so sorry." She stepped back into the doorway, looked up at him and bit her lip. "He won't have me seeing you."

"I know he blames me."

"He's wrong, Robert, but…"

"But what?"

"He is my father…"

"What are you saying?"

"I don't know."

"You don't want to see me anymore?"

"Yes I do … I don't know. I don't know what I want."

"But I love you Bel." The words were out before he had thought about them." He looked directly into her eyes, but she turned away. "Do you not love me?" he asked.

She hesitated.

"I see." He was crestfallen.

"Please, Robert." But he was already turning away. Then he turned back to face her. "It's alright Bel. I am sorry to have been so blind." He walked away.

"Wait, Robert…" she called after him, but he was shattered. He walked down the path and did not turn back.

Two days later, shortly after work had begun Captain Peters arrived, coming down by horse from the direction of Malia. He walked up to Riley and Robert who were on the keep platform.

"Gentlemen. You will be relieved to hear that we've got him."

"Walker?" asked Riley.

"Yes. He was taken by my men on the Kabri road. And he has admitted to the whole business."

"Well! That is a relief. What did he have to say?"

"He seems quite unhinged if you ask me. One minute he was placing the entire blame on you, Mr. Riley. The next, he was asking that we try to get you to consider taking him back."

"I don't believe it! Out of the question."

"Of course. He's not going anywhere. We have him in the lock-up at Haifa and he'll be put on trial for assault and abduction… and for the theft. I will need you to formally press charges."

"Of course. I can come down tomorrow afternoon."

"That will be excellent."

"Thank you for letting me know, captain."

"Yes. Well, I'll be off. I have other business to attend to this morning and a long ride back." He went back to his horse tied on the path beyond the moat.

11 WALKER'S ACCOUNT

Walker's account from the torn-out pages, written in the police station

It is a good thing they left me the pages I had torn out from the diary and stuffed in my pocket, and I was lucky enough to be able to steal a pencil from the sergeant's desk. The fool didn't even notice! Well, I shall keep a record of this. I need to remember everything that is done to me so that I can prove that I have been mistreated, first by that American and now by the police.

It is dark. There is just enough light to write. They have put me in a miserable cell. The walls are filthy and there is only a hard bed to sit on covered with a flea-bitten, straw mattress. It is stained and stinks of mould. I can't sleep, but at least I have time to think.

How could I have let myself be caught?

I have to get out of here. They have no right to lock me up. They're all fools…

The officer said they would contact my father. They have no right! Why can't they leave him out of this? He certainly won't understand. He never has understood me.

It is all Riley's fault, anyway. You would think that they would see that. I was driven to this by that damned American. Can't they see that I am being victimised? I should know better than to expect any understanding from the police. Of course, they would support him against me.

It's so unfair! It has always been this way, ever since I was a child. I was always being blamed.

God, this place is awful. I'm trying to ignore the smell but it's no good. It stinks of piss. Damn them!

I should kill myself... Then maybe they would see how unfair they have been. They will regret having treated me like this... locking me up.

I was so near getting away. I should have been more careful. I thought they wouldn't look for me in the mill. I hid my pistol under a fallen tree, but didn't have a chance to recover it when I saw the troops approaching. Still, I had the rifle. I got away just in time. God – that was close! I climbed the hill on the northern side of the stream, skirting the path along the valley and crossing back over downstream, well beyond the camp. Then I climbed up towards the Kabri road. I was going to cross the fields to the coast without being seen. And I was careful at first, but by the time I reached the road I had become overconfident. I should have been more careful! I didn't think that I would run into anyone, and I began walking quite boldly down the road. Why did I do that? I suppose I never thought those fools would look for me. But they did. I got to a point where the road crossed a dirt track and suddenly, out of the bushes on the side—four armed men. There was no point running, with no cover and an unloaded rifle. I was taken to a motorcar they had parked down the road and driven to the police station in Akko. Hours in waiting in this bloody cell... the whole morning. They didn't even give me anything to eat or drink!

I was a fool! Maybe I wanted to get caught?

I don't understand any more what is happening to me. It seems as if everything is pressing in. Everyone is out to get me!

I haven't been unable to sleep for a while now. At camp I was often awake all through the night. It's not just that. When I was able to drift off to sleep, I would suddenly awaken in a panic, terribly shaken, perhaps from a nightmare, though I could not recall having dreamt anything. I would be trembling and in a cold sweat. Lying alone in the dark - Riley and Palmer were in a separate tent - I found myself overwhelmed by anxiety. Afraid of the dark... like when I was a child. Afraid of the empty hills all around. It was as if they were closing in on me... and afraid the Arabs, afraid they might try to harm me. And that American... that he was plotting against me! Perhaps he was.

Things have got out of control. I get so scared. I can't understand it. It's never been as bad as this before... not like this. The strange thing is, generally by morning I feel relief, as if it was all nothing and that I am in control. I sometimes even feel a sense of elation! But, invariably, in the afternoon the depression returns. And the nights... the nights are the worst.

12 EXTRACT

Extract from the police report of Captain Peters, 9 June 1926

*I saw the prisoner at six o'clock. Sergeant Guy unlocked the
cell and told the prisoner to follow him. We walked into an
adjacent office, and I told him to sit down. A guard remained
standing by the door. I asked him if his name was Lawrence
Walker. He answered with impertinence - You know that! I
asked if he knew why he had been arrested and he answered
that he did not. He denied having stolen equipment from the
camp at Montfort, including the rifle that we had found on
him, claiming that he was given it by Mr. Riley. When I chal-
lenged him that this was not what Mr. Riley had told me, and
that Mr. Riley had said he had also taken a camel and other items from the camp, he protested, saying that these were
lies. I then asked him about the burning of the tent and the
abduction of the camp-boy, warning him of the seriousness of
these charges. At this point he began to break down. He stat-
ed that Mr. Riley and Mr. Palmer were ganging up on him
and trying to silence him because he had threatened to expose
Mr. Riley to the head of the Antiquities Department as having mishandled the excavations. He claimed that these were
trumped-up charges. When I said that the camp-boy support-*

ed the charge of abduction and has the bruises to show for it, he made a remark about the boy being an Arab and therefore an unreliable witness. I answered that I believed the boy, and that I thought he was not aware of how serious the charges were. I also mentioned that it was suspected that he had killed the villagers' dog. He vehemently denied this as well. I said to him that the dog was not important, but the forceful abduction certainly was. At this point he gave himself away. He said that it wasn't forceful. I took advantage of this slip and asked him if he was admitting that he had taken the boy to the mill. He did not deny this now, but said that I misunderstood his motives, that he was trying to get Riley to take him back and that he thought he could approach him through the boy. I asked if he thought he would achieve that by dragging the boy at gunpoint and beating him, and when I asked why he had burnt the tent he said that he had not meant to do that. By this stage he was in tears. He no longer denied anything. I had the sergeant bring him a glass of water. When he calmed down, I repeated to him that he was in serious trouble. Regarding Miss Knowles, he claimed that he had done nothing to her and had not intended her any harm; and from her statement it seems that this was probably true. She was not physically attacked by him. He admitted that things had got out of hand and said that he was sorry. He asked to speak to Mr. Riley and seemed to think that Mr. Riley would drop the charges and take him back. But when I told him that that was hardly likely, he quite suddenly changed his attitude again and dropped all appearance of remorse.

13 WALKER'S DIARY

Walker's Diary from the torn-out pages, written some time after the events described

I couldn't eat the food that had been given me, nor could I sleep. In the middle of the night my mouth was dry, and my eyes were on fire. A centipede crossed the floor and I got up and crushed it under my shoe. At first, I had only felt anger, but as the night wore on, I sank deeper into despair. At some point I began to think about taking my own life. It was only an idea I was toying with at first, but after a while in that miserable cell, I found myself thinking more practically about it, about how I would go about it. I reckoned I could tie the sheet to the window bars, which were high enough to serve my purpose. This window looked out over the courtyard of the police station. There was a full moon. God, that moon! It was huge and seemed to be mocking me in my miserable state.

I settled on this. They would come by in the morning and find me – dead! Then they would see the mistake they had made. That was my plan… I suppose it had become a plan by then. The only trouble was that the guard came down the passage outside my cell every so often and was likely to see me before it was done. But in my mind, I guess, I was not entirely *decided on carrying it out, and the idea of discovery before it was too late held its own appeal. I would be found, and they would finally understand the injustice. Why should I try to kill myself unless I had been in the right, unless I had been unfairly treated? They would have to understand…*

What a fool I was to think that!

There was enough light in my cell from the lamp in the passage and from the moonlight coming through the window. No one was about. I pulled the sheet off the mattress and twisted it around several times, then pulled its ends to test its strength. It seemed satisfactory and I stepped over to the window. But it was too high to pass the sheet through. I tried several times, to no avail. I thought of dragging the bed over to the window but found that its legs had been set into the concrete floor. Maybe someone had tried this before? I looked around for something else to climb on but there was nothing. Nor was there anything else to tie the sheet onto except for the bars of the cell's door facing the corridor: the top bar was level with the ceiling and there was not enough space to pass the sheet through, while the parallel bar ran across at waist height. I couldn't very well hang myself from a waist-high bar, unless, as it suddenly occurred to me, I did it in a half-seated position. Perhaps that would work… why not? I looked across the corridor. The guard had not returned, so I took the sheet, twisted it several times to form a cord and tied it in a slipknot around my throat. I was in a kind of trance. I pushed the sheet through the bar, tying it tightly and close enough to leave only a short length that would not be enough to allow my head to slip down to the floor. I would release my full weight and would stretch my legs out in front of me so that I would hang from the bar. It could work. And what else could I do? As I recall, I took a deep breath then. I thought that I was ready but at the same time I half-feared that in another minute I would change my mind. What had begun as a sort of a game had somehow evolved into something that was actually taking place. I had no control over it and was merely a participant. I thought that perhaps it would not hurt if I slowly eased myself down into a hanging position, so I bent my knees crouching down. The sheet was already taut, pulling at my neck and I felt the pressure increase. Then in a second of resolve that immediately, but too late, dissipated, I threw out my legs, all my bodyweight pulling the sheet tight. Immediately I panicked. I tried to pull myself up, but my feet slipped on the smooth concrete floor, and I slid forward which made the short length of the sheet pull tighter, turning me over on my side. I kicked out, trying desperately to regain balance, grasping at the sheet with one hand, the other thrashing out to get a hold of the bar... but I had slid too far forward. Terrified now, I tried to get my fingers between my neck and the sheet, at the same time struggling for breath to cry out, but this only increased the pressure on my throat caused by the weight of my body pulling down. Again, I tried to shout, but could hear my voice as a thin croak, and the lack of air made me start to lose consciousness. There was a pounding in my ears. I was sinking, drowning, and at some point, I suppose, I stopped fighting. Then there was darkness. The next thing I recall is that I was on the floor and two men were leaning over me and saying something. I tried to sit up, feeling the soreness round my neck and the pressure in my lungs.

14 DISAPPOINTMENT

Albert seemed crushed after the interview with the grand commander and the castellan. All the colour had drained from his face and he appeared ill and tired. I tried to encourage him.

"Do not despair. We can keep looking."

"No, Hermann. It was foolish of me to have involved you in this."

"Not at all," I said. "I am grateful to you for allowing me to help."

"You should not be. It is a fool's errand. I have come here for nothing, and I have endangered you." He looked into my eyes. "You are a good boy, Hermann, and I am very grateful for your kindness and your fidelity. But I was wrong. I should have listened to my wife. My son is lost." He was completely despaired. "He is certainly dead. I will never see him again."

I attempted to distract him from these thoughts, remarking on the strange manner of the grand commander and his apparent subordination to the castellan, and suggesting that the latter had some other agenda, so that his words should not be taken too seriously. I pointed out that, after all, he had said nothing definite, and what he did say carried no real weight. But I could see that Albert was not persuaded by my arguments. He had given up hope.

Afterwards I spoke to Brother Walther, and I brought up our conversation with the castellan. He immediately became reticent, as if I had entered some forbidden ground. But I was intent on pursuing the matter.

"Why does the castellan say we cannot leave?"

"Clearly the danger is much greater than I had believed it to be. We will no doubt learn of the situation at chapter."

"And why is Grand Commander Eckhart so deferential towards the castellan. I appreciate that Castellan Jordon is an important man, but this is most unusual behaviour."

"You should not involve yourself in these matters, Squire Hermann."

In spite of Walther's censure, I was bold enough to continue:

"Squire Thomas showed me the castellan's private garden. What is the important work he is doing here?"

"Thomas had no right to speak to you of the castellan!"

"He said nothing, Brother Walther." I regretted having said what I had, and kept to myself the other things of which Thomas had spoken, but pressed him on this: "I had asked him what was behind the wicker fence."

"There are things best not interfered with. I will say only this, and then we shall put an end to this discussion. The castellan is doing very important work for the Order. He is a man of vast erudition and is knowledgeable of the relevant Greek and Arabic texts, and I believe that he is attempting to create something that will improve our chances of overcoming the enemy, something that will save our castle... perhaps even save what remains of the kingdom."

"A device? A weapon?" In Acre I had heard mention of new ballistic weapons that the Saracens had developed, and my curiosity was greatly aroused.

"No. A substance, if I am not mistaken, perhaps something like the Greek Fire... only of far greater vigour." Then he caught himself, "That is enough. *In multiloquio non effugies peccatum.* I should not have told you this much. These are not matters for the likes of us to discuss."

15 DISCOVERY

Robert immersed himself in the fieldwork, and the remarkable developments that now began enabled him to put aside his distress over his separation from Bel. About a week after they had begun digging in the large cistern, the men had cleared what turned out to be a broad chamber partly cut into the rock but, at shoulder height constructed with finely tooled ashlars forming a ribbed ceiling. It was so well built that, although neither Robert nor Riley was knowledgeable of the construction of medieval cisterns, it seemed to both of them to be rather too well-made to have been intended solely for that purpose alone, even though the walls were covered with the same layer of pinkish hydraulic plaster that covered the other cisterns in the castle. Work was extremely slow. Riley had unwittingly assigned the three laziest workers to clear the chamber. When Ra'ed or Riley were not around these men would do nothing at all and, as a lot was going on at this time in other parts of the castle, they had plenty of opportunity to take advantage of these absences. However, such deception could not go unnoticed for long. On the third day Riley realized what was going on and spoke to Ra'ed. After a rowdy discussion between the foreman and these men, they were split up, and new workers were brought in, six now, in order to make up for lost time. A ladder had been lowered into the shaft and baskets of soil and rubble were lifted up by rope and pulley. The complete exposure of the vaulting of this fine construction of the cistern had initially awakened Riley's interest in it, and now he spent most of his time overseeing the work there. The floor still was buried but the middle of the chamber was cleared to some depth, and Riley ordered the men who were doing the heavier work to leave the central area and to work out to the sides in order to level off. As they did so there was a sudden noise from one side of the chamber as a large quantity of soil that had remained attached to part of the northern wall loosened and fell away, exposing a previously unobservable section of the wall. One of the workers called excitedly to Riley, who was on the other side of the chamber. Coming over with a lamp he saw that at the level of the springing of the vault, between two ribs that rose from simple stone corbels, there was what appeared to be a sealed opening. It was not very large and was hardly noticeable at first, but some of the plaster that had covered it had come away with the soil. This had revealed an arched frame sealed with cut stones, but of dry construction with no mortar. The plaster, apparently a hurried attempt to hide it, had been roughly applied. In the light of their lamp, they could see how the colour did not entirely blend in with the surviving plastered sections of the vaulting around it. It appeared to have been done in haste, sometime after the walls had originally been plastered.

Riley put one of the men in charge, giving strict orders not to touch the opening, but to keep clearing and levelling the chamber. He went to look for Robert. He found him in the western hall.

"Robert. I've something to show you," he said breathlessly.

"What is it?"

"Possibly what we have been waiting for. It looks like," he paused for dramatic effect, "an entrance to a secret chamber."

"No! You're joking."

"Not at all. Come and see for yourself."

They hurried back to the cistern and climbed down the ladder into the cool darkness. As soon as his eyes adjusted to the dark Robert could make out the blocked arch.

"Oh... yes! I see it," he said excitedly. "This is wonderful!"

16 WALKER'S ACCOUNT

Walker's account on the torn-out diary pages, probably written in hiding

I was moved to the Italian hospital and placed in a private room with a guard at the door to make sure that I did not escape or try to hurt myself again. I lay on the bed staring at the ceiling. I got to know every crack, every stain on it! I refused to speak to the nurses or to the guard who came into the room on occasion. There was no way that I was going to play their game. In the afternoon, the captain who questioned me yesterday came by, but I refused to speak with him as well. Later Townsend arrived. At first, I didn't speak to him either, but he was persistent. He pulled up a chair by the bed and told me that my father was going to come the next day. This was the last thing I wanted to hear. I told him I did not want to see him. He tried to make excuses for him. "He is your father. He cares for you." But what does he know? My father doesn't care about me. I told him that. I told him the only reason he wanted to come was to try to smooth things over. He was worried that I might damage his reputation. Townsend said that this was not true. He said my father is a good man. What a joke! He began to lose patience with me. He said he couldn't *understand why my father bothers about me. I didn't need to hear that. I told him that he has never had any time for me. Never! I have no doubt that he would have been quite happy if the police hadn't interfered, if they had let me die. I told Townsend that and he said it was not true. But it is true! I know it. He said my father was horrified when he heard about what I had done. But I knew what to say to that. I asked him why he wasn't here now. He couldn't answer that. "I'll tell you why," I said. "He is too busy with his own affairs." He said that wasn't fair. Not fair! His son nearly dies, and he will <u>try</u> to come down tomorrow!*

But I was wasting my time. Townsend is my father's friend. He doesn't understand me, and he doesn't understand our relationship. He knows nothing of what I went through as a child.

He went on blaming me. He said I was selfish. Then he really annoyed me. He said it was a good thing mother hadn't lived to see this. I told him to shut up about my mother and turned my back to him. That kept him quiet for a while. When he spoke again, he asked what I was playing at and why I was so determined to ruin my life. He said I could make something of myself. I have to admit that I was almost taken in. For a moment I thought that perhaps he really cared. I tried to explain how everything had been going well enough and how things just somehow got out of hand and that it was as much Riley's fault as mine (God knows why I said that. It was entirely his fault!) but naturally he took the American's side, saying that I couldn't go on placing the blame on other people, and that I had to start taking responsibility for myself. That is so typical! I was trying to tell him what happened, and immediately he blames me. He said that Riley had told him I had been drinking. I denied it but he did not believe me. I had been drinking, but so what! I asked him what was going to happen to me.

Then he came out with some nonsense that my father and he would do their best for me, but that if Riley or the camp-boy should decide to press charges, there was not all that much they could do. He suggested I write Riley a letter of apology. Some chance!

My father came in the afternoon. I was lying on my back staring at the ceiling. He walked over and stood by my bed. I knew he was there but didn't turn to face him.

He spoke very quietly. He said my name, but I didn't answer so he raised his voice, asking what I had done. I turned then and told him that I was sorry if I had caused him any trouble. That got him. He said that he didn't care about the trouble, but about what I had done to myself. He told me to look at him. I asked him why he cared, and he said, "I am your father. Of course I care." I wanted to believe him. I really did. He pulled up a chair by my bed. He said that he wanted to understand. I don't know why, but I took him at his word and opened up to him. But it was no different from the way it always has been. He heard, but he wasn't really listening. I told him what had happened but all he had to say when I was finished was that I could not do things like this, that Riley was in charge and it was up to him how to decide to run things. He even said that Riley was a very competent man. That's a laugh! I knew it. I knew he wouldn't understand. It's always like this. He always understands the other side. Anyway, he was silent for some minutes and then said that what he really didn't understand was what I had tried to do to myself. He asked how I could do it, how I could try to hurt him like that. He asked if I thought that my death would have meant nothing to him. I didn't think it would mean much, I told him. That really hurt him, I could see, and I half regretted having said it. By now he was standing with his hat in his hand. He began saying, "If your mother were alive…". Before he could

*finish, I said that if she were alive, she would have understood
me. I saw how sad he looked then, and was sorry that I had
said it. He turned to the door. As he walked away, he turned
again and said that he would speak to the police officer in
charge and see what he could do. Then he was gone.*

*At three o'clock, after the nurse brought me a cup of tea,
I suddenly became aware that the guard that had been sta-
tioned at the door of the room had left his seat. He might have
been standing just outside the door, but it occurred to me that
there might now be an opportunity to get away. The nurse
had left the room and the other beds were empty. I suppose
the other patients had been moved elsewhere because of me.
I was careful to make no noise. I eased myself out of the bed,
glad to find that my suicide attempt had left no effects other
than a little stiffness about my neck and a slightly sore throat.
I walked over to the open door and looked out. The guard was
leaning against a wall down the corridor, smoking a cigarette
and talking to one of the nurses. This was too good. It seemed
almost as if my escape had been prepared for me. I actually
thought for a moment that this was some type of trap, but I
made a decision. My clothes were on a chair by the bed, and
I quickly dressed and then approached the door again. The
guard had not moved. He was alone now but was facing away.
I eased out of the door and hurried down the long corridor in
the opposite direction. I recall feeling a rush of excitement, like
a child absconding from school. I passed several nurses and
patients, but nobody paid any attention to me. At the end of
the corridor was a large double glass door. I walked right out
and down a path through the small garden, trying to appear
as calm as possible, even nodding a greeting to a fellow standing at the gate. I walked out of the gate and onto the empty
street. Then I broke into a run.*

17 SUSPICIONS

I could find out nothing more about Castellan Jordon, and other matters took over my attention. Since our audience with Grand Commander Eckhart and the castellan, the condition of Albert had deteriorated. At first, I thought that this was only the despondency resulting from his realisation that nothing was likely come from his efforts to find his son at Montfort. He hardly spoke and seemed to be sinking into lethargy, asking to be left to his bed through the entire day. He had no appetite and declined to attend meals, only accepting some wine and biscuits that I brought him from the collation after Vespers. But then this decline began to manifest itself in bodily symptoms. He found it difficult to walk or even stand and would lose consciousness on occasion. He was increasingly unable to fall asleep at night. I asked the infirmarer to examine him. He came to the dormitory, and I helped him lift the old man into a seated position. He gave him a beverage made from a mixture of artemisia and wine, the juice of various fruits, flower petals and spices. The infirmarer warned him that the taste was bitter and not at all pleasant, but Albert did not complain.

"It will help you sleep," the infirmarer said.

"Thank you. You are very kind, Brother Simon." He said feebly.

We could not have left the castle now, even if conditions had been safer, and it had become apparent that the words of the castellan indeed carried weight. We were constantly hearing from those arriving at the castle reports of attacks on travellers by the advance troops of Saracens, and it was now told among the brothers that one large force of the Sultan's army was already on its way along the coast, approaching the Ladder of Tyre. Some were saying that they had turned inland to Safed and that the immediate danger had subsided, but Safed was already in the Sultan's hands, and it was told that he now kept his siege machines there.

Over the following days I saw the castellan on two occasions. The first time, he was approaching the great tower accompanied by the grand commander and a brother that I had not seen before. They were in a great hurry; the castellan in the lead and the grand commander trying to keep up with him, appearing to be in a state of considerable agitation. I heard only a few words as they hurried past. It was the castellan who spoke:

"I have no time to deal with this," he said. "Please look after these matters yourself."

The grand commander stopped in his path, appearing greatly distressed and raising his hands in a gesture of exasperation. Meanwhile the castellan hurried on, the attendant brother hard on his trail. This brother held a small sack, but I could not see what it contained.

The second time I saw the castellan, I was engaged in conversation with a knight I had befriended, Brother Johan, a man of about my own age. We were coming out of chapel after high mass and saw the castellan leaving the castle by the north portal where a path led out onto the slope and down to the stream. He looked around furtively as he left, and I could not help wondering at this. I expressed my observations to my friend:

"There is something very strange and secretive about the castellan."

"Do you think so, Squire Hermann?"

"Yes. Do you not?"

"Come here." He took me aside to a place by the wall of the chapel where a small tree partly hid us from unwanted observation. "What do you know of Castellan Jordon?"

"Practically nothing. Only that he is said to be a man of great abilities, but is very proud of spirit and behaves with considerable superiority… and also that he seems to have some hold over the grand commander." Then I caught myself. "Perhaps I have been too outspoken."

"Yes, Brother," he said, "You should be careful… but you are not mistaken."

I looked at him closely and waited to hear more.

"Castellan Jordon is constantly disappearing from the castle. And when he is here, he spends most of his time in the great tower. But not in the tower chapel as you might think, and not in the hall above. I know this because I followed him once." Johan stopped speaking for a moment and bent his head to look out under the branches of the tree. Then he turned back to me and whispered conspiratorially. "He usually has a brother with him who stands at the entrance to the stairs and stops anyone from entering while he is there. One time the brother was away, and I followed him into the great tower. There was no one in the chapel and he had not seen me at the doorway. I saw him lift a wooden hatch in the floor and climb down into the cistern. He must have lowered a ladder down beforehand. Thankfully, he had not notice me observing him. I fear to think what may have happened had he seen me, and of course I dared not follow him down. He had closed the hatch from within."

"Indeed! He went down into the cistern?"

"Yes, Squire Hermann. I waited outside, opposite the entrance to the chapel pretending to be occupied with something. I was there for some time, but he did not emerge."

"Do you have any idea what he might be doing down there? And is there no water in the cistern?"

"I have no idea on either of those questions."

"But that is extraordinary! And if there is no water in the cistern, if the castle is attacked, the tower would be of no use as a refuge! Do you think the grand commander is aware of this?"

"I do not know. But I will certainly not be the one to tell him. I fear too greatly the castellan's wrath. There are some brothers who are paying dearly for having questioned him. And perhaps there is some logical explanation that we are not aware of."

As the weeks passed, I could sense the tension building up among the brothers of the garrison. There had already been a degree of unrest when we arrived, but now there was a growing anxiety, and even anger that resulted from the feeling that we knew nothing, that nothing was being told to us. We had no real knowledge of the imminence of the dangers facing us, or of the true location of the Saracen army. Nothing had been told to us since we had attended the chapter that I have already described. Had the great Crac of the Hospitallers been taken, or had the Saracens fallen back before that huge fortress? Was there any truth in the rumour that they were already in the Galilee? And was there still hope of aid from overseas? No one was now permitted to leave the castle, except, as I had seen, the castellan. There did not seem to be any contact between the castle and the other German properties. For all we knew, Acre itself might have fallen. We might be the last outpost still in Christian hands.

I did not believe this was the case, but for Albert it had become irrelevant. Since the audience with the grand commander and the castellan, his condition had steadily declined. I had seen despondency overtake him, and I saw how the remarkable energy that I had witnessed in Acre had been replaced, at first by apathy, now by bodily infirmity. I was watching an old and broken man dying and

I knew of no way to help him. Albert was now at the infirmary, and I visited him several times every day, but there were other things occupying me.

Once it became apparent that I was to remain in the castle, I began to take my place in the regular activities of the garrison. I was given various duties which occupied most of my time between services. Among my other tasks was the requirement to perform guard duties. These mainly involved patrol on the lower wall-walk or in one of the towers. It was on one of these occasions that, entirely by chance, I overheard a surreptitious argument that took place between the grand commander and the castellan, that threw light onto the true nature of the castellan's activities and put a new perspective on what he had said at the first chapter that I had attended. I was on duty in the inner gate tower with another knight, and, as was our practice, I had left him alone for a while at the base of the tower while I took position on the roof. It was a quiet afternoon, the hour before vespers. The tower was small and there was room for no more than two or three men on the roof. I stood some time on the battlements overlooking the northern valley, and at one point, tired of standing in the heat, and seeing no apparent movement in the valley, I squeezed out into a narrow side chamber, a type of stone hoarding, to rest for a few moments. It was a tiny space, not visible from the tower roof. Hardly had I squatted down to rest when I heard hushed talk and realised that someone had come out onto the tower roof just where I had been standing moments before. I dared not show myself, fearing that I would be criticised for not being on guard on the roof itself. I waited where I was, greatly apprehensive of being discovered, apprehension that increased as I realized that the voices I was overhearing were those of the grand commander and the castellan.

It was in this manner that I was witness to the following conversation between them, which began in low tones but grew in intensity. From his sonorous voice I recognised the grand commander who spoke first:

"We can talk safely here," he said. "The guard will not hear us at this height." He paused for a minute, and then continued. "I need to know, Jordon, how you are advancing with your experiments? Time is of the essence. You have told me nothing."

The voice of the castellan came in a distinctly irritated tone.

"You cannot expect me to constantly inform you of my progress. This is a slow and difficult labour."

"We do not have time." The grand commander's voice displayed an urgency that made me aware of how important this discussion was. "I need to know where we stand. I have received very, very bad news this morning from the supply caravan from Acre. Crac has fallen."

"Indeed?"

"Yes. It may be that the main Saracen army is already on its way south. Now, Jordon, I must know… now. Have you a formula?"

"I am working on it. A few weeks more…"

"We don't have weeks."

The castellan raised his voice. "What do you think I'm doing? Playing dice? I can't make this happen according to your whims."

"Keep your voice down, Brother Jordon. This is no whim. It is our only hope of survival. I have given you all the support I can and now I am wondering if I have not misplaced my faith in you. Was Brother Matthew right? Should we abandon the castle? Be truthful with me!"

"Abandon the castle? Are you a fool?"

"I will thank you, Castellan, even here, to remember your place!"

"We cannot abandon the castle. I will do what I can to speed up the process. That is all I can promise you. It means that I will have to work in the open. It will cause a great deal of noise and create disruption."

"So be it then. We have no choice. When the Saracens arrive, there will be a much greater disruption than anything that you might cause. Work in the open if you need." He paused for a minute. "And I want to inspect the laboratory."

"What! On no account!"

"What do you mean? I will remind you once again castellan. I am commander here. Not you. I want to see for myself what you have done."

"Do you not trust me, Grand Commander?" Jordon sounded shocked and even more angered.

"Of course I trust you."

"Any intrusion into my work will only delay it. Do you wish to be responsible for that?"

"I don't see how my examining the laboratory…"

"It cannot happen. The work is too delicate. I can suffer no intrusion, not even from you." Jordon had raised his voice and the grand commander, fearing again that they might be overheard, acquiesced, and continued in a lowered voice.

"Alright, Jordon, alright. But I must have your word that you will…"

At this point, although the conversation continued, I could no longer hear it clearly and I realised that they must be on their way down the staircase in the outer wall. I was relieved at not having been discovered but was very concerned by what I had overheard.

The following day the effects of this covert conversation became known to all. At chapter, the castellan was absent. The grand commander rose and spoke to us. Without mentioning the fall of Crac he warned us that the situation had deteriorated and that our fate was in the hands of God. He said that the castellan was working at a great pace now to alleviate our position and that in this regard he had decided that the area of the herb garden and the castellan's garden were out of bounds to all. No one would be permitted to approach these areas without the castellan's authorization. An alternative route to the outer ward through the inner gate tower and the sally-port on the south was to be used by those who needed to reach the outworks on the south and west. He warned us that a great deal of noise would likely be produced by the castellan's work and that we should not be concerned by it, nor should we be inquisitive as to its cause. It seemed to me that this was rather like telling a cat to pay no notice to a mouse.

No exceptional noise was heard that day, nor in the days immediately following, though a great deal of activity could be observed by anyone passing to the lower ward, where the castellan and a number of lay workers were to be seen on their way to and from the gardens. It was only on the fourth day, just after morning mass, that a very loud roar was heard which shook the walls of the guests' chapel, sent flocks of pigeons into the air from the columbarium, and startled the livestock and the horses in the stables. I later heard from Brother Johan that, following this noise, the castellan was seen hurrying frantically from the garden and appearing as white as if he had seen the devil himself. The workers who had been with him were not to be seen, and word spread amongst the brothers that something terrible had happened to them. Indeed, the following day it was whispered that the men who had gone down that day to the castellan's garden were not the same men who had been there on the former days. After that, no more loud noises were heard and the castellan was hardly seen; only occasionally, late at night when no one but the guards were about, was he noticed entering the great tower.

Over the next week the heat came like a glove. In all my time in the East I had not become accustomed to it, and in its increased intensity it was not only disagreeable, but seemed like a bad omen that, for me at least, added to my sense of foreboding.

At the next chapter, the castellan was once again conspicuous in his absence. It was perhaps his outburst on the earlier occasion and the violent nature of his argument with the cellarer, that made his absences so noticeable - this and the fact that everybody's thoughts were upon him and his rumoured activities over the past few days. The grand commander rose to speak. He now looked pale, tired, and agitated, and he leaned against a podium as if he had not the strength to support himself. Indeed, his appearance did more than all the rumours that had been going around to produce a sense of looming disaster among the brothers. He informed us that because of the danger of travel between Acre and the castle, supplies were no longer getting through on a regular basis. Even though the Saracen army was still not seen, it had become gravely dangerous to leave the fortifications. Some of the local Saracen villagers, realising our plight, had taken to attacking our caravans and those few settlements in the countryside still retained by our Order. Even the farmlands and the sugar plantations to the west around Manueth, which the Hospitallers had allowed us to harvest, had to be abandoned because of these raids. This was particularly worrying because, for almost all of our supplies we were dependant on whatever could get through from Acre. If the road to the coast was cut, we would be entirely isolated. Hunting expeditions in the surrounding forests, which had supplemented our food supplies with venison, wild fowl, and boar, had ceased altogether. Therefore, the grand commander told us, he was instigating a rationing of food until such time as conditions improved and regular supplies could get through. This speech, in particular the last comment, created much consternation among the brothers.

18 WALKER'S DIARY

Walker's diary from the torn-out pages, apparently written while at the cave

I got away undetected. By the time that the fool of a guard would have returned to the ward I must have left the hospital far behind. I ran through a small pine grove beyond its fence, slipping and almost breaking my neck on the damp stones. I passed a few houses and made my way to the centre of the town. I had thought of stealing a horse or even a motorcar, but the opportunity did not arise. I skirted the centre for fear of being seen, made my way through back streets and then out of town, heading north below the Carmel. I made sure to keep to the fields, away from the road, where there was enough low scrub to hide in if necessary. There were occasional travellers on the road, but they probably could not see me and in any case, no one seemed to be in pursuit. I moved away from the hill, heading across the sand and swamps near the bay. I was tired and thirsty and had not eaten since the morning and had no money. It was already becoming dark when I saw in the distance a small group of houses on the plain across from the road and made my way towards them. It was a new Jewish settlement called Kfar Ata. I approached the nearest house on a dirt path, thinking that I might knock at the door and ask for help. I knew these settlements were guarded since the riots of 1920, and thought that the best chance of getting something to eat and find a place to spend the night would be by direct approach. I tried to think of an explanation for my situation, but nothing believable came to mind. In the end I settled for a story that did not seem entirely plausible, but was the best I could come up with. As I approached the house the door was opened by a young woman with blue eyes and dark hair tied back in a scarf. She asked what I wanted. Like many of the Jews, she spoke broken English with an Eastern European accent. I told her that I was a surveyor for the government; that I had come down from Jerusalem and was planning to carry out a survey of land further down the coast. I said that my motorcar had caught fire some distance down the road down and I had lost all my equipment and my money.

I was amazed that she seemed to believe me, as the story sounded less and less plausible as I told it. She said she would call her husband, and I was certain he would send me packing. I had half decided to steal what I needed when the husband came to the door. He was a little bit older than me, dressed in farming clothes, and he seemed friendly enough. The woman returned and stood behind him in the doorway while I repeated my story. To try to gain his sympathy I put on a wonderful display of innocence and despair. No doubt my youthful appearance helped. I told him that I was new on the job and would be in a great deal of trouble over this. I realised that it would be unlikely for the police to look for me here so I made bold and asked if I could stay in their house for a couple of days while I did what I could of my surveying work. I never thought for a minute that he would agree, but they spoke together in some foreign tongue and then the husband told me that I could sleep in one of the sheds behind the house for a few days. I told him that I was greatly in their debt. This would be the perfect hideout, at least for the moment. The small settlement seemed so cut off. I even felt no fear of using my own name. They invited me into their kitchen, and the woman asked if I was hungry. She made coffee and fried some eggs, and I sat with them at the kitchen table. I wove a life story, partly true but mostly imaginary, and managed, it seemed, to gain their complete sympathy. Later the man took me out to show me where I could sleep. We carried out mattress and bedclothes, and once I was set up, he brought me a pen and some writing paper that I had asked for in order to add plausibility to my story. Later they invited me to their meal table. I thought it would be prudent to be as unobtrusive as possible, and following the meal I said that, after the upsetting incident with the motorcar and the long walk, I was ready for sleep. I told them I would be setting out early in the morning on my survey and would return in the afternoon. I thought that I would leave before they rose and that, for safety's sake, I would seek an alternative hideout for the following night.

In the event it was well after sunrise when the woman woke me. She asked how I had passed the night and I repeated that I greatly appreciated their help and that the shed was quite comfortable. In fact, it was very stuffy, and I suffered from the mosquitoes; I was also quite certain that I heard rats scraping around in the dark.

She gave me some breakfast and then I wandered off, out of sight. But I had changed my mind. I had somehow gained the confidence of these people and they had accepted my story and were not suspicious. They would not inform on me. Why not stay on there for a while longer?

Over the following days I holed up in a tent they had set

up for me behind the house. It was more comfortable than the shed; airier. I had nothing to do but pretend that I was going off to survey, and I had time to write up some of these notes. I ate meals with them and even helped at some of the farmwork. I got along well with them despite what must have certainly seemed a rather strange presence among them. The Jewish settlers do not generally look favourably on representatives of the government, even lowly ones such as I had presented myself as being. I was biding my time and I began, under my guise of surveyor, to make plans.

In the course of those days, I made a discovery that would be of great use to me. When I had set out along the lower slope of the Carmel on the first day, I had seen a small quarry on the mountainside, and it occurred to me that quarries use dynamite. On my third day at the settlement, I headed out to the quarry. It was a long walk. Keeping away from the road I made my way back towards the mountain. After some time I reached the fence surrounding the quarry grounds. I edged around the fence under cover of eucalyptus trees that had been planted along the side of the property and investigated the area. I made two discoveries. At one point along the fence it would be possible, with not too great an effort, to move aside the wire and squeeze my way through. The other discovery was that there was a small wooden shed located not far within where the path ran up towards the slope of the mountain and the quarry face. This shed was partly cut into the ground, and it looked to me the most likely place for explosives to be stored. I spent a couple of hours watching from beyond the wire, but saw no activity. On my way along the perimeter of the property I had seen a guard at the gate and a few men walking along a path that led to the quarry beyond, but on the whole, there did not seem to be very much of a presence. The following day I returned around noon and saw a truckload of workers driving up the path from the gate. There was still very little activity at the shed, but my expectations rose considerably when, hidden behind some bushes, I watched while a man approached, unlocked the door, and removed a wooden crate. From the manner in which he carried it, it appeared to be quite heavy. I was certain now that this must be dynamite, even though on the two days that I had been around the quarry I had heard no explosions. I found a spot under a tree and dozed off in the warm half shade, waking after a few hours. I then returned to my position near the fence. No one was about now. I ventured out near the fence and looked carefully over the area between the fence and the shed. I would have to remember any obstacles on the way as it seemed most practical to attempt a break-in at night. I had with me safety matches and a candle that I had been given by the woman. That would be of help getting to the shed, though I realised I had better be careful with the candle once I got in there, if indeed, as I hoped, it contained dynamite.

In the event, I did not need the candle. I wandered off and slept under a tree for most of the afternoon, returning towards nightfall. I waited till it became dark. The moon was nearly full, and after overcoming a bit of fencing rather more stubborn than I had anticipated, I had no trouble in making my way to the shed. I stopped against its wall and crouched down listening for the sound of the guards. There was none. The door was locked with a large Yale lock. Before I attempted to break in, I waited in silence for at least ten minutes, but there was no sound of anyone approaching, only the distant barking of jackals on the mountainside. After waiting in this position until my knees became quite painful, I stood up and approached the door. There were no windows, only the single wooden door.

I had nothing to try the lock with, so I put my knee against the door and attempted to wrench away the lock. Not surprisingly, it was strongly built and would not give. I found a fist-sized rock and tried to knock the lock free by striking it on its side, but the noise was greater than I had anticipated, and I quickly retreated behind some nearby trees.

I must have waited for at least another quarter of an hour before I felt certain no one was coming. Then I approached the shed again and another idea occurred to me. The door was constructed of horizontal wooden planks. I lay down on the ground placing my feet on the second lowest plank took hold of the other end and forcing with my fingers at its edge pulled with all my strength. At first nothing happened, but I felt a very slight give that encouraged me, and I increased my effort to lever the plank free, pushing with my feet against it. As I increased the effort, I could feel the pull of the iron nails against the wood. Then came a high-pitched screech as they worked free, sending a shiver up my arms and the back of my neck. The plank curved slightly away from the doorframe and loosened. I bent it back. It was hanging only from the nails on one side. Again, I waited, listening in the silence. Then I began to work on the next plank up and freed that too. The third plank not only screeched in coming free but cracked loudly. Again, I froze and waited. I almost panicked, but still there was no sign that anyone had heard. I lay against the wall, breathless from the effort, my heart pounding in my chest, ready if necessary to get up and make a run for it. Several moments passed. Eventually I got up. Enough planks on the lower part of the door were now bent away to enable me to squeeze through. I took another look around and then eased myself in.

Inside, the shed was pitch dark. The little moonlight that came through the hole at the base of the door did nothing to

*illuminate the interior. I was forced to take a risk and light the
candle. With great care I huddled down on the floor and lit
the safety match close to my chest, then passed it to the wick of
the candle which birthed a tiny yellow flame. I let it grow and
holding it up I could just make out the contents of the room.
Wooden crates were stacked against two walls. I bent down,
let some of the wax spill on the floor near the centre and stuck
the candle to it. Then I stepped over to one of the crates and
opened it. In it were sticks of dynamite, placed in neat rows. I
opened a second box. It was the same. Then I saw what appeared to be a cloth jacket thrown over one of the boxes. I lifted
it and could hardly believe my great good fortune when a large
and heavy revolver that had been wrapped in the jacket fell
out. I picked it up and held it in my hand. It was beautiful, like
an unexpected gift. I opened the cylinder and found that it was
fully loaded. I looked around to see if there was any more am-
munition in the shed and found a couple of boxes of cartridges.*

*Everything went perfectly. I took a single crate. It was
marked "DANGER:EXPLOSIVES" in large red letters. It was
quite heavy, and I carried it with difficulty, hiding it away under a thicket of thorn bushes a few miles from the settlement.
But I kept the revolver with me, and the jacket, and slipped
unnoticed back into the tent. With the jacket under my head,
I lay awake for some time, breathing heavily with the excitement. Eventually I calmed down enough to fall asleep.*

*I rose very early the next morning. I needed to get as far
away as possible from the quarry. The break-in would certainly be discovered very soon, and the police might come around.
They might even make the connection between my escape and
the theft.*

*I knew that the settlers rose early, and I decided to leave
openly. I washed at a pump in the yard and walked up to the*

house. I thanked them for their hospitality and told them that I found I could not do the survey work without equipment, that I had decided to return to Jerusalem and face my superiors. They invited me to have coffee with them before I left, and then I had another remarkable stroke of good luck. While they went out to bring in water from the pump, I looked through the things on a dresser and found a hidden roll of banknotes, which I pocketed. This might seem ungrateful after their hospitality—and I have to admit that they were unexpectedly kind to me—but my need was greater than theirs.

When I left the settlement, I knew I could not walk very far carrying the heavy crate of dynamite. I was uncertain about what to do. It seemed a pity to take just a few sticks and leave the rest, knowing I would need them, so I left the crate hidden in some bushes with the intention of returning. It occurred to me that I could take the horse stabled behind the house, but I feared that I could not do so without being seen. I decided instead to return towards nightfall. I would need to be especially careful since by then they might have discovered that the money was missing and would be on the lookout for me or perhaps even have called the police. After covering the crate with leaves and branches I headed south, following a path along a dry stream bed, and when the valley opened up I moved slightly uphill to make sure that I would not be observed.

The police are certain to be looking for me by now. They undoubtedly will have linked me to the theft of the explosives and the gun. They probably expect me to return to the castle, as indeed I intend to do, but in my own time. Now, however, I will take greater care and will not be caught. I will show them who I am and what I am capable of.

I have found an ideal place to hide out. After I left Kfar Ata I made my way inland, across flat land and uncultivated fields. I kept to small tracks and walked cross-country for most of the morning, stopping only occasionally in secluded places to rest. It grew warm and I had to wipe the sweat away from my eyes. At one point when I looked up from the stony track, I saw a motorcar approaching in the distance. I dropped to my hands and knees. It came along a dirt road to my left, but fortunately no one had seen me.

I moved away from the road then, and when I felt I had distanced myself enough I slowed my pace. The plain opened out to a broad vista, but fortunately not a soul was about. There were no villages, just a dusty expanse stretching north and south, bordered in the distance by mountain ranges. At a certain point I discovered this cave at the foot of a slight rise; a mound rather than a hill. On the edge of it are several stunted pine trees, and near its base there is a sandstone ledge, almost invisible in the low bushes and long grass where the cave has its opening. The entrance is quite high and after a few steps the roof rises even higher. The cave has the sour smell of rot and mould, but it is pleasantly cool. I am pretty certain no one will find this place. It will serve my purpose.

19 SIEGE

Our expectations in no manner lessened the surprise when one morning word spread like fire in a dry field that the Saracens had arrived and were taking up position on the hill to the south. The atmosphere in the castle was volatile. Like many others, I wished to see for myself, but all the brothers who were not part of the permanent garrison were confined to the north side of the castle, and from here there was no sign at all of the enemy.

Once again, I was assigned to duty on the south wall. The tension among the brothers was palpable. Everyone had something to say, and many claimed to have seen the Saracens for themselves, though I doubted if all the reports I heard were true. Some said that the entire hill to the south was covered with soldiers, and huge siege machines were being erected, while others said there were just a few machines on the top of the hill. When the cellarer appeared at about midday, we fell upon him and demanded to know what he had seen. It was true, he told us, that the enemy had arrived, and siege machines were indeed being constructed on the slope of the hill. We asked why we were being confined to the north if there was no threat here and he told us that it was the decision of the grand commander and that enough men were in position in the south. He said that there was no way of knowing if the sultan was going to move part of his troops to the north, although this was far more difficult terrain for launching an attack, and siege machines could not be employed here at all.

"What about the castellan?" one of the men asked. "What about the promised weapon?" This query was accorded a chorus of support by the others.

"I cannot tell you," Brother Matthew answered. "I wish I could. As far as I know the castellan has not been seen all morning."

"But he promised us… the grand commander promised us that he would protect the castle."

"Promises are more easily given than kept," said Matthew despondently.

"Then we are lost."

"I do not know," Brother Matthew said wearily, shaking his head in exasperation. "I have done what I could to prevent this." He was silent for some moments and then added: "Perhaps I am wrong. Perhaps we shall yet bear witness to the castellan's efforts," but none of us really believed that.

In the afternoon I went to see Albert in the infirmary. He was lying in the cot, very pale and barely responsive. I told him what was happening, but he hardly seemed affected by it. I spent most of the afternoon and much of the following night on guard on the wall. We could hear nothing, and no news reached us after the visit of the cellarer. We were told that there would be an emergency chapter in the morning, but nobody really knew a thing and it almost seemed as if we had been abandoned here.

The following morning, just after daybreak, word came that all the infidels' great machines had been erected overnight and were lined up in a clearing on the south. The anxiety amongst us rose to new levels. Those knights and sergeants who had slept took up their weapons, while others went to rest after a long night's vigil but did not take off their armour. Men were sent to carry equipment to the positions along the walls, and much activity began around us, accompanied by little talk, even less than usual.

Shortly before the hour of Terce some of us were called to take part in the defence of the main building. I was among these and here at last, I could see the enemy and their monstrous machines. An atmosphere of imminent disaster hung over the castle, and there was no longer any talk of an emergency chapter. The first sign of the approaching battle came shortly after I had taken up my position on the roof defences. All at once there was a tremendous commotion from across the valley; a loud noise that was a terrible mixture of trumpets, drum-rolls, and shouting. From where I stood, I could see men in the Saracen camp running about like disturbed ants, and shortly a hail of arrows and crossbow bolts rose in the air and whistled down in the area of our outworks with a loud collective hiss. The guards on the southern wall took what cover they could, and all eyes turned to the machines as they swung up and down. A whoosh, as rock projectiles came hurtling across the valley, followed by reverberating thuds as they struck the ground. I heard the cracking of wood and the crash and crack of stone as some hit the lower outworks on the western side of the hill. Then glass shattered as one missile struck the upper wall of the chapter-house and a great thud as another landed on the roof.

These first stones brought a wild cheer from the Saracens that travelled with them across the valley. Then there was a short lull, and a second volley came. Projectiles flew up and fell within the outworks. They seemed to be directing their missile attack at the most splendid part of the castle—the Great Hall and the grand master's apartments above it. There were no defensive rooftop positions on that building. This may have been an oversight on the planners' part, for although the hall could be fairly well defended from the adjacent battlements, little could be done against this barrage of missiles. One volley struck the south wall of the hall and came crashing down on a group of defenders who were just running back from the outworks. There was a horrible cry that filled me with terror. A neighing of horses came from the stables behind us, and more cries and shouting from the round tower at the western end of the outer wall. Now, finally, there began a movement of men from the northern defences to positions facing the south. Someone had at last given the order. We could see the knights and sergeants running frantically through the southern portals, and from what I could make out, they had been directed to retake positions abandoned after the first barrage. They also moved towards the makeshift walls in the open area below the Great Hall and all along the undefended northern extension of the castle. This was the weakest part of the defences, on which so much effort had recently been expended, and as was now clear, these efforts had been left too late. Our archers occupied all of the battlement positions and arrow slits in the central building and the great tower.

I joined these men and applied my long-dormant skills in the use of the crossbow. As the defences had not been completed, there were too many brothers to man the available positions on the outer wall, and archers were being pulled back to the inner wall and to the roof where I was standing. I could see a company of Saracens approaching the outer defences. They wore iron mail and chainmail on their helmets and bright red and green caparisons decorated with Saracenic heraldry. I saw how our archers on the outer wall opened fire on them from behind and heard the cries and the loud rattle of the arrows that for a moment split their ranks (although there was, in any case, little regulation in their formation because of the difficult lie of the land). I saw how they reformed on the hill and moved forward in the clearing before the wall, and how panic and confusion returned on our side. One Saracen—a man of high rank, I think, for he seemed to be leading a group of others close behind, his sword raised, suddenly stopped as if frozen for a moment, his arm still high and his mouth open as if he had said something or shouted, though it was too distant and the noise of the battle too great to hear him. He fell, an arrow protruding from his head, but those behind him did not stop, clambering forward and past or even, so it seemed from my vantage point, right over his prone body, and others joined them. Soon the steep place, between the trees on the distant slope where they had held their line, was filled with shouting men. From my position I could clearly see our men running from the lower wall to new posts further behind and could hear the shouting.

There was so much commotion and disorder in the castle that, after attempting to make some use of my bow, I realised that there was nothing effective that I could do. With a number of other men, I stood behind the merlons as a spectator, passively watching the Saracen progress.

Now and then my thoughts strayed to the old man. Was he safe in the infirmary? With no reason to remain in my position, I decided to look for him. I descended the staircase to the basement and went out along the path down on the northern side to the outer ward. Much of the sound of battle was blocked by the tall buildings behind me, but there was a great deal of commotion here as well, with men running in all directions. I reached the infirmary and found the old man entirely alone in the chamber lying in his cot. When he saw me, with an effort he lifted himself up and spoke in a thin, broken voice:

"What is happening, Hermann?"

"I am afraid that the Saracen attack has begun."

"I feared as much when the others left."

"The attack is on the other side of the castle, but this building is against the wall. It is too exposed. Will you come with me?"

"Where do you want to go?"

"There is no safe place. But if help does arrive, we will perhaps have a better chance if we hold out in the tower. I saw others going there. Do you think you are able to walk?"

"I will try," he said.

I helped him out of bed. He was very weak and put all his weight on me. We made our way up towards the great tower, entered the inner ward by the main portal, slowly climbing the staircase to the chapel on the lower level. The effort had left him breathless, and we sat for a long time on a stone bench. Occasionally I went to observe the fighting through an arrow embrasure in a narrow passageway within the thick southern wall of the tower. The barrage continued throughout midday and into the early afternoon. Volley after volley of stone projectiles and barrels of Greek Fire were being hurtled through the air. The Greek Fire caused the greatest unrest; the noise it created, and the brilliant glare was enough to make the devil himself tremble with fright. I could see that trees on the lower slopes were alight, but there was no fire as yet in the castle itself. The air was filled with the stench of sulphur. The Saracens also fired arrows dipped in Greek Fire, and every so often these flashed across the valley, but they seemed to cause little damage. In the meanwhile, the Saracens had set up additional machines, having hacked down trees and levelled out another area further down the slope. From there they directed their fire at our outer wall. At a position at the top of the hill a colourful pavilion had been erected, presumably for the sultan, and a path had been cleared from it down through the trees. Within a few hours it had been extended all the way down to the firing positions. Their men formed a human chain and were passing down wooden beams to construct yet more machines. I could also make out the stone projectiles and barrels of what must certainly have been more of the inflammable liquid.

Sunset had always been a splendid hour at the castle. Now the sky was doubly ablaze, and in the dark that followed it retained a bloody red glow. As the evening commenced, I helped Albert to the embrasure. The chapel itself had become crowded with despairing men and I was glad that we had managed to find this small, unoccupied refuge. Albert was terribly pale. His skin had taken on a greyish hue and his eyes were half closed. I asked him how he was feeling:

"I am alright, he replied. "Do not worry about me," though he was almost inaudible. He asked me if I might get him some water, and I left him and went into the chapel. I spoke to some men, but when I mentioned water they were up in arms on the subject. It appeared that the castellan had ordered the cistern to be sealed. The trapdoor on the chapel floor was covered with heavy wooden beams and a great iron lock. When I saw this, I recalled the words of Brother Johan. However, they told me that water jars had been brought from the cistern in the kitchen. I found these stacked at the door to the chapel, filled a small flask and brought it to Albert, but he hardly responded when I helped him to drink. I feared for him, he seemed so weak, but he said that he was just tired and needed to rest. His eyes were moist and red and seemed to have sunk even deeper into his skull; his skin was like parchment, almost translucent and very tight at the bridge of his nose and on his forehead. There was no bench or pallet on which he could lie. I told him to lean against me. I feared that at any moment we would be told to move out of the embrasure, but apparently the fighting was still too distant to make this an effective firing position, and we were able to remain here, at least for the moment. Albert soon fell asleep, while I sat, with mingled horror and fascination, watching through the loophole.

A thick, heavy darkness spread over the valleys and hillsides around the castle and seemed to match the darkness that spread over our minds and in our hearts. For some reason, perhaps an in-

tentional ruse to lull our defences into unpreparedness, perhaps
having decided to wait out the night, the Saracens quite suddenly
stopped their attack on the outworks, and the hillside where they
were positioned became eerily quiet. It almost seemed as if they
had packed up and left.

I watched for some time, expecting the fighting to flare up
again. My mind began to wander. I was thinking about the past
weeks, about our meeting with the Preceptor's chief clerk, Brother
Matheus, at the palace of the Hospital in Acre, how Albert had held
onto his hopes and how these had been raised again when a clerk
at the Court of the Chain claimed to remember meeting Prior Bernard after he had disembarked in 1266. That had been the first time
that someone had actually recalled his son, and Albert's eyes had
lit up, as if we were about to meet him. The clerk had remembered,
although it had been five years earlier, Bernard's intention to visit
the German house. I recalled that I had tried to keep Albert from
becoming too hopeful. It was then that he had decided this fateful
course of action that had brought us to Starkenberg. If we learnt at
the castle nothing of the whereabouts of Bernard, he had reasoned,
if nothing came of it, we would return to Acre, and he would sail
in the spring passage for Limassol. And if nothing was to be found
there, he would return to Germany. It was now unlikely that Albert
would ever get to Cyprus or find his son, let alone return home to
his wife. Indeed, I was doubtful if either of us would return from
here alive, and even if we did, whether the kingdom itself would
survive. With the increasing success of the Saracen attacks, Tyre
and Acre were certainly under direct threat, perhaps were already
under attack, and it seemed that the whole kingdom was collapsing
about us like the walls of this very castle.

As I was engaged in these thoughts Albert broke into a sudden paroxysm of coughing. I gave him some more water from the flask and helped him to lie down, first placing my cloak across the hard, stone floor. He was almost immediately asleep, but a return to my reminiscences was hindered by a renewal of the attack. This new volley of mangonels was of greater intensity than before and far noisier. A pure cold fear overtook me. Leaving Albert for a moment, I went into the chapel to look for reassurance among the other men gathered there; the archers and sergeants passing through on their way to or from the battlements. But their faces reflected the same fear that I felt. I returned to the embrasure. At one point there was some commotion in the chapel, and I went back to see what had happened. From the dark doorway I saw all the men were being ordered to leave. Then another group of men entered the empty chapel. They appeared not to have noticed me in the shadowed doorway. Two of them unlocked and lifted the trapdoor over the cistern and lowered ropes into it. They had a number of large wooden chests. One of the men climbed in and they lowered the chests. The castellan was not there but I recognised one or two of the brothers as men I had seen accompanying him on earlier occasions. Watching these events, I wondered what was in the chests.

In spite of my curiosity, I feared being noticed. I went back into the dark embrasure and returned to observe the fighting. When I came back later to look inside the chapel, the men were no longer there, and the cistern had been re-sealed. The chapel remained empty for some time, and I was briefly seized by the fear that we were entirely alone in the castle. Outside the sounds of battle continued unabated.

The night brought no respite, but in the morning, it appeared that despite the damage caused on the previous day, the machines had not entirely destroyed the outer walls. The onslaught continued, but was broken by intervals of up to an hour, flaring up again when, with a loud hiss, a barrel of Greek Fire snaked up into the sky. During the night these barrels illuminated the castle almost as daylight, trailing tails of fire like those of comets, and shedding showers of gold sparks as they screamed across the valley. Now their effect was less dramatic, but yet enough to instil fear in any observer. Some of the Saracen machines remained aimed at the western buildings and the central ward, while others hurled stones at the lower outer wall and the higher inner wall that curved around the western end of the castle. At one point I caught sight of a group of enemy sappers advancing through the dry grass and approaching the outer wall. But even though they were quite close they did not appear to be under fire from the wall, which meant either that they had not been noticed, or that our positions on the wall had already been abandoned. For a moment I considered going into the lower castle to give warning. However, it soon became clear that these men did not fear discovery. They were walking upright, and it was obvious that our men had indeed already moved back from the outer enceinte and repositioned on the main wall. With no problem at all the Saracens occupied the outer wall and towers and signalled for their reinforcements to follow.

Now, as the morning progressed, the impossibility of our position had become clear to all. A general flight had begun in the direction of our refuge in the great tower. Here would be the last stand. Already the chamber was filling up once again with men coming up the stairwell from below, then climbing the stairs to the upper chamber and the roof. The enemy must have known about this movement, and from where I watched I could see a new mangonel position being set up opposite us. More volleys of arrows came whistling against the castle walls. These were aimed against the battlements, but the Saracen archers were still too distant for them to be effective, and the positions on the top of the great tower were out of their range. Nonetheless, the rain of arrows rattled horribly and with surprising volume against the outer wall of the tower. I had to abandon the position I had taken at the loophole and move back into the embrasure.

As I turned my attention away from the fighting, I realised that something dramatic was once again going on within the chapel. Keeping out of sight, I saw a group of men that included the castellan and the grand commander entering the chamber. They were with two or three important looking men and two labourers who were again lifting the large wooden hatch that covered the opening on the floor of the chamber. There was no attempt this time to keep the brothers away. I wondered - was there no longer a fear of anyone witnessing whatever was going on, or was it simply that the rush of defenders into the tower made secrecy impossible? However, only few brothers stood by to watch as most were hastening to the upper storey and the defensive positions above. The castellan and grand commander were arguing heatedly, or rather, the grand commander was arguing and the castellan, for once, was listening without interrupting. Standing unobserved in the doorway to my passage, I tried to hear what was being said above the din of battle and the rush of men towards the stairs. The grand commander was clearly livid, almost ranting, but the noise in the chamber was so great that I could catch only a few of his words. At one point he raised his voice enough for me to hear him say:

"You have deceived me. You have betrayed my trust."

Jordon answered him but I could not hear him over the general commotion. The grand commander's voice, however, rang out clearly: "This is your doing? I would have given orders to abandon the castle. Do you realise how many lives your treachery will cost? What have you done, Jordon?" He shook with rage. "What have you done?"

The castellan appeared almost humbled, so in opposition to how he had been until now. Now I could just make out his reply: "I was almost there."

"Where? On the verge of making gold?" shouted the grand commander.

I wondered what he meant by this.

"You have not produced a weapon. You have not even managed to turn your lead into gold. It is on your conscience, Jordon. Your conscience! But if I live, I shall make certain the Grand Master hears of this."

I wondered, what did he mean about gold? Before I had time to reflect on this, I saw one of the knights approach the grand commander, after which he turned and vented his full anger on the castellan with these final words:

"He that touches pitch shall be defiled therewith!" Then, taking up a lantern and uncharacteristically pushing aside the men in his way, he stepped onto the ladder and descended into the shaft. The castellan said something to the other men with him whereupon they hurried out of the chapel. Then Jordon climbed down into the cistern after the grand commander.

At this very moment there was a loud crash from the direction of the embrasure. This put an end to my speculating of the remarkable scene that I had just witnessed. I crawled back into the embrasure beside the prone body of the old man and approached the arrow-slit. A barrel of Greek fire must have struck the southern wall of the tower just to the right of the arrow-slit. The wall seemed ablaze in a white conflagration, and the embrasure filled with smoke and the overpowering smell of naphtha. It seemed that the full brunt of the attack had now been directed at us. I moved back to the safer position where Albert was lying. Despite the noise and the smell, he was quite still and seemed to be sleeping, albeit fitfully. I remained beside him for some time, then returned to see what was happening in the chapel. The first thing I saw was the castellan ascending from the ladder in the cistern. He looked pale and frightened. Noticing me he scowled, his visage most frightening, but then hurried out of the chapel. No one else ascended from the cistern. I was wondering what all this meant, and why the grand commander had not come out with him. Perhaps he had ascended while I was within the embrasure. It must have been so, for the castellan went off and shortly thereafter returned with some labourers. I was careful now, that he should not see me observing him from the embrasure.

"Seal everything," I heard him say. "Seal the room and seal the passage. Do not go into the room. A word of this to anyone and I will see you dead."

It seemed an empty threat in our current situation, but his words were startling, nonetheless. What was he sealing, what passage, and why at this time was it so important?

I returned to sit beside Albert. He had not moved. After an hour or so I returned to the chapel, and Brother Walther who was passing through to the upper chamber stopped to tell me the bad tidings. Hopes of a rescue force reaching us in time had been abandoned. It might be only hours before the castle fell. A delegation had set out for Acre earlier, but it now seemed clear that this move had been taken too late.

"There might be an attempt to negotiate with the sultan," he said. He asked how Albert was, and I told him that I was worried about him and that he seemed to have slept through all the noise.

After Walther had ascended to the upper chamber I returned to the embrasure. I now felt a need to take a more active role in my own fate. It was obvious that this would end badly and that it would end quite soon. What would happen to us if we were taken into captivity, I wondered. I had heard talk about the barbarity of the Saracens, particularly of the terrible torture and slaughter that the people of Antioch had suffered and how the sultan had put to death all but two of the defenders of Safed, beheading one thousand and five hundred men on a nearby hill.

But perhaps there was still the possibility of escape. I did not think that this would be cowardly. Many of the other brothers had already given up any show of trying to defend the castle. I tried to awaken Albert, shaking him gently by the shoulder. At first it was to no avail, but eventually he opened his eyes and struggled into a sitting position.

"We need to leave," I said. "It is not safe, even here."

"Go then, Hermann," he answered in a very weak voice. "Go. But without me. I am too ill. I will follow later."

I tried to explain the gravity of the situation: "The castle is falling. We have to find a way out before it is too late." He just shook his head and smiled:

"Dear boy. For me it is already too late. Please go."

"I cannot leave you."

"But you must, Hermann. It is alright. I am resigned to my fate. I know that I will not find my son. It is my destiny to die here in this castle. Perhaps I will see him soon, in another place. It is God's will, and I am not afraid. But you must save yourself. You are young. You have much to live for."

"I can help you," I pleaded. "We can leave together. Please let me help you."

"I will not go with you," he said, "but do not let me die knowing that I have caused your death as well. I am so grateful to you for the aid you have given me. Do not go against my wishes now. I beg of you. Leave. Go now!"

I was torn, but I could see that he was resolute and that I would not be able to change his mind. The sounds of the battle were growing louder. Albert lay down again and closed his eyes. He had made his decision. I had to make mine.

20 WALKER'S DIARY

Walker's diary from the torn-out pages, written at the cave

I risked heading back to Haifa today and purchased some food and a bottle of whiskey. After that I hid out until sunset, when I decided to take the chance of returning for my dynamite. On reaching the outskirts of the settlement, I approached with great stealth and surveyed the settlers' property from behind some cypress trees. Once again lady luck was on my side. The horse was saddled and tied to a wooden stake outside the stable. It was grazing on a bit of dry stubble. When I was certain that no one was watching, I made my way over, untied it and led it away to the place where I had hidden my stash. I lifted the crate of dynamite onto the saddle and mounted the horse behind it. By now it was growing dark, and I trotted out onto the road, one hand holding the reins, the other supporting the crate, and when I had covered some distance, I somehow got it into a steady gallop using the end of the reigns as a whip. When I arrived at the hideaway I dismounted, set the crate down on the ground and led the horse by the rope to the cave. At the entrance it raised its head and blew in protest, but I whispered to it and led it in. Its breath was warm against my cheek and loud in the narrow

confines of the cave. It would be best to keep the animal hidden,
I thought, in case someone should chance this way.

After securing the rope I walked outside. There was still
a little light, but it was rapidly waning. The heckling of small
birds in the trees continued through the dusk until at last it was
quiet. It was only then that I felt safe. I carried the crate into
the cave and stepped out again. I took the revolver and held
it with both hands, feeling the power in its weight. I thought
that I might shoot something, just for the pleasure of it and
to release the tension, but for all the isolation of this place, I
feared to be heard.

21 WALKER'S DIARY

Walker's diary from the torn-out pages, written at the cave

Yes! I have made my first attack. This is only a foretaste of what will come.

I took the revolver with me. The dynamite is safely hidden away, and I have hidden the other items that I purchased with the settler's money in the cave. This morning I felt that everything was ready. I knew exactly what I was going to do. I set out very early, before dawn, taking the revolver with me. I rode the horse much of the way, then let it go, for fear of being too conspicuous. I won't need it again anyway. It was well into the afternoon before I got to the top of the hill. I saw the white tents of the camp and I could see the guards there, smoking. No one else seemed about. I nearly gave myself away when there was a sudden commotion in the bushes in front of me and a heavy thumping of wings as three of those bloody chukars ran out frantically from between the rocks and lifted into noisy flight. I nearly had a heart attack! I may have even cried out, but fortunately no one noticed.

I scrambled through the forest following the hilltop above the camp and adjacent to the castle. After a while I was exactly opposite the castle but rather higher, and I descended the slope until I was at the same level. Hidden by the trees I could see the entire length of the ruin and observe any activity on that side. I took off the heavy pack, lowering it carefully to the ground, and sat on a rock watching the men moving about in the castle. They were working in the middle part and in the keep. I knew their daily schedule - I had been the one to set it up in the first days of work. I knew that they were now after their morning break and would work steadily through until one o'clock. Then they would take a two-hour break, returning at three and finishing at five o'clock. It was this two-hour break that I was waiting for. I had reckoned the time it would take to climb down the slope and then ascend to the castle. I would have to skirt around to the east in order to approach unseen. Some of the workers would still be in the castle during the break but the majority would climb the path to Malia to take their rest in the olive grove. All I needed was to get into the castle unnoticed and then about ten minutes to do my work.

I watched for some time, waiting for the break. Suddenly I was distracted by something rather odd. On the ground near where I sat there were a number of large, almost perfectly round stones. Were these ancient catapult stones? I suppose something of the archaeologist remains in me. Absorbed in such thoughts, I had briefly lost sight of what was going on in the castle. The men were beginning to move off for their break. My plan was to wait for about half an hour after they climbed up the path between my vantage-point and the castle. Then I would make my move. Something else, however, now caught my attention. There was a lot more activity than usual on the keep, and all the men were hurrying that way. Someone, it might have been Riley, was walking to the edge and shouting to someone across the castle. I could hear this only faintly and could not make the words out, but I did distinctly see a second figure running across the central part of the castle and climb up into the keep. I wondered what was going on.

The time came when the men would normally have left for their break, but no one did. It seemed they had all gathered in the area of the keep. At first, I was annoyed. But then I began to think that this could actually work in my favour. If everyone was located at that end of the castle, I could climb up on the west side unobserved, do what I planned to do, and the effect would be all the greater. Yes, this was definitely a good development, but I would need to be especially careful. I hitched up my pack and walked back along the hillside until I was opposite the western hall. From this distance it certainly appeared to be unoccupied. I decided to make my move and began cautiously to descend the hill. Reaching the path on the north, I skirted the castle and climbed the steep slope, coming around behind the outer enceinte. The ascent was very hard, but the trees completely hid me. I passed the outer gate tower and very carefully approached the upper part of the castle. All the time I was aware that if seen and recaptured I would be thrown back in prison and face a much more serious charge. Only my unbending desire to take revenge on Riley made me go on.

As I had expected, I found the western side of the castle unoccupied, and I quickly got to work. I squatted down on the ground near the high wall between the central building and the hall, placed the satchel down on the ground and pulled out of it three sticks of dynamite wrapped in oil-stained paper and an outer wrapping of cloth. I laid them on the ground and twisted the wicks together. Then I took out of the satchel the additional length of wick that I had found in the crate and twined the wick from the dynamite onto it. Carefully placing the sticks on the ground, I covered them with a pile of small stones. I spread the length of wick from the dynamite across the hall as far as the entrance in the high wall. Then I put the satchel back on, walked over to the opening in the wall and stood there looking across the central part of the castle. When I was certain no one was coming and that my escape route was open I walked back, took out of my pocket a box of safety matches, and lit the extended wick. Then I exited through the opening, slipped down the path on the north, and jumping over rocks and obstacles, half running, half sliding down the hillside, made my way quickly back the way I had come. As I ran, I expected that at any moment I would hear the blast of the dynamite. On the path to the west of the castle I stopped for a moment to catch my breath. Nothing!

I was debating whether or not to turn back when it finally came… a loud, thundering boom above and a hurtling of rubble and dust into the air. I stood watching for some moments as the dust cloud rose and cleared, my sense of elation tinged with disappointment when I saw that the wall appeared to remain standing. Damnation! I had been certain it would come down. I headed quickly up the hill to the south from where I would be able to see better the damage I had caused and observe the response to my action. But the dense forest that gave me good cover also prevented me getting a good view of the castle until I was finally back at the level I had been earlier. Then I could see that a number of the men had crossed back to the hall. A cloud of dust was still hanging over the edge of the castle, and slowly settling onto the slope.

It was less than I had hoped for, but it would do for a start. Now I hurried uphill to the very top, where I stopped again for one last look. I could see the workers scuttling about. I turned and hurried off across the top of the southern hill, heading south.

Soon it was dark, and I found a place for the night in an old, abandoned house. The roof had fallen in, but it gave me some shelter and I had a blanket in my pack and some provisions that I had bought in Haifa. Rising early, I walked for much of the day and finally arrived back at the cave. Everything was as I had left it. I pushed aside some stones and the woollen cloth covering my stash and found it all untouched: the wooden crate neatly packed with several rows of dynamite sticks encased in strips of paper packaging, and the bottles and tins of food that I had purchased in Haifa - the return to Haifa was a risky business in itself. I have become remarkably daring, and I cannot believe that I could have done these things before. But I have a purpose now.

22 WORK

When the explosion occurred Riley and Robert were deep in the belly of the cistern. The workers had just begun to remove the stones blocking the opening, and excitement was at a peak. Neither of the men knew what they would find, but such a construction had clearly been done with the intention of hiding something, and the fact that it had been blocked and plastered over suggested that this might be the depository of something significant. Riley had read somewhere that the treasury of the Order may have been located in the castle; he knew from the contemporary sources he had read, that after the castle fell the archives had been taken by the knights back to Acre, but there was no mention of what had happened to the treasury. He could not help considering the possibility that they had stumbled on its hiding place.

The sudden explosion, somewhat muffled, was loud enough to startle them. Even at this distance the walls of the cistern shook.

"What on earth was that?" Riley called up to Abdul, who was still standing by the opening on the floor of the keep. The workers had gathered there expectantly to see what would be found when the blocked annex was opened. "What has happened?"

"An explosion Mr. Riley. Behind the wall."

The men in the cistern hurriedly climbed up the ladder. When they came out into the light, they could see the smoke and dust rising above the high wall at the far end and could smell the dynamite in the air. Abdul and a number of the workers had already descended from the keep and were running back across the centre of the castle. Riley was reluctant to leave the cistern unattended.

"I'll see what's going on," said Robert. He ran down the stairs and hurried across to the opening in the high wall. The men crowding around the breach in the wall moved aside to allow him through. The hall was entirely filled with a cloud of dust and a number of rocks were scattered across the floor, but despite the apparent intensity of the blast there did not appear to be any serious damage apart from a large crater in the floor. Robert stood beside Abdul.

"See this?" he pointed to the remains of the fuse. "It's Walker. He must have been released. When did the men leave this side of the castle?"

"About half an hour ago."

"Then he must have come up just after that. That means he cannot have gone very far."

"Yes sir, but far enough to take cover. I don't think we will be able to find him. We don't know which way he has gone."

"He might still be here. Listen, Abdul… take the men and check to the north and south. See if there is any sign of him. And take a rifle with you. I'm going to speak to Mr. Riley."

Robert headed back across the castle, climbing up into the keep where he scanned the hills to either side, but he could see nothing.

"What was it?" asked Riley, as Robert descended the ladder back into the dark cistern.

"An explosive charge. Don't worry. It was badly placed and only caused minor damage to the floor. It can only have been Walker. He must have been released."

"Released! And he had dynamite? My God! What is he playing at?"

"The fellow is clearly deranged."

"Where on earth did he get the dynamite?"

"I have no idea. I never thought he would go this far."

"Neither did I."

"There is some history to this though. You remember what Professor Gilford said."

"Yes, but nothing like this. Do you think we can rely on the police? He could have got someone killed."

"That may have been his intention."

"What!"

"He might have been intending to kill someone."

"No... I don't think so. He's just trying to scare me," said Riley. "He is clearly unstable but..." He was silent for a moment and then added, almost as if speaking to himself: "He was disagreeable from the start, but he didn't seem insane!"

"Well, it's pretty clear that he is, and we might be in real danger. How are we going to go on?"

"We just will."

"Are you sure you appreciate what has just happened?" Robert looked into the older man's eyes. "He used dynamite, John!"

"I don't mean we shouldn't take precautions. For one thing, we will get Peters down here with his men. And I'll tell Abdul to set up a guard now. We have a few rifles. That should be enough till the police arrive."

"Alright. But do you think we can go back to work in the cistern."

"We have to. I'm not going to let this lunatic get his way and destroy our work. There is too much at stake."

"Yes... alright. But we need to deal with this before he does anything more serious." He paused for a minute. "Listen, John. I don't mind going up to Haifa. You set a watch here and keep working in the cistern."

"I don't want to go ahead without you."

"Well, one of us has to go."

"I can send one of the men up to Malia and get someone there to inform the police. Perhaps Father Nicephor will help us. He has a motorcar, I think."

Abdul had come back, and they called him over.

"Any sign of Walker?"

"No, sir."

"Look, Abdul. Can you think of someone who could go from Malia to Haifa and inform Mr. Townsend and Captain Peters of what's happened?"

"I could go."

"No. I want you here."

"It's not a problem. I can send someone to speak to Father Nicephor. He has a motorcar. Not a very good one, but it can get to Haifa."

"Yes. That's what I was thinking. Would you do that, please?"

"I'll go now."

"Good fellow! When you've done that, I want you to organise a watch. I want men on all sides of the castle and a group to join Salah at the camp.

They sat on the castle wall, gazing across the valley to the south. There was no movement except for the gentle sway of the breeze through the branches and an occasional flight of birds. After some time, Abdul returned and spoke with the workers. Then he came over to Riley.

"I have sent a man up to the village and have spoken with the workers. They will set up a guard here, and in the camp as you asked. I went down to see Salah. He said that he had not seen anyone and heard nothing until the explosion. He is very frightened. I told him not to worry and that we will send some men down to join him."

"Good." said Riley. "You had better do that now. The boy has had enough of a fright already." As they spoke, several of the men, some of them armed with rifles, took up positions on the walls to the north and south; two of them, using a rope ladder, climbed the high wall on the west from where they would have an excellent lookout over the countryside.

"I guess we can get back to work," said Riley. Turning to Abdul he said: "Listen. Mr. Palmer and I are going down into the cistern again. You stay out here with the men. If you see anything at all, call us immediately."

"Yes, sir," Abdul answered.

"We will give you a shout if we need you."

Riley called for two of the younger workers to join him, and they climbed the stone stairs back up into the keep, then down the ladder into the cistern. Two hurricane lamps were lit, and attention focussed once more on the alcove. Using a crowbar, Robert knocked off the remaining plaster. It came away in a single piece, like a thick white board. They could now see the full size of the blocked opening –it was large enough for a man to stoop and enter. With the crowbar he began to loosen the stones blocking the entrance. One of the boys helped him to pry the stones loose. It was hard work and created a great deal of dust, which hung in the still air. Although the blockage looked as if it should be fairly easy to pull apart, the stones turned out to be very closely set, and it took considerable effort to loosen them. Eventually they managed to lever them loose and with a final knock send them thumping down into the space beyond the blockage. Robert climbed onto the narrow ledge and peered into the opening they had made.

"You won't believe this," he said with a wry smile on his face.

"There's another layer of stones behind it! The entrance is still completely blocked."

He got down and Riley climbed up to look in.

"You're right. There's nothing to be done. We will have to knock out all of these stones and then get to work on that layer."

"That's going to take a long time. I am beginning to think we have raised our hopes too high. There may be nothing but more stones."

"That wouldn't make any sense. Why would anyone go to all this trouble if there is nothing there? This opening is carefully built. And consider... why is it here in the first place... in a water cistern? Look how much trouble they went to, blocking it and then hiding it with the plaster. It has to be important."

"You would think so," answered Robert. "Pay no attention to me," he laughed. "It's just that this seems to be so big, and of late I have come to expect disappointments."

Robert was thinking of something else. In spite of the excitement that the discovery of the secret opening in the cistern had aroused, he still found his mind wandering back to the recent disappointment in his personal life.

"I can't believe you're going to be disappointed this time."

"What do you think we are likely to find?"

"I've no idea. But to be so well hidden... it seems that it could only be something that was considered to be of great value. What I find strange is that this cistern must have been out of use, at least while this entrance was open. If there was water in it, access to the passage, or chambers, or whatever is beyond this wall would have been difficult... or impossible."

"That's true."

"Which means that there would have been little or no water for the defenders if they were holed up in the keep during a siege.

That would have been an unacceptable situation. Surely the keep would have had to have an independent water supply."

"There may be an answer to that," said Robert. "Take a look over here."

Holding one of the lamps, Robert showed Riley something he had noticed earlier when the men had brought in the hurricane lamps. On one side, against the wall of the chamber where the workers had exposed a section of the stone flooring there was a square-shaped aperture blocked with soil. With the lamp held directly above it, the opening became more obvious.

"I thought I noticed this earlier, but with the excitement of the discovery I didn't really pay attention to it. Don't you think it might be a shaft down to a second cistern located further below this chamber?"

"I suppose that is possible. Yes. You could be right! Well done, Robert," Taking up one of the picks Riley swung it and struck the soil, which came away and even subsided. It seemed indeed that this was indeed debris that had collected in what had formerly been an open shaft.

By nightfall they had made some progress at the blocked arch, but the opening was still too small to allow access; it would have been possible to continue using lamps, but they reluctantly decided to call it a day. It was tiring work and they were anxious to know if there was any word from Haifa. Riley had Ra'ed organise a guard to keep watch on the keep through the night and the two men made their way down the hill to camp.

At sunrise the following day they were back up at the keep. Before getting down to work, they sat in the cool mountain air drinking Turkish coffee. Riley set down the small china cup.

"Ra'ed says Townsend and the police will be here this morning. I will be glad to have that worry out of our hands."

"It won't be, unless they manage to catch him," said Robert. "The fellow seems to have the ability to vanish into thin air."

"Well, at least we won't have to have our men guarding the place, and we can get back to some of the other work that still needs to be done. Anyway, being down in the cistern without knowing what is happening up here is not at all satisfactory."

He slowly pulled himself to his feet, took the cup and threw the coffee grinds out over the edge of the platform, then walked over to the wooden ladder that protruded from the hole in the floor. "Get the lamps, would you."

"We left them down there yesterday. Don't you remember?"

Following Riley, Robert climbed down the ladder into the darkness. The workers had begun to arrive. Ra'ed with two other men joined them, and they were soon back to work, loosening the stones in the blocked arch. As they worked their anticipation was re-awakened. After about an hour they had managed to take down nearly all the stones of the outer layer. Behind it, by the light of the lamps they could now see the inner face of a wall a foot or so back, covered with mud-mortar that seemed to have been hastily thrown against it. This had to be chipped away before they could effectively work on the inner construction. Ra'ed had some picks lowered into the cistern, and two of the workers began hacking away at it. There was little space to manoeuvre on the narrow ledge they had cleared, and the mortar was so hard that parts of the stones they had removed earlier still adhered to it. Every so often Robert took over from one of the workers. After most of the mortar had gone, they got to work again with crowbars, loosening the rocks near the top of the alcove arch. When one of these stones was loose, Robert tried to ease it out with his hands, but when this failed, he instead—as he sometimes did with a difficult cork in a wine bottle—pushed it in, using the back end of the pick shaft. The rock flew easily back and disappeared with a thump, leaving a dark hole.

"No Robert. Don't do that!" said Riley. "We don't know what's behind. If there is anything fragile you might damage it."

"Yes, of course," said Robert. "Sorry. But look. It went some way in. This is a deep recess. Perhaps a chamber... or a passage!" To pry free the stone next to the one he had pushed in, he knocked it back and forth, then pulled it carefully out and handed it down to one of the workers, who dropped it to the floor. The stone next to that was likewise dislodged, and now the hole was big enough to peer into. Riley passed him up a lamp. The atmosphere in the dark vault was electric. Robert lifted the lamp and held it in as far as he could reach, looking past it into the depths of the space that was exposed in the yellow light. It was not strong enough to illuminate very far beyond the entrance. Nonetheless, he could see what appeared to be a narrow, low-ceilinged chamber. On the floor of the chamber were some shapeless dark forms, but these could easily be fallen rocks. From the little he could see, the chamber appeared to be empty, though in this light he could not make out its far side.

23 REFUGE

The noise of the fighting became louder and more fearsome. No one had remained in the chapel; all the brothers had either gone to take refuge in the upper level or had fled to other parts of the castle. At one point an arrow whistled right through the narrow shaft at the end of the embrasure and barely missed striking the prone figure of the old man. I tried again to wake him, but he was in a deep sleep. He had become very cold, and his breath was loud and uneven. I gently shook him again and finally he opened his small watery eyes and gazed up blearily into my face.

"My son… it is you?" he asked. "Praise God!" He smiled weakly, I felt faint. He thought that I was Bernard. "I knew that I would find you," he said very softly. I tried to correct him but he merely repeated: "My boy. My dear, dear boy." I held my tongue. Perhaps this was better. He closed his eyes then and fell back into a slumber. I lifted him gently into a sitting position, surprised at how light his small body was. I did not even try to waken him again and nothing would shake the oblivion that had engulfed him. I pulled him as far away as possible from the arrow-slit and carefully lay him back down against the embrasure wall. He was almost motionless, only the faint rising and falling of his frail ribcage and an almost in-audible whistling breath exhaled from his half-open mouth. I took his thin hand and could feel the weak beating of his heart. Quite suddenly I remembered the death of my father that for so long I had put out of mind.

At this point a small group of knights and unarmed men came in a noisy rush down the staircase and entered the chapel through the open arched door in the wall opposite our embrasure. As they passed through one of them looked across the chapel into the passage where I was sitting at the edge of the embrasure holding the old knight. He came across as the others ran out towards the western door. It was the boy, Thomas.

"Why are you sitting here?" he asked.

"What am I to do?" I said, gesturing at the old man who lay against me.

"What has happened to him?"

"He is ill. He is dying."

"Then you should leave him," he said. "You need to save yourself."

"I can't leave him."

"Then take him to the upper chamber before they seal the door. The brothers up there are preparing for a last stand."

"What are you going to do?"

"We are going to try to get away before the Saracens break in. You must join us. It will be soon now. The castle is about to fall."

"I don't know what I should do."

"Come with us. The Saracen troops are all ranged on the south and west. There don't appear to be any on the north. It may be possible to escape down the hill into the valley."

As we spoke the sounds of the battle were becoming louder and the walls shook. Through the embrasure the sulphurous air was heavy with smoke and ash. There was no doubt in my mind that the fall of the fortress was rapidly approaching, and I thought about what would happen if I remained. Albert was certainly at death's door. At least he would be spared whatever terrible fate was in store for the rest of us if we fell into the Saracens' hands. I regretted that we had not tried to get away earlier. I had waited too long.

"Let me help you take him up," said Thomas, "…quickly, before they seal the door."

Thomas and I carried him up the stairs but at the top we found that the massive wooden door had already been sealed and bolted from within. No one answered when we shouted and pounded upon it. The iron plates nailed to it must have muffled the sound of our banging and there was an inner door beyond it. It was hopeless. Even if they had heard us, they might have thought that we were the enemy. I shamefully admit that fear overwhelmed me now. I felt like a trapped animal. The Saracens would enter the chamber below and kill us here in this narrow staircase. We carried Albert back down and gently laid him back on the embrasure floor. He was entirely cold now and not responding at all; I was almost certain he was already dead. After some moments of hesitation, I followed Thomas down the stairs and out of the tower. As I stepped out I suddenly felt quite weak and realised that I had had nothing to eat for over a day. I had not even thought about food until then. But there was no time. We hurried across to the main door that led out to the north. The battle noises were still muted on this side. I could see some brothers entering from the western part of the castle. This was a relief, for in my terror I had become quite certain we were already alone. My fears had raced ahead of me. We stopped at the gate, and as we waited there I tried to calm myself. My thoughts returned to the old man: perhaps he was still alive. Could I be certain that he was dead? How could I leave him? I began to believe that I had not checked sufficiently whether he had truly stopped breathing. I turned to Thomas:

"I'm going back," I said.

"What? Where are you going?"

"I have to be certain he is really dead,"

"He is dead!" he answered.

"I must go back!"

"No, Squire Hermann. It will be too late."

"Don't wait for me, Thomas. I will be alright."

In truth I was terribly afraid. I ran and climbed the stairs again. Albert's body was as we had left it, lying on my spread cloak on floor of the embrasure. I went over and took his wrist but felt no rhythm of the heart. I held my hand over his open mouth and against his nose. I could feel no breath, and I knew now that he was gone. Sorrow opened in me like a chasm, so great that for the moment I forgot my fears. I lifted the body, light as a small animal. Hesitant as to what I should do, I carried him further into the embrasure, then lay him gently on the floor. Would there be an opportunity to return and take the body away for burial? Then I ran back down the stairs. I could not see Thomas. He might have made his escape, but I wondered if perhaps he had entered the service rooms to the west. I passed through the kitchen and cellars calling his name, but there was no response. The walls were shuddering as missiles struck with increasing frequency. Heavy thuds reverberated from above and dust shook loose from between the stone joints in the walls and the vaulting. I turned back and made my way through the empty basement chambers and out to the gate, reaching it just as a shower of arrows rained down on the open space outside. It would be dangerous to cross it: even if I were not struck by an arrow, I might have to make my way on my own beyond the tower gate; a disconcerting thought. Perhaps I would fall into a trap. It was possible that the Saracens had by now moved guards to this side. Perhaps they had occupied all the hills around the castle.

When I stepped out into the doorway to take a better look, I saw for the first time the full horror of what the battle had wrought. In the space between the inner and outer walls were many prostrate bodies lying as they had fallen in the rain of arrows. None of them moved. There were no injured; all were dead. There must have been thousands of arrow shafts, and the soil where the dead lay was dark with blood pooled around the bodies.

My legs began to shake uncontrollably. Finally, some other men arrived, and a debate began regarding the best course of escape. I listened to them, but looking across the bloody place, I could not believe that it would be possible to get through. Meanwhile there had been a lull in the fighting; the arrows had almost ceased to fall. Some of the men chose this opportunity to make a run for the outer gate. I have to admit that I was too scared to join them, and in my fear sought any excuse to remain where I was. I recalled the prisoners in the underground cells that we had passed when we first arrived at the castle and turned to one of the men nearby:

"What about the prisoners?" I asked. "Do you think they have been released?"

The man I spoke to was a brother I had seen several times in the refectory. He looked at me uncomprehending.

"The prisoners?" he asked.

"The people incarcerated in the cells below the Great Hall," I said. "Do you think they have been released?"

"I don't know," he answered, as if it were a matter of small importance.

"Should we not see?"

"No!" He seemed annoyed by my suggestion. "There is no time. Do you want to be killed?"

"But we cannot just leave them."

"They will have been released. Anyway, we don't have the keys. We could not help them if we did go back."

"I don't know," I said. "I will go to see."

"Don't be a fool," he said. "There is nothing you can do for them." But my fears were so great that I would rather turn back than venture out into that open space of death. I hurried back through the basement, further than before, and saw what I had not seen then. Some of the dust had settled and to my horror I saw that parts of the vaulting had collapsed, leaving a great gap in the ceiling through which I could see the destruction of the upper chamber, where even the sky was visible through the collapsed roofing. I went out through a portal and took the path down to where, I recalled, the subterranean cells were located. The height of the Great Hall protected this path from missiles, but the thick smoke and dust burned my eyes, and I could hardly see my way. As I ran, more knights came fleeing from the southern defences. I was pushed aside and nearly flung down as they passed. I went on, and finding the cell windows, called into the dark. There was no sound from within. When I pushed at the great wooden door it gave way easily and I realised that the prisoners had indeed been released.

It now occurred to me that I was probably one of the few people still in this part of the castle. I turned back the way I had come, and when I reached the doorway to the north, I heard my name called. It was the boy, Thomas. He stood across the open space at the outer portal.

"Quickly Brother," he shouted. "You must hurry." He was signalling for me to cross, and I almost began, but hesitated again, seeing the bloody bodies in the bailey. The shame of my utter terror and panic is still with me. When I finally found courage, it was the wrong moment. As soon as I began to sprint across that open space, I heard the terrible sound above, and the air was again alive with a great whooshing and hissing, then the clatter and ping of iron striking stone all around me. I ran across what seemed an endless space, hearing the cries of someone calling out nearby.

"Take cover! Take cover!"

I felt the first sharp, burning blow on my left shoulder and was knocked and wheeled around by the sudden pain. Then another flash of heat on my thigh, and another. I cried out, surprised by the sound of my own voice. I raised my hands to protect my face, and still on my feet tried to reach the outer wall. Then my legs buckled, and I sank to the ground, trying not to fall on my wounded arm and leg, but the shafts in my thigh were thrust in deeper, and I twisted in agony. My vision clouded and I must have lost consciousness. When I came to, the pain was like a great heat.

There came another lull in the firing, but I could not drag myself to safety. I could hear Thomas calling to me. He sounded far off, and I felt the rapid drumming of my heart as faintness overcame me and I lost consciousness again.

There was darkness all around me, but then a small light, a whiteness gradually appeared, and began to spread, and grew increasingly whiter. I thought I could still make out objects—trees, walls—but all substance was disintegrating. I became convinced that I was dying, though I could see vague forms again, perhaps the bodies of the dead that had fallen around me. Yet as I glanced about, this too dissolved into the whiteness and there was no form, and the whiteness was spreading over everything.

Then I felt hands upon me. I was mortally afraid, but slowly grew calmer with the certainty that this was not a thing to be feared, not the whiteness, not the hands that were lifting me and carrying me out of that place of death. A warm sensation, which began in the places where I had been hurt, spread like the light till it filled my whole being. I felt I was rising above and away from the place where I had fallen. The light enveloped me like a soft and gentle caress, and it turned from white to gold, and it seemed that I had been taken from the battlefield and set down in a vast field of grain that stretched as far as the eye could see. Above me the sky was a deep blue. An absolute peace came over me. It occurred to me that I must indeed have died, and curiosity made me wish to raise myself up and look about, though I knew, that I could not do so, that I was no longer a physical being and that my bodily form had been replaced by this non-corporeal warmth.

As I became aware of these things the heavens gradually darkened. Heavy clouds came racing in from the distance, black and terrifying, and with them a horrific rushing sound that grew louder and louder. I heard a distant howling like that of wolves, and numberless black ravens or bats came, filling the sky in swirling masses that spread until they covered the entire firmament, then descended and swarmed around me. And as the heaven and earth turned black, the golden field turned black as well. As I was certain now that I was indeed dead, I understood that I was not to be in heaven, then, but in purgatory, and with this knowledge I was overcome with intolerable sorrow, loneliness, and remorse. I recalled my sinful life, my faithlessness, how I had abandoned those who loved me, and I wept in repentance, though without tears, for I had no eyes, and no sound issued as I had no mouth.

Then, as I looked on, the black flying creatures turned into ash, and a fresh wind came up and scattered it about, blowing it across the plain, off the rocks and cliffs and out into the caverns and rifts. It rose and then it was gone, and the sky grew steadily blue again. The field became golden once more and I knew that I was going to live. Someone touched my shoulder. It was Albert. He stood bending over me and he was his old self, his face radiant. He told me that I need have no fear, and I believed him.

I was later told that I had been dragged out of the open area and into the shelter of the forest. With great bravery and at considerable risk, I and the other wounded had been carried down through the gate of the lower enceinte, escaping on the northern side of the castle hill. Because of the steepness of the hill and the thickness of the forest, this side of the castle remained open, and the men passed unseen, within a stone's throw of the battling Saracens. Following a path along the stream to Casal Imbert, the retreating group then turned southward to Acre.

Many of our brothers were killed in the battle. Those who were taken prisoner when the castle fell were later escorted back to Acre by the sultan, and there released in an unusual gesture of compassion (unusual for, although their release had been agreed upon between the defenders and the Saracens if the former laid down their weapons, such promises of the sultan had often been broken). The grand commander must have died in the castle, for he did not return with the garrison and his body was not seen by those who returned. Nor did anyone recall having seen him. But I recalled that last time that I saw him, descending into the cistern followed by the castellan. I had not seen him emerge when the castellan did so, but he surely must have done so. As for the castellan, he did not survive the battle and I think few regretted his loss. He had been among those struck by arrow-fire in the place where I had fallen.

I imagine that the body of poor Albert remained where I left him, deep in the embrasure. I have often wondered about this. It was in heavy shadow, and it is possible that no one would have seen him there. The Saracens broke into the great tower and attacked the barricaded brothers. I have since spoken to some of the knights and sergeants who were captured and later allowed to return to Acre. No doubt they had been too fearful at the time to take in anything around them, but none of them recalled seeing the body. It may still have remained deep in the embrasure when, a few days later, the Saracens began to bring the tower down. The sultan made certain that we learned of his dismantling of the castle. It was told that there hardly remained stone upon stone. If this report is true, then the old knight must lie buried beneath the rubble of that great edifice.

24 WALKER'S DIARY

Walker's diary from the torn-out pages, written in a shaky hand and strained, perhaps with whiskey

One good thing about this business is that I can drink this whiskey without anyone criticising me… and it's pretty good stuff! Perhaps I'll save the bill for Mister John Riley. Ha! Why not?

I suppose that was not too bad for a first assault. That is all it was… a first assault. But it is a pity it didn't do more damage. I thought that the whole wall would topple down. I wish I knew more about explosives. Anyway, next time I'll use more. I am going to knock down that entire blasted castle!

There is something else that bothers me. What was it that had caused the workers to remain on the site during their break? Something must be going on in the keep! They must have discovered something of importance. If so, I have to find out what it is. There is no way that I am going to let that American get the better of me. He will pay for what he had done. If he has made a big discovery, I am determined to sabotage it. Then perhaps I'll deal with Riley himself.

God, this whiskey is good…

I need to think about what I should do next. They are bound to have extra guards on after today, and they will certainly get the police in again. If they have found something of value, it will not be left unguarded. I should deal with that first… before it's too late. I'll just have to take care of the guard. I'm not afraid of using force if that is the only way.

Yes, perhaps someone will even have to pay with his life. That isn't my fault… Everything could have been different. He could have shown me some respect. But what can you expect? The American is a fool! It's Gilford who's really to blame. He, at least, should have known better than to put an amateur in charge. And then to take his side against me! I can't believe how he was taken in. And to have me arrested! Me! It is so unfair. Sometimes I feel I'm going to explode at these injustices… At least I can write all this down. It helps. This way I will not forget. I will not forgive them. Not Gilford and certainly not Riley. Why, I might even kill Riley!

Damn, damn. Must get hold of myself. It's this whiskey. I should drink less… But it is so good. Yes. I might kill him. Why not? It would be justified. He calls himself a father… my father! Ha! He should be made to pay for what he has done to me… even with his life… Some father… some… some… Wait, no… no, I don't mean him. Riley. Damn it. It's Riley. He should die. The whiskey is confusing me. Riley should die. Yes. But he would have to see everything in ruin first. He would have to know that he is about to die… and that it is because of what he did to me. How can I make certain he knows?

I might destroy the entire castle. Blow it to smithereens. Riley will be aware of who is behind the destruction, but he won't be able to do a damned thing about it!

No! It's not enough. He has to pay with his life. That is

*the only way to overcome the humiliation. I have to do it – I
have to kill him.*

*I must not forget to destroy these notes. But not quite yet.
They help me make my decisions.*

25 A LETTER

A letter written by Moufazzal

(Author's note: This description is based on a recently discovered letter written by Mufaddal ibn Abi'l-Fadā'il [Moufazzal], a Coptic Christian who lived during the reign of Sultan al-Nāsir. He is known for his history – **Al-Nahj al-Sadīd wa al-Durr al-Farīd fī mā Ba'd Tārīkh ibn al-'Amīd** [edited by E. Blochet Paris, 1920] – a work describing the life of the Sultan from the time of his coming to power [i.e., it is a continuation of Ibn al-'Amīd's history that ends at the beginning of the Sultan's Baibars' reign]. In this letter Moufazzal describes to an unknown recipient, the Sultan's actions in Syria in the summer of 1271. The language is rather poor, the sentences are disjointed and there are numerous grammatical errors, and it is doubtful perhaps whether Moufazzal ever intended to include this description in his history, if indeed it predates that work. Aside for its descriptive value, the chief significance of the letter lies in the fact that, whereas in his history Moufazzal follows closely earlier sources such as Muhyī al-Din, Ibn Shaddād, Ibn Wāsil and Baibars al-Duwaidar, the information found in this letter, or at least in the section in it pertaining to the destruction of al-Qurain [Montfort Castle], is *not found in any of the other fourteenth and fifteenth century histories, so that it almost certainly preserves some earlier lost source. The complete text of this letter was recently published by Professor Walid al-ʻUmari in JMS vol. II 13, 2004 pp. 213-22.)*

This is how the castle of the Franj was destroyed by Sultan al-Malik al-Zāhir Rukn al-Dīn Baibars al-Bunduq-dārī al-Sālihi. The Sultan gave orders for the dismantling, and sappers were set to work at various places on the lower walls along the north side and below the great building on the south, while other men cut quantities of timber and brush and carried these into all of the chambers. These were stacked into piles in the centres of each chamber on all levels and were set alight. Meanwhile, one group of sappers using ladders, set to work dismantling the wall below the Great Hall. They worked there for a full day, but the stonework was so solid that they hardly made any headway. The Sultan was greatly vexed by the slow progress of their work and in order to encourage them he promised a reward of a gold dinar for every stone they removed. The stones of this wall were not large, but the mortar that the cursed Franj had used in its construction was extremely hard and the sappers had only managed to pluck out smaller stones in a level section running near the base. They ceased work when falling rubble and ash from the fires above became a hazard, temporarily abandoning the position with the intention of returning later.

These fires, after they were set, first on the upper levels and then on the ground floor, caught rapidly, and the men who had been charged with igniting them were impelled to flee, rushing out of the buildings, and distancing themselves down the hill to the south where they stood below the Sultan's tent to watch the effects of their work. In the cellars the flames raced up the piles of timber and brush, and quickly spread to the wooden mezzanine. The whole level exploded in a tempest of flame and swirling smoke that filled the vaults and poured out with a tremendous roar through the ground floor windows, throwing sparks and ash into the air. The upper floor took longer to catch fire, there being fewer inflammable furnishings on that level, and the piles of wood burned within for some time before the flames spread and began to do any real damage to the structure. The fires burned throughout the afternoon and the night, lighting up the whole valley between the surrounding hills in a bloody red glow. By morning, the ground floor was beginning to show signs of imminent collapse, but the fires had fairly much burned themselves out and the men waited till early afternoon when it was possible to enter the castle again and then set about introducing more timber into the basement and setting it alight for a second time. The result of this was surprisingly immediate. As soon as the new fires were fully ablaze the greatly weakened superstructure collapsed in a tremendous roar of dust and ash that piled up into the sky in a tumult of rolling grey and black in the form of a giant dragon that spread out, and then settled slowly down onto the upper slopes of the hill. Never before had such a sound been heard in these hills. The large stones of the outer walls rolled down the slopes, those to the north and west came crashing up against the outer walls, collapsing the wooden beamed roofing of the structures inside the wall and piling up on their ruins as high as the top of the wall and its battlements. Parts of the outer wall then collapsed under the strain and all of the stone and rubble that had gathered up behind it crashed down the slope. After the destruction of the central part of the castle, came the turn of the great building to its west. The sappers returned and continued to work on the horizontal trench they had excavat-

ed into it. They managed to deepen it considerably in spite of
the iron-like hardness of the mortar, but the wall above still
showed no sign of weakening and eventually they abandoned
these efforts altogether.

Nonetheless, the Sultan was very pleased with the thor-
oughness of destruction. The interior of the castle was entirely
destroyed. The fire in the western building spread rapidly. Piles
of brush that had been placed there and the left-over naphtha from the Greek fire that was poured onto these, ignited
with ease, burning with a brilliant vigour. There were enough
wooden furnishings to help set a tremendous blaze. The heat
shattered those of the glazed windows that had survived the
blows of our mangonels, and the fire in the vaults roared like
wild beasts. This gave the Sultan, who was witnessing the dismantling from across the valley, great pleasure. From his tent
the conflagration appeared like a great, three-horned crown. It
swept through the western building until its vaults collapsed,
bringing down two stories, the upper one being where the lead-
er of the Franj was wont to reside. In this palace the painted
plaster blackened and peeled from the stone. Wooden tables
and benches blazed and crumbled, flame ran through cloth,
lamps shattered and fell. The weight of the collapsing vaults
brought down the walls on three sides, and with them the
north and south walls of the basement where only the great
barrel vaults remained standing and where a huge pier that
had held up the rest remained at last, on its own like a monument to the sultan's glory.

In the end only the tower on the east remained standing. It
was now all the more impressive for its great height against the
shattered ruins. The Sultan had intentionally kept the tower
for last, and he himself took charge of its destruction, coming
down from his tent for the first time since the work had be-

gun. He regarded this as the most important part of the dismantling as it would finally and for all time render the castle
unusable. This had been his procedure in many other towns
and castles that we had occupied. He had no intention that the
Franj should have the opportunity of returning with a strong
army to reoccupy their castles as they had done in the time
of Salāh ad-Dīn Yūsuf ibn-Ayyūb. If the Franj should return
they would find no walls standing and no vaults remaining.

The walls of the great tower were ten paces in width, and
it was constructed of enormous cut stones, perfectly joined and
filled with hard white mortar and rubble fill. For the destruction of this building the Sultan called in more teams of sappers and had battering rams wheeled up through the broad
moat at the base of the tower. The men were at work for a
whole day and most of the next, the Sultan himself carrying
stones and working the crowbars. When enough undermining
had been done the massive structure opened out like a flower.
The men ran for cover and there was a moment of eerie silence
followed almost immediately by a growl like that of an earth
tremor or a caged beast. The immense stones came down on
the south and north, crashing through the lower walls, piling
up or pitching down onto the ruins and into the moat. The
men shouted in delight, but their shouts were drowned by the
roar of the collapsing tower. The walls at the base that had not
been damaged by the rams were forced out in whole sections
with the tremendous weight of the collapsing tower, and the
stones and mass of rubble shook the whole valley as the tower
fell. Although the dismantling had been carefully planned, it
came down so suddenly that a number of men were unable
to get away in time and were buried under it, may God have
mercy on them. Stones larger than the size of a man plummet-
ed down the hills into the valley to the south where the men

ran for cover. Some of the stones fell all the way down on the southern side then continued in the hollow of the valley to the west. Others collapsed down the steep slope to the north, some of them falling onto the roof of the mill that the Franj had erected by the river, causing that structure to collapse as well.

26 ENLIGHTENMENT

Ra'ed brought down additional lamps. Robert and Riley came down from the ledge and one of the men was put to work on the wall, using in turns an iron bar to loosen the mortar and a pick. He worked for half an hour before any real progress was made. Then, quite suddenly and unexpectedly a large part of the obstruction came away, and the opening was big enough to step into. Riley passed up the lanterns for Robert, who climbed up and managed to squeeze through. He found himself in a narrow passage or elongated chamber that extended back for at least as far as the frail yellow lamplight. Apart from some large stones near the entrance, all he could see were a number of ceramic sherds on the floor. Robert bent down and picked up a few. They had a dark green, shiny glaze. There were also pieces of glass, likewise greenish in hue, with an iridescent patina like fine gold that flaked away at the touch. It appeared he was standing in some kind of passage. But a passage to what?

Riley called from below:

"Don't leave us in suspense, Robert. What do you see?"

"Well … nothing actually. Just a few rocks, I think, and a bit of broken glass and pottery."

"How far can you see in?"

He stepped into the dark and held the lamp out ahead of him.

"Not far. Only a few yards."

"Does it look very deep?"

"I can't really tell from here. Come up and take a look."

Riley climbed up the ladder onto the ledge, pushing himself through the remains of the blockage, and Robert made room for him, passing him the lamp. Riley held it at arm's length in the opening and looked in.

"So…" asked Robert, "what do you think?"

"It's quite narrow."

"Well… you can only see the opening. It could broaden out. And there may be something further back. You can't see enough with this light. Ra'ed," he called, "pass up the other lamps."

The workers handed up additional lamps and the light in the passage was substantially increased. They could now make out the stonework of the walls and the ceiling, which was formed of large blocks of stone set like a gable.

"I'm going in to see how far it goes. Take a look at these."

Robert handed Riley the sherds and pieces of glass that he had picked up and taking a lamp in each hand he began to move back into the passage. The light of one of the lamps flickered out and he tripped over some obstacle on the floor, almost losing his balance. It was only a stone. Next to it he saw more broken glass and something thin and elongated which he picked up. It was a tube, red brown in colour and looking like rusted iron. He moved on several yards. Then he saw something small moving in the light of the lantern and, holding it towards the ceiling, he found that he was not alone: the roof of the passage was occupied here and there by some long-legged spiders that, as the light fell upon them, broke into a nervous shaking on their webs.

"There must be another opening," he said. "The air is not as close as you would expect if this chamber had been blocked for centuries. It seems to go on for some way."

"Wait a minute, Robert," said Riley. "I'll join you."

Thoughts of hidden treasure were receding, but their anticipation and excitement had in no manner declined. Riley took his lamp and followed Robert, carefully sidestepping the stone over which Robert had tripped, and they began to advance together deeper into the passageway. A thick layer of dust rose around their feet as they moved. After the first few steps the passage had begun to slope very slightly downwards, and every few yards there was a shallow step, hardly noticeable because of the thick accumulation of dust.

"What do you think," said Robert.

"I wonder if we are not perhaps in some sort of escape route."

"You recall that Walker had mentioned something about the villagers believing there was a secret passage from the castle down into the valley."

"If I had not seen this, I wouldn't put much weight on anything Walker might have said," said Riley.

"No. But it does appear that he may have been right about this. Perhaps the villagers have been down here sometime."

"Now that I think of it," said Riley, "in the mail that you picked up for me there was a copy of a nineteenth-century description of the castle that recorded a subterranean passage descending to the mill. We should ask Ra'ed if he knows anything more about these tales of the villagers."

"But there is something quite odd here. I mean, if it was an escape route, why would it have been sealed? It seems to me that the work of blocking it so carefully would only make sense if it had been built not as an escape passage but in order to hide something… something of great importance, with the hope, perhaps, of eventually getting back and recovering it."

"Or alternatively, it was originally intended as an escape route, but for some reason at the last moment it was used in order to hide something."

They took more steps, altogether about twenty paces from

the opening, and there was now a deeper layer of soft dust on the floor that billowed and filled the small space, making breathing increasingly difficult. They took care to tread softly. In the light of their lamps, they could now see a wall ahead of them, and a narrow, arched opening. There was room for only one of them to pass through it. Riley took the lead, and in the light from his lamp he found a narrow staircase descending from the arch. There were about six steps before he encountered an encumbrance of soil and dust entirely blocking the passage below him. He descended as far as he could: there was just a small gap left below the stone slabs that formed the roof of the passage. He turned back to Robert who was at the head of the stairs and asked him to call up one of the workers. There was not enough room in the passage for more.

Now began a slow process of clearing the staircase; slow because there was hardly any room to manoeuvre, but also because the air was rapidly filling with the soft grey dust. All three men were soon coughing, and even with a handkerchief tied over his face, Robert found it difficult to breath. Although it was quite cool in the passage, Robert saw that Riley's forehead was beaded with perspiration.

"Are you alright?"

"No. I don't think I am," Riley answered. He staggered and leaned against the wall. "This is a bit too confined for me. I'm going out. I need some air."

Another man climbed in after Riley had left and joined Robert and the first labourer, who had begun to scoop the soft dust into baskets and hand them back. Robert then passed them on to the new man. They worked like this for some time, filling the baskets and then passing them back to the men outside. Eventually breathing in the passage became impossible and they had no choice but to take a break to allow the dust to settle.

When the three men descended from the passage, Riley and

the other workers could not control their laughter. They were completely covered with dust, only their red eyes showing through where they had rubbed them clear.

"I think you fellows will be in need of a bath," laughed Riley.

"Yes. I rather think so," Robert answered between coughing fits. "We had better leave this till tomorrow."

They lifted the last of the baskets out of the cistern and covered the entrance with a board and some heavy stones. Riley, Robert, and the other men then took the path that circled the hill and followed it all the way down to where the stream formed a series of shallow pools. They stripped off and plunged into the cool water. While in the cistern they had lost all sense of time and it was already getting quite late. However, the water was a delicious pleasure, and they continued bathing till it became dark. Then they headed back to the camp.

27 REPORT

From Captain Peters' report

Walker waited eleven days for his next attack. He must have realised that he could not wait too long, and he would have been aware that the expedition was approaching its end. Possibly he thought that enough time had passed for our men to be caught off guard, perhaps he even thought they might have left the area. He chose a Sunday (27 June). I believe this was because he knew that there were no excavations on Sundays and normally only a single guard would be at the site.

We subsequently found the cave where he had been hiding, as I confirmed later from the diary he had kept throughout the time he remained at this cave. He had stored food and water there. He would have considered this an ideal hideout from many standpoints. For one thing, although it was a long way from the castle, it was also distant enough to be out of the range of our patrols. For another, the land around the cave is generally quite flat in all directions and it would have been a good vantage point to observe anyone approaching. He may have been here previously and seemed to have known that very few people passed this way. The weather was also in his favour. He appears to have slept against an outcropping outside the cave where there are some rather dense trees. There we found the remains of a campfire, cigarette butts and the half-empty crate of dynamite that had been stolen from the Carmel quarry. On the whole, this would have served as a fairly comfortable and convenient base.

Walker had clearly planned to carry out more than minor disturbances. He had enough explosives to cause real havoc and we know from his diary (attached pages) that he intended to physically harm Mr. Riley, apparently even considered killing him. He wrote there that he planned to reconnoitre first, to see where an explosion would do serious damage and to find a hidden location to shoot from. When we later found his pack, it contained fifteen sticks of dynamite neatly wrapped in paper and cloth, together with safety matches, a length of fuse, a canteen of water and a small pick.

28 UNCOVERING

In the early morning a thick mist settled over the camp. Then the air began to clear, the mist moved up the hill, and by the time they had drunk their coffee and climbed up to the keep, it had mostly vanished. The day turned bright, and had it not been for the excitement of their discovery, they would have been reluctant to go back down into the cistern.

Soon they were in the passage again, removing the accumulated dust from the stairs. Riley put more men at work now and they were better equipped with handkerchiefs over their faces and a good supply of water in tin buckets, which they sprinkled on the ground to settle the dust before starting work. This proved to be effective, and they made steadier progress than on the previous day.

Robert worked on the staircase at the far end of the passage while the other men formed a chain, passing the baskets of soil back out into the cistern. Riley remained near the entrance, overseeing the lowering of the baskets. By midday they had cleared about thirty steps of the narrow staircase and still saw no end to it. Robert headed back to Riley, and they told the workers to take their lunch break, then climbed the ladder back into the brilliant daylight.

"I am convinced now," said Riley. "This must have been constructed as an escape route originally, whatever it may have been finally used for."

"Yes. So it would seem. But we still don't have any idea why it was blocked."

"Probably the only way we are likely to find the answer to that is by clearing out the whole thing."

"Do you think we have time for that?"

"The plan was to excavate for just one week more. I will have to go up to Jerusalem again to see if I can get an extension."

"Why not get Townsend out to take a look at the passage? He could inform Professor Gilford and explain to him the need for an extension. It would save you the trip."

"Yes. That's a better idea. Frankly, I'd rather not be absent just now."

"I wonder where the passage is going to lead to. I lost my bearings down there. Do you think it could really go all the way down to the stream?"

"Well… the opening is to the east, but the passage turns slightly north, and at the entrance to the staircase there is another half turn to the left, so I would say we are pretty much heading to the west. If there is another turn to the right, that will mean that we are heading north, down the slope. In that case, perhaps there really was a secret passage to the mill."

Riley was silent for a few minutes. He seemed to be trying to find the best way to say something. Finally, he spoke:

"Listen, Robert… I want you to go on from here with the digging. You and Ra'ed."

"What do you mean?"

"To tell you the truth, I am finding it too claustrophobic in there. I'm not good with closed places."

"Oh… I see. Well… it's not a problem."

"In any case, I would like to keep aware of what is going on outside; at least until we know what's happening with this Walker business."

"Alright. Perhaps I will take a few more workers to carry the debris back out of the cistern."

"Yes. Let's bring in the team that was working in the cistern. That will give you ten men. And another thing, Robert. I don't want you to take any risks. We don't know how deep this thing goes or how stable the roofing is. Remember, all the superstructure of the castle on the north side fell in this area. If at any time you feel uncertain, don't take any chances. Come back out and we'll decide how to go on from there."

In the afternoon, the men brought in stacks of baskets and digging tools and placed them on the side of the passage. They brought up more water in tin canteens and a number of hurricane lamps.

Riley had admitted to Robert his fear of being in the narrow confines of the passage but had not told him the extent of his phobia. This was partly out of embarrassment. He knew his limitations, and that he was not a brave man, and he accepted this as part of his character, but he did not always find it easy to admit the fact to others. There were three fears that he had experienced during the excavation: the first was a mild vertigo that had overcome him on the first day, when he climbed up to the top of the high wall dividing the two sides of the castle's central wing. His purpose had been to see the site from this vantage point, but also to test himself, to see if he could overcome a mild fear of heights.

His second fear was of snakes. Once, when they had first begun to excavate in the middle chamber of the castle, he had climbed up onto the thick outer wall on the southern side, intending to jump down to a level area a few feet below. He stopped and froze at the very edge. Directly below were two long, pale-coloured vipers entwined in a carnal act. He leapt back, overcome with terror, and had not had the courage to return to that spot since.

His third fear was one that had plagued him as a child when he heard stories about people who had been buried alive. An over-active imagination had allowed this last fear to reach extreme proportions. In adulthood he had to put this behind him, but on the few occasions when he did find himself closed in, the old panic returned. This had happened twice during the work in the chamber. The excitement of their discovery at first enabled him to overcome this anxiety, but he was greatly relieved when they had come out and it was something of a relief to admit his problem to Robert.

Judging the distance that they had advanced from the keep and the extent to which the passage descended and turned west, Robert estimated that they must now be working more-or-less below where the outer ward had been, against the outer fortifications, in the area that lay under the rubble of the castle's northern side. He estimated that the part of the outer ward they were under would be buried below collapsed stones and debris several yards deep.

They came now to a place where the passage appeared to level off. Taking a compass out of his pocket, Robert noted in the light of a lamp that it continued due west, which meant that it was running along the contour of the hill. They were entering a series of small, narrow chambers, each ending in two or three steps down to the next. There was nothing very remarkable in these chambers other than their existence, the fine quality of their construction and the fact that the first two were almost entirely clear of debris, even of dust. The floor of the third chamber, however, was covered with a thin layer of soil. It was groin-vaulted and a circular opening on the ridge of the vault was blocked with fallen stones and soil, and a fine network of hair-like roots hung down in the centre of the room, reaching almost to the floor. On the paving below the opening was a pile of soil that had fallen through, and a slow drip of water was seeping down from the stones. The plaster of the walls had long ago peeled away and disintegrated. They moved ahead, more quickly in this section because there was little need for clearing. They had additional lamps brought in, and some of these were left in the passage and chambers to increase the spread of the light. When they looked back, they could see part of the passage before it turned away and rose too high to be observed. After the third chamber, the passage narrowed again, still advancing west, evidently still under the outer ward. A short way further along they found that it was again partially blocked. They could hear water dripping in a dark open flue on the inner wall, which seemed to indicate a water source above, another cistern perhaps. Robert wondered whether the flue extended to another passage further down within the mountain. A pervading dankness filled the chamber, but the air was still breathable. They reached the end of this section on their knees because of the build-up of soil on the floor. When they had cleared enough to get through, they found that the passage then took a ninety-degree turn and began to descend once again, now to the north and down the mountain slope. From here it took the form of a narrow and steep staircase.

They had advanced only a short way before it was again necessary to remove the accumulated debris. This was becoming more difficult because of the considerable distance they had come and the narrowness of the passage. The human chain was no longer effective, and every so often they were compelled to stop work altogether and carry the collection of full baskets all the way back to the entrance of the passage in order to empty them. In places the passage was only just wide enough for one person to work in or pass through. Robert had one of the workers remain at the lowest point they had reached. The others were organised to carry the full baskets back. This resulted in a very slow pace in the clearing of the passage. It could perhaps have been alleviated by bringing in more workers, but Robert thought that conditions in the passage would become too difficult. In spite of the fact that the construction appeared to be sound, and in no place they had passed through did there appear serious damage, they could not be certain that part of the structure might not collapse.

They worked in this manner throughout the day. When Robert finally made his way back through the chambers and passage and climbed down into the cistern, he saw that Riley was not there. He turned to one of the workers who was carrying a basket over to the opening.

"Where is Mr. Riley?" The man did not understand. Robert climbed up the ladder into the brilliant daylight, rubbing his eyes as he emerged. Another worker was standing at the entrance preparing to descend in his place. He addressed his question to this man.

"He is not here, Mr. Palmer," the fellow answered.

"Yes. I can see that." Robert climbed the stairs from the keep down into the area that had been the kitchen. Two young labourers were sitting against one of the walls, smoking. When they saw him, they stood up and picked up their tools.

"Have either of you seen Mr. Riley?" They both shook their heads. "Where is Abdul?" They shook their heads again. He made his way across to the castle chambers, through the opening in the high wall and into the western hall. No one was there. He walked over to the edge of the platform that commanded a good view over the entire northern slope of the hill. No sign of anyone. He then walked around to the west and then to the southern edge; nothing there either. Looking down towards the camp in the distance, he could just make out a figure, apparently Salah, moving about between the tents.

29 REVELATIONS

Most of our wounded had been sent to the great hospital of Saint John, but it turned out that my wounds were not as grave as they had first appeared to be, and I was brought to the German infirmary. Nonetheless my recovery was slow. Looking at it in retrospect, I believe this was in part because of an illness of the mind that accompanied the physical one. As I lay in the infirmary my thoughts were constantly on poor Albert, and I was plagued by the guilt of having failed him. I felt that I had given him poor advice and that I had not had the wisdom to get him away from the castle in time. The idea of his poor body left in the tower haunted my nights.

Slowly I recovered from my physical injuries. I was no longer able to raise my left arm above shoulder height, and from that time I have walked with a slight limp. Brother Walther came to visit me in the infirmary, and it was from him that I learnt the true nature of the castellan's activities. My speculations regarding what I had witnessed at the castle were confirmed. He told me what he had learnt on the last day of the battle.

When the fighting had reached its peak, he had been on the inner defences, aiding the knights who were fighting a losing battle against the advances of the Saracens under the unceasing bombardment of their position. At one point, the marshal gave the order to fall back to the area of the inner gate below the Great Hall, and that was the moment when, like many others, Walther made the decision to attempt to save himself. He began then to make his way back through the castle.

By now the enemy had been heavily bombarding the area of the Great Hall and the domestic wing, causing considerable devastation to the upper levels of these two structures. When he was passing the entrance to the staircase that led up to the apartments of the higher dignitaries, Walther almost ran into the cellarer. Brother Matthew was a highly educated man, no less so than the castellan himself. At first, he had been Jordon's protégé, but in recent weeks, as I had myself witnessed at the chapters, he had come out in clear opposition to the castellan. His opposition had become more intense as the castellan grew increasingly secretive about his work. Matthew now came hurrying down the stairs from the castellan's apartments. There was smoke in the stairwell above him and a loud crashing sound as something collapsed. He was carrying in his arms several heavy tomes and a pile of vellum scrolls. Walther's curiosity was aroused and despite his haste he asked the cellarer what these were.

"I think you will not believe it if I tell you!" Matthew had answered. "Take a look at these!" and he laid the volumes and scrolls down on a large fallen stone. "I was sent," he said, "to retrieve these from Brother Jordon's apartment. I was told not to look at them and to show no one."

"But I see, brother Matthew, that you have done so nonetheless?"

"Well, brother," the cellarer had answered, "I no more trust the castellan than I imagine do you. But even I did not expect this."

"What have you found?" Walther asked him, and he answered excitedly:

"There are works by Albertus Magnus. Here is the fourth book of his *Meteora* and the *De rubus metallicis et mineralibus*. And there are also treatises on alchemy. Here is a part of Michael Scotus' *Ars Alchimie*, and these are translations of Arabic alchemical texts by

Gerard of Cremona, and the Latin translation by Robert Castrensis of the work of Morienus". He showed Walther the title: *Morieni Romani, Quondam Eremitae Hierosolymitani, de transfiguratione metallorum, et occulta, summaque antiquorum Philosophorum medicina, Libellus, nusquam hactenus in lucem editus.*

Walther was astounded:

"Brother Jordon was involved in alchemy?" he asked in disbelief.

"So it would seem," the cellarer answered. I think that our good castellan was not working on Greek Fire at all, or at least, not exclusively. I think he has been trying to make gold. That would explain the quicksilver and the sulphur that he had purchased, at great expense to the convent. I saw these items myself. How could I not have suspected this?"

"But, Brother Matthew…" said Walther, "Are you certain? Sulphur… is it not an ingredient in the Greek Fire? And quicksilver has many uses. And there was that loud noise coming from his garden, and the smoke. These treatises may be nothing more than evidence that he is a man with an inquisitive mind."

"Believe that if you wish," the cellarer answered. "I think that these texts are proof of his real interests. I did not find a single one relating to combustible liquids! And look at this, Brother." He took out of the stack of scrolls a leather bag and, opening the string that secured it, poured out onto the stone a pile of gold coins, necklaces and bracelets of turquoise, amber and gold. Had the castle not been collapsing around us, Walther told me he would have been astounded by the cellarer's audacity in taking those objects.

"Why does the castellan have these among his possessions?" brother Matthew had asked.

Walther answered that perhaps they were to pay for the purchase of materials for his experiments on weaponry.

"You are an honest fellow, Brother Walther," the cellarer returned, "but far too naive."

Walther asked what Brother Matthew intended to do. He

would, he said, at last be able to open the eyes of the grand commander, albeit too late to save the castle.

At that very moment, Walther told me, a horrible whistling had warned them of a renewed barrage. Matthew hastily gathered up the volumes and jewels and ran for cover. Walther noticed he had missed a chain of fine amber beads on the stone, but as he was about to reach for it, a great burst of flame in the stairwell above made him abandon the necklace and seek cover himself.

30 SECRETS

Just as Robert was despairing of finding him, Riley came up from the undercroft.

"There you are," he said. "I was beginning to worry that something had happened to you."

"Oh, I'm sorry. I was just below. I've been thinking about what we have found, and what we said earlier. We have a secret escape route that would have enabled the knights to get away into the valley during a siege. They must have spent a great deal of time and expense constructing it. And yet, not only did they not use it when the castle came under siege, but they blocked it from within, taking great pains to hide its entrance under the layer of plaster..."

"What if it was intended for the high-ranking officials to escape and was hidden by the garrison in order to cover their escape route before the castle fell?"

"That seems very unlikely. What would be the point? I can understand that they would conceal the outer exit into the valley, so that it would not be discovered by an enemy, but why hide it from the inside? Whoever sealed it would have had to have been in the secret but would not have been able to benefit from it. And think of the location. It was within the strongest building of the castle where the knights would make their last stand. This entrance would be discovered by the Muslims, if at all, only after the castle had fallen. By then, anyone using it would have had enough time to get away. It would no longer matter if it were found. No… It only makes sense if it was indeed, as we were thinking earlier, used to hide something."

"I suppose you are right," agreed Robert. "The only reason there could be for blocking the passage on the interior is if they had decided not to use it to escape. But then what were they hiding, and from whom? They… somebody… must have wanted to hide something that was within the passage, something that was not to be discovered by the enemy… or perhaps, by others in the castle."

"But we haven't found anything—even though, as you can see by the blockage of the entrance, it was never broken into!"

"Unless from another entrance. We have to go through it again. Whatever we are looking for might be farther along down the passage, or perhaps we have overlooked something."

"It's not very wide. If there had been anything to see, we would have seen it."

"Perhaps. But we didn't really examine the walls. And we didn't have much light with us. I think we need to take a second look at the section we have already cleared."

"Alright. I agree," said Riley. "We should buy some more lamps."

"When do you want to do it?"

"As soon as possible. I'll ask Ra'ed to get the lamps and we can go back over the passage systematically from the entrance, examining the walls, the floor and the ceiling."

"From what I could see, in many places the floor was the levelled bedrock."

"Perhaps not all of it. You mentioned seeing a flue down to a lower level. Anyway, if we're going to do this, we should make a thorough job of it."

"Sounds like a good plan."

Robert walked the length of the passage, advancing slowly, examining every surface. As he went, he picked up pieces of ceramics and glass and placed them in a basket. He found the rusted iron object that he had noticed earlier and examined it. It was very fragile and came apart in his hands. Close by was a second, similar object. It appeared to have once been part of a mechanical device of some type, like the interior of a lock mechanism. It had two thin flat bars, still held taught by a piece of copper. He placed it carefully in the basket. Then, quite unexpectedly, he found what they had been looking for.

Just before reaching the staircase at the end of the passage's first section, he noticed a slight change in the alignment of the wall. In the stronger light of the additional lamps, he saw what he had missed before. There was a blind arch on the wall, quite easy to see now. Once again it was partly covered with plaster, which over the centuries had crumbled away. It might be another passage or chamber. Examining it carefully, he saw it was not as carefully disguised as the outer entrance from the cistern. Perhaps, he thought, this one had been considered safe from discovery. Nonetheless, it too had been blocked.

Robert placed the lamps on the floor and pulled a small trowel out from his pocket. He began to work at the remaining plaster and the mortar that held the small stones within the arch. It was damp and soft, crumbling easily. Within a few minutes he was able to work one of the stones loose. Then holding a lamp up to the opening, he peered in. He could see nothing however, so he left it on the stone and headed back to call Riley.

"John. I think I've found what we're looking for. You should come."

With help from Ra'ed, Riley climbed up and followed Robert back through the passage. When they reached the lamps, Robert showed him the basket that was half full of broken shards and glass as well as the fragments of metal.

"Look at these. I hardly noticed them before." Riley looked over the items in the basket. Then he put it down and looked at the wall where the lamp stood. He immediately saw the blockage.

"It's déjà vu," he said. "What do you think this time? A second passage?"

"I have a feeling we are finally going to find out what this is all about."

"Perhaps." There was a hint of doubt in Riley's voice.

"You don't think so?"

"I don't know. I must admit that I'm a little sceptical now. I was almost certain we would find answers when we broke through from the cistern. Now I have a feeling, we are going to find more questions."

The stonework was much easier to break through than that of the entrance from the cistern, and after about ten minutes enough stones had been removed to enable them to crawl through and into the tenebrous space beyond. Robert climbed in first and gave a short cry. He had vanished into the dark and the light from his lamp flickered out.

"Robert! Are you alright?"

"Damn! Sorry… Yes, I'm alright. There are three or four steps here. I almost fell headlong." He appeared back at the doorway.

"Pass me another lamp. And mind the steps."

Riley passed in three additional lamps and climbed carefully through the doorway. The two men stood in the shadowy chamber and looked around. It was an oddly shaped room, almost round. The air was close with a heavy smell of mould. The ceiling was a low dome, at its edges about the same height as the passage but rising to the height of two men at the centre. When their eyes had adjusted, they could see that it was octagonal, or more precisely, square but with four very broad arch ribs, one in each corner. These arches rose from the angles to support the dome. Robert held up one of the lamps to examine the ceiling. At the meeting point of the four arch ribs there was a stone with a simple boss carved with an eight-pointed star. Between each point of the star was a roundel, and Robert remembered seeing this same design on a stone mould they had found under the chamber below the hall. On one side opposite the door, he saw a dark shape which, when he approached, turned out to be a large, dome-shaped brick oven with a chimney rising above it into the ceiling. Holding a lamp to the hearth, Robert found it was completely blocked with soil and small stones that must have come down the flue and spread onto the chamber floor. There was also a slight accumulation of debris, about a yard wide, around the perimeter of the room, but that was all. The floor was almost clear of dust. It seemed as if this chamber had hardly been affected by the passage of over six and a half centuries.

It was the debris around the walls that caught their attention as they took all this in. It contained many sharp, thin objects. Riley bent down and began to pull out of the dust large pieces of glass.

"Look at these!"

Robert joined him and together they began to pull more glass fragments from the soft dust heaping them in a pile. The glass was almost colourless with no patina, and in the lamplight appeared to have a faint green tinge. They were mostly slightly curved pieces, and some were flat but rising towards the centre.

"These look as if they were pretty large beakers," said Riley. "Industrial … laboratory vessels, I would say."

"These too," said Robert, clearing the dust from two small basalt mortars that lay side by side. "Do you think this might have been some sort of laboratory… a secret laboratory?"

"There's pottery here as well." Riley held out a few large shards, mostly glazed with a monochrome dark green. Among these were some pieces of friable, chalky ware with a thick alkaline glaze decorated with turquoise and dark blue designs. "These might be albarellos."

"Albarellos?"

"Yes. Jars that were used to hold chemicals, spices, and medicines. I've seen jars like this in the museum in New York."

They also found in the dust several pieces of metal, the same rusty red brown as those found earlier by Robert, and numerous viridian-coloured fragments of oxidized copper, some with distinct shapes: small cones tubes and rings. And there were some lumps of powdery substances, large yellow pieces of sulphur, others of white and grey and a vitreous black material. Suddenly Riley called excitedly.

"Robert. Take a look at this."

Riley was holding a small, spherical ceramic vessel. It had a conical base and narrow neck, and the mouth was blocked with what appeared to be unbaked clay. It was surprisingly heavy. Other similar vessels lay broken on the ground. Robert picked up a piece.

"Look how thick this is," he remarked, holding it up to the light. It had a grey, stone-like appearance. They placed the vessels with the growing pile of glass and metal objects and left a lamp beside these so as not to trip over them in the semi-dark.

As they moved around the room, their light fell on walls that had retained their original plaster, and they saw what at first appeared to be a varying pattern of fine dark incisions that covered the lower parts of the walls up to the level just above their heads.

"My God…" said Riley suddenly. "This is some type of writing!"

Robert took up his lamp and like Riley held it up to the wall. The light exposed masses of finely incised script together with various designs and patterns.

"This is remarkable! What do you think it is?"

"I have no idea."

They examined the walls more carefully.

"You know," said Riley. "Whatever this chamber was, there is no doubt that it was considered very important. Perhaps this writing has something to do with why it was concealed."

"Do you think this may tell us why the passage was blocked?"

"Perhaps… if we can find out its meaning…"

To make the most of the light, they held the two lamps close together. Almost every inch of the plaster on the lower parts of the wall was incised. Perfectly preserved, the inscriptions stood out quite clearly. Some dark substance, perhaps charcoal, had apparently been rubbed into them to make them more easily visible. On the other side of the room they found beside the chimney a small area had been left without graffiti: here a single design had been carefully incised near eye level. Unlike the written inscriptions, which were all formed using a fine stylus, this had been executed with a thicker implement. It consisted of two squares, one within the other and turned at a forty-five-degree angle to the outer square. Beside it were two smaller versions of the same design, one with the inner square the same size as the outer so that together they formed an eight-pointed star.

"I know that sign," said Riley. "It's the Philosopher's Stone."

"The what?"

"It's a symbol of alchemy. It represents the relationship between the four elements and four properties. You see … there are two squares, one inscribed within the other and placed diagonally to it so that its angles touch the mid points of the outer square. Each angle represents an element or a property". Riley pointed to the angles on the larger symbol. "The elements are fire, air, water and earth and the properties are hot, dry, moist and cold. According to Aristotle, air is primarily wet and secondarily hot, fire is primarily hot and secondarily dry, earth is primarily dry and secondarily cold, and water is primarily cold and secondarily wet."

"That's fascinating. But what does it mean?"

"Well, I'm not entirely sure … it was thought to be the formula for turning base metals into gold."

"Gold! You amaze me, John. How do you know all this?"

"I once read a little on the subject, but I'm no expert. Perhaps there is a decent library in Jerusalem, and we can find out a bit more?"

"So, an alchemy lab! Do you think that is what we have found?"

"It does look like that may be the case." Their excitement was peaking with these thoughts.

They moved around separately now, examining the walls and the floor. Suddenly Robert let out a low whistle sound.

"What is it?" said Riley.

"There are bones here. If I am not mistaken, I think they are human!"

"Bones? Let me see."

Riley stepped over to where Robert was standing. In the light of the lamps, they saw in one corner of the chamber the articulated remains of a complete skeleton doubled over against a stone step. Observing the way it was positioned, the skull, ribs and other bones of the upper torso lying over the legs, Robert asked:

"Do you think someone has moved it?"

"It may simply have been the way the fellow had been seated on the step and leaning forward when he died. Something caught their light in a yellow flash.

"And look … there's a ring."

It lay in the dust next to one of the hands. Riley leaned over, picked it up and rubbed it gently on his sleeve. "It's gold! Look Robert, and blue enamel. Oh… It's beautiful… and there's a design."

The ring was as clean as if newly made, and it was inset with a finely rendered black fleur-de-lis on a blue shield.

"I've seen this type of work before. There are similar pieces in New York. I think they come from Limoges in France. Do you realise the significance of this? Whoever this man was, he must have held a very elevated status to be in possession of such a ring… and yet he was sealed in here… sealed in here!"

"My God… you're right. I wonder… do you think he might have been alive when the door was blocked?" Robert was horrified by his morbid thoughts.

"Well, either that was the case, which would mean he was cold-bloodedly murdered, or else perhaps he died beforehand or was killed and for some reason left here instead of being taken out to be buried."

"There may not have been time to bury him. He may have died during the siege."

"But Robert… Why seal him in here? Why, for that matter, was the chamber sealed at all?"

"Perhaps whoever did this hoped to return. Whichever way you look at it there is something highly irregular here. We'll have to think this over some more."

Riley carefully wrapped the ring in a handkerchief and put it in his pocket."

"Should we collect the bones?"

"I would rather come back and photograph them before we move them."

"You're not going to have enough light for photography in here."

"Well, perhaps, you're right. But at least we can bring more lamps, and you can make a careful drawing to record the position before we remove them. I think we should come back for this on Monday."

Back in camp, Riley spread the finds from the box across the sorting table. He took the ring from his pocket admiring its workmanship, then wrapped it in a small piece of cotton and placed it in a cigarette box. Robert picked up the heavy ceramic bottle.

"Any ideas what this held?" he asked.

"Well. Let's open it and see."

"Surely you don't think there will still be anything inside?" asked Robert with incredulity.

"There is definitely something," he said. "Here. Shake it."

"Shake it?" Robert looked at him doubtfully.

"Go on. Gently."

Robert held the vessel in one hand and gave it a slight shake. He could feel the sway of a liquid within.

"Oh, goodness… you're right! There *is* something."

"Can you bring a glass jar from the tent? There should be one there with a screw top."

After a minute Robert returned with the jar and Riley used a pointed screwdriver to carefully prise the clay stopper out of the narrow mouth of the ceramic vessel. Then he held it over the jar and shook it slightly: little silver beads fell, bouncing and shimmering into the jar, joining together in a trembling mass.

"There you are. Just as I thought... mercury." He pointed to the large powdery yellow lumps of substance that he had placed in a cardboard box. "So, we have mercury and sulphur... two of the basic components of the alchemist's art!"

31 CLOSURE

For a long time after I left the infirmary I carried, together with my injuries, an immense weight of sorrow and guilt. Surely, I could have somehow prevented Albert's death. At the very least, I should not have abandoned him in the end. No amount of reasoning by my fellow brothers in the German house enabled me to shake off the despondency into which I sank; not even by Commander Ulrich, who himself visited me in the infirmary, nor my own awareness that I had only left him when I knew he was no longer alive, and that I could have done no more for him. Gradually an understanding grew within me that only if I myself could fulfil Albert's quest, and find his son, would I begin to find any peace of mind. I resolved that as soon as I was sufficiently strong, I would carry on the search, however unpromising it seemed. When I spoke with Commander Ulrich, he pointed out that with the Mamluk advances it was increasingly dangerous to leave the city. He did, however, permit me to go on making inquiries in Acre itself. This I did, even though I had already been through most of the city with Albert. I was determined to complete the search.

Remembering that Bernard had been prior of a Premonstratensian abbey, it occurred to me that I should speak to someone at the Premonstratensian house. Albert, I recalled, had spoken to the Premonstratensian abbot, and the matter had even been raised in their chapter, but nothing had come of it. As soon as I was able, I made my way there and asked for an audience with the abbot. He repeated to me what he had already told Albert. He himself had long been absent from Acre and had only recently returned to the city. But if I wished to pursue the matter, he said that I might speak to the prior, Michel, who had been in the Acre house longer than anyone else.

Prior Michel was a small, stout man, with white hair thinning around his tonsure, bright eyes, a round face and perpetual smile that suggested a very kindly disposition. I told him who I was and about Albert's mission and his death. I was stunned when he answered my enquiry by informing me that he indeed remembered Bernard.

"You do!" I answered. This was not at all what I had expected to hear.

"Oh, yes indeed. As you are an emissary, as it were, of his father, I will show you where he is buried if you wish."

"Buried?" I was caught off guard. Although both Albert and I had realised that as likely as we were to find Bernard alive, there was the equal, perhaps greater possibility that we would find he had perished. "Then he is dead?"

"Yes. Oh. I am so sorry Brother," he answered, observing my reaction. "I thought you were aware of that."

"No, not at all." I felt a wave of sadness, as if this man whom I had never met had been my own brother. I thought of the old man and of the love that had brought him, at the end of his days, to make this futile and danger-filled journey. I thought of his faith and courage and remembered those last moments of semi-consciousness in the tower when he had thought that I was his son. Prior Michel saw how shaken I was.

"Squire Hermann. Please, sit down."

"No. There is no need," I said, pulling myself together. "It's just a bit of a shock. But I would like to see his burial place."

"Then I will take you. It is not far. We can talk when we get there." He led the way to a small graveyard in a plot of land between the Premonstratensian house and our quarter. The cemetery was enclosed by vine-covered walls, and we passed through its arched gateway. There were not many graves and the prior walked directly over to the tomb. I noted that someone had paid for a rather fine stone, one of the larger ones in the cemetery. It was in the form of a large marble sarcophagus shaped like a miniature building, with a gabled roof and shallow arched recesses bordered on all four sides by miniature columns, each with tiny capitals. Engraved on one side of the gabled lid was a three-line Latin epigraph: †HIC IACET BERNARDVS DE VLME, PRIORVM DE MONASTERII S. PETRI IN AVGIA DE PREMONSTRATENSIVM: CVIVS ANIMA REQVIESCAT IN PACE. AMEN. It had been here all the time, so near to where Albert and I had passed. Indeed, we must have walked right by this very cemetery at least twice during our perambulations. Perhaps, I thought, this was for the best. Albert had died without finding his son but still with the hope that he was alive and even, at the end, with the belief that he had found him. Now, in any case, I had a sense of having fulfilled my debt to the old man. Despite our failure, I felt that I had done all I could. I stood for some time beside the tomb, and then turned to Prior Michel who had been standing by, silently waiting for me.

"Do you know how he died?" I asked.

"I think so," he said, "but, for both our sakes, I would ask that if I tell you what I know it should go no further, but be buried here in this small cemetery with the prior."

I readily agreed. The father and his son were both dead, and it was only through curiosity and as a sense of personal need that I was pursuing the matter.

"You have my word, brother." [Indeed, I have kept this promise until this very day. However, there is no longer any harm in putting down these words as, shortly before I began writing this account, it came to my knowledge that the present prior in Weissenau is aware of these facts and, in any case, our house and that of the brethren of Saint John have now been lost to the Saracens.]

"Then I can tell you what I know—it is not very much and is in part conjecture. You are acquainted with Prior Bernard's mission?

"Yes. He came to the East to try to obtain for his monastery a famous relic: the arm of Saint John the Baptist, which, I understand, was in the possession of the custodian of the relics of my house."

"That is correct. He arrived here in the spring passagium of 1266 and he stayed with us. He met with the German commander and with the custodian, Brother Hubert. He also met the Hospitaller sacrist, Geoffrey.

"The sacrist!" I interrupted. "We spoke to him. He told us that he had never met Prior Bernard."

"Then he misled you. I know this from Brother Hubert who is entirely reliable, although he was, not surprisingly, quite reticent on the matter. He gave me only a very brief account of what he knew. He said that a violent argument had broken out between Bernard and the Hospitaller sacrist in his presence. After that, Prior Bernard left and was not seen or heard of again. Several weeks went by. When Brother Hubert asked Geoffrey if he had any knowledge of the missing prior, the sacrist admitted that he had later spoken with him, and that Prior Bernard had told him the price for the relic was too high; he was therefore relinquishing his bid and returning home. As there was no alternative offer, the relic was purchased by Geoffrey. However, Brother Hubert admitted to me that he had suspicions that something was amiss." Prior Michel hesitated. "I don't know if I should tell you this."

"Please, Brother. You have had my word."

He then continued, but in a hushed voice as if he feared, although we were entirely alone in the cemetery, that somebody might be listening:

"Through his ties with other Hospitaller brothers—who, I might add, have no love of their sacrist, and in some cases even despise and fear him—Hubert discovered that Geoffrey had established connections with the Ashishin. Have you heard of them?"

"No," I answered. "That is, I have heard the name, but I don't know much about them."

"They are a Saracen tribe of hired murderers. Around the time of the crusade of Emperor Frederick, these Ashishin had become tributary to the Hospitallers for the annual sum of 1,200 dinars. Five years ago, the Sultan had released them from the tribute. However, shortly before that, it seems that Geoffrey had made an agreement with them according to which he promised to intervene on their behalf and have the tribute lowered. For their part, the Ashishin would make certain that no rival party thwarted his efforts to obtain the relic of Saint John. In their overzealousness—not untypical, I should point out—they had very nearly assassinated the German custodian, but it seems that Prior Bernard was the target that Geoffrey had in mind. This is all hearsay, of course, but the fact is that Bernard's body was found, stabbed, and badly mutilated on a dung-heap outside the city near Mons Suspensorum. We would not have been able to identify it but for a letter of introduction from the abbot of Weissenau, which was found near the body. I had him buried here and an appropriate tombstone set on his grave, but I decided, in consultation with our former abbot, not to pursue the matter any further, and not to make any demands against the Hospitallers. This was, I am ashamed to say, because our Order was deeply in debt to the Hospitallers at the time. In exchange for our silence on the matter, the Hospitallers agreed to annul our large financial debt. But the grand master refused to have the sacrist removed from office, and in spite of our abbot's protests, he has retained his position in the Order to this day."

"But how was it that word of the prior's death failed to reach Weissenau? Even the emperor knew of his mission!"

"I will tell you that, but, Squire Hermann, I remind you again, this must go no further. I have only told you about this and shown you this place because I was told in advance by a friend in your order about your quest and the efforts you had made, and I could see from the moment I set eyes on you that you are a person of honour."

"I will say nothing of it to anyone."

"It was the decision of our former abbot. He believed that if it were made known the abbot of Weissenau would be certain to demand retribution. This would have created an undesirable tension between our house and the Hospitallers, and perhaps the agreement between us would have been revoked. You must understand that the situation between us was very volatile at that time. The abbot in Germany would not have understood this. I informed him, God forgive me, that Prior Bernard had never arrived. He must have assumed that he had died during his passage to the East. The whole matter was rather shameful, and I am not at all happy for the part that I have played in it. The only thing I could do was ensure that Prior Bernard was buried with an appropriate tombstone. I was not permitted to inform the other brothers and, as the cemetery is rarely used now, there was little danger of anyone who knew the prior becoming aware of his grave there. When our abbot returned to Germany and the new abbot was elected, I maintained my silence as I had promised. I am telling you this now because some years have passed, and it is a matter I wish to confess to someone. I trust you and believe that you will keep your word."

32 DISCLOSURES

The day after the laboratory was found, Robert and Riley left the castle and drove to Jerusalem. They stayed once again at the new American School. Riley stalled on his meeting with the director of the Department of Antiquities. He knew that it would be necessary to report on their discovery but had decided to do a bit of research before he spoke to the professor. He wanted to find out more on the subject of alchemy. Soon he would be returning home and it seemed that all the important work still lay ahead of them. He also had letters to write. In the morning it was decided that he would join Robert later at the British School of Archaeology, which was located in a building called Way House. The school was known to have a good library.

After breakfast Robert walked to Way House, where he was greeted at the door by a young woman and shown into the library. There, almost hidden behind a huge stack of papers and books was a figure he immediately recognised. It was the gentleman they had run into during the ceremony of the Holy Fire at the Church of the Holy Sepulchre. His appearance had considerably improved since then. He now wore a clean white shirt, a neat, dark bowtie, a grey waistcoat and a long grey overcoat which, when he moved his stubby arms, exposed a crimson silk lining. In this dress his figure appeared even more baggy-shaped, expanding greatly at the mid-point, narrowing at top and bottom, His head was fairly small, and like many portly people, he had remarkably small feet and hands. His white hair was neatly combed, and he wore old-fashioned, metal-rimmed reading glasses low on his nose. His cheeks were flushed pink, which gave him the appearance of a character from a children's book—a cheerful gnome perhaps—and although at first, he appeared almost bothered at being discovered, he immediately recovered his good humour, smiled broadly, and standing up, greeted Robert in a loud welcome. Fortunately, there was no one else in the library except for the young librarian who had shown Robert in and seemed oblivious to the gentleman's inappropriate loudness.

"Ah… greetings my dear. The archaeologist, isn't it?"

"Yes. I'm Robert… Robert Palmer. And you?" Robert asked in a whisper.

"My name is Felix… Felix Riedl. How are you, Mr. Palmer?"

"Very good, thank you."

"Splendid. No need to whisper, my dear. Hardly anyone uses the library. We have it all to ourselves." Robert looked across again at the librarian. She was paying no attention to them at all, but was busying herself over a pile of volumes. "What have you come for? Perhaps I can help."

"I don't know. Do you think there might be something here on alchemy?"

"You are interested in alchemy?" He looked strangely intrigued.

"Well… yes."

"Then you must come to my library. You will find nothing here on alchemy."

"You have a library?"

"Yes, indeed. I have a wonderful library, unique in fact. Many rare volumes. You must come to see it."

"I would like that very much."

"We could go now if that suits you. I am more-or-less finished here."

"Are you certain? You look as if you are in the middle of something."

"Ah, yes. Well… that can wait."

"Actually, perhaps I should stay. My friend is supposed to meet me here."

"Your friend, the other archaeologist? No problem. We will tell Miss Wharton where you are. He can easily find us. I am always happy to show my library. Come. I will take you there now. It is not very far."

After speaking to the librarian, Robert and the old fellow left Way House and made their way back in the direction of the city walls. As they walked down Museum Road, Robert learnt something about his companion. An only child, he had been born in Frankfurt-am-Main and had studied theology and medieval Church history at Heidelberg University, where he completed his dissertation on the Influence of Neoplatonism in the Sermons of Meister Eckhart. He had spent a number of years at the Sorbonne, and later studied for some time at the Faculty of Divinity at Cambridge University. Reading between the lines, Robert came to understand that Riedl had been financed as a young scholar by his father, but as he grew older and failed in his attempts to get a position in an academic institution, his father had refused to continue supporting him, demanding that he find some form of employment. Eventually he returned to Germany. Still unmarried when his father died, he found that he had been left nothing, and all hope of financial salvation abruptly ended. He eked out a living as a private tutor and in his middle years, mainly out of curiosity and a love of the Bible, Riedl had come to the Holy Land. At that time Palestine was still under Turkish rule and, as a German, he was well received. He settled in Jerusalem, remaining there after the Great War, and spent his time teaching French to the British and English to the Arabs. He lived a humble existence in a small house in the Old City, where he had the two things he most cared about: his library and his cat, Peter.

Passing through the New Gate into the Old City, they made their way through twisting passages and narrow lanes. Riedl's house was in a stepped alley in the Christian quarter. The house was half-hidden behind a high stone wall where wild snapdragons and capers sprouted in the spaces between the stones, and young ailanthus trees sprung up at its base. Behind the wall oleanders had already produced a mass of pink and a mulberry tree cast a deep, speckled shade over the stone paving and potted geraniums.

When he unlocked the door the two men were greeted by an obese tabby cat that rolled over, displaying a broad, soft-furred belly to be rubbed, then stretched and preceded to rub against their legs so that they very nearly tripped over it.

"This, my dear Robert, is Peter, beloved companion of Felix in his otherwise solitary life, and, as you can see, like his master a lover of good victuals. Off with you, my dear," and he gently pushed the cat aside with his foot, though it continued to press between their legs as they ascended the dark staircase to the library. This was a large, airy room with a wooden-slatted balcony at one end overlooking the garden and the street below, and a broad arched window at the other end that filled the room with light. Robert was struck by the number of books it contained. From the floor to the high ceiling, every space was covered with bookcases packed with volumes, many of which appeared to be ancient. There was a rich smell of paper and leather as one finds in old book shops. Enough space was left at the centre of the room for a large oak desk on which were stacks of leather-bound tomes, files of papers covered with neat handwriting, a pipe stand, a Turkish ceramic tobacco jar, pens, a glass inkwell, and various small objects of mixed antiquity, including coins, clay lamps and the very same lead ampulla that Riedl had shown them at their previous meeting.

While Robert was looking around the room Riedl sat down heavily in a deep armchair and the cat came over, clawed the already tattered upholstery on the side of the chair and curled up beside his feet.

"So, Robert, my dear. You are interested in alchemy, are you? I happen to have a very old copy, sixteenth century I think, of the famous text of Morienus, a hermit, here in Jerusalem. It was translated into Latin from the Arabic by Robert of Chester in the twelfth century. Let me see if I can find it."

He pushed himself out of the chair and looked over the bookcases, pulling out here and there a volume, until at last he exclaimed:

"Here it is!" He held in his hands a small book. "Do you understand Latin?"

"No, unfortunately not," Robert answered.

Riedl began to translate the text on the title page. "This is a record of the revelations of the hermit Morienus to the Arab king, Khalid Ibn Yazid Ibn Mu'Awiyya, in which he describes the secrets of the art of alchemy." He held it out to Robert. "This copy dates from 1564."

The book had a binding of blind-stamped pigskin and was labelled in a fine cursive script with the title, MORIENI ROMANI QVONDAM EREMITAE HIEROSOLYMITANA ** Paris, Gulielmum Guillard, PARISIIS, M.D.LXIIII. Robert held the little volume reverently. He opened its thick pages and looked at the neatly printed, old-fashioned lettering.

"I wish I could understand this," he said.

"If I am not mistaken, I read this through once and summarised the process that Morienus describes. Let me see."

Robert handed him back the book and Riedl leafed through.
From near the end of the volume he pulled out a small, folded piece
of paper with tiny handwriting on both sides. He sat back down in
the chair and began to read to himself. After a while he spoke.

"Yes. Yes, I remember this. It seems quite simple. Of course,
it is not really simple at all, and many of the terms he uses are ob-
scure and open to interpretation, but reading it through you might
imagine that the process is no harder than baking a cake... well,
perhaps somewhat harder, and it is considerably more time-consuming and would have taken several weeks to carry out. Imagine
if it took several weeks to bake a cake. Ha... what a precious cake
that would be!" He smiled at the thought and then caught himself.
"Felix. You old fool. This young man does not want to hear your
ramblings... Am I right, my dear?" and without waiting for an answer he continued. "If I summarise the process in simple terms, it
is this: One takes the base material... the base metal that is, and
extracts the water from it so that, in the words of Morienus, it begins to putrefy."

"Putrefy?"

"Yes. That is indeed what he says. I suppose that the removal
of water causes it to smell, though possibly the smell was caused
by the use of manure to achieve this extraction. In any case, when
it has putrefied and whitened it must then be infused with spirit or
fire. This is so that, as he says, the tincture descends and enters it. I
imagine that this means the material changes colour, closer to red
or gold. It is by now so cleansed and improved that there are no
longer any impurities in it. Next, he calls for adding to the material
a fourth part of the ferment, or milk –- I have no idea what that
means—and placing it in the sun, or in dung, to dry it out. Then
begins the next stage in the process: one part of the substance is
taken and cooked for three days. Morienus warns that one must be
careful to be exact about the time and the level of heat at this stage.

Otherwise, the whole process will fail. Now it is necessary to wait for seventeen days, after which the pot must be opened and the liquid changed, and all of this must be repeated three times, until it is reduced by half and the fermentation is finished. After another twenty days it must be removed, dried in gum arabic, and placed on the furnace. At this stage it needs to be moistened daily with a fourth part of the remaining mortified matter. Care must be taken that the flames do not touch the pot as this would destroy it. The final action to be taken is the placing of the pot in a large furnace with a fire above it. This baking must continue without diminution for two days and nights. And that is it. The process will be complete, and the base material will have become pure gold."

"Well, phew! Thank you so much. That is most enlightening!" Robert laughed. "I don't think I will be trying it out, however."

"Ah… And why not?" Riedl smiled.

"Well. I could hardly understand any of what you said. This base material - what is it? And you say it has to putrefy, for goodness sake! And then the tincture descending into it… what on earth does it all mean? And, even if one could understand these things, the formula is not very exact with regard to details. You would have to know what type of furnace to use, and what exact temperature and… well, I mean, it's all nonsense anyway, isn't it?"

"It must seem that to you. A lot of highly intelligent people thought it could be done."

"But surely you don't?"

"What do I know, my dear? I am a very simple man. I can't even bake a cake! Anyway," he went on, "the catalyst to transform base metals into gold was the so-called Philosopher's stone. It might have been a combination of fire and water, or other materials, and it could take the form of a powder rather than of stone. Indeed, it is also known as 'elixir', which comes from the Arabic al-Iksir, meaning powder."

"So… they added this elixir, this Philosopher's stone, to the substance. At what stage?"

"I don't know. Oh… my dear, you are laughing at me for being so naive," he said good-humouredly.

"No. Not at all. Well, certainly not at you. But you must admit, it does sound pretty absurd."

"I suppose it does. Anyway, this doctrine of a catalyst, of a material which enables the transmutation process to be performed, was not entirely speculative. It had been based on successful experimentation and was supported by practical evidence, and it found much favour over the centuries with many great minds. In any case, you know, experimentation seems to support the possibility of transmutation of metals. For example, it was found that galena, which is lead sulphide, a material that possesses the appearance but not the properties of lead, when heated acquired its malleable and fusible properties—in short, it can be successfully transformed into lead. If this can be done with galena, why not with other metals? And if indeed, as Aristotle asserted, all metals are of one family, why should it not be possible to transmute a base metal into gold?" He put down the little volume.

"So, you are saying that you believe this could be done? On a practical level, I mean, in a laboratory?"

"I don't know what to believe," Riedl laughed. "But in the thirteenth century it was certainly considered by some to be feasible, just as it was in the seventeenth and even by some people today! But what do I know? As I say, I am a very simple man. I understand nothing… absolutely nothing."

"I'm sure you know a great deal."

"Why thank you, Robert, my dear. Well… I do know that there are a number of different methods referred to in Byzantine and Arab sources. For example, there is the mercury-sulphur method. In mercury, water and earth are both present; in sulphur, there is fire and air. Thus, a combination of these two substances would contain all of the four elements. Mixing of clean and pure mercury and sulphur in a close compound generates heat and causes a maturing, or cooking if you like, and this process results in the creation of various metals. If the quantities of the two substances are ideal and the ideal amount of heat is achieved, it is believed gold will result. If, however, coldness enters before maturation is achieved, the result will be silver. If the combined material dries too much in the process, the result is copper. Another method is the use of what I referred to earlier as the elixir, which is made from mineral, animal or vegetable matter applied to a base metal that has been transposed into a black passive condition. The elixir permeates it like yeast pervades dough and transmutes it into gold."

He stopped speaking now and sat back. Then looking directly at Robert, he said: "Perhaps, as you say, this is all nonsense. But tell me please. Why does it interest you?"

"Can I rely on your discretion?

"Ah… You greatly interest me now! Yes, my dear. I will be most discreet."

"Then I will show you something." Robert opened his bag and brought out several rolled-up pages. "This is something we have found. I could not photograph it because there was not enough light, but I made these copies."

Robert handed him the pages. Riedl unrolled them and laid them out in front of him. He leafed quickly through them, then he put them down on the table and began to examine each one more intensely. He opened a drawer, pulled out a large magnifying glass and continued to study the pages in silence for some time. Finally, he spoke:

"These are most interesting."

"I copied them myself. They all seemed to have been done by the same hand," said Robert.

"Really? There are some letters I have never seen. Whoever wrote these was very knowledgeable. To judge by the style, they are of thirteenth or fourteenth century date. Are there more?"

"Many more. I copied only a few. Can you read them?"

"I can read them my dear, but can I understand them? That is the question."

"Some are in Latin, some in German, others are Greek."

"Yes. Recognising the language is not difficult ... but interpreting them, that is something else."

"And can you interpret them?"

"Let me see. Ha! This ..." he pointed to one line, "This is part of the formula I just described." His mouth opened in an expression of incredulity. "How remarkable! But it is somewhat different. And this one ..." he pointed to the line below, "This I can read, but I have no idea whatsoever what it means. But my dear... you must tell me where these are from?"

"This is where your discretion is called for."

"You have my word. I will not tell a soul."

"You recall my mentioning that we have been exploring a castle in the Galilee. These are from a secret chamber we discovered beneath the castle. We found them incised on the walls. I wanted to know if, as we suspected, these are connected with alchemy."

"Why did you suspect alchemy? You say that you cannot read Latin, and I assume you cannot read the Greek?"

"No, that's true enough. I can't read any of these. But, my friend, the dig director, Mr Riley—you remember, he was with me at the Holy Sepulchre—he told me that he had in the past come across a paper on alchemy, and when we discovered a design incised on the wall, he immediately recognised it."

"Your friend? Yes, of course I remember. And a design, you say?"

"Yes... this. May I?" Robert sketched the design on a piece of scrap paper.

"Ah! Yes! The formula of the *lapis philosophorum*. You found this incised on the wall?"

Robert sat next to him, and they looked again at the sketches he had made.

"You see here," said Riedl. "The symbol of the sun and the symbol of the moon. The sun represents sulphur, the moon mercury." Then he was quiet again. After a moment he spoke: "You say a laboratory?"

"Well, we think so. You see, the room where we found these contained an oven and on the floor were the remains of many objects that perhaps had once been on wooden shelves or tables: glass jars and metal pipes and the like. There was nothing left of the tables, but the nature of the objects certainly seems to suggest that this was a laboratory. The room had been sealed at some time."

"A laboratory... a laboratory of an alchemist, no less. This is quite a remarkable find, indeed sensational. I would like to see this laboratory."

"Perhaps we can take you sometime."

"I would appreciate that very much."

Riedl picked up the papers with the drawings and studied them again intensely for several minutes. Suddenly, he pointed to a few lines of text:

"This seems to be something else."

"These came from the wall nearest the door," said Robert. "There were no other inscriptions there."

"This is very interesting. Perhaps our unknown scientist was not only involved in alchemy. Three substances are recorded here; *sal petræ*, that is saltpetre, *carbo, carboneum* or carbon, probably in the form of wood ash, which was used to refine the saltpetre and purify it of the deliquescent calcium salts, and our old friend, *sulpur*, sulphur. This gives the exact portions: seven parts of saltpetre, five of carbon and five of sulphur. This is familiar to me."

"It is not connected to the other materials?"

"I don't think so. But I know I have seen this formula." He sat quietly, a concentrated look on his face. After a while he broke the silence:

"I don't know. I can't place it."

They sat for some moments without speaking until Robert broke the silence:

"Tell me, Felix," he asked. "Who was that gentleman you were with at the Holy Sepulchre when we first met you?"

"Gentleman? Ah, yes. He is a friend of mine whom I hold in affection and esteem."

"Really." Robert was taken aback. "Excuse me for saying so but it hardly appeared so when we met at the Holy Sepulchre!"

"Appearances, my dear, can be deceiving. His name is Gustav Neumann. He is a theologian and orientalist and perhaps the greatest Aramaic scholar alive. My dear Peter was a gift from him."

"You seemed quite at odds with him on that occasion."

"We usually argue when we meet. It means nothing. He enjoys antagonising me. I do the same to him. He, by the way, would be most interested in this discovery of yours."

"Perhaps it would be better to wait until I speak to Mr. Riley before you mention this to him."

"Of course, my dear."

The cat stretched, then it lazily jumped into Robert's lap. Amused, Robert ran his fingers through the thick, soft fur between its ears.

"I see that Peter has taken to you, my dear."

After he had left Riedl, promising to be in touch with him again, Robert walked back to Way House, reflecting on the conversation. Had he said too much, he wondered? Riley might not approve of his having confided in Riedl at all. I am a fool, he thought. I had no right to speak about our find without his approval. It would be a pity to lose Riley's trust, perhaps even his friendship, which until now had been so warm. The man had been so friendly and knowledgeable. But I don't know anything about him, thought Robert.

As he approached the school, he decided to admit his imprudence to Riley, apologise and hope for the best. However, Riley was not at Way House and, according to Miss Wharton, had not been there. Mildly surprised, he walked back to the American School and found Riley in the dining room.

"Ah … there you are," Riley greeted him as he entered. "Sorry I didn't meet you. I ran into Professor Gilford."

"Really!"

"Yes. I hadn't planned to speak to him yet, but as he came by and we got into a conversation, so I updated him on the find. It was nearly noon by the time he left, so I decided not to go to Way House. Come and join me."

Robert helped himself to a plate of soup and sat beside Riley.

"He was quite excited," he went on. "He will try to come out later this week. Did you find out anything at the library?"

"Look, John," Robert said. "I may have done something foolish. I hope you won't be angry with me."

"Why? What has happened?" Riley looked concerned.

"Do you remember that chap we ran into at the Holy Sepulchre?"

"Oh yes, I remember. There were two rather odd fellows."

"And one of them showed us the Crusader ampulla."

"Ah, yes. He seemed to know a lot about the ceremony."

"That's right. Well, I came across him at the library. We started talking and he asked me what I was there for." Robert went on to explain the course of events. "One thing led to another and ... I hope I haven't been foolish ... I told him about our find."

"Oh ..., you did?"

"It was very stupid of me, I know. It just came out. I asked him to be discrete, but thinking about it afterwards I realised that I hardly know the fellow."

"Well. I wouldn't worry too much about it," said Riley. "Do you think he is reliable?"

"Actually, he seems to be a very decent chap, and extremely erudite. And he has an amazing library."

"Then I really don't think there is a problem. Anyway, to tell you the truth, I'm fed up with all the secrecy you come across among scholars—everyone keeping everything close to their chests. I saw it in New York all the time. You could never discuss a discovery with anyone. Nobody would ever open up on their work until it had been published."

"Well, I'm relieved you're not angry."

"No, of course not. So, tell me, what did he have to say?"

"He went over the basics of the technique, not that I understood what it all meant, and he agreed with our conclusion that this was a secret alchemic laboratory. You know, I've been wondering a lot about that. Why should it be secret? From whom was it being hidden?"

"What do you mean?"

"Well ... what we discussed before. It was located in the sealed-off passage. The passage, it seems pretty clear, was originally intended to be used as an escape route from the castle down into the valley on the north. Who was the passage intended for? For the entire garrison, do you suppose? Perhaps for the leaders alone. In which case they may have had an interest in hiding it from the rest of the garrison. That would explain why it was built in the cistern, but not why it was blocked. And then what about the laboratory? Why was it located in the secret passage? Was it also hidden from the brothers? Or perhaps there was opposition to whoever was experimenting in alchemy. And was the laboratory so important that it was worth sacrificing the escape route for? And then we come back to the question, why was the laboratory sealed? Did somebody hope to get back and recover whatever was in there without the Muslims, or perhaps someone else, finding it? And... whose was the body we found?"

"Slow down, slow down!" Riley laughed. "You've got my head spinning! Did your friend have any suggestions?"

"I didn't ask him. Do you think the Order was opposed to involvement in alchemy?"

"Probably, I don't know. These organizations were pretty strict about what was permissible."

"You know, Felix—that's his name – is really quite well informed. He may have knowledge of such matters. You should come with me to meet him."

There was, however, no need, for the next day the eccentric Riedl himself appeared at the American School, asking for Riley and Robert. Coming down to meet him in the garden, they found him in a state of obvious excitement.

"Oh, my dears. I am so glad you are here. Hello, Mr. Riley, yes? How are you? I am so glad to have found you both. I never asked where you were staying. Miss Wharton at Way House suggested I look here."

"I'm sorry," said Robert. "I completely forgot to tell you we were here. John, you remember Dr. Riedl?"

"Yes, of course."

"Please, please ... call me Felix. Gentlemen, forgive my bursting in on you like this. But I have remembered, my dears! I have remembered and I have found it!"

"What have you found?" Riley asked, amused at the gentleman's boyish excitement.

"The formula, of course! I have found the formula ... the other one. You remember?" He turned to Robert. "The one you showed me—on the paper. I have found it and it is most interesting. I knew that I had seen it somewhere."

"Well—what is it, for heaven's sake?" Robert laughed, then turning to Riley he explained, "He is referring to the text that we found near the door."

"You will not believe this" said Riedl. "It would appear that your good alchemist was also experimenting in creating an explosive material ... gunpowder, no less!"

"Gunpowder?" said Riley. "But I thought gunpowder was invented in China and that it only reached the outside world much later..."

"No, no! Not so, my dear. There was much work done in the Islamic world on developing gunpowder, and even in the making of primitive types of canons. An Arabic text written by a Syrian—al-Hassan al-Rammāh—was published just about the time your castle fell. It was titled *al-Furusiyyawa al-Munaseb al-Harbiyya* which would translate roughly as *The Book of Military Horsemanship and Ingenious War Devices*. It included over a hundred methods for making gunpowder. Al-Hassan attributed these to his 'fathers and forefathers', so the knowledge was already well-established in the Islamic world at this time. Indeed, it would seem that the formula for gunpowder had even reached the West, where scientific studies were, generally speaking, far behind those in Arab lands. Not surprisingly perhaps, the same men who were delving into the art of alchemy were also occupied with developing explosives: Albert Magnus, perhaps, and Marcus Graecus and Roger Bacon. Bacon published a treatise in the middle of the thirteenth century, called *Epistolae de secretis operibus artis et naturae, et de nullitate magiae*. In it he recorded the formula in a cipher or anagram. It was one of your compatriots, my dear Robert, who unravelled it. This is how I found the connection. I knew I had seen it somewhere. I have in my library a book published a few years ago by a British officer, a Lieutenant Colonel H.W.L. Hime. He decoded Bacon's formula, identical to what appears in your inscription: seven parts of saltpetre, five of sulphur and five of carbon... and there it is... gunpowder!"

"Why did Bacon write it in cipher?" Riley asked.

"The Inquisition, my dear. There was a thin line between science and magic, and magic was considered as bad as heresy."

"So, let me understand. Someone in the castle was involved in attempting to convert base metals into gold, and at the same time he was trying to develop gunpowder?"

"Yes, so it would seem. But, as I said, these disciplines were of a very similar nature and were quite often attempted by the same men. Marcus Graecus for example wrote on alchemy but also had some remarkable ideas on incendiary weapons which he published in his *Liber Ignium*, the Book of Fires, perhaps a little later than your gentleman." He pulled out of his pocket a small book and opened it to a page he had marked. "Listen to this." He began to read in an amused voice in Latin: "Alius modus ignis ad comburendos..." then he stopped. "I'm sorry," he said. I forget myself..." He continued in English, describing a formula for setting fire to the enemy's camp by smearing crows with a mixture of petroleum, pitch and sulphur and sending them off at dawn to perch on the tents. The heat of the sun rising would ignite them. A second formula, supposedly invented by Aristotle when he travelled in dark places with King Alexander, was for a material that would burn continuously for at least one year, while another type of fire, also invented by Aristotle, could last for nine years – it could burn houses on a mountain and the mountain itself!" Riedl shut the book dramatically.

"Those are indeed interesting," said Riley, "…and quite entertaining! But what I find extraordinary is that in that dire situation, somebody in the castle might have been involved not only in making incendiary weapons but also in alchemy. You would have expected them to give priority to the former, or, more likely, to abandon the alchemy altogether. And why, in any case, would a member of a Military Order be trying to make gold? Did that not go against the monastic ideals followed by those Orders?

"Yes, it did. But as you know, these were very wealthy organizations."

"And," Robert added, "since alchemy would no doubt be a low priority during a siege, is it not more likely that those inscriptions were from an earlier time, when there was no immediate threat to the castle."

"Yes, precisely!" said Riley. "It may be that this person—obviously a very knowledgeable man—who had been involved in alchemy turned his efforts to work instead on explosives when the threat of siege became a reality."

"Perhaps," agreed Riedl. "Or alternatively, he was delving in alchemy in secret, without the awareness of his masters. This is pure speculation, of course, but perhaps he was taking advantage of his knowledge and the materials provided by the Order to produce weapons, to do a little of his own work, on the side, as it were."

"An interesting idea," said Riley, "and one that might better explain what we have found."

33 REPORT

From the report by Captain Peters

Since his escape, Walker had dropped out of sight, but I was certain it was only a matter of time before he reappeared at the castle. We were aware from his last attack that he was again armed and that he had managed to obtain dynamite. This fact would link Walker to the break-in reported by a guard at the new quarry on Mount Carmel, where an entire crate of dynamite and a revolver were stolen from a storeroom. I decided to take no chances and asked Jerusalem for additional troops but was informed that there was no spare manpower available.

I urged the director, Mr. Riley, to put a hold on the excavations until Walker could be apprehended, as he was clearly in a dangerous mental state, but Mr. Riley was opposed to this because he could not indefinitely extend his leave of absence from his employment in New York. I decided against imposing a halt to their work, but advised him and his assistant Mr. Palmer of the risk and updated them regarding our investigations. I then placed my men in groups of three or four in strategic positions on the slopes around the castle, in particular on the more approachable sides to the south and east, and three men at the expedition camp. These positions were held *for the following four days, during which nothing exceptional occurred. There was no trace of Walker in the vicinity of the castle or anywhere in the district, and no sightings were reported from Haifa or Acre. I could not keep the men on this type of duty indefinitely, and on the 23rd I reduced their number, redeploying the remaining men more thinly, and concentrating them on the southern slope near the camp. Patrols were set up along the roads and tracks to the north and south, including the area where we had previously apprehended the suspect.*

34 VISITORS

The little party made its way down from Malia, first by car as far as was possible, then on foot. Robert, and Abdul walked briskly ahead and the three older men, Riley, Professor Gilford, and Doctor Riedl, followed a short way behind. Riedl was soon puffing for breath, and after a short rest they continued at a more leisurely pace. The day was mild and in the shade of the forest the walk was pleasant. Riley updated the professor and the doctor on the archaeological developments, and events relating to Walker; Riedl expounded on the importance of the newly discovered laboratory. They followed the bed of the valley sloping down through the forest until, at one point, Robert and Abdul led them off the track and into the trees so that they could follow the overgrown medieval road, a rock-cut path on the side of the hill that had been used by the German knights to carry stone from the distant quarry during the construction of the castle. This road led to the narrow chasm of the outer moat, and they walked through it, arriving at the castle around midday.

As they came into the area below the keep, they saw the two guards who had been placed there by Captain Peters, sitting in a high arched window in the wall at the far end, smoking. They stood up as the group entered, then, recognising Riley and Robert, waved, and sat back down.

"What a remarkable castle," said Riedl, surveying the majestic ruin in its setting of forested hills.

"This is your first visit, here, I imagine," said Robert.

"Yes, indeed it is."

"Have you been here before, professor?"

"No, I have not, though I have viewed the castle from the hill across Wadi Qura'in."

"Then, gentlemen, let us show you around. We will take a look at the excavations and leave the cistern and the laboratory to the end. Then we'll take you down to the camp and look at some of our finds."

Riley and Robert led them through the excavations in the castle kitchen and down to the west where they had uncovered what might have been a chapel. Passing through the ruins of the Great Hall, they went down a path on the north side to the huge basement vaults, on to the gate tower and finally, retracing their steps back to the keep. Abdul greeted them there with the finjan, and they stood and drank coffee while Riley told them about the events leading up to the remarkable discovery in the cistern.

"So, it isn't really a cistern at all," Professor Gilford said after Riley had described the discovery of the second shaft on the floor of the chamber. "That is certainly very interesting!"

"The actual cistern appears to be below it, and this chamber was apparently constructed in order to conceal the presence of the passage."

"That must mean that the chamber and passage were constructed from the beginning when the keep was built, and not as later additions built when the castle was under threat."

"Yes, that's correct… at least with regard to the chamber. The passage must have been intended from the beginning, but it is not under the keep. It could have been completed later. And the laboratory may have been added at any time."

"I've often heard claims of such secret passages in other castles,"

said Professor Gilford. "I always thought they were local folklore…
myths."

"And now, gentlemen…" Riley placed against the wall the cane
that Salah had whittled for him, to replace the one broken by Walker, "Would you like to come down and see our little discovery for
yourselves?"

"That is particularly what we have come for," answered the professor with a laugh.

Abdul handed out lamps and one by one they made their way
down the ladder into the cool darkness of the subterranean chamber. A second makeshift ladder gave access to the mouth of the passage. Riley, who for this historic occasion had resolved to overcome
his difficulties, led them single file along the dark passage to the entrance to the laboratory, where he stopped. When they were assem-
bled in the small space, and the combined light of their lamps filled
the narrow chamber, he spoke again:

"This is the entrance. Take care as you enter. The laboratory is
a little below the level of this passage. There are a few steps down."

In the centre of the room, the gathered light illuminated the
chamber to the extent that some of the inscriptions on the walls
were already visible, and holding up his lamp, Riedl stepped close
to examine them.

"Be careful, Felix," said Robert. "Don't go too near the wall.
There is a lot of material on the floor that we will want to examine.
Do you see? Some collapsed shelves, perhaps."

He pointed to the debris adjacent to the walls, and Riedl stopped
in his tracks.

"And, gentlemen," Riley added, carrying his lamp over to where
the skeleton was located. "Be especially careful over here. It seems
that someone was left behind… perhaps our alchemist?"

The intake of breath of the two visitors was clearly audible in
the closed space.

"Really?" said the professor.

"Whoever this gentleman was," Robert added, "It would appear that he was sealed in here..."

"Which perhaps suggests foul play!" added Riley.

"What do you mean? asked Professor Gilford as the men stood over the skeleton.

"Why would a body be left here? The passage and the chamber are sealed, and do not appear to have been discovered by the Moslems, which means that it must be a Christian. If it were a natural death, the body would have been removed for burial before the chamber was sealed and not left lying here unburied."

"And..." added Robert, "we have not examined it yet, but you might notice what looks like it might be a knife blade in the dust below the ribs."

"Oh, yes... I see," said the professor. Well... foul play then. This is interesting!"

"Perhaps. I'm not really sure it is a blade at all."

Meanwhile, Riedl had been drawn back to the graffiti, taking care to keep away from the debris that skirted the wall. He was muttering to himself, entirely absorbed by what he saw. Finally, he turned back to the others.

"So... Doctor Riedl... What do you think?" asked the professor.

"Please, professor. Call me Felix."

"Very well, Felix," said Professor Gilford and he smiled but did not suggest that Riedl adopt the same familiarity.

"I think that this is indeed what Mr. Riley says it is, and what I understood it to be when young Mr. Palmer here showed me the drawings in Jerusalem. This is certainly the laboratory of a scientist, a very erudite man with the most up-to-date knowledge in the arts of alchemy... and, it appears, explosives. It is extraordinary to think that he was located here in this isolated castle."

"It is even more extraordinary to think that he may still be here!" added the professor, glancing down. Then he turned to Riley. "Well, John. What is your plan of action?"

"This discovery has taken us onto in a whole new path. I never expected to find anything like this. I have sent a telegraph off to New York to ask for an extension of leave and more funds. I imagine that I will get the former. I'm doubtful about the funds."

"I might be able to help you a little with that," said the professor. Riley brightened.

"That would be wonderful," he said. "Then we could systematically excavate this chamber and have Doctor Riedl... Felix... do a proper study of the inscriptions."

"Yes. Yes indeed," added Riedl excitedly, without shifting his gaze from the walls.

"Well, gentlemen," said Robert. "The air is getting rather close in here. Let's continue our discussion out in the open. Come along, Felix. Tear yourself away. You will have plenty of time to examine these walls."

35 FINAL ENTRY

Final Entry in Walker's diary (June 27) from the torn-out pages, apparently written in the cistern under the keep

I managed to reach the hill south of the castle without being observed. Even with those fools everywhere. I could hear their whispering as I crouched in the bushes. My heart was pounding… but I don't mind if there's an audience!

On the hill I took the backpack off and remained in the bushes for a long time, nearly an hour, I think. All the time I could hear them murmuring, but they had no idea I was there!

Before, I felt hunted. Now I am the hunter! The forest was all I needed…

Down to the bottom of the valley and then up to the level area between the two moats. Still, no one had seen me. I made my way across to the western side above the moat. Nobody was on the keep, but I hid there waiting for perhaps another hour. The forest was completely silent. I could see right across the keep to its eastern wall. If anyone was there, I would have seen him. I slipped into the moat and came around on the north. Those fools in the valley had left the castle completely unguarded! This is more than I had hoped for. I climbed the *keep and went down a ladder into the darkness of the cistern. I stood there a few moments, just for the feeling of it, then lit a candle. They had left hurricane lamps. I lit one. That was when I saw a ledge and a place in the wall that had been broken through. So! This is what they had found – a secret passage, just as I thought! I had said as much to Riley, but he didn't believe me. Now he thought he would take all the credit for it.*

I climbed up and through the broken wall into the passage. I wanted to see where it went. A bit strange being entirely alone under the ruins of the castle. I walked along the passage to where it ended in steps going down began to descend as a staircase. Not enough light to go on. I nearly fell.

What have they found here? Gold, perhaps? This was my discovery, not Riley's! He thinks I can be pushed aside. I'll show him. There should be enough dynamite to bring the whole damned thing down. Now I'll deal with this. I must think…

36 REPORT

From Captain Peters' report

At 3 o'clock my two men were in position behind the western wall when Walker came up from the cistern. They had seen him enter and signalled to me as we had arranged. We saw him move into the centre of the floor above the cistern and bend down. We could not see what he was doing but I was afraid that he might be setting another explosive charge (as turned out to be the case). I called out to him and he stood up and seemed to freeze momentarily. He had seen my two guards, and I came out from behind the wall. I ordered him to stop but he just shouted something, grabbed his pack, and ran off. He climbed down the rocks on the eastern side and headed to the north. We were in close pursuit, but he was very vigorous and was able to put several yards between himself and my men. He ran up to the east, stumbling on rocks and bushes. As we approached the top of the rise there was a tremendous roar behind us, and I realised that he had indeed set off a large explosive device in the cistern. There was no point turning back at this stage as no one was in danger there and it was imperative we apprehend him. We continued our pursuit in a north-easterly direction, as far as Wadi Qura'in, where the cliff drops down several hundred yards. The terrain there is very difficult, but we were now quite close behind him. At this point he turned to look back, still running, and a branch caught his face. He must have been blinded for a moment, and he stumbled onto the rock outcrop. He was unable to stop in time. I saw him try to grab the branch of a tree growing at the edge, but it came away in his hand. The weight of the back-pack probably added momentum, propelling him forward and off the edge of the cliff.

37 CONCLUSIONS

The two men stood above a gaping hole that had opened on the north slope just below the keep.

"I can't believe this," said Riley, shaking his head. "There is nothing left. The poor fool! He wanted to get back at us, and that he certainly has! He has destroyed an amazing discovery and has got himself killed. What for? I never imagined, even after the other things he did, that he would go this far. I should have realised something like this could happen."

"Don't blame yourself, John," said Robert. "What more could you have done? Peters and his men were here. It's not as if we hadn't taken measures."

"I know. I just don't understand," he said gesturing over the destruction with his hand. "It's all gone. We have nothing but your drawings. Thank heavens we made those. I should have had it better guarded."

"Perhaps we should dig down? It might be possible that some of the plaster with the graffiti has survived."

"I don't think so. The explosion must have been very powerful to bring down the entire chamber and leave a crater like this. The plaster would have turned to powder. In any case, I cannot now justify delaying my return to America."

The week leading up to Riley's departure was taken up with minor time-consuming matters: returning the equipment and the tents to Haifa, paying outstanding bills, finishing drawings, and writing up a preliminary report based on the field diaries. Robert helped Townsend to pack those finds that were to be shipped to the museum in New York. He felt now, as he had after leaving the gendarmerie, that he was poised on the edge of an emptiness in his life. What should he do, he wondered? He considered the options of other employment if he remained in Palestine, but more and more his mind was turning towards going back to England.

One evening shortly after he had returned to his house in Haifa, there was a knock at the door. He was not expecting anyone and generally had very few visitors. When he opened the door, it was Bel. This was so unexpected that for a moment he was at a loss for words.

"Bel! What are you doing here?"

"I heard you were back." Strands of her hair blew across her face in the slight breeze, and she pushed them aside and smiled. He felt a pang at seeing how lovely she was.

"Yes, I'm back," he said. "But I'm being rude. Come inside. When they were in and had sat down on the sofa he spoke again. "We have wrapped up." He hesitated for a moment, then spoke again: "I… I thought…"

"I know. I should have spoken to you. I knew it was not your fault. I never blamed you, Robert. My father… He is so overprotective. I should not have let him control me."

"Can I get you something to drink?"

"No. I just want to talk."

"I don't understand... I didn't understand. You seemed so self-confident. That is part of what I admired in you."

"It's not entirely untrue. I am very rebellious at times. How can I explain it? I wanted to speak to you but at first, I was so shaken... you have to understand... that business at Malia, and then father had had a letter from my mother. She is very ill. I felt such pity for him. I let myself think he was right. I am so sorry, Robert. I should never have let those things colour my feelings for you."

"Perhaps it was what you wanted?" He was still hurt and unsure.

"No. No, Robert. I didn't know what I wanted. But I know now."

Early on the afternoon of his departure for Alexandria, Riley drove Robert and Bel up to Malia, and the three of them walked down to the castle for a final time. They sat around a fire drinking beer that Salah had brought up from its cooling place in the stream. Conversation steered away from the remarkable events of the past month, and they spoke mainly of what lay ahead. Riley spoke of the work he would have waiting for him in New York, Robert and Bel of their plans to leave Palestine for a while. As dusk approached, they left the castle and headed back for Malia. It was their last night. They climbed up above the castle to the east and sat for a while on the escarpment beyond the ditches, watching as the sun's gold globe sank through a thin orange band of cloud just above the sea, silvering the clouds' edges, then moving below until the base of it touched the sea and broadened at its amalgamation with the horizon - like an alchemist's dream - then narrowed until it was gone. And after it was gone it remained for a while still in their minds.

EPILOGUE

The stones of the keep lay in the cool, dense growth of trees and vines, covered in the spring by a blanket of emerald moss and small ferns, occasionally trampled on by wild boar coming up from the valley for the rich harvest of acorns from oaks around the outer side of the enceinte. Every so often a small stone would loosen from the walls, tumble down the slope with a cascade of soil, and drop into the hollow where the hidden chamber had been. The castle fell back into its old solitude, its silence broken only by the scuffling of the boars in the early morning and the howl of jackals after sunset.

POSTSCRIPT

It is a decade since I wrote this novel, and in the intervening years I have continued the excavations at Montfort Castle that led me to write this fictional account in the first place. One or two things that I have learnt in those excavations would slightly change the picture presented above if I were to write it today. For example, the ceremonial Great Hall of the castle in which squire Hermann and Albert met with the Teutonic grand commander, was in a state of ruin in the year that this event takes place in the novel and would indeed have been so since the first siege of Montfort by Baibar's generals five years earlier in 1266. This fact only became apparent to me in 2017, seven years after I wrote this description and it seems to me that, this being a work of fiction, even if based very much on historical fact, I am able with clear conscience to leave it as I wrote it. Another possible discrepancy that occurs to me is that the castle of Castellum Regis was in all likelihood already in Muslim hands in 1271, the year in which the events in the novel took place.

A.B.

Made in the USA
Monee, IL
10 August 2021